A Broken Path

A Broken Path

Ann Pilling

NEW ENGLISH LIBRARY

The author and publisher gratefully acknowledge permission from William Trevor to quote from *The Silence in the Garden*.

British Library Cataloguing in Publication Data
Pilling, Ann
  A broken path.
  I. Title
  823.914 [F]

ISBN 0-450-54984-4

First published in Great Britain 1991

Published by New English Library,
a hardcover imprint of Hodder and Stoughton,
a division of Hodder and Stoughton Ltd,
Mill Road, Dunton Green, Sevenoaks, Kent TN13 2YA
Editorial Office: 47 Bedford Square, London WC1B 3DP

Typeset by Hewer Text Composition Services, Edinburgh
Printed in Great Britain by St Edmundsbury Press, Bury St Edmunds, Suffolk

for Phyllis

'Mrs Rolleston, do please try to rest. No matter how it was, it belongs to the past now.'

'The past has no belongings. The past does not obligingly absorb what is not wanted.'

The Silence in the Garden
William Trevor

1

Friday 17th October

John Peacock was pretending to be blind. He often did it along this track, and sometimes in Richmond, down one of the side roads. In Richmond you could feel the pebbles through your sneakers because the streets were all cobbled. Big round cobbles they were, like duck eggs, and they'd come from the bed of the Swale.

Dad had told him that. 'The things your father knows,' parroted his mother, blind with love, if he ever came up with a useless scrap of information, like Frenchgate being paved with river pebbles. He really was useless now because last year he'd suddenly died on them. He'd left no money, and a farm that was going to be sold off next spring for a fancy price, and John was going to have to live in Darlington, with Auntie Win and his mother.

It was all right for her, she'd never liked living at Park Head. There were big shops in Darlington, and plenty of folk around. It was people she'd missed most, she said, when his father had first married her and brought her to the valley, people, and cars going by, something she called 'life'. Now she would have 'life' again, because of death. He was glad he'd not seen his father in his coffin.

To act blind you needed to get your bearings first and he opened his eyes so wide they became two mouths, sucking in the shapes of the burning land, all the lights and the darks of it. A month ago the trees in their valley had been that listless green which marks the fag-end of summer; now everything flamed before him. On top of the waterfall Dad's little birch tree glowed dappled vermilion, shimmering gently as though lit up by an inner lamp. Yet there was no sun today and the thick sky sat heavy on the fell tops. In autumn that tree had always been Dad's 'burning bush'.

Now he was rotting under a raw hump in Keld graveyard. The boy shut his eyes suddenly, blacking out the flaming trees, and the tears spilled down. He swayed for a minute on the stony path, then walked forward boldly.

His eyes stayed shut until he came to the fork in the track. He could tell he'd reached it because of the smell from the old cow-house. She had wanted to buy that too, the woman, said she wanted to make it into a 'guest house' for when her friends came. But Mr Metcalfe wouldn't sell. He might now, though. He seemed more in a selling mood. If only Dad had bought their farm off him twenty years ago, when he'd had the chance.

John didn't want to go and live in Darlington but his mother said she was glad. That was only because she was depressed. She took little green pills with all her meals and bright blue ones at night, to get her to sleep. They made her do horrible snoring noises. He could hear her through the wall.

She was still asleep now. Uncle Maurice would wake her up when he came to do the cows and when he'd finished he'd take her down to his place, to spend the day there. John would get off the school bus in the village, and they'd have tea together. Then Uncle Maurice would drive them back, eightish, because the nights were drawing in, and she would swallow her blue tablets and go straight to bed. That was the pattern now.

He hated it but at least they were still in the valley, and the long winter, with its massive snows and its mean little spurts of daylight, lay endlessly before them. Perhaps, before spring, Uncle Maurice would talk to Mr Metcalfe again, about not selling the farm. Let the winter go on for ever, otherwise. Let it be like the dream he'd kept having, after his father died, when he woke up each morning to find the sun had altogether forgotten to come up, when the suffocating darkness against the windows went on and on.

If it was a hard winter, like people were saying, Dad wouldn't change much in Keld churchyard. Cold preserved things. If they opened the coffin they might find the flowers Mum had put there still in his hand. Auntie Win had let it out, about those. In murders they did open coffins sometimes. He'd read about it.

Since Dad, he always woke early and he would rather be out of the house than hang round listening to his mother's awful snoring noises. His watch told him there was another twenty minutes before the bus came. That was good, because he wanted to check out the woman again. Yesterday she had been at her work by seven-thirty, hunched over her big table with the papers strewn all over it and the wireless on full blast. It had sounded like Radio One.

It was an unusually large brass keyhole, and the woman had been polishing it. He hadn't been able to see very much, apart from a little piece of her back in a bright blue jumper, a bit of gingery hair and, beyond her, Dad's burning bush framed in the window like a picture postcard, with the water churning down over the rocks. Through the keyhole the little tree looked as if it were floating.

She had bought Foggett's because of its view of the waterfall and a silly price she'd paid for it too, according to his father. It had always been very damp and in the years it had stood empty the floors and the ceilings had rotted. She'd had all that seen to straightaway, though, before she'd moved in. Mr Metcalfe had kept very quiet about the rats, but Dad had warned her. They were much worse here than at Park Head because they came up from the river, loads of them. John had seen them himself.

He was at the back door now with his eyes wide open, staring down at his feet. There were rat droppings on the ground and the bottom of the door looked as if it had been chewed. A hungry rat would eat anything. She ought to get the pest people up again, from Richmond. You could catch diseases from rats. They had always kept them down, at Park Head. His father had been a very careful farmer.

The back door was painted olive green now and hand-carved lettering on a new wooden tablet said 'The Rock'. That was stupid for a start, even his father had said so, and he never used to speak ill of people. The cottage had always been Foggett's because of the folk who had built it, just as theirs was Park Head because they were that bit higher up, and because a man called Elias Park had built the first farmhouse there with his own hands. It said Foggett's and Park Head on all the maps; the woman was trying to change history.

But 'The Rock', she had told them, was a lovely place she had once seen in Wales. Foggett's was even lovelier, and it really was on a rock, wasn't it? 'The absolute peace and quiet' was the reason she had wanted it, after the view of the waterfall. She needed the quiet, she said, for her writing. The books obviously made her a lot of money. Her bunch of flowers was the biggest of the lot, when Dad went. She had written a letter too. Stone-faced, his mother had put it aside without reading to the end.

Again, today at only twenty-five to eight, she was already sitting at the table with its litter of papers. He could see the same bit of gingery hair, the same key-hole shape of blue jersey, and Radio One was on full blast. 'Sometimes, John,' she had told him, 'I just sit and think. I might go a whole day and not write anything.'

After his father's death Uncle Maurice had invited her to Park Head, he said it wasn't right not to, after the flowers and the letter. But his mother would not speak, and the next time the woman came, knocking on the door with another bunch of flowers, she ran upstairs and hid. The woman never came again.

It was strange that someone who liked 'absolute peace and quiet' should play pop music so very loudly. Perhaps she didn't really hear it, when she was busy doing her writing, or perhaps she was a little bit deaf, like Auntie Win. She wrote with a fountain pen, a thin black one with a gold clip. She had shown it to him specially, so he could tell his teachers at school. They all read her books. But he couldn't see her hand moving across the papers. Only Dad's tree moved behind her head, and the water, crashing down. Then, in the still room, something long and dark began creeping across the table.

He half ran along the meadow path, away from the cottage, leapt the gate and started climbing the broad track up to the road. It was not true, and he had not seen it. Or, if he hadn't taken his eye away from the keyhole just at that moment, he would have surely seen her start up, throw something at it, scream. But he ought to go back and help her. His mother wouldn't answer if she came knocking at Park Head and rat's piss could give you a terrible disease. A sewer man had died of it last year, in New York. It had been on the telly.

In a minute the school bus would come down from the dale head, sweep him inside and carry him off to Richmond. He'd got two cigarettes today, nicked from Uncle Maurice's jacket. It was only since Dad that he'd smoked, but he needed them now. He would squeeze on to the back row and light up the minute the bus got going. The driver must be able to smell it but he never said anything.

In the long grass by the main gate Daffy Bayles had left the woman her daily pint of milk. Seeing their cows she had walked up to Park Head on her first morning, with a jug. When Dad explained that they weren't registered to sell milk she'd gone a funny colour, dark red, angry-looking, and she'd asked a string of questions before going away. His father was annoyed too, because she hadn't believed him. She thought he'd said no just because she was an incomer, she didn't seem to understand that they didn't have a certificate to sell.

His father had gone straight inside and rung Bayles's for her. 'Daffy'll leave you a pint by the gate, each day,' he'd said. 'It's all right, nobody'll pinch it.' And she was sorry then because he'd been kind, tried to pay for the phone call, gone the funny red colour again. 'That's all right,' his father had said quietly, in his shy way. 'Come up to us if you've got any problems. There's usually someone around.' 'One of Nature's gentlemen' Michael Peacock was, according to a man at the funeral. His mother wept when she heard.

In the high lane a lone tree had shed its leaves, crisp copper coins that drifted about, rattling in the small wind. John looked up and studied the sky. There was big rain coming later, enough rain to brown the river as it threshed down over the woman's waterfall and to turn the glowing leaves round his feet to a dark slime overnight. He leaned against the gatepost and listened for the bus. In the silence of the valley he could always hear it coming, miles away, but today it was late.

He poked about aimlessly with his feet, parting the long grass round Daffy's bottle. Something clinked. He bent down and pulled out three more bottles, all full. Two were already quite solid, the third was still runny but a light mould had formed round its top. Carefully, he lined them up along the wall. Today's bottle made four. Silly Daffy, not to have gone to Foggett's, to speak to the woman. But then, Daffy Bayles was daft, that's where he got his name from, though his real name was Eddie; twenty-five-years old and sixteen stone, fit for nothing but mucking out and delivering the milk. Some people said that when he was a baby his mother had dropped him on his head, on the stone flags in their back kitchen, but Dad said he had been born like it, and that you had to understand.

But Daffy wouldn't understand that four milk bottles meant that the woman wasn't there, wanting a delivery. She *was* there though, she was doing her writing at the table, looking out over the waterfall, with the wireless blasting through the cottage. She had been there yesterday too, at just before half-past seven. He had done a time check on her because, now and again, the bus came early. If he wasn't there waiting it pipped twice and drove off. Everybody knew about his father and that he couldn't come to school if Mum was having one of her bad days.

He knelt down in the road, put all the bottles back and pulled the grass over them. As he straightened up he heard the bus changing gear at the top of Swinner Hill. In two minutes it would be at the gate, and the door sliding open to admit him.

Slowly, with that uncanny, disembodied feeling he knew only from dreams, he saw himself open the red iron gate, walk back through it and retrace his steps along the track. At the cow-house he heard the bus sounding its horn, but he went on, through a second red gate and along the meadow path, his strides measured and even, a regularity strangely at odds with his wildly fluttering heart.

In the keyhole he saw the now familiar pattern of ginger and blue with the white of the papers behind it and his father's burning tree. Complete stillness otherwise, apart from the endless rush of water over the rocks.

He went slowly round the side of the house, noticing that the leaves from the big sycamore on the corner were heaped up, dark and sodden, on the bonnet of her car. This was more than a day's leaves, surely, and it was more than a day's milk by the gate. Feeling slightly sick, he edged his way down towards the river.

The front wall of Foggett's was great boulders at the bottom. They had built the house on a rock above the water and in the tiny cellar underneath the main room the floor was bare limestone, and never dry. That was how the rats got in. His father had advised the woman to fill the whole thing up with concrete, and forget it, but she'd just laughed.

The cottage only had one door, at the back, and it opened into a small kitchen. The large front room, where she wrote her books, had the window with 'the view'. Under the sill the wall dropped away and disappeared into a litter of great stones, all heaped up anyhow. From across the river it looked as if someone had hurled them there in a rage. Dad had told him that they shifted sometimes, and that cracks came in the cottage walls. But the woman had wanted it so badly she hadn't even called in a structural surveyor. That was daft of her, you should always do that, especially with old places.

There used to be a wire fence between the front of the cottage and the back meadow, because of the sharp drop down, on to the rocks, but she had got somebody to remove it. She had not wanted to rent off the field for grazing and she had no husband, and no children. No one would come to see her, she said, whom she wouldn't warn about the drop, and nobody was likely to go sleepwalking in the garden. She had laughed about it that time with Uncle Maurice at Park Head. She laughed at quite a lot of things.

He had always wanted to get himself up the heap of rocks and look into her special writing room. Now he was doing it, but with the dumb inertia of nightmare. When he reached the top he had to stretch right up, pull himself on to the stone window ledge, and huddle there. It was hard, because the drop was much greater than it looked from across the river. He had often hidden there in the bushes and stared across at her lighted window as the sun went down. He wanted to know what a famous person did, when she was on her own. He had only seen her properly that one time, in their kitchen.

Now he was seeing her close to, perfectly still at the table, and her bright blue eyes were staring straight at him. But there was something awfully wrong with her face. It was all swollen, as if somebody had stuck a pump in her neck then blown it up hard, and there was a great green bruise down one cheek, the exact shape of a pear, green, but turning black at the edges.

Her mouth was open in a perfect round and there was some white inside it, not teeth, but what looked like a big ball of paper. Some of the papers in front of her were torn up into strips and from the ball a

6

solitary strip hung down, moving slightly, as if a wind were blowing in from somewhere.

Her left hand rested on the table, its fingers fanned out over an open book, tight swollen fingers like the face, sausage fingers now. He couldn't see the writing hand because of the two dark creatures busy there. One lay stretched full-length, quite easily, along the blue woollen sleeve, its tail relaxed, curled round in the crook of the woman's arm. Its mate, much smaller, was more crouched up, head down, body quivering. Both were quietly intent on feeding.

Suddenly he opened his hand flat and banged on the window, shattering two panes; the rats streaked away as glass showered into the room. At her table the woman toppled sideways and the right arm moved towards him, showing its gnawed, untidy stump.

The boy's long cry sounded through the empty valley, weaving its echoes into the steady rush of the arching water. Then he jerked back in a single movement, stiff and almost perpendicular, on to the heaped rocks below, then rolled over and over slippery green stones until his body rested on the gritty shore of a small pool fringed with young mountain ash, a secret place where he had once watched the woman bathe naked.

His head rolled from side to side, jerkily at first, with eyes wide open, then, as they fluttered shut, slower and more rhythmically, like a spinning coin that comes to rest at last. His knees, drawn up for a minute as if he were in pain, sagged down again and fell apart. His left arm was twisted under him, his right lay stretched towards the pool. He had torn his fingers on the rocks as he fell and they were bleeding into the water.

2

Tuesday 14th October

Grace was greatly looking forward to seeing the cottage. On the day the purchase was completed Anna had sent her a key through the post. 'This is your own personal key, darling,' she had written, 'and the place is *yours* and for *your use* whenever you want. You must come first, as soon as the builders have finished. Why not take The Girls over for a holiday?'

It was obvious that 'The Girls' rather amused Anna: Ba Savage, whose library job she had used in her novel *Harriet Harker*, and Marian Stoker, who worked for a nursing agency. Both would celebrate their fiftieth birthdays this year. Grace was thirty-five.

She had known of The Girls and of their special, rather exclusive relationship for some years because, like her, they went regularly to St Saviour's church. But she had only started to know them as friends through Marian, who had nursed Mother in the final weeks of her illness. Then Ba had got her to play the piano occasionally for Torch Bearers, the youth group she ran at church. This summer she had been invited to join them on their annual holiday, two quiet weeks of bed, breakfast and evening meal at a farmhouse in Wensleydale. Grace, grateful for the company after the sudden loneliness of White Lodge, had enjoyed it all, the letter-writing by the fire, the gentle walking, the cream teas in the pretty stone villages. This week she had joined them again, to see the autumn colours. She was becoming one of The Girls.

Before going into private nursing Marian Stoker had delivered babies. Anna had giggled about that. 'It's quite the wrong name for a midwife,' she had told Grace, 'they don't *stoke*. She doesn't push in, she pulls out. I might use that, it's funny.' Please don't, Grace had wanted to say, not Marian too, it's not fair. Now, though, at breakfast, she was watching Marian's large horse teeth munch toast with some distaste.

Marian was unmarried 'and grateful to be so', a phrase always delivered with lip-smacking emphasis, as if her singleness were sparing her some tiresome or terrifying ordeal. Grace wondered about her. Perhaps it was her lack of husband and lack, therefore, of what Mother used to refer to coyly as 'the sexual side' which had led her to abandon midwifery.

One of her own private griefs, shared with nobody, not even her best friend Anna, who scorned the state, was that she too was not yet married. With the child-bearing hips and the heavy breasts of the plodding, rather lumpy heroine of *Harriet Harker*, she was surely made for it, and she could not imagine a marriage without children. But she remained philosophical, believing that the Lord had a plan for her life and that this plan included a husband. She even felt she could predict who the man would be. It was Stephen Allen, though so far as she knew he was still married to Lynn. How all that would be resolved she could not begin to conjecture; but she knew that her life was in God's hands, and that she was precious to Him.

She had set today aside for visiting Anna, while Marian and Ba had earmarked it for shopping. When they all met at breakfast a thick rain was hurtling into the dale from the fellside and Grace inspected the weather in some alarm. To reach the cottage she had to drive from Wensleydale into Swaledale over the high Buttertubs Pass. There she must find a lane which led out of the main valley to Anna's cottage. The map marked it as a dead end and there were only two buildings along its five-mile length, Park Head, the farm at the far end of the valley, and her own cottage, Foggett's, half a mile nearer the road.

Anna had mentioned that it was a difficult lane to find and because she was uncertain of her map reading Grace asked The Girls to advise. Marian rose to the challenge at once, serene and smiling as she produced a neat pencil case, extracted black and red felt tips and drew an immaculate map. Life, generally, Marian Stoker seemed to find vastly amusing, for she smiled blandly at each new turn, displaying the quite enormous teeth. Even at Mother's death she had smiled. But Grace had ascribed that to embarrassment, to her not quite knowing how to cope with a grieving daughter who had unexpectedly become a friend. All this jollity must surely be a refuge from some private hurt, something Grace knew nothing about, as yet.

Ba mentioned again that she had once done a walk up to Park Head Farm, and that the valley was very beautiful. 'There was a marvellous waterfall,' she said, 'and a little bathing place all ringed with mountain ash. We walked right down the stream, I remember, till it joined the river at the bottom. I'd love to see it again.'

Grace was careful not to respond. Ever since their arrival Ba had

9

been hinting that she would like to come along with her today 'just to see the cottage'. But it was obviously Anna she wanted to see. She knew all about the Anna Beardmore phenomenon, how her modest sales had suddenly taken off after *Saddleford General*, about the first TV film, the tours and the interviews. She must surely have read *Harriet Harker* and seen that the heroine, who bore a suspiciously close physical resemblance to Grace, worked in a public library, like herself. Could she, too, have missed the description of the little mad woman who was always coming in to complain, the woman who had so upset Harriet that she had called in Mr Illingworth to advise, unhappy Mr Illingworth who had ended up in her bed? Grace remembered the description quite clearly. The mad woman had tight grey corkscrew curls, 'a keen, tanned face and made small rapid movements, like a foraging squirrel'. It was Ba. Anna must have gone into the library on some pretext, observed her, then gone home and made notes.

And yet Ba wanted to meet her, very much, apparently. 'I'd love to do that walk again,' she repeated, rather plaintively this time. But Grace merely folded the map and put it in her handbag.

'It's not walking weather, dear,' Marian observed crisply, 'and anyway, we're shopping.' She boomed rather and, as she cut toast into four neat squares, the smile came again. Grace was trying very hard but she didn't like her very much, she was too managing. Of the two, she much preferred Ba.

She left the farmhouse rather earlier than she needed, while The Girls were still drinking coffee, nervous of the drive ahead. If it was misty on the pass she must go very slowly and if the cloud got too thick she would simply turn round, go back to the farm and ring Anna. She would not want her to take risks.

Visibility was not brilliant but at least the road over Buttertubs was a proper highway, and very clearly marked. At the beginning of the long ascent she tucked herself in behind another car and stayed there. It was the safest policy, in mist.

Last night The Girls had enthused about the stupendous views she would get from the top of the pass, but now everything was blotted out by low-lying cloud. Twice the car in front stopped altogether, and she saw sheep ambling casually away, sooty-faced and fantastically horned, their long fleeces hanging down like unkempt hearth-rugs.

When the car she was following signalled left into a lay-by she went too, gratefully. She was still very early. Anna often wrote into the night, then slept in next day. She mustn't arrive to find her still in bed. Coffee time, they had agreed on the telephone last night, so she ought not to get there before eleven. Anna had her little routines and she would be ruffled if Grace found her unprepared.

The other car now opened its doors and four people got out, a young couple and two small children, a boy and a tiny girl, her walk still a stagger. The father swept her up rather brutally before she had moved two inches and yelled to his wife, 'Hold on to Jonathan, we don't want any accidents. There's nothing fencing the bloody things off.'

Grace left her car and followed at a discreet distance, suddenly embarrassed to be a woman on her own, seeing the sights. The lay-by must mark the location of the famous buttertubs, huge circular holes gouged deep into the limestone by underground rivers, millennia ago. By the fire last night Ba had shown her photographs, drawn diagrams to explain just how nature had formed them. A butter tub, or churn, was traditionally of that shape, big Marian had brayed, barging in as usual on the quietly informative Ba.

Grace stared down at the massive holes, saw the smooth rounded sides frilled here and there by bright green fern, heard the plashing of water far below, and marvelled. *When I consider the heavens, the works of thy fingers that thou hast made, what is man, that thou are mindful of him?* At her side the small boy stepped forward daringly, and threw a stone. 'Fucking well cut that out!' the man yelled, pulling him back and taking a side swipe at him. Grizzling, the child ran back towards the car. When she heard her brother, the toddler-in-arms began to cry too, a loud penetrating howl that the wind took up and magnified, tossing the desolate sound along the empty sheep-bitten hillsides. Grace made her way back to her own car and started up the engine. The sound of the crying child was strangely bitter to her, though she did not know why, except that it made her think of Stephen and his estranged wife Lynn, now up in Scotland with their children. She loved Stephen's little girls dearly. 'Auntie Gracie' they called her, loving her back. She so longed to see them again but whenever she phoned, Lynn made excuses, though it was not as if she would see Stephen if she visited. Nobody knew where he was.

It was clearer in the valley bottom and she followed Marian's neat map without difficulty. Just above the hidden lane she noticed something, left the car in a gateway and walked up to it. On a small concrete platform, a few yards above the road, someone had placed a seat, very recently because the wood was still raw and new, and there were dribbles of fresh concrete in the grass.

She sat down on it and looked at the view, two great cheeks of hillside tufted along their lower slopes with flaming autumn trees, and through them a glint of water where the Swale rushed towards

11

the complex of falls in the valley bottom. In the foreground a grey stone bridge sprang elegantly over a wide pebbly beck. On its green banks fat black-faced sheep grazed peacefully. In the absolute stillness she fancied she could hear their regular tearing chewing noise, mingled with the low bubble of the stream.

She stared at the view for a long time, her heart steadily expanding as it took in the great spread of greenness, the burning trees in the deep cleft of the hillside, the music of the water over the stones. All this she must store and keep, for the drab lonely winter in Peth. More and more these days Anna was subject to whim and change, and Grace was uncertain when there might be a second invitation to visit. She had a key but she felt too nervous to borrow the house and live in it alone, and she didn't know The Girls well enough yet to suggest they might share it.

Only when the view was fixed and she had drawn courage from it did she rise from the seat, turn round and look at the small metal plate screwed on the back. It was rather cheap-looking, with cramped, ugly lettering, and she guessed that Anna would have already ordered something better. The inscription was undated and very short. 'In memory of Guy Beardmore, who loved this Dale.'

It was some minutes before she felt composed enough to walk down to her car and negotiate the narrow entry into the lane. When she glanced in the driving mirror she wished she had brought something to clean her face. Anna might notice that she had been crying.

On reaching the cottage door, after a slow and cautious drive along a stony track, and a muddy walk across a large field, she nearly cried again. On the outer gate a crudely-painted sign still said 'Foggett's', but for Anna some craftsman had carved a new name plate. 'The Rock' it said, against the fresh green paint, in chubby capitals.

Anna did not believe but she was always telling Grace how she 'needed' *her* faith. It seemed some kind of folksy superstition, as if, by believing in Grace, she somehow caught a bit of God from her. Guy had always been more direct in his agnosticism. 'Say one for me,' he would call after her, with a sneer, as he watched her preparing for Sunday morning church. At fifteen he had sloughed off religion and all its works with a thoroughness that had grown over the years into a paranoid loathing.

Anna, in her first letter to Grace about Foggett's, had described its situation in minute detail. 'And it really *is* built upon a rock, darling,' she had written. ' "I have set mine house upon a rock." I feel it augurs well for me.'

12

But Grace had not known till this minute that she had actually renamed the cottage. She stared at the wooden plaque and fresh tears came in a rush of love and pity for her friend; but through them she felt hope. *Behold, I have graven thee upon the palms of my hands. Heaven and earth may forget thee, yet I will not forget thee.* He would not. Anna also was in his hands, in her anguish about Guy. Patting her face dry and pulling her scarf straight under her coat collar, she knocked on the door.

When nobody answered she checked her watch. It was ten minutes past eleven and there was no way Anna could still be in bed. 'I had a very good morning,' she had told Grace on the phone the night before. 'Nothing down on paper yet, but I think it's there. I can see the shape underneath now.'

Just once Grace had heard her address an audience about her writing, at a winter lecture organised by the Peth Lit. and Phil. Society. It had been in the very early days and nobody had really heard of Anna Beardmore. She had been shy and awkward.

Asked how a book 'grew' she used the image of stone being steadily cut away layer by layer, until a general shape emerged. Then that shape was refined by smaller and slower movements as the writer worked on finer and finer detail. '*Not* very original,' a woman near Grace muttered, quite loud enough for people to hear. It was Geraldine McEvoy, and *she* was Peth's 'writer', on the strength of her weekly literary column in the local newspaper, and some limp verse which she had published at her own expense. Anna, not knowing her audience, innocently warned against the pitfalls of vanity publishing. Geraldine, a large woman who always attended local functions in flowing, lurid-coloured clothes and dramatic hats, had left before the end, with much noise. Anna's first really bad review, describing her second Peth novel as 'indifferent airport literature', appeared in the *Gazette* a few months later.

Grace remembered that it had been a large and curiously eager audience and that she had heard whisper of the Beardmore parents first from one, then another, as Anna walked on to the platform with the aged chairman of the Lit. and Phil. What had happened years ago at Firs had not been forgotten in the small uneventful town of Peth. People were anxious to see how those remaining had survived, especially when they proclaimed themselves in books.

'I rewarded myself with a long walk this afternoon,' she had told Grace on the phone. 'It was absolutely glorious. I'm dying for you to come. But listen, we'll have to eat out. I've not managed to organise the cooking yet. I keep forgetting that it's ten miles to the nearest shop, and I missed the travelling butcher yester-day.'

'So what will you do tonight?' Grace was interested in the way other lonely people spent their time and The Rock, though spectacularly set, was also spectacularly isolated. Anna had a radio but no television. Grace did, and she watched it rather more than she should. It was a habit she had somehow drifted into, since she had been alone.

'I may write a bit more, or type up. Then I'll *clean*.' This was said with a giggle. White Lodge, where Grace had lived all her life, always looked immaculate, thanks mainly to the efforts of old Mrs Lumb, the daily help, whereas Anna lived in hand-to-mouth chaos whenever she came to Firs, the house she owned next door. She was always apologising to Grace about her 'messes'.

'Don't bother to clean up for me, Anna. It's you I'm coming to see,' Grace had said reassuringly. She meant it. Isolating herself at The Rock, to start drafting the book about Guy, had been something Anna had talked about for so long that Grace knew she was frightened, not of the physical isolation which she always sought when a book was under way, but of what she might find, when she began cutting away the stone.

Grace herself could not look at Guy's death yet. All it meant, in terms of the life he had lived, spoke of such pain for Anna, the friend of her life, that she could hardly bear it. For herself, it was all thrust far back into semi-consciousness where it would remain until she was given enough strength to look at it whole. She had always rather disliked Guy and in his last years she had come to detest him, for all that he had done to Anna. She did not begin to understand what he had become, at the end.

But Anna had been his sister and his twin. Often, in the months after The Tragedy, when she had stayed with Grace at White Lodge and Guy was away at school, she would stop suddenly, out on a walk, or when they were doing homework at opposite ends of the large oak dining table, to say, 'Grace, I'm sure there's something wrong with Guy.' More than once Daddie had telephoned the school to set her mind at rest. It was never very serious but yes, Guy had been concussed in a rugby accident, or yes, he was in the San with mild food poisoning. Anna always knew.

Strangely, she had not felt his death. When they brought the news she was staying with Grace at White Lodge. For days she had absolutely refused to believe it. She had wanted to see him for herself.

But Dr Lucas had not allowed her to go. In all the circumstances, he told Grace, in language strangely unmedical for the tense, rather tight-lipped elderly man she had known since childhood, it would be 'too heart-breaking'. In any case, Anna's presence was not necessary. Identification of the body had been made by Stephen Allen who had been sharing a flat with him at the time.

They had been friends almost as long as Grace and Anna, ever since Guy, after his expulsion from Cambridge, had done a course at Peth Art College. Stephen, a year or two older, had taken a job there, unable to live solely by selling his paintings, not even in the grim lodgings he'd found himself with old Mrs Dutt. Their friendship had always puzzled Grace, the unassuming gentleness of Stephen, Guy's thrusting loudness and irrationality, his bursts of sudden violence. Stephen had definitely been the stronger influence, for all Guy's bombastic, theatrical behaviour, and when she had seen them together she'd noticed how respectful Guy could be, how anxious to please. He had rather modelled himself on the slightly older man, she and Anna had both noticed it, and Stephen, though he surely had less to gain from the friendship, had always been tolerant of Guy's excesses. He must have needed Guy in his own way, for whenever, over the years, their various women failed them, they invariably sought each other's company. And Stephen had been there at the end. It was he who had opened the bathroom door.

Oh, Stephen. When she had heard what he had been forced to look at, and to endure, she had wanted to go to him. But within days he had left the flat and she had not seen him since – unless that distant figure on the crematorium path had been his, on the day of Guy's funeral. Even now she could not be sure.

She knocked on the door three times but got no response, so eventually she put her ear against it and listened very carefully. Little sounds were drowned out by the steady pouring of the waterfall, muffled by the thick walls of the cottage but still loud enough to make detecting movement inside rather difficult. After a minute she bent down and put her eye to the polished keyhole. The door between the tiny kitchen and 'The Room' as Anna called it, because there was only one, was open and she could see the large pine table where she obviously sat and wrote. Behind was the window with its vision of rocks and rushing water, and a little tree perched right on top of the fall, its frail autumn leaves rippling gold and black in the sunshine.

She could see a single sheet of paper on the writing table but otherwise, from what she could make out, Anna had certainly tidied up. The bit of kitchen framed in the large keyhole looked immaculate, with its neatly folded tea-towels and its rack of pretty blue and white china. 'I adore it,' Anna had written, after her first night at The Rock. 'It's absolutely *me*.'

No doubt the paper would be a note explaining where she was. Grace herself would have stuck such a thing to the door, but that was not Anna's way, she enjoyed certain little rituals with her friends. She had made a great point of sending Grace her *own* key and she would now, wherever she had rushed off to, be deriving a certain satisfaction from the thought of her letting herself into the cottage, poking about, admiring everything. 'You are my only true friend,' she had written, after Guy's death. 'Dear Grace, you are more myself than I am. Please don't leave me.'

For months she had treasured that note. Slipped in between two pages of the diary she wrote up every night before she said her prayers, it had become frayed and thin. She particularly valued it because Anna had never spoken in such a way of their friendship before, and, as she had become more and more successful with her books, the Peth links seemed to be slipping away, and Grace with them. It was one thing to cherish your old and trusted friend in silence, another, infinitely more precious, to give the thought voice.

But then, driving herself out into the world again, after Mother's death, Grace had attended the first winter meeting of the Lit. and Phil., and, in his opening remarks about *Wuthering Heights*, a book she had always been meaning to read, the speaker had quoted exactly what Anna had written to her. 'Nelly,' the woman in the book had said of her lover, 'he is more myself than I am.'

That night she had slipped the precious letter out of her diary and scrutinised it. The quotation was not acknowledged in Anna's punctuation, and Grace felt cheated. Why had she not said that she was quoting from another book? It was because she had relied on Grace's ignorance.

And suddenly the whole letter, with its melodramatic 'please don't leave me' had seemed trashy and cheap. With uncharacteristic spite Grace had torn it into small pieces and burned them on the kitchen stove. There were aspects of Anna's character that she definitely mistrusted now, less and less did she seem to resemble that numbed and desperate girl who had lived with them for so long at White Lodge, after The Tragedy.

For example, 'You absolutely *must* meet Julia,' she said, every single time she came to Firs, jubilant from a successful editorial meeting. Julia Wragg was her publisher in London. 'I would love to,' Grace always replied, and she meant it; for although such an event would make her nervous – how would she dress, how would she avoid appearing dull-witted and ill-informed? – she very much wanted to meet the elderly woman who now seemed to wield such power in Anna's important life.

But no meeting was ever arranged and the most hurtful thing now was that Julia was soon to spend a whole week at The Rock with Anna. For Grace, the friend of her life, she had allotted a single day, and even this was already eaten into, for she was not at home.

Grace took the cottage key from her handbag and inserted it into the new steel lock, incongruous above the much larger keyhole with its thick brass plate. It was possible she would not get in because Anna had twice been burgled, and she had talked of fitting new security locks to her various properties, to Firs, to her house in London and now, perhaps, to The Rock also. But the olive green door creaked, then swung inwards, admitting the curious Grace to the house she had heard about so often in excited letters from Anna, to the place which had 'restored her soul'. In the old days she had been rather touched by the way these letters were so liberally sprinkled with scriptural references. Now she felt that what she held most dear was somehow being held up to ridicule.

The minute kitchen was very neat, for Anna. On a dresser, below the racks of blue and white china, there was a tray set out with coffee cups, percolator and a packet of Bourbon biscuits. Grace smiled, forgetting her hurt. That was a reminder of the old, heady days. Mother had always bought Bourbons for White Lodge.

She went through to The Room, her eyes drawn immediately to the magnificence of the waterfall, framed in the small deep window opposite the inter-connecting door. 'Ideally,' Anna had written, 'I'd like to have a huge picture window knocked in, it's such an incredible view. But apparently I can't. It's a listed building and I'm in a National Park. Of course, I could always just *do* it. You know me.'

Grace did know her, well enough to predict that she would have her modern window when she judged she had lived at The Rock just long enough to be established. Anna had always liked things to go her way, and now she was so very successful she sometimes behaved as if her way was also her right.

As yet the cottage was still quite sparsely furnished. Her writing table dominated the room and by the fire there were two ugly wing chairs upholstered in a hard green velour. Grace recognised them from the breakfast room at Firs, even though Anna had draped bright camouflaging rugs over the backs. In the stone fireplace, its high jutting mantel filled with bits of characteristic Anna rubbish, letters and pencil pots, a small torch, half a bar of chocolate, she had arranged firelighters, sticks and small coals, ready for Grace. 'We'll have a real fire,' she had said gleefully on the phone, 'but I shan't light it till you actually arrive.' Proper coal fires were like the Bourbon biscuits; they were about White Lodge days, and the past.

New pine bookshelves, fitted into the recesses on each side of the fire, were already filled to overflowing with tapes and compact discs, as well as books. Grace didn't inspect the titles, her eyes moved instead to an odd-looking poster tacked on one wall, above a chest of drawers. Skirting the table she went up and looked at it more closely.

From the information printed along the bottom it seemed to be a picture of some modern sculptured object, a pavement tiled in black and white diamonds, the whole thing so photographed as to reveal the various layers of cinder and small waste on which the pavement had been laid. Underneath was the earth itself. The section of diamond pavings with their underlying layers made up the entire photograph except that in the middle there was a jagged break, splitting the tiles, damage done, perhaps, by the dropping of some very heavy object from a considerable height. Towards the bottom of the picture, as if its owner had suddenly abandoned his walk along the pavement, was a solitary, dirty gym shoe, its toe pointing down to the floor. In the bottom right-hand corner Grace read 'Broken Path'.

She stared at it, puzzled. Most of the objects in this room were quite familiar to her. The furniture had come from Firs though the bright rugs and curtains were new, bought from a shop Anna had described as 'a gorgeous cheap little bazaar place, in Richmond'. Her attitude to the spending of money was still very cautious. She could not, she had recently told Grace, really believe that she was *rich*. She felt it was a dream from which she was soon to be rudely awakened. Therefore, as yet, she still spent prudently.

This curious poster was not only new, it was somehow definitely not 'Anna'. There were several pictures on the rough white walls, a set of Victorian water colours from Firs, a fine early engraving of Peth parish church that Mother had given her, on her twenty-first birthday and, over the fireplace, one of Guy's oils, even then an aping of Stephen's technique and a pathetic remnant of his abandoned career at art school.

Grace looked away, staring out over the tumbling yellowish water in an effort to compose herself. The emotion was unexpected, and she must not weep again. If she did, Anna would choose that moment to walk in.

But where on earth was she? The short day was already dribbling away and she didn't want to drive back over that high pass in pitch darkness. When she felt calm again she went back to the table and picked up the note, holding it at arm's length. Anna's writing had never been very legible and this, no doubt, would have been scribbled in her usual tearing hurry. It would contain revised times and new instructions, a different meeting place. She would not have stopped long enough to consider the feelings of her oldest friend.

She expected to see 'Grace, darling . . .', Anna's usual opening these days. Instead, in clear though shaky capitals, she read: 'SUICIDE IS SIMPLY THE MOST EXTREME AND BRUTAL WAY OF MAKING SURE THAT YOU WILL NOT BE EASILY FORGOTTEN.'

3

The brief burst of sunshine that had set the little tree burning had now spent itself, and The Room was dark again. The window over the table was small and the one in the kitchen smaller still. In the real depths of winter The Rock would need artificial light in the daytime hours. Anna had spent several thousands on the fabric of the place and it was now supposed to be rot-proof and thoroughly free from damp. Even so, standing in the shadows by the lifeless grate, Grace felt an intense cold strike through her.

She did not touch the note again because it was not intended for her; it belonged to the material Anna was collecting for her book on Guy. 'Novel Seven', she had printed on a notebook. Grace looked at the blue cover thoughtfully. So she had finally decided on fiction. When they had first talked about her new book she had been undecided whether she would work something out in letters or in the form of an extended essay. An actual novel had not been mentioned. All Anna would say was that it was to be her first 'serious' book and that Julia would probably not know how to market it, after the Saddleford series.

On top of the blue notebook was a fountain pen and two new lead pencils, each sharpened to a very fine point, and on the right of the note one of the familiar small red boxes she used for her card indexes. Anna's thoughts on Guy interested Grace far more than the Peth novels but they never talked together in any detail about what she was writing. Even now she still worked with her left arm hugging the paper, her hand ready to hide the script from prying eyes, like a little child that is saying 'don't copy'.

In the front right-hand corner of The Room a thick green curtain hung on polished rings. Grace stretched out a hand, hesitated, then pulled it aside, the sudden clacking noise sounding obtrusively loud in the still room. It revealed one very deep step, then a short flight leading up to the floor above, bare grey stone and treacherously steep, just as Anna had described in that first ecstatic letter. 'They are the *original* steps, darling, and over three hundred years old. But I must have some kind of hand-rail fitted, for the more doddery visitors. I can just see poor old Julia falling headfirst otherwise.'

Grace squinnied upwards. A thick bar of smooth dark wood had been screwed to metal fixtures cemented into the wall. There was a square of light at the top but it was hard to tell whether it was coming from a window or from an electric bulb. As she stood there, trying to gather courage to ascend, there was movement. A bar of shadow flitted across the lighted square and there was a faint squeak, as if something up there had put very slight pressure on one of the beams.

She retreated, pulled a chair out from the writing table, and sat down heavily, her heart pumping. Anna had told her, unwisely, that before she had taken it over The Rock had been overrun with rats, but that they had since been thoroughly dealt with, holes sealed up, bait laid, every inch of the property checked and re-checked. She had absolutely insisted on that. 'But I did get a shock on my first night,' she had confided in a letter. 'I must have heard the one that got away, rooting about in the roof. It was terribly loud, Grace, like someone in long clothes dragging their skirts across the ceiling. Lovely Mr Pattison came first thing next morning and saw to it. They're marvellous up here.'

In winter rats always sought warmth and food; Grace knew that because they had once had a rat at White Lodge, in the wash-house. Daddie had killed it but she'd had a terror of rats ever since. Guy had played on her fears rather cruelly, chasing her round the garden with an old fur glove shouting, 'Rat, Rat.' Anna would obviously have to summon this Mr Pattison again. She could not go up those stairs. She had once heard of a rat cornered in a barn, going for a man's throat.

The prevailing smell of The Rock was faint must and damp. She could smell fresh coffee too. Anna had obviously ground the beans earlier and filled the percolator. There was also the faint smell of Firs, the Beardmore family home that Anna had recently bought back. Every house had its own characteristic odour and that of The Rock reminded her very strongly, now she analysed it, of the gloomy buried house next door to White Lodge, its gothic upper windows masked in creeper, its drive quite lost in trailing shrubs and neglected grass.

The Firs smell must be coming off the wing chairs, off the carpet too, perhaps, which she recognised from Dr Beardmore's study. It had obviously been very recently cleaned and the dark blues and mauves of the geometric border design stood out richly against the fainter blue ground. The cleaning had not eliminated the ink stains, though. Anna's father used to wipe his fountain pen on the inside of his jacket, then flick it irritably on to the floor, to get the ink flowing. She was just like him. The cottage was only neat and tidy today because it was her new toy and she was playing house. Soon, thought Grace, it will be as chaotic as all the other places she has lived in.

As well as Firs she could smell alcohol. This surprised her because Anna, who had drunk rather freely before, had stopped completely after Guy's death. She had always blamed Stephen Allen for his drink problem, unfairly, Grace thought. They both knew perfectly well that Guy had been in trouble for under-age drinking when he was still at school; it had certainly not been initiated by Stephen, whose own drinking always came on with his bouts of depression. When he was well, and able to paint, he hardly seemed interested in food or drink. When he had lived with Lynn on the island they had not drunk at all.

Grace looked all round The Room for an empty glass or bottle but found neither. In the kitchen the fridge contained a bowl of tomatoes, some cheese and half a can of baked beans. Anna was no cook but she liked these, mounded greedily on thickly buttered toast. Grace found a bowl, decanted the beans into it, then looked round for a rubbish container. Anna often left food to go bad in tins and she had once got acute food poisoning from doing so.

There was a new red plastic pedal bin in one corner of the kitchen. She opened it and threw away the can. There was no empty wine bottle inside but she could see ash, and several cigarette butts on top of some screwed up paper. As she stared down at them something behind the bin moved suddenly, then streaked into the shadows. She stepped back, her hand over her mouth, stifling a scream. She did not want to stay here a minute longer. Mr Pattison from Richmond was 'lovely' no doubt, but he could not have been quite thorough enough. The thing behind the bin had been much too large for a mouse, or a shrew.

She went back into the main room and fingered the note uncertainly. Unless she opened the red box to find a blank card she would have to write on the other side of this paper and she absolutely couldn't do that. What Anna had written was the seed and the starting point of her essentially private work about Guy. Merely reading the note had felt like a betrayal. To scribble some trivial message on the back of it was not possible.

Walking on tiptoe, lest she disturb another of the creatures which she had no doubt were in the skirtings or under the floorboards, she made her way to the stone staircase again and looked up. The same square of light still patched the wall, unbroken now. The only movement in the place was at her back, in the steady pouring of the great waterfall beyond the window.

Terrifying thoughts came to her as she stood with her foot on the deep stone step revealed by the clacking curtain. She knew that she ought to ascend the narrow stairs and investigate the upper storey, to reassure herself that all was well. Anna could have had intruders in this lonely place. How else could she explain the unaccountable smell, the ash in the kitchen? Yet there was no sign of disorder in the two lower rooms.

Trembling now, she climbed up one step. It was not possible, was it, Lord, that Anna, swept beyond her controlled, rational self in these tortured investigations about Guy, had, in a moment of peculiar anguish, followed, twin-like, along the same road? That she lay up there on the ancient Victorian brass bed she had described so minutely in a letter, beyond help, beyond prayer?

No. Grace would not believe it. Clutching the new hand-rail she resolutely mounted the second step. She would investigate thoroughly, reassure herself that all was well and perhaps, too, find the innocent explanation for Anna's absence, after their telephone arrangement. What was slightly annoying her now was having to return to The Girls as it were empty-handed. She would feel foolish, confessing that there had, after all, been no meeting, especially after Ba's impressed enquiries. Perhaps she would not tell them.

There were only eight steps to the upper floor but Grace stopped half-way, and retreated. She had not only seen shadows again, barring the illuminated square, she had heard something quite distinct above her head, not creaking beams this time, more like a pulling noise across a wooden floor. 'The one that got away,' she recalled from Anna's letter, 'like someone in long clothes dragging their skirts.' But that had been in the floor space over the bedroom. Now the creature seemed to be in the room itself.

She must get outside. Nerves, hunger after a small breakfast, and a deep fear about Anna that she could not, in spite of everything, quite thrust away, were all combining to bring on that curious, swimmy feeling that often signalled one of her little 'attacks', those alarming turns she had occasionally, when her heart raced so. She had not worried Anna with it but tablets had been prescribed by Dr Lucas, and he had advised her to lose a little weight.

She reached the kitchen door and pulled it open, swallowing down great gulps of cold air. Over her head the dragging noise had started up again, but louder now, as if pursuing her.

Banging the door behind her Grace fled, stumbling as she ran along the meadow path, away from the cottage.

Friday 17th October

As she drove home she was listening to a radio programme about dustmen. It was warm in the car and she'd recently made a rule that she wouldn't listen on motorways any more. She had once nearly fallen asleep, found herself only inches from the car in front and come to a screaming halt. The driver had turned right round, making an obscene gesture; the whole incident had unnerved her.

But today she was fretting about Anna and it would be a good two hours before she reached Peth. Radio 4 could fill in the gap, time she would otherwise spend worrying. She'd not told The Girls about Anna's not being at The Rock on Tuesday, now she rather wished she had. But they were on their way up to Scotland for the second part of their holiday. She had not been invited – not that she really minded. There were things to do at home.

The minute she got there she would go next door to Firs, to see what was happening. It was quite possible that Anna had suddenly decided to come south for some reason. It would have been just nice if she'd told Grace about the change of plan. She'd phoned every day since Tuesday, but had never got an answer. But then, Anna was very much more casual these days. She could have easily cancelled Julia Wragg, and gone straight back to London.

Now a man was describing what people sometimes put into their dustbins, babies' nappies full of you-know-what, sanitary towels and chicken carcasses. They were the worst, he said with evident relish, because, if they got too warm, maggots bred in them.

Grace's hand hovered. If the conversation got much worse she would switch off. Mother had been cremated so she had no worries there, but Daddie had been interred, in the old family grave at High Peth. He'd been dead for nearly fourteen years. How long were maggots active, though?

'That's not my bin,' one peevish old woman had told the speaker. 'Mine's got a green lid.'

'This *is* a green lid.'

'Well, it's not mine. I want my own back, if you don't mind.'

All the speakers sounded like the people up in the Dales, though the accent was flatter. It was certainly Yorkshire, but probably further south. Anna would know, she was clever at placing accents.

Her own had undergone subtle changes in the last few years, 'cultivated northern' she called it, with a certain embarrassment, though it didn't sound in the least northern to Grace. It was all the TV and radio, she decided. The naked exposure of live television was nerve-racking, Anna said. You needed to 'merge'.

'Once,' began a dustman, 'I went to this house and a man and a woman were having a bit of, you know, on the settee. Well, t'bin were right under t'window so I had to fetch it. Woman shoved her hand up when she saw me. "Leave us two bags, love," she shouted, just like that.'

24

By their dustbins ye shall know them, pondered Grace. The interviewer was on to his third subject now, according to whom the lower-class areas had bins filled with grease, dogdirt and used toilet paper. Again, her hand moved to the off button. She was feeling uncomfortable now and the disgusting details had made her slightly queasy. If she had one of her little attacks at the wheel of the car it could be much worse than the screeching brakes and the man who'd gestured at her.

Someone said, 'We were once called in to move a bed and when we got upstairs we found there were a dead man in it. "Hey," I said to the young feller who'd rung up. "Hey, what are you playing at? There's a dead man in this bed." He said, "I know" – right thick he was – "it's me dad. I didn't know what to do with him, like. I thought perhaps you could shift him. He's been dead three weeks."' Grace pressed the off button and drove steadily on.

Soon she passed the boundary sign which marked the transition from Cumbria to Lancashire. Anna, whenever she saw the modernist red rose sign, always raised her fist in salute, then smiled at Grace. The smile meant, 'We are Lancastrians, you and I, we inhabit Peth. Hurrah for the red rose county.' And Grace duly returned the smile, but only because she was loyal. Anna hardly ever came to Peth these days and she didn't need Lancashire any more, though in the early books she had drained it dry. The lifeless, bleached grasslands up which the great road now climbed were an image of what she had done to her 'red rose county'. Grace no longer made herself read the stories, though she always received an early copy with the same unvarying inscription in the front. 'To Grace, in love and friendship.'

She had tried with the novels for a long time, but she always found the fat books rather heavy going. Even so, there was a special shelf reserved for them in Daddie's large mahogany bookcase and she had recently shown them to The Girls with some pride. She had wanted to like the novels for Anna's sake. But then *Harriet Harker* had been published, and after that Grace no longer quite trusted her.

There was no doubt that she was the model, worthy, plodding Harriet with her flat splayed feet and her broad hips. Harriet too was lumbered with a tiresome invalid mother and she worked in a lending library like Ba. To Grace it had seemed insensitive of Anna to have used one of The Girls' jobs so blatantly, turning Ba into that little mad woman who haunted the romantic fiction shelves, not to mention Harriet/Grace herself. Why couldn't the heroine have been a shop assistant, or something vaguely medical like an occupational therapist? The hospital world held great appeal, according to Anna. *Saddleford General* had been one of her big early sellers, though the television series was largely responsible for that.

25

In using her best friend Grace for Harriet, Anna had not been kind. It was not only the splayed feet and the hips, it was what she had called 'the facial problem'. 'There was a slight hairiness about the face,' she had written in her opening paragraphs, 'and it was dark hair. By fifty Harriet would have the beginnings of a fine moustache.'

At this page in *Harriet Harker* Grace's copy automatically fell open, she had looked at it so often. Sometimes she wept over it. 'Oh, don't be so *silly*, darling,' Anna said defiantly when she had timidly ventured, after much prayer, that Harriet . . . in some ways . . . rather resembled . . . But Grace was not deceived.

The Lord had answered her petition about *Harriet Harker* and it had not been taken up by the television companies. Nobody, it seemed, had been much attracted by its slow-moving and incipiently moustachioed heroine. *Harriet* 'lacked drama' according to one letter, forwarded from Anna's London publishers to the house in Peth. 'Look at this, Grace,' she had said irritably, passing it over. 'What *stupidity*. Harriet's one of my better creations, I think.'

But she was not so much a creation as a rather cruel borrowing. Thanking the Lord that he had spared her the ordeal of seeing herself, through Harriet, involved in various distasteful sexual exploits on the television screen, Grace had held the letter silently, in her large hands. These too had been minutely described in *Harriet Harker*, hands which, after The Tragedy, Anna had taken so often into her own soft little paws, for comfort. Guy, jealously watching, had made strange faces to show that he did not approve. He had disliked Grace's family from the very beginning, in spite of her parents' kindness.

Now Anna could creep up and hold her friend's large hands whenever she pleased. Guy was dead. The postman no longer went to Firs with his long, incomprehensible letters, letters which Grace was under orders to destroy. Nor did the telephone ring any more in the middle of the night. There was no silence like death.

About thirty miles from Peth she stopped in a service area, filled the car up with petrol, then went to the cafeteria for a cup of coffee. It was silly, not waiting until she reached White Lodge. Mrs Lumb would have lit the stove for her, she could sit in the warm kitchen with Binkie on her knee, and open her post, instead of which she was perched uncomfortably on a shiny plastic seat which seemed permanently angled downwards, in an effort to get her out of the place as quickly as possible. With her coffee she munched on a Danish pastry. Dr Lucas had said no cakes or buns, but she had a sudden nervous urge to cram her stomach, a need for sweetness, for comfort. It was Anna. She couldn't stop thinking about her.

It was dark and she didn't like night driving, especially on a motorway where lights from the opposite lane flashed endlessly into her eyes. Rain made everything worse, the way it magnified the water on the screen, and it was raining now. Nevertheless, before setting off on the final leg of the journey home, she was definitely phoning Anna again. As she sat drinking her coffee it had come to her with absolute certainty that Anna was back at the cottage.

She dialled the number and let the telephone ring for a very long time, quite long enough to tell her that she was wrong. But she was determined to get an answer, and she did not replace the handset. Mother had always laughed at what she had called Grace's 'funny little hunches'. Ba Savage, not usually given to expressing strong opinions, felt that these psychic intuitions, granted to Grace at odd times in her life, might well prove accurate, but they were not 'of The Lord'. Please would she *not* mention them to the Torch Bearers, Ba had pleaded. There was too much emphasis on the occult in modern children's literature, and young impressionable girls were bound to latch on to it.

Grace let the telephone ring for a full sixty seconds, timing them on her watch. At last, genuinely puzzled, she removed the receiver from her ear and reached out to replace it. Then the phone at the other end was picked up, obviously dropped, then secured again. 'Hello?' she said. '*Anna?* It's Grace. What happened, on Tuesday? I've rung so many times.'

There was no answer. All she could hear was a light quick breathing and the muffled pouring of the waterfall in the background. 'Anna?' she repeated rather shrilly. '*Anna?*'

'She's n – n – not available j – j – just now,' someone stammered, a male voice, Scots, extremely quiet. 'I think she's t – t – t – taking a shower.'

'*Is that Stephen?*' Suddenly she found herself breathless, hardly able to speak. In the sheer relief of hearing his voice again, of having proof positive that he was all right, *alive* after all she had secretly feared, she forgot she was angry with Anna. Nor did she think, in the sheer relief of the moment, about what his presence there might mean.

She knew that Stephen had once been a lover of Anna's, though when and how the relationship had ended she was unsure. Anna had always been rather secretive about him because, Grace sensed, she really rather despised him. Latterly she had dismissed him as 'a bit pathetic' and Grace suspected they had quarrelled. While she worried, Anna seemed rather relieved that he had disappeared from their lives. It was tactless because she knew all about Grace's tender feelings towards him, confided long ago in the intense early days.

And now he was alive, and at The Rock. He had not yielded to one of his awful moods of darkness and taken his own life, which was what she had begun to fear, after his long silence. 'It's marvellous to hear you, Stephen,' she said warmly. 'But what on earth have you been *doing* with yourself? It's been months.' But there was a sudden click and the phone was replaced at the other end.

She immediately redialled and got the engaged signal. Either someone else had phoned in those few seconds or else Stephen had left the receiver off the hook. Anna might be bathing (there was no shower, she thought) as a possible prelude to further lovemaking. She had once described to Grace in some detail how she liked to prepare herself for it, her small, rather watery blue eyes flicking sideways on to her friend's face, to see if there was a reaction. Grace had noticed that, when Anna had no man on the go, she seemed to need to talk about sex; there was evidently a particular satisfaction from speaking about such things to a friend of her persuasion, someone the same age but a virgin, a woman who would believe in chastity before marriage.

But for all their years of friendship she misread Grace in this. She didn't need to eavesdrop on the finer details of sex for her own fullness of life. She supposed, though, that what Anna had written of her in *Harriet Harker* must be true, that she could be 'infuriatingly matter of fact about the passions'.

She was still passionate about Stephen and to her what Anna's novels described as 'passion' bore no resemblance to what she felt. The marvellous God-given word was surely misused when applied to the ludicrous fumblings of a character like Mr Illingworth, in the Saddleford series. Perhaps the new book would be different. Perhaps that was why Guy had had to die, so that something 'enduring' – that was Anna's word about her new novel – might come from her pen.

But here Grace's faith failed to shed light. On the holiday Ba had talked to her about something she called 'creative suffering', and of her own brief marriage to a younger man who had treated her shamefully. She had come to see, she said, how God had used the hurt and the lone-liness. She had the library, Torch Bearers, Marian, and everyone had been so supportive. Out of the wreckage had come hope and goodness, even a kind of joy. Grace had listened but her heart was troubled. Then was the Lord in that sordid London bathroom, a year ago, in the night-mare on which Stephen had stumbled? Was this what Ba was saying?

If it was, she did not understand. There was an outer darkness round her faith which sometimes frightened her; all round the clear and simple picture, the constant, steady light, hovered something else, tangled and many-layered, full of inexplicable threat. Ba's wrecked marriage was part of it, and Guy, and the old tragedy at Firs. All she knew was that such things could not be of the Lord, in whom was no darkness, neither any shadow of turning. Yet she feared that if she once looked properly at the threatening layers she would be engulfed by them. The Girls were rather brisker about their faith. Marian would quote at her, no doubt, if she knew of these feelings: *Lord, I believe, Help thou mine unbelief.*

Well, God Almighty was outside her little human time scale, Grace understood that much, and outside Anna's. Only at the end of her writing life would anyone be able to fit the pieces together and judge how much Guy's life and death had contributed to what she had achieved – if indeed she emerged as the 'important' writer she now seemed set on becoming.

For now, though Anna had failed her again, she felt at peace. Stephen was alive and they were together at The Rock. His living presence was of more significance in the scheme of things than were her irritations at the vagaries of Anna Beardmore. Anyhow, it was not the first time she had been let down like this. She ought to have anticipated it.

Only five miles short of the first Peth exit she found herself immobilised in a gigantic traffic jam which delayed her for nearly an hour. For a while she listened half-heartedly to the radio, then she switched off and prayed that Anna might be at The Rock, or at Firs, and that all manner of things would be well with her, and with Stephen. When she finally crawled up to the top of the hill that looped round the last bit of sooty moorland before the road dropped down into Peth she saw a glittering skein of red brake lights ahead, more or less stationary. She signalled left, came off the carriageway early at Peth North and took the ring road round town. At last, two hours later than she had expected, she swung off Manchester Road into Birch Grove, the broad tree-lined avenue that led to their own Beaumont Crescent, to White Lodge and to Firs.

On the corner was a small newsagent's, still open. She stopped, collected a copy of the *Peth Gazette* from a stand, went inside and paid for it, exchanging desultory remarks about the weather with an elderly man behind the counter as he rooted about in his till for change, glad of a customer and taking his time, talking about the nights drawing in, about the nippy evenings and the inconvenience of the one-pound coin.

Worrying again, about Anna's whereabouts, she walked out hurriedly while he paused for breath, got into the car and drove off as the evening paper boy pedalled along the pavement with his empty bag wetly flapping. In his front basket was a radio tuned into a local pop station, blaring loudly. It was just eight o'clock and an excited voice broke into the music with the news headlines, leading with some story about a Lancashire celebrity who had been involved in something succulently described as a 'lonely cottage horror'. But Grace had already passed by.

4

Grace went to bed very early but set her alarm for eight o'clock. There was no sign of Anna's car at Firs and the house was dark, but she planned to go round there first thing tomorrow, to check for signs of her having called in. It was not impossible that she had spent a few hours there, then driven on to London. She never stayed very long in her old home, Grace had noticed, she always complained that it was too cold and too uncomfortable. Not that there was any shortage of money to put things right, not now. But Grace was certain that Anna didn't want to, she had obviously finished with Peth; she would probably sell the house soon. Why had she bought it back in the first place?

She slept badly and at two in the morning took a sleeping pill. She had thrown the rest of Mother's tablets away but keeping these in a drawer for the really impossible nights was easier than bothering Dr Lucas. Besides, he would nag her about her weight, and the heart thing.

She did not particularly like the thick black sleep the pills induced, nor the way they pulled her down into dreamless oblivion from which, when day came, she must crawl her way to the light, clawing upwards as from a deep pit. If she explained to Dr Lucas he would no doubt give her something that suited her better. But she felt that she must endure. Besides, she balked at the thought of talking to the familiar elderly doctor about how she was feeling, of how the pain about Mother was still curiously intense, and of how she feared for her own future, the sheer loneliness of it.

He would simply say, 'But Grace, you have so much to do, you have the business to keep your eye on, and that large house; you have your church work, all your friends,' he who knew her and her family so well and had always been, under the brusqueness, extremely kind. How could she tell him that this was the point, that it was the sheer endlessness of her own future that terrified her? Dr Lucas would not understand. Besides, to admit such things would be letting the Lord down and she must walk close to him now, till the darkness passed.

Still feeling thick-headed and heavy at half-past ten next morning, when some far-away noise woke her up, she pulled on her dressing gown and climbed up the stairs to the third floor. From the attics there was a clear view of the drive and front door of Firs. If Anna had come back in the night she would be able to see the car. But the weedy half-circle of gravel was empty and dead leaves from the trees along the drive lay in deep drifts round the front steps. There was obviously no one at home. Unaccountably, Grace shivered, pulling her robe around her. She was thinking of Stephen's voice on the telephone and therefore of Anna, safe and having her bath at The Rock. But an uncertainty still lingered. Then, up through the house, came a repetition of the noise that must have dragged her up from her deep sleep. Someone was ringing the front door bell and, getting no reply, pressing it more insistently, and for longer. She walked slowly down three flights of stairs, clutching the banister very tight because she felt nervous suddenly, and feeble. On the lowest step she paused, staring at the front door down the long shadowy hall with its pattern of black and white tiles, each diamond still perfect after ninety years, suddenly remembered the strange poster pinned on to the wall at The Rock, the shattered paving, the dirty shoe.

Through the coloured glass of the upper panes she could see a head. She advanced slowly, undid top and bottom bolts, turned back the double lock and opened the door the few inches allowed by its thick brass chain. It could be Anna in which case, come in, coffee on the go immediately and let's sit and natter by the kitchen stove, back to the old days, all hurt forgotten. Then through the crack a timid voice said, 'Grace? It's Breda, Breda Smith. Can I come in?'

She paused then unfastened the chain, half opening the door and stepping back slightly, disconcerted. Of course she should have realised that it couldn't possibly be Anna who, without shoes, was only five foot two and whose small curly head would not have come half-way up the coloured glass. Breda, whom they had both known at school, was nearly six feet tall and very thickly made. She had a plain flat face, heavy legs and hands and feet so large they made Grace's own rather clumsy extremities look almost delicate. She had topped the other girls by a good head and her figure in those days had been a perfect triangle, small breasts, spreading waist, massive hips, all supported by trunk-like thighs. Grace had always felt rather sorry for Breda Smith though she had once played Herod magnificently in a school nativity play, wearing a great black beard with determined cheerfulness.

At eighteen she had gone to college in the Midlands and trained to become a teacher. Then, in her mid-twenties, she had changed career, entered the police force and done surprisingly well in it. Mother, who was small and pretty, had always referred to her rather distastefully as 'that very *big* girl'. But she had still clipped out anything that mentioned her from the *Gazette*. Grace knew that it was Mother's selfishness which had kept her at home, through the long hypochondriac years of widowhood. It was hurtful when she'd pointed out other people's achievements.

Anna was the great exception. Such a glamorous, worldly success had proved too much for Mrs Bradley to swallow. She did not collect clippings about Anna Beardmore, nor often speak about her, in spite of the way they had taken her and Guy in, after The Tragedy.

Grace said, 'Why, hello Breda, long time no see,' and she pulled rather self-consciously at the neck of her dressing gown. 'Sorry I'm in this state, I had rather a bad night so I slept in. I should be at Sainsbury's, monthly shop, *ugh*,' and she laughed, rather nervously, trying to remember just when Breda Smith had last called at White Lodge. It was New Year's Day two years ago, she thought, when burglars had gone over several of the larger houses in Beaumont Crescent. Breda had come round collecting information from the residents. She did not socialize with Grace, though they still exchanged Christmas cards. She had been in uniform then.

Now she wore a smart camel trench coat with a Paisley scarf knotted at the neck. Though you could not trade in feet or hands, or heavy legs, you could always lose weight and Breda had shed several stones. Grace was impressed; her own attempts to diet were not going too well. She said generously, 'You look awfully smart, Breda, and you're so *slim*. Listen, why don't you come in for a minute?' and she held the door open.

'Grace, I'm sorry, but I'm afraid this is official,' and Breda produced an identity card encased in plastic. It revealed that she was now Detective Sergeant B. Smith of the Lancashire CID. 'My boss'll be here in a minute,' she said.

'*Boss* . . . who's your boss, Breda?' Grace's voice had dropped to a whisper. *Policemen*. Her broken sleep and that hammering on the front door. The dressing gown. It was death again and already, after Mother and Guy, she was choked with it. Last week, in the Dales, The Girls had helped her to take her first, uncertain steps back to the light. Now this. Who was it this time, old Aunt Celia in Lichfield? A god-child? Marian and Ba, killed on the motorway? She stared up into the police-woman's face, the deeply mournful expression in the large flat eyes quite chilling her, and she tried to say casually, 'What's all this about then, Breda, more break-ins?' *But she knew*, and suddenly she had no spit and couldn't make words. She stepped backwards into the hall and sank on to the nearest seat, a Victorian chair with a finely reeded back on which Anna and Guy had huddled together, the day of The Tragedy, Guy turning his mother's wedding ring over and over in his hands. Daddie had removed it, before they took everything away.

Breda loomed over the chair, her kindly, ugly face still more troubled now, one hand stretched out. Then car tyres crunched to a halt outside, and a door slammed. 'This'll be my boss, William Buckle. He's a Detective Superintendent, he's new.'

Someone came into the hall fast, almost at a run, a slight, neat man rather shorter than Grace and a few years younger, his round already balding head only just skimming Breda's shoulders, immaculate in dark grey with a pink rose in his buttonhole.

'*Right*, is there somewhere we could all sit down?' he said rather abruptly, addressing his remark to Breda.

She immediately snatched her hand from Grace's shoulder and flushed. 'I've . . . I've not had a chance to explain to Miss Bradley yet,' she began, and her voice shook. 'I don't think she can have heard the news.'

Grace went on staring, motionless on her chair, watching a large tear roll slowly down Breda's face. 'It's about Anna, isn't it?' she got out at last, in a funny little croak.

William Buckle was showing her his identity card but she didn't look at it. 'I think the central heating's playing up,' she whispered, touching the radiator behind the chair. Now she thought about it the whole house felt like an ice-box. It was the cold that must have wakened her, cold, and the ringing of the front door bell. 'I think we'll have to sit in the kitchen,' she added, closing the front door and making her way along the hall. 'I've an all-night stove in there.'

Breda followed, clearing her throat elaborately, to cover the silence. Behind came the man with the rose. 'It's not much warmer in here, is it?' he remarked, taking papers from a briefcase and spreading them out on the table. Then he rubbed his hands. His delivery was curiously tight, his movements jerky as Grace watched him arranging himself for the interview.

'I slept late,' she said, in a dead voice. He had not contradicted her remark about Anna. 'It just needs banking up, that's all.' But she stayed where she was in her usual chair, placed sideways to the garden so that she could see the birds, while she ate her solitary meals. Her ears were making their familiar buzzing noise now, a weird little noise that she could produce at will, to blot out external sounds. She did not want to hear what these people had to say to her.

'I'll do it, Grace,' offered Breda. The man made no move, except to

34

unscrew a fountain pen and write something on a sheet of blank paper. But Breda got down on her knees and riddled the fire energetically. Then she put fuel on, piece by piece, poking and riddling again. She stayed hunched over the stove for a considerable time, sweeping up grit and ash, arranging and rearranging shovel and fire-irons, replacing the rubber hod on the special square of blue linoleum assigned to it by the fastidious Mrs Lumb.

'So, are we ready then?' the man said at last. His voice sounded no kinder and his fingers had started drumming the table top. He was staring very hard at the silent Grace.

'Oh, sorry, Boss. Yes, that's burning nicely now,' Breda muttered, through her back.

When she turned to the table Grace saw that her red face was faintly streaked where coal dust had settled in the path of her tears. She herself could not have wept at that moment, not if all the coals in the gently glowing stove had been taken out and heaped upon her naked flesh, one by one.

Buckle was appalled that Smith hadn't managed to break the news before he entered the house. Now he must do it himself, and he was afraid, of hysterics, of awful weeping. Before coming to White Lodge he had spent a full hour grilling the police-woman, in his office. She had been at school with Grace Bradley and Anna Beardmore, and she knew of their friendship. People did, she said, it was a small town, Bradleys was an old-established jewellery business and the father had been a local councillor. Anna Beardmore was famous.

He leaned across the table and proffered his ID card yet again but Grace didn't look at it, nor at him. Turning away her face she stared out into the garden.

He said, 'My name's William Buckle. I'm a Detective Inspector here in Peth. But I'm here this morning on behalf of the North Yorkshire police. They're conducting an enquiry into your friend's . . . your friend's *death*.'

He had spoken it. It was brutal, breaking such news like that, but for him there was no other way. Still she did not move, only in her throat there was a small convulsion as she swallowed something down. A brief sunburst suddenly brightened the heavy greenery outside the window and he could hear the heartless busy twittering of small birds.

Silence was thick in the room. She didn't speak but she was still doing things inside her throat, there was a kind of faint clicking noise. 'She was found yesterday morning,' he said, 'by a schoolboy, in her cottage. I'm very much afraid it was foul play.'

Now she looked at him, her eyes narrowing, and he heard a sharp catch of breath. Breda moved closer, scraping her chair along the kitchen tiles, stretching out an arm. But Grace shook it off and huddled away from them both, like a terrified child, bunched up in her seat. 'Somebody has *killed* her?'

'Yes, Miss Bradley, I'm afraid that someone has indeed killed her.'

Now he took refuge in his notes, impersonally reading, avoiding her eyes. 'It almost certainly happened three days ago, that is on Tuesday, but they're not absolutely sure. Changes in body temperature are crucial when one has to establish the time of a death, and the cottage was extremely cold.'

'I know, I went there.'

'Yes, and we must obviously talk about that.'

'What happened to her, please?' She had lifted her head and he felt great dark eyes on him, devouring his face. The child-like request made him want to weep. He had been cowardly, hanging about in his car at the end of the drive until he was sure Smith had told her. She mustn't know everything yet. She wouldn't be able to bear it.

'It seems she was strangled.'

'*Seems?*'

'Look, I can only tell you what's in this report, Miss Bradley.' He could hear a familiar shrewish irritation in his voice and he hated himself for it. But he felt powerless, and his sudden hardening, after the initial soft-footing, was clearly like a blow to her. She jerked away, covering her mouth. Breda's arm crept round her shoulder, gently squeezing, and this time she did not resist. Her body yielded, and she closed her eyes.

Buckle looked at the two women as they clung together, loathing his clumsiness, envying the protective arm of the awkward Breda. He too should have offered softness and comfort; instead he had repulsed her.

The unnerving silence of the immaculately ordered house with its lumbering, heavy furniture awakened old memories, and with them a practised restraint, and he lowered his voice to little more than a whisper. He said, 'You see, Miss Bradley, this isn't actually our case. Investigations are going on in the area where the body was discovered. That's normal procedure. Only, yesterday evening you were on your way back here, I gather, while the police were, er, busy at your friend's cottage. Keith Hallam – he's the Detective Superintendent in charge up there – contacted us this morning, and asked me to speak to you, in the first instance. I used to work for him. He'll be sending someone down in due course, I've no doubt, but for now – '

36

'I would like to know what it says in the report, please,' Grace interrupted. She was sitting upright now, her hands neatly folded away in her lap. Breda remained close.

He looked at his papers. 'Well, they have the post mortem result.'

'*Already?*'

'Oh yes. They don't waste time, in a case like this. Death was by manual strangulation.'

'Manual? How else could it be done?' Her voice was a harsh croak, the whole of her suddenly bird-like, a large bird, glossy-dark, brooding in measured silence before it swooped. She unnerved him.

'Well, with some kind of ligature. But the bruising, and other details, suggest that this particular killer used his hands.' He didn't want her to ask about the 'other details' so he read rapidly on, but Breda suddenly interrupted. '*Bill* . . .' Grace was fainting.

Watching her fall was something he never forgot. Smith had warned him she was a 'nervy' type, and excessively religious, a woman who had acted the dutiful daughter far too long and forfeited her chance of any independent life, spending endless sacrificial years with a demanding invalid mother. Always, afterwards, he regretted the brutality of the way he must have delivered the few facts he had chosen to give her, the very words. 'Cold', 'post mortem', 'strangled'. He heard again his own voice, officiously enunciating, as the scene before him suddenly changed, from a colour version, as it were, to black and white.

At a stroke the woman's face suddenly lost all its blood, as if a great wave had washed over it, sucking it empty. For months afterwards, whenever he thought of her, he saw again the puffy white cheeks under thick dark hair, the black kimono dressing gown with its scattering of pale embroidered flowers, the shiny expanse of black and white checked Formica between them, the glossy white wall behind. Without warning she fell sideways from the waist, her entire trunk momentarily rigid, only just caught by Breda as it sagged and crumpled, as the police-woman leapt up, knocking her own chair over, sinking with Grace on to the cold floor.

He picked up the pencil and the spiral notebook, its appointed page still virgin. Then he got up and began searching fruitlessly in the cupboards for alcohol. Breda, who had managed to get Grace's head down between her knees, suggested he try the drawing room. She remembered mince pies and mulled wine in there, one Christmas, when Grace and her Junior Church friends had organised charity carol singing. Breda had been thrilled at the invitation to join them. She had always liked Grace and she secretly hoped they might become friends. But after the Beardmore tragedy it was all Anna and Guy, and she realised there was no chance. She had not liked Anna, she was always too thrusting, too full of her own selfish schemes. Guy she had hardly known because he went to a different school and, after The Tragedy, had been sent away to board. Now both of them were dead and poor Grace like a big rag doll in her arms, in this cold and silent house. But she was coming round, with weird little moaning noises. As Breda heard Buckle walking back along the hall, clinking glass, she tried to pull the saggy white-faced heap nearer to the warmth of the stove, pushed the hair back from the damp forehead and tightened her arms round the limp shoulders.

Grace didn't like spirits very much but she kept a small selection of the usual bottles in, for other people, following her mother's pattern. Now, though, she drank obediently from a large tumbler of brandy. As it warmed her, the wild thumping of her heart gradually calmed and inside her head the contents of her skull stopped hurling themselves about, as if they had been somehow detached from their inner lining. She opened her eyes and found she could focus. She was sitting on the floor. Buckle was back at the table with a pen in his hand. Slowly, she got to her feet, helped by the police-woman.

'I'll get up, now,' she told her.

'Sure?'

'Quite sure, thank you. I'm all right.'

Taking her time she drew up a chair, sat down and faced them both. '*God is our refuge and strength,*' she was repeating silently, '*A very present help in trouble. Therefore will we not fear, though the earth be removed, and though the mountains be carried into the midst of the sea.*' She did not allow her ears to stop their dinning noise until she had taken every word to herself. Only then was she prepared to hear more. As they talked she felt Christ himself was by her side, his hand outstretched lest she should fall again.

He said, 'I apologise, Miss Bradley, I mean, for any clumsiness. I realise what a great shock this appalling news must be to you.'

'It's all right. How can it be your fault? I'm sorry, did you tell me your name? Buckley, was it?' Already she felt calmer. Thank you, Lord, she said.

'Buckle, as in shoe.' From his pocket he took his ID card and passed it over.

'Oh yes, *Buckle*, Breda did say . . . William. My father's name was William.' He too had been smallish, spare, fastidiously neat, like this man. She had loved him, infinitely more than she had loved Mother which was why the pain of her death had been so unexpected.

Buckle took the card back and turned over several pages of the report faxed to him by Hallam, knowing that he must tread carefully. He was not going to tell her that her friend's body had been found propped at a table with its right hand severed and that the hand had been found earlier this morning, inside the railings of a primary school, lying in the middle of the asphalted playground; nor that rats had been seen feeding on the body; that the woman's mouth had been stuffed with paper; that she had been sexually assaulted, possibly after death. She would hear it all soon enough, from others. Besides, she was someone who, in her loneliness, perhaps dwelt too much on the dead. She had just mentioned her father who had died years ago, according to Smith. It was cruel that this new, horrific death should touch her now.

'I do need a few details from you, Miss Bradley, about where you have been in the last few days. Now, I gather from this that you saw the v – your friend Anna on Tuesday?'

'*No.*' Her voice was harsh and cawing again. 'And why . . . why do you want to know what *I* was doing, Mr Buckle?'

'Miss Bradley, this is a murder enquiry. You were in Swaledale last week and I understand that while you were there you visited the deceased. These questions are routine, I assure you. Everyone who might have seen your friend, or been to her cottage, will be interviewed. In the process some valuable piece of information could emerge unexpectedly, and give us a lead. Therefore we are bound to question anybody who might be able to help us.'

As he spoke he felt a faint prickle of physical excitement. It was the first big murder in which he'd had any kind of role, and the first time he had actually pronounced that particular speech, until now only familiar to him from police training videos, and from the television. He hadn't wanted to work in Peth but he had very much wanted this promotion, so he had accepted the posting; and now, because he'd once worked for Keith Hallam, a chance to be in on this case, if only temporarily, had suddenly dropped into his lap. It could prove sensational, the rape and mutilation of a writer whose name was more or less a household word.

'I gather from Miss Stoker and Mrs Savage that you visited your friend for the day on Tuesday, and that you had, er, "a lovely time". Is that correct?'

'Are The Girls back then?' Grace rapped, still harsh and loud. In spite of her prayers for calmness a huge panic was steadily gathering inside her, threatening to break. 'They can't be, they'd have phoned, straightaway.'

'The Girls?'

'Marian and Ba. They were driving on, yesterday, up into Scotland. They weren't coming straight home.'

'That's correct.' From the report both 'The Girls' appeared to be nearing fifty, one was a nurse, the other a librarian, sharing a house. 'But they had left a forwarding address,' he explained, 'with Mrs Fawcett at the farm in Wensleydale. The police have already interviewed them. Now it says here that you very much enjoyed yourself, on Tuesday.'

'Yes, yes I did, but on my own, I meant. Anna wasn't at the cottage so I went back. I drove back into Wensleydale and decided to visit Miss Bruce. Breda knew Miss Bruce, didn't you Breda? She used to teach us.' In her attempt to control the rising panic she could hear her voice getting louder, and higher.

The police-woman nodded and made soothing muttering noises but she did not raise her eyes from a notebook where she was intently scribbling. Grace felt a tension between her and Buckle. Was it simply embarrassment at his inept handling of the situation, his thinly disguised irritation and his helpless staring on, after the faint?

'Her address is Miss Winifred Bruce, care of Holm Firth Residential Home for the Elderly, Askrigg, Wensleydale, North Yorkshire,' she said, enunciating every syllable, in a kind of mockery, Buckle felt, of his own crisp delivery. 'Check with them, that I was there on Tuesday, if you don't believe me, but don't go worrying Miss Bruce. She's not well, she wouldn't understand.'

'Of course I believe you, Miss Bradley,' he said testily.

'She was marvellous, Miss Bruce, she taught RE. She put these plays on, every Christmas, and we were all in them. Breda was Herod once – *weren't you, Breda?*'

The police-woman scribbled on. Then she said rather timidly, 'Yes, I was. But Grace, I do think we ought to get on . . .'

'And Anna was in one, *The Dayspring from on High*, it was called. Don't you think that's a marvellous title? Anna was always on the lookout for good titles, for her books. She used to ask my advice, sometimes.'

'Marvellous,' Buckle muttered in bewilderment. She was running away from him now, escaping into her safe, unsullied childhood memories.

'Claire Dearden was Abraham and Anna was Isaac. Anna brought a knife from home, a real one. It was Guy's. He had this collection of weapons, you see, on his bedroom wall, and she just took it. There was an awful fuss because some boys got hold of it in the playground and started to fool around. One of them was hurt and Miss Bruce

40

got told off by Miss Druckett – she was the head mistress. People said Miss Bruce cried.'

She had cried again on Tuesday, when she saw Grace, big helpless tears for her unwilling incarceration in the minute institutional bedroom at Holm Firth. Now Grace saw the tears again, and heard the terrible keening. At least Mother had died at home.

'It's an awful place,' she said, *'awful.'* Then, *'When thou was young thou girdest thyself and walkest whither thou wouldst: but when thou shalt be old, thou shalt stretch forth thy hands and another shall guide thee, and carry thee whither thou wouldst not.'*

They stared at her. 'Grace?' Breda said. 'Are you OK?'

'Jesus said that, to St Peter. He was crucified too, upside-down.' Quietly, she began to weep.

Buckle waited for a minute, making mild noises of sympathy, until she seemed calmer, then he ploughed on. 'I would like to go back to Tuesday morning, if I may.' He hoped his voice did not betray him for his flesh was prickling again, with a kind of exhilaration. There was an inconsistency between Hallam's report and what she had told him. This rather hefty spinster who sat sniffing before him, plain, apart from the thick dark hair and enormous dark eyes, a passive sort of woman who, in her nervousness and shock, had at first seemed unable to string two sentences together, had almost certainly visited the scene of the murder on the day it had happened. These 'Girls' had told the police. Yet she had denied it.

'You had "a lovely time",' he reminded her 'at the cottage, we assumed, and so I – '

'At *The Rock*,' Grace interrupted shrilly. 'She'd renamed it The Rock, it's from the Psalms.'

'I'm very sorry, The Rock.' Hearing the signs of panic he poured another inch of brandy and edged the glass towards her. 'Now, Miss Bradley, could you just tell me what you did, that morning? Take your time.'

She laid her large hands flat on the table, thinking of how Anna had grasped them once in this very kitchen, holding them against her trembling face for comfort, and of Guy huddled on a stool, warming himself at the stove. He said he had never been warm again, after that day.

'I drove over from the farm into Swaledale.'

'When?'

'After breakfast. I'd phoned Anna the night before, just to check that it was still all right for me to go.'

'Why shouldn't it have been all right?'

Grace hesitated. 'Well, because she was extremely busy, with her

41

writing. Sometimes she had to change her plans at the last minute.'
Latterly, Grace had learned to check and doublecheck. Anna had
a habit of setting up arrangements to come to Peth, arrangements
that involved Mrs Lumb doing extra cleaning, Grace switching
the heating on, preparing special meals, only to scrap them when
something 'important' came up in London. But she was not going
to let Anna down by talking of her disappointment and hurt to this
detective. There was a kind of suppressed violence in him, a hostility
which, in the awful circumstances, she did not understand.

'And what time did you phone her?'

'After our evening meal, at about half-past eight.'

'And did anything unusual strike you about the conversation? I
mean, did she sound her normal self?'

'Yes, I think so.' Fizzy in fact, almost too much 'on top'. It had
sounded to Grace as if she might be back on the pills prescribed for
her to 'cope', after Guy's death. They didn't give her very much
sleep but she quite liked that. The small silent hours were when she
wrote best.

'So you drove straight to her cottage?'

'No, I stopped, twice. I had a quick look at the Buttertubs first,
those holes on the top of the pass. They're a big tourist attraction.'

'I know them,' interrupted Buckle. 'I used to go walking up there.
And then?'

'Then, when I'd found Anna's lane, I sat on a seat for a bit.'

'A *seat*?' Buckle knew Swaledale quite well. It was beautiful, but
wild and windswept. Most of the time up there it rained, blew or
snowed and there was a definite shortage of flat land. It wasn't the
kind of place where they provided little shelters for trippers.

'She'd had a little seat put up, on a bit of flat ground overlooking
the river. In memory of her brother. I just wanted to see it.'

Buckle studied his notes. The dead woman's brother had committed
suicide ten months ago. Someone called Stephen Allen, an artist friend
with whom he'd been sharing a flat, had found him dead in a bath,
wrists cut, fifty sleeping pills and a bottle of whisky inside him. No
cri de coeur, that one, but a real belt and braces job, absolutely no
chance of being rescued, brought round and comforted, like half the
people who tried it. Buckle dreaded suicide cases. All that weeping.

Fearfully he glanced across at her. The brother and sister had died
within a year, both violently, and between them her own mother, and
all of it to be borne alone, in this silent house, ritually cleansed and
ordered, Smith had told him, for nobody at all. He felt the sterility
of it all, the waste. He had no religion whatever but he was glad for
her, that she held such passionate beliefs.

42

'You knew the brother, I take it?'

'Oh yes, Guy.' She pronounced the name with a certain distaste, he thought.

He glanced down at the report, but he was thinking more about her. She was beginning to interest him in the way that what had emerged from his notes as a suffocatingly dull life, manacled to an invalid mother, had been intertwined with the life of someone famous and celebrated, with the brother's sordid self-murder and now with a rather more spectacular murder of the sister, by persons unknown. He looked up at her, suddenly realising that they had met before, in the pages of a novel called *Harriet Harker* which he had picked up some weeks ago on a station bookstall, to while away a long train journey. He'd chosen it because Smith had told him that Anna Beardmore wrote about Peth, the dreary unpromising town to which he'd come on promotion.

But hadn't the woman in that novel been exceptionally heavy and plodding, and hadn't there been a rather cruel detail about facial hair? Grace was certainly quite large, taller than he was, and heavier, but then, he had always liked large women. What was she like, underneath? There must surely be more than he had seen so far. Anna Beardmore had had a lifetime's friendship with her.

He could see the faintest of shadows on her upper lip but it didn't worry him. Fran had had a large mole on her face and he had liked to kiss it away, loving it because it was part of her, calling it her 'beauty spot'. Fran was sandy and freckled while Grace Bradley had the most wonderful deep colouring, a flawless skin and thick heavy hair that fell in careless unbrushed loops over her shoulders. Out of the dark frame came a remarkable face which, in *Harriet Harker*, Beardmore had surely dismissed as 'plain'. He stole another look. The eyes were enormous, deepest red-brown, the whites a milky blue, the nose large but shapely, the mouth generous. Dressed all in black and white, and stilled by the shock of what she had just heard, her features had set, assumed a definite severity. But he marvelled at the evenness of the face in its solemn repose. If only she would smile at him.

In leaning forward to listen to his questions she had let her kimono fall open, revealing a loose, low-necked night-gown and the beginnings of breasts. He looked away but she had seen his eyes flit down. Pulling at her clothes she flushed scarlet.

'So then you went to the cottage?'

'Yes.'

'And she wasn't there?'

'No. I knocked several times and waited. Then I let myself in.'

'How?'

'I had my own key.'

'Really? Why was that?'

'Anna sent me one, when she first bought the place. She wanted me to use it for holidays. She knew she wouldn't get up there all that often herself, she was based in London. It's much nearer for me. I can do it in two hours, up the motorway.'

'That was very generous of her.'

'She *was* generous, she was my best friend.' Grace stumbled over the words and Breda flashed her a quick nervous smile. 'Best friends' were very useful, Grace had realised, as she'd watched Anna's new prosperous pattern of life emerge, indispensable when one had several properties to maintain and when one was never around oneself. She had always known that Anna used people, even at school, and people's characters became set very early. Why should it have been any different in the later years, with her? And she had, after all, had the time, tied to Mother and to White Lodge. She had been glad to help.

'But you had never actually been to the cottage before?'

'No. I'd planned to but then my mother had another stroke. I was needed here full time, then.'

'I see. And did everything seem in order, when you went in?'

'Oh yes. It was all very neat, in fact.'

'Unusually neat, would you say?' The cottage, when the police had broken in, had given the appearance of having been thoroughly scrubbed down. If the hand had been cut off in one of the rooms there was no obvious trace of blood. Either it had been done elsewhere, then the body brought back and propped in its ghoulish position at the table, or the murderer had swabbed and scoured every washable surface in sight. Forensic tests were already being carried out on materials taken from the cottage.

'And was this typical?'

'Well, yes, at least, when she had something new it was. She liked to show her things off, and I think I was the first proper visitor. She'd had a lot of work done to the place and she didn't want anyone to see it till it was finished. She promised on the phone that she was going to tidy up. She laughed about it, actually. Normally, she was a bit untidy.'

'And it looked as if she had been waiting for you?'

'Yes. There was a coffee tray with biscuits on and everything, the kind my mother always bought, for ours.'

'Can you remember anything unusual at all, Miss Bradley? Did you see anything . . . smell anything?'

Grace hesitated, remembering the smell of the alcohol and the cigarette ends in the rubbish bin. But the police would have surely been over the cottage in minute detail and made those discoveries for themselves. She breathed deeply, silently praying that she might remain calm, for she was about to deceive him, deceive *the police*, in a murder enquiry into Anna's death. She knew that it was wrong and she had been wrestling with her planned dishonesty ever since she had recalled that final phone call she'd made, from the M6. Stephen had been at The Rock yesterday.

She ought to tell Buckle, *now*. But there had been traffic noise in the background and Stephen's gently-accented Scottish voice had come over the line very faintly. How could she be sure? She was, though. There had been an initial hesitancy, then the stammer, an impediment from which Stephen had suffered since childhood.

She could feel Buckle's eyes on her now and she kept her head bowed, and stared into the palms of her hands. She could not tell. Whatever Stephen had been doing at The Rock could have been nothing to do with Anna's death. On that certainty she would stake her own salvation. Telling this man about the phone call would only set them all off along false trails, make them waste precious time which ought to be concentrated on finding Anna's killer. Let them find Stephen for themselves, and ask their interminable questions. She hoped they would not for he had suffered too much in his life, and she loved him. 'No,' she said calmly, though as she spoke her heart gave a queer little flutter at the outrageousness of the lie, in such grave circumstances. 'No, there was nothing unusual.'

He paused, sensing that this was wrong and that she had more to say. But she remained silent.

'In the main room,' he said reluctantly, at last. 'Was anything out of place there?'

'Not really. There was just – it looked as if she'd been writing.' Anna's desks and tables were always very tidy, Grace had noticed, contrasting bizarrely sometimes with the clutter all round her.

'Just what?'

'There was a piece of paper with her writing on. I only looked at it because I thought it might be a note explaining where she was. I should never have read it.' Her throat constricted painfully, swallowing tears down. At that moment the most terrible thing of all was that she had broken in on Anna's private world. There had been no murder. She was still alive somewhere, and Grace had violated her trust.

'What did the note say?'

'It was something about suicide, about its being the best way of making people remember you.'

45

It was. She could see Guy Beardmore quite clearly as she spoke, huddling over their stove on the day of The Tragedy; bloated and drunk on television, the night of the Pritchard Awards; little Guy in his new green grammar school blazer and short trousers, buying a Parker fountain pen from their shop; Guy Beardmore in all his incarnations.

' "Suicide is simply the most extreme and brutal way of making sure you will not readily be forgotten." ' Buckle was reading the quotation from his report. The paper had been stuffed intact between the victim's lips, and left trailing down. 'Did it mean anything to you?'

'She was planning to write a book about her brother,' Grace said, 'but she told me she was frightened of making a start. She kept putting it off and putting it off. She said she didn't really know where to begin. It was obviously about that.'

'I see. Did you go upstairs?'

'No.'

Involuntarily Buckle clicked his teeth. Although he kept reminding himself of the conventions, that he must be patient, remember what this woman was going through, the news was a blow. Hallam's theory was that the assault had taken place in the cottage but the murder and the mutilation elsewhere. He wanted details about the state of the upper rooms. It would have been quite something to have faxed those to Yorkshire.

'Why not?'

'I was frightened.'

'What of?'

'I heard something in the room overhead, something quite big, and I thought it might be a rat. There had been rats before Anna bought it. I didn't want to . . . to see anything. They can attack you. Once, in our wash-house – '

'I see, I see,' he cut in impatiently, not wanting any more childhood reminiscences. 'So you stayed downstairs?'

'Yes.'

'How long for? How long would you say you were in the house altogether?'

'Ten minutes, fifteen, at the very most. I wanted to leave when I heard the – whatever it was.'

'And you went back to your car?'

'Yes.'

'Was Miss Beardmore's car there?'

'I didn't notice. No, I think it wasn't. I'm sure I would have seen it, it's red. I know Anna's car.'

'Could it have been parked on the far side of the cottage?'

'I suppose so. I didn't see it, anyhow. I think she usually parked in the lane, because of all the mud. No, it definitely wasn't in the lane.'

'All right. So then you drove back into Wensleydale, to see this old lady?'

'Miss Bruce,' Breda prompted.

'Yes.'

'You drove straight back?'

'Yes.'

'And did you see anybody, in between leaving the cottage and getting into your car?'

'No.'

'Are you quite certain, Miss Bradley? Nobody answering this description for example?' He gave her a slip of paper.

Grace read, 'Male, heavy beard, thin face, five feet eleven inches tall. Camel duffel coat, striped (?) scarf.' It was an accurate description of Stephen and of the clothes she had seen him in so often; even at the crematorium on the day of Guy's funeral he had been wearing that filthy old coat. The description omitted to say that it was very dirty and the scarf in ribbons at one end, where it had once got caught in a bicycle wheel. She shook her head and handed the paper back. Then she covered her face with her hands. She could feel her cheeks burning and in these vital minutes it was imperative that she should give nothing away. Stephen had obviously been seen in the vicinity of The Rock, though the paper did not say when.

He had answered the telephone there, yesterday, Friday. He had stammered out, 'She's not available just now,' and then 'I think she's taking a shower.' *But according to this man Anna had been dead for three days by then.*

Knowing that she was holding something back, and with an apology for 'procedural tediousness' Buckle now took her through the whole thing again, Breda adding copiously to her notes, her expression of professional mourning now distinctly apologetic. His questions were rather barked out, second time around; he could hear the hard edge in his voice as the woman cringed away from him, faltering, stammering out the same answers as before. He couldn't help it, he was no good at this, and especially not with women, not now.

He made no attempt to disguise the fact that he didn't believe she could remember so little about her visit to the Beardmore cottage, and that he felt she could say more. 'You are probably the most valuable witness we have so far,' he said reproachfully, she, who had 'witnessed' nothing and who must, for Stephen's sake, withhold her one useful piece of information, at least for now.

They did not leave until Breda had read out everything she had written down. 'This will be faxed to Keith Hallam in Yorkshire,' Buckle explained, 'and later today someone will bring round a typed copy which you must sign. I'm not quite sure where things will go from here, or whether you'll see either of us again. As I said, someone from North Yorkshire may well come to see you, I just don't know. Also, we'll need to take your fingerprints. Obviously you touched things at the cottage and we have to eliminate them. Someone will be round to do this. Is that all right, Miss Bradley?'

There was no answer. With her hand on the front door, which she now held open for them, she was staring down the gravel drive. Anna was walking up it, swinging an embroidered Indian bag that contained school books. No regulation satchel or neat leather case for her. Mrs Druckett had complained endlessly about her Bohemian untidiness, her breaking of rules; but Anna didn't care.

'Miss Bradley? Is that all right?'

Slowly the gay youthful figure faded away. *Not dead, but sleeping.* Anna had merely gone into the next room, to rest. When these people had driven away she would go up to the attics and lie on the bed that had been hers in the old days. She could not let her go yet. They hadn't said goodbye.

The detective seemed to be repeating something about fingerprints and a typed report. 'Yes, that's quite all right,' she said dully, 'but I really must go now. I would like to rest.'

As he revved up his car engine she was already half-way to the third floor, climbing slowly, immensely weary now, hardly able to lift one foot in front of the other, or to lift her face, to look at the door of the room Anna had once occupied, with all her things.

Neither Buckle nor Breda Smith spoke until they reached River Flats, the new block in the centre of town where, by coincidence, they both lived, Buckle alone, in a small apartment on the top floor, Breda lower down, in a larger flat she shared with Sal Griffin, a psychotherapist at Peth General.

She had been excited when she'd heard about Buckle's appointment. He was more or less her age and apparently unattached. She was always on the look-out for a suitable man and when she discovered he was actually renting in River Flats she'd become rather excited. But from the beginning she knew that nothing could happen between them. Even if they'd warmed to one another – and she hadn't cared for him at all, he was so off-hand and remote – their physical disparity ruled out any kind of 'relationship'. At six feet Breda needed a man on an altogether grander scale and Buckle was slight, and rather dapper. She'd wondered at first whether he had somehow cheated his way into the police force because she doubted that he was the necessary height. Grace was taller than he was too, though Breda had sensed, jealously, that there was a certain male interest on his part. She had seen him look at her breasts when the kimono had fallen open.

The minute he had turned off the engine he reached behind for his briefcase. 'Well, what do you think?' he said, slapping it on to his knee.

She paused, then said simply, 'I just feel desperately sorry for Grace. She's a sweet person, Bill, I've always liked her. "One of life's nice people" – that's what my mum used to say about her.'

'I dare say she did, but I don't mean *that*. How do you feel about the interview, that's what we're talking about.' He was still snappish and horribly curt, almost as bad as he'd been with Grace, an unpardonable irritability, Breda had felt, in the circumstances. She hesitated, not wanting to expose herself to the lash of his tongue. She had heard his character-assassinations of some of the dimmer people, at work.

'I'm not sure. What did you think?'

He was pulling at his chin, a firm, square chin, neatly cleft. Everything about him was neat, rather too much so, she suspected. That degree of control and care hinted at some inner uncertainty, beneath it even some private terror. Sal had once discussed that syndrome with her. She might ask her about it again.

'Funny woman,' he muttered, 'funny life she's led, don't you think?'

'Oh, I don't know . . .' She suddenly felt intensely loyal to Grace. At school some of the cleverer ones had poked fun at her, calling her 'Holy Joe'. Breda knew how cruel schoolgirl ridicule could be.

'For heaven's sake, there she was, stuck in that depressing house, year in year out, with the mother. It's gruesome. She's never had a life of her own.'

'But Bill, if you'd known her as long as I have . . .'

'What do you mean?'

'Well, she was always so willing and cheerful, the sort that gets put on by people. It's her religion, I think. It means everything to her. She's got this overdeveloped sense of duty.'

'And the mother cashed in on it. She sounds to have been a bit of a bitch.'

'Yes, I think she was. She was very pretty, even when she was an old woman and, you know, petite. I think Grace was an embarrass-ment.'

'Was Anna Beardmore a bitch too?'

Breda was silent. She found his sudden hardening and curious changes of mood unnerving and instinctively she was cautious. Just what was he trying to get out of her?

He said testily, 'Oh come on, Breda, you said you'd known them both for years.'

'All right, I detested Anna. I'm sorry she's dead, well of course I am, but that's how I felt. So did a lot of other people. And it was pathetic the way Grace trailed round after her. I don't think it was because of the books or anything, she wouldn't set much store by that kind of achievement, it wouldn't actually *interest* her. But Anna Beardmore had this, oh, this *hold* over people, especially men. She could make them do whatever she wanted, they just, you know, sort of . . . fell to her. And it was the same with Grace. You could see exactly how Anna manipulated her. It was awful.'

'How did two people like that ever become friends in the first place? It seems extraordinary to me.'

'I told you, they were next-door neighbours for years and years, and then Grace's parents took the twins in for a bit, when the parents died. There weren't any relatives to do it, apparently. Actually, Anna was there for quite a time, I think. Guy was packed off to board somewhere, but she had to stay at our school. She always blamed Peth High School for the fact that she didn't get into Oxbridge. Guy did, you see.'

'But it doesn't explain why they remained friends. I mean, Beardmore was obviously a bright spark whereas Bradley – '

'But that was part of it,' Breda interrupted, hating the slick professionalism of the surnames. 'Anna was really rather brilliant at school, and she had to be the star, *always*. She just pushed her way to the front in everything. People didn't like that much, I can tell you. There was only Grace to stick up for her and she was a part of it all, somehow.'

'Bathing in the reflected glory?'

'That kind of thing, I suppose.'

'So Bradley took a vicarious pleasure in Beardmore's achievements? They made up for her own boredom, her own inadequacies?'

'I wouldn't put it quite like that,' Breda said, suddenly bolder.

'All right, how would you put it?'

'Well, I don't think it's a sign of inadequacy to be a person everybody likes. Brains aren't everything.'

'Point taken. So what about Beardmore, then? What was in it for her?'

'I've told you, Grace was useful while Anna went swanning about.

She was always in Peth, to do things. Anna's most recent crackpot scheme was buying the family house back. Grace was very useful there. She had some idea of living in it again, I think. Also . . .' But here Breda stopped, suddenly aware of her own physical shortcomings. What she'd been going to say was rather close to home.

'*Yes?*' Buckle barked at her.

'Well, Sal Griffin, the friend I share with, would call it the Beauty and the Beast syndrome, I suppose.'

'Meaning?'

'You know, meaning Anna would get a subconscious kick out of going about with Grace. She was awfully glamorous, not beautiful, but she certainly knew how to make the best of herself. On TV last time I hardly recognised her, and of course, she had plenty of money so clothes weren't a problem, whereas Grace . . .'

'Plain Jane?'

'Yes.'

'Cruel, I'd say.'

'I know. But Anna Beardmore was.'

He said, with some warmth, 'I don't find Grace Bradley plain at all. Do you?'

She was silent, remembering his eyes on the black flowered dressing gown, the defenceless white breasts.

Fishing in his briefcase he produced the local newspaper with its picture of Anna Beardmore, also a paperback novel. '*She's* the plain one,' and he handed both items across, jabbing at the photo. 'Have you read this, by any chance?' It was *Harriet Harker*.

'Oh yes, I've read the whole series. They're all set in this town.'

'I know, you told me,' Buckle said irritably. 'So you knew Bradley was used for this book?'

She said slowly, 'Yes, I suppose I did.'

'Why didn't you tell me?'

'Was it important?'

'It could be. Someone has killed the writer of this story. Everything's "important", potentially. I mean, in theory, Grace Bradley could have killed Anna Beardmore. Has that possibility occurred to you?'

'*Grace?*' She stared at him in disbelief. 'Bill, that's insane.'

'Thank you.'

'Well, I'm sorry, but I can't – '

'Please don't apologise. Of course it sounds fantastic but remember one thing, everything's happened in the history of criminology and I do *mean* everything. For example, Grace: the poor woman could have suddenly flipped her lid. She could have been brooding over it all for years, been in love with Beardmore and felt she had finished with her.

51

Or she could be named in the will. It'll be quite a packet, I should think.'

Breda sat silent, feeling that he was simply mocking her now, playing intellectual games, out of boredom. Clearly, she bored him as a woman. She said doggedly, 'Anna was raped.'

'Yes, but it doesn't necessarily cut someone like Bradley out. She could have been in it with somebody else, one of Beardmore's cast-off men. It was you who told me about them, remember?'

She opened the car door. 'I'm sorry, Bill, but I don't think any of this is very serious. It's just too fantastic. And anyway, if you really thought Grace was involved you wouldn't have given her any details, would you? Now if you've nothing more for me to do I'd like to go in.'

'No.' He leaned across her and pulled the door shut again. 'Just a minute. *Motive*, Breda, let's think about motive. Why didn't you tell me about Bradley appearing in the book?'

She hesitated. 'Well, I suppose I didn't like to think that Anna Beardmore did that, especially to someone like Grace, someone who trusted her, adored her, actually. It was so cruel.'

'Well, at least we agree that the victim was cruel.' He flicked through the pages of *Harriet Harker*. 'And inaccurate. I mean, in this, Harriet's made out to be some kind of ugly, hairy lump with nothing between the ears and Bradley's rather handsome, if you like that kind of thing,' he added indifferently.

Undeceived, Breda watched him putting the book back into his briefcase. He said, 'Are you religious, by any chance? Are you like her?'

'No, I don't believe. That's not to say I don't try to do my best by people,' she added sententiously.

'Would you lie, if you were religious?'

She faltered. 'I'm not sure . . . I mean we all lie at times.'

'I'm certain she lied just now. There's something she's not told us, about this man Allen. Tell me about him. Is he a friend of hers?'

'Well she *knows* him, through the Beardmores, but I'm sure there's never been anything, you know, romantic. Stephen Allen used to go around with Anna at one time. He got to know them through Guy, when he was teaching at Peth Art School. I should think he was the only friend Guy Beardmore ever had, well, the only one that stuck to him.'

'And last Christmas he discovered Beardmore's body in a bath. *Yuk.*'

She shrank from him, and from the childish word that suddenly rendered him inadequate. Perhaps this was the professional hardening that they'd warned her about, when she'd opted for the police force, warning her how the major tragedies of other people's lives would soon cease to shock. At first they were disgusting, then they became merely tedious, matters of routine.

He said, leaning across her and pushing open the door, 'OK, have a few hours' break. I'm going back to work. We have to check out her movements Tuesday through Friday. Hallam's got most of it already, I gather, from those friends of hers, The Girls or whatever she calls them. She was with them for the rest of the week. So there's not much more to do, but I'd quite like to keep Hallam's lot away for a bit. It'd liven this dump up, don't you think? Perhaps we could go back and see Bradley again. Anyway, I'll be in touch. See you.' And Breda was dismissed.

She stood on the damp forecourt of River Flats watching him reverse his car and drive off. He intrigued her though she liked him even less now, after his incredible theorizing about Grace, and she'd hated the harshness of the way he'd handled the interview, the relentless battery of questions.

She didn't understand his tension, his extreme irritability in a situation where all should have been as low-key as possible. It was highly unprofessional. Was it frustration because he wasn't really part of the enquiry or was it something personal? She knew little about his private life except that his only 'family' was a mother on the south coast whom he occasionally visited. Office gossip had it that he avoided women in general because he was still raw from some protracted relationship that had gone disastrously wrong, though nobody seemed to know any details. But he was definitely interested in Grace and her instinct was that if there were any further visits to White Lodge they would not include Breda Smith.

As he drove towards the town centre Buckle felt guilty about the way he had snapped at her and rather more about his clumsy handling of Grace Bradley. He had been unnaturally tense and he knew that the source of it all was a deep personal anxiety. She had interested him and no woman had done that since Fran; he had simply not allowed it to happen.

Three years ago, one week before their wedding, she had walked out of his life into the arms of someone who had surfaced from her past, gone to live with him in France and never seen Buckle again. The shock and pain of it had been so intense it was how he imagined the loss of someone much beloved, a thing he had never experienced. His only loss so far had been that of an aged father who had always been a remote figure to him. Fran was alive, she and the new man had a house in Brittany, there were twin boys. But to him her going was still like some awful death and he often dreamed of her, always drowning and being swept away from his arms on a great sea. Now there was this woman Grace. He must not let himself be drawn into love again.

The oddness of today was the massive incongruity of it all. Grace Bradley was awkward and clumsy, slow-moving, rather over-weight – and most definitely a virgin who, even if her religion allowed her to experiment, would probably be terrified of sex. From what Smith had told her she wasn't too bright either, and he admired clever women.

But she had been in some pain, much of it compounded by his own clumsiness, by his inability to reach out the hand of comfort as the lumpy police-woman had done, to say, 'We are here, and we care about you in this horror; let us help you.' It was what she called his emotional 'sterility' which had lost him Fran, or so she had argued. But it was not his fault.

He was the only son of elderly parents, born when his mother was forty-five years old, his father nearly sixty. To this day he didn't know if he had come as a longed-for child or was never meant to be and was therefore something of an embarrassment. Neither had ever talked to him of these things and now Father was dead and Mother a very old woman. They had talked very little to each other, they were quiet people who had lived quiet lives, lives of minutely-established routines into which, always biddable, he had simply fitted.

He supposed they had been proud of his steady progress at school, and of his university degree, but they were not given to praise. His father had died in the year he took his finals and since then his mother had lived on alone in the same sea-side town to which they had gone on their marriage. Death had changed nothing except that his father's small tobacconist business was sold and the money put into a trust for his mother's lifetime. Nobody had consulted him. As the only child he supposed he could have been resentful, but that had always been their way. It had simply been a matter of 'arrangements', spoken of cautiously in the same manner that his mother had talked to her friends of 'the womb' and 'the change' when, as a small child, he had played tidily with his toys, at her feet. He had *had* toys, and bicycles, and boxing gloves. At least they had seemed to know that children required such apparatus. But they had never talked to him very much, or touched him, and when he had cried in rage or disappointment his mother had told him to 'be a brave boy' or, later, to 'control' himself and that he must be 'grownup'. Not in all his life had either of them ever said 'I love you'. He had never seen his mother weep, not even at his father's funeral. She was a large strong woman, more like a man. Though they had provided for him, and taken a certain interest, he now felt it had been all duty.

White Lodge had reminded him of his childhood home by the sea, in its polished orderliness and its sense of routine, its very silence. Perhaps, subconsciously, that had awakened his first sympathies with Grace because it was an imprisonment he understood so well. He thought of her now and her soft, wounded face swam up to him in all its immense vulnerability. He wanted to see her again; he must.

He had deeply sexual dreams that night, dreams about which, on waking, he felt confused. He had coupled with Fran under water, as the gathering tide tried to pluck her out of his arms, and with the dead Anna whose elfin face had stared out at him from every newspaper that day. The hefty Breda he had beaten savagely, then mounted from behind; only with Grace had there been any gentleness.

When Grace had let them out she slid the brass chain back into position and sat down again on the reeded mahogany chair where Anna and Guy had clung to each other, and to her father, that night. Breda had been very kind but the detective had been hideously on edge. There was surely something very wrong with him, some private unhappiness that he seemed to be working out on her; and she had not liked it when he had looked at her breasts. If she was to have sexual thoughts she wanted them to be about Stephen.

She knew that it was outrageous of her to have kept back the information about the telephone call and it was obvious that Buckle hadn't believed her anyway. He was bound to come back, and the people from Yorkshire might come too. What if, because she had kept silent, a second woman died? And a third? She *must* tell someone, but she felt unable to do it yet.

She stood up, turned round, knelt down on the cold tiles and tried to pray, tried to think only of the Lord Jesus Christ, wanting him to come to her in his power and his wisdom, in his simplicity. She needed courage, and for the way to be made clear to her. When the police came back she must definitely tell them. It was terrible, wicked, to withhold such information.

If Anna had been lying dead at The Rock on Tuesday then he must have been the person who found her. But why, then, had he not alerted somebody? Either she had been mistaken, and she had spoken to Anna's killer, or else, in his horror at finding her, he had done what she herself had done, when Daddie died, and acted as if nothing at all had happened.

That morning she had left her mother with the Sister in charge, slipped out of the hospital and gone into Peth, knowing that they must eat that night, in spite of death, and that there was no food at White Lodge. In the covered market she had met a girl she knew, fresh-faced Carole Newton, back for her first long vacation from Sheffield University. 'How's your father, Grace?' she had called casually, across the bustling stalls. 'Mum told me he'd been in hospital.'

'Oh, he's fine now,' she had answered cheerfully, almost yelling above the din of shoppers. 'He sat up and had some ice cream yesterday, it was marvellous.' Which was true, and it had been truly marvellous. But today, not an hour before this, he had had a second massive heart attack and died. She had watched her mother close his eyes.

Had Stephen, in shock, simply stayed with Anna at The Rock, just *stayed*, numb and unbelieving, unable to lift the telephone, unable to do anything at all? For hours? Days? He had been through the same horror when he had found Guy. How could the Lord let this happen to him a second time?

Grace closed her eyes tighter and pressed her cold palms hard against each other. In this hour she must hold fast to all that was good. But she had no words and the darkness had started coming in on her again, lapping up, threatening to engulf the simple light; she needed to know for herself, in this hour, that her God was a very present help in trouble.

She prayed aloud the words of the General Thanksgiving, her favourite collect, but the precious cadences felt hollow and meaningless, and she knew that the Lord didn't want to listen to this; he was telling her quite clearly to explain the whole truth about Stephen, to admit that in her interview with Buckle she had left undone those things which she ought to have done.

Yet she could not bring herself to listen. Not now, Lord, she argued with him, in her agony of mind. They would surely find Stephen, she persuaded herself, if indeed it was he she had spoken to, they had a clear description. They didn't need her.

In the kitchen the stove was burning low again and it was starting to feel cold. So was every radiator in the house, and the answering service at Hibbert Engineering informed her that nobody could deal with her call until Monday. She unhooked her Scottish Nature calendar from the back of the door, brought it to the table and studied it. Today was the first Saturday of the month. She was down to arrange the church flowers this afternoon, and to polish the lectern eagle. It was also the day for her big shop at Sainsbury's and there was a pencilled reminder to phone Frankie at the shop,

to tell her which days she would be coming in. She had promised
The Girls that she would make next week 'the first week of the
rest of her life', Ba's phrase and one she'd found helpful when her
marriage had ended. Daddie's jewellery business belonged to Grace
now, they had reminded her, and she could be very useful to it, with
her good business head. Difficult Frankie was only the manageress,
after all, and she really had no right to tell her how the shop should
be run.

Grace hadn't ever told them she'd got a 'good business head', but
they seemed to know that this had been Daddie's view. They had
been so sympathetic during the week away, especially Ba. Both felt
her self-image was low, Marian tracing her mood briskly, without
question, to Mother's death. 'Nothing to worry about, dear,' she'd
said, 'you'll come up again. Death's absolutely natural.' Grace had
endured in silence, knowing that all death was hideous, unnecessary
and not planned by the Almighty, who had said 'Let there be *light*', not
dark. Death was not 'natural' and therefore the pain of grief suffered
by His creatures wasn't 'natural' either. But she had realised early on
in her friendship with The Girls that such dangerous concepts could
never be discussed with Marian Stoker. Ba was much easier to talk to,
though there had been few opportunities to be alone, without Marian,
who was extremely watchful and ill at ease if they started a discussion
without immediately involving her. But Grace had managed to confide
to Ba about Daddie's plan for her to run Bradley's, how she'd once
started a business course at the Tech, but how everything had come
to an end with his death and Mother's long years of illness, so that
the opportunity to involve herself in the affairs of the shop had so far
escaped her. During her week away, though, urged on by The Girls,
she had made a firm decision to confront the awkward Frankie and
assume her rightful place.

On the window sill her little cat mewed to be let in. She opened
the glass and it jumped down, purring hopefully against her legs.
She spooned out the remains of the tin left by Mrs Lumb, poured
fresh water into its drinking bowl, made herself a hot-water bottle
and went back upstairs. She took four of her mother's sleeping pills
from the bathroom cupboard and swallowed them down, hoping they
would give her a few hours' more sleep after the broken night. Only
as she drifted peacefully off into the blackness did she remember all
the brandy Buckle had made her drink, and then the faded mauve
lettering on the bottle saying 'avoid alcohol'. Well, she might feel
rather sick, vomit even, on waking, but she wouldn't die.

While she slept the phone rang several times, first The Girls, then
Mrs Lumb, then Frankie from the shop. All of them had heard about

Anna. Breda Smith rang, unofficially, 'as a friend', she'd planned to say, 'just in case you wanted to talk', and a policeman came round to take her fingerprints, hammered on the front door for a long time, then went away again.

It was dark when she woke up. Binkie, the little tabby, overjoyed to find a warm body in a bed again after its cold lonely week in the wash-house, crept under the duvet purring rapturously, pawing at her for more food. Its breath wafted against her face in warm fishy little puffs and she woke thinking of Anna, remembering the days of miraculous closeness in this house, this room.

And at last she began to weep, not the civilised controlled weeping she had allowed herself for Mother but a hard hysterical crying, an obscene and ugly noise that gradually swelled up, turning into a succession of great screams, sounds that were torn out of her, like someone being flogged, and as she wept she banged her head repeatedly against the panels of the bedroom door.

Down in the hall Mrs Lumb stood staring at the ceiling with a doorkey in her hand. It was nine o'clock and she had been phoning White Lodge all day. Getting no answer she had finally decided to come round. She did not usually venture out at night, because of the drunks and the muggers. It had meant two buses, then a long walk along the badly-lit avenue that led to Beaumont Crescent; but she thought Grace might need her and she had brought her overnight things in a shopping bag, just in case she was asked to stay.

As she stood listening down in the hall a door banged over her head, the cat came racing down towards her, then Grace herself appeared, swaying about rather drunkenly at the top of the last flight of stairs and making a curious low crooning noise, like a lonely child that sits comforting itself, all noise and passion spent.

'Mrs Lumb,' she whispered, staring down, 'Oh, *Mrs Lumb* . . .' and a sudden awful howling filled the house. Putting her shabby market bag on the nearest chair the old woman made her slow way towards her, holding out her arms.

5

The Girls were marvellous, cutting short their Scottish jaunt and rushing home to Grace. Both had work to do in the following week; Ba was due back at the library and Marian had a ten-day nursing engagement in Staffordshire, looking after a broken hip. But the few days of holiday they had left were given over entirely to her.

She felt overwhelmed, the first meeting was so excessively emotional. Marian seemed quite to fill the large hall at White Lodge, blotting out the light from the garden and crushing Grace against her as she wrapped her in a suffocating embrace, murmuring 'our poor, dear girl' and pressing her face up against her cheek, sandy and bristly, Grace noticed, at the moment of impact, not soft and slightly furry, like her own. Ba hovered nervously on the inside mat, waiting for her own chance to offer comfort. When she did it was a quick squirrel-like hug and the briefest of kisses. But her small dark eyes were full of tears as she whispered, 'I'm so sorry, Grace, about this terrible thing.' Marian's eyes remained dry, and the curious bland smile came and went, as before.

They spent hours in the kitchen with cups of coffee. The ancient central heating boiler was broken beyond repair and Grace had ordered a new one. She was not used to spending large sums of money and the cost of it appalled her. Her shock was not lessened by the fact that Hibbert Engineering sent their estimate on the same day that she received a visit from Edward Pollitt, the family solicitor, whose firm had also acted for Anna. She had been planning to find someone in London but Pollitts she had found were 'deliciously old-fashioned', and of course Grace was always on hand to deliver messages.

Grace, it seemed, was to inherit her entire estate, the capital, the investments, the houses, the royalties. Her most recent will had been made before Guy's death, but only just before, after that monumental quarrel during which she had thrown him out of the house. Grace was going to be very rich indeed, Edward told her. He seemed rather stunned.

She decided not to tell The Girls about the will. Marian, who had 'views' on everything, would offer immediate advice, and she felt too

59

tender. Some tablets prescribed by Dr Lucas had calmed her down a little, stopped the embarrassing bouts of crying and enabled her to sleep; but she still felt unable to deal with anything beyond the immediate day in hand, she was too deeply shocked. Nor did she feel she could attend Anna's funeral service. She was frightened she might faint.

'I'm afraid you'll have to make the arrangements,' she told The Girls, 'unless we leave it to the undertakers. They'll do everything for us, if we ask them. They can consult with Pollitts. Anna didn't want a religious service, I do know that.' Only ten months before Harvey and Paine in the Manchester Road had cremated Guy, and, more recently, Mother. She could not face another visit to that hideously discreet office with its fake wood panelling and its canned church music, its vase of dusty arum lilies, or to talk to Mr Harvey with the shiny slipping teeth about the relative merits of ash or English oak, to look at a coloured booklet depicting assorted designs of shroud. She had done it for Guy, with no love for him in her heart, only for love of Anna and because the smart new friends had been conspicuously absent. That love must suffice Anna now. Others, who were stronger, must act for Grace.

Marian spread herself across the kitchen table making a long list of things to be done, and asking about the whereabouts of any Beardmore relatives, noting down Grace's answers in bright blue ball-point, underlining headings and subheadings. Ba, holding her hand under the table, seemed to understand more. 'We'll deal with it, dearie,' she whispered, and the kindness made Grace want to weep anew. 'If there really are no relatives in this country to take over we can deal with it. And you certainly mustn't come, not if you're still feeling like this; don't blame yourself.' For Grace was blaming, because she lacked the necessary courage.

There was a dearth of blood relatives in the Beardmore family, though Grace thought there was a cousin in Canada, an evangelist who worked for some big religious charity. Anna had always been very sneery about Uncle Harold's 'Bible bashing' activities. 'He didn't come to Guy's funeral,' she told The Girls, 'and I don't suppose he'll come to Anna's.'

'Oh, he well could,' Marian said confidently, 'he'll stand to inherit, you see. I mean, who else is there? There'll be a fair amount of money, I should think.' But Grace made no reply.

'They've been here, of course, the police?' Marian went on.

'Yes, I told you. It was a local man, William Buckle.'

'Oh *him*. We've had a dose of him too. Cold fish. Didn't like him at all.'

'I think he might just be a bit shy,' Grace began tentatively. He'd been pleasanter on the telephone, the day after that first interview, anxious to make amends, she felt.

Marian snorted. 'Huh. I don't care for any of them, or their methods. I mean, we were terrified on the M6, when they flagged us down, flashing lights, sirens, the lot, and all totally unnecessary. I told them, didn't I, darling?'

'They were only doing their job, Marian,' Ba muttered. 'I thought they seemed a bit embarrassed, when they realised who we were.' She glanced uneasily at Grace. 'It is a *murder* enquiry.'

'Oh I know, I know . . .' but Marian was still angry. 'They took us through every minute of our week in the Dales, every second. It was outrageous.'

'But it was the same for me,' Grace said. 'It's only routine, Marian. They've been here twice, actually. First William Buckle came, then Keith Hallam sent one of his own people down, a woman, Gloria – quite high up, I think. She was sweet.' But she hadn't told Gloria Medlicott that she had spoken to Stephen on the Friday afternoon, from a call box on the M6. Now she felt her cheeks burning.

Marian was eyeing her suspiciously. 'You never told *us* Anna wasn't at the cottage on Tuesday. Presumably the police took you through all that?'

'Yes. Twice.'

'*Why* didn't you tell us? We thought – '

'Oh, Marian . . .' Ba murmured warningly with a kind of desperation as the other woman barged on.

'I just didn't want to talk about it,' Grace said flatly. 'She was always doing that to me and I felt, you know, a bit let down.'

'By her standing you up, you mean? *Huh.*'

Grace, feeling she had been disloyal, shrank away. She rather wanted Marian to go home now. She was so noisy, so *big*. She felt she was being suffocated by her.

'Anyhow, they put you through the third degree too, did they?'

'They certainly asked a lot of questions, yes.'

Ba said, with unusual spirit, for her, 'Marian, they explained everything. I don't really see your objection.'

'Oh yes, they *explained*. They explained that nobody could be ruled out. That's what they *explained*, my dear.'

Grace stared at her. 'You mean, they thought *you* could have had something to do with it? Or *me*?'

'Yes, technically. And they'll be back, you see if they're not. As I said, it's outrageous.'

'I really think we've got to talk about next Thursday,' Ba said wearily. She had confided to Grace, in a guilty moment, that dear Marian, though the salt of the earth, could be curiously obtuse about some things, when her temper was roused; and she was clearly very angry about the police.

'All right,' Marian snapped. 'Well, I don't know what Grace feels but I don't think we can have a secular funeral.' She spoke as if there could be no argument about it. Grace didn't like the 'we'. It was as if Marian were appropriating Anna, and Anna was hers.

'But that's what she wanted,' she said, though timidly, for she was putting the burden of the affair on them, because of her own cowardice. 'She didn't really believe in anything. Neither did Guy, in fact he hated religion.'

'You had hymns at his funeral, dearie,' Marian reminded her sharply, 'you told us all about that.' If she had not been a Christian Grace felt Marian Stoker could easily have been the sort of person who would have buried suicides at a crossroads, with a stake driven through the heart, or a great stone on the breast, to stop the unhappy spirit from rising.

'But she *wanted* them then,' Grace pleaded, 'in the shock of it all. She said she'd like something comforting, for those that came. She left it all to me.'

Marian didn't reply but her face left no doubt at all as to what she personally thought of Anna Beardmore, even though she was now prepared to order her funeral.

Grace had arranged Guy's bleak little service entirely alone, dreading that nobody but herself and the undertakers might be there. At the time of his death Guy Beardmore seemed to have lost the few friends he'd managed to hang on to, over the years. But a few people had come all the same, salvaged from school and college days; some of Anna's publishing friends had turned up too.

Anna herself had spent the day with Julia Wragg in London, wanting to put distance between herself and the event. 'Forgive me, Grace,' she had written. 'I know it's terrible, just going away, but I can't bear it otherwise. I know you'll cope.'

Coping. That was the special word Anna had always used of her. 'I hope you're coping, darling,' she had written, when Mother died at last. She could certainly have come to that funeral, there was nothing harrowing about it, the merciful release of an old woman from pain and sickness, an end Grace had welcomed. But she had been on holiday in Spain, with Julia, 'fleeing the good old British winter'. 'Don't feel you must come back, Anna,' Grace had said on the phone, though Mrs Lumb was already warming up Firs, in preparation. But she had not broken her holiday.

Funerals. What she remembered most vividly about Guy's was that fleeting glimpse of Stephen. As she walked into the fresh air out of the stale overheated air of the chapel she saw an unkempt bearded figure in a camel duffel coat, hovering on the edge of a gravel path. 'Stephen!' she shouted. Everybody stared and she heard her own voice, anguished and embarrassingly loud, releasing into the bitter air the internal horror of the comfortless devotions inside the ugly chapel. Two great black birds clattered up from a clump of bare trees by the path. '*Stephen!*' she called again, but he turned away his face, his body swaying uncertainly for a moment, as if he wanted to come to her, but then he ran off, into the trees. It was the last time she had seen him.

Now she listened as Marian outlined her ideas for Anna. They had already been told that, now formalities were over, the body was to be 'released' for burial, so that they could make their arrangements.

Grace dreamed nightly of that 'release'; for some reason Anna was not part of it. It involved, instead, Guy and his mother and father floating about peacefully over the moors above Peth, their faces young and unconcerned. As they drifted round, Anna was at home bent over her typewriter, busy on a new book and annoyed when the telephone rang, with news of their several deaths.

The Girls told her very little about the service. Marian was obviously all set to embark upon a blow by blow account when Ba, seeing Grace's expression, put out a warning hand and frowned. Silenced, Marian rather huffily produced some sheets, printed on her home computer, listing all who had been present plus, when she had been able to find out, details of who they were and why they had come. It was a surprisingly long list and at the last minute the service had been transferred to the larger of the two chapels, to accommodate everyone.

Several publishing people had been there and others with London addresses who were simply noted down as 'friends'. Grace knew very few of the names and it came to her painfully that for years now, Anna had conducted her own separate, private life in which she had had no part. For all the effusive protestations about their being 'best friends' she had sensed for a long time that Anna was losing interest. Her glamorous writing world was consuming her more and more, and Grace was never invited to share it.

Buckle and another colleague were at the service, they said, someone from Keith Hallam's office, and a man called Maurice Peacock whose address was Low Farm, Swaledale. Two of Ba's older Torch Bearers were there too. 'They sang so nicely, darling,' she assured Grace, 'I was glad they came. The singing's usually so awful at funerals but they're grand little Christians.'

'Yes, they were *thrilled*,' boomed Marian.

So there had been singing, in spite of Anna's wishes, and in spite of all she had said. She stared at Marian accusingly.

'Just one hymn . . . well, there had to be *something*, dearie.' Marian was unrepentant.

Unwillingly, fearing the pain, Grace glanced at the Order of Service. They had sung *O Love that wilt not let me go/I rest my weary soul in Thee*. It was a fine hymn, yet she wanted to scream at Marian, who understood so little. Anna's mood had been coming up again when this hideous death had happened; when the lunatic had broken in on her she must have been happily writing. Grace was certain now that the killing must be the work of someone mentally deranged, though she still didn't want to know more than the essential details. Everyone had respected that, particularly William Buckle.

She had decided that his initial awkwardness had come from some problem of his own. Anna had always warned her that she was too open and trusted too easily. 'Never give all the heart,' she would quote at her. But Anna had had no *enemies*. Stephen was just one of many men friends whom she had eventually dismissed. She got bored easily, Grace had always known that. But she had never injured anyone so deeply that they would be driven to take such an appalling revenge. Nor had she been locked in that awful interior darkness which must, out of a clear blue sky, have suddenly descended on Guy, and led him to take his life. On the telephone, that Monday evening, she had sounded bubbly. It had not been a matter of 'resting her weary soul' in anything.

She said, 'Thank you both, thank you more than I can say,' and she put the service sheet and the list of mourners away in a drawer. All this was for later, when she was alone again. The strange unreal time with The Girls round at White Lodge every day, and Mrs Lumb sleeping in the house each night, must end soon. Then the real loneliness would come.

'I'm glad Mrs Lumb was there,' she said, catching sight of the name as she closed the drawer. Against it Marian had typed 'cleaning woman'. Grace would have preferred 'helper'. She honoured Mrs Lumb, faithful to Mother and Daddie over all the years, now faithful to her, in her solitariness. Against her name, when The Girls had gone, she would write 'valued friend'.

Julia Wragg had not come to the funeral. She had phoned The Girls and explained that she had just come out of hospital and had not been allowed to travel north.

'What's wrong with her?' Grace asked fearfully. *Not more bad news, please, Lord.* Julia was one of the few links left with Anna, and she was determined to meet her now.

'Oh, some woman's complaint, I gather,' Marian told her, oddly coy for someone in the nursing profession.

'She didn't go into details, Grace,' Ba said, rather more kindly, 'but she promised she'd be in touch with you, very soon.'

But would she? Grace was doubtful. For years now the prospect of meeting Julia Wragg had been dangled before her by Anna. 'We want you to meet,' she had said, so many times. 'We' meant that the friendship with Julia was becoming more and more important, pushing Grace out, and she had grown jealous. She too was becoming boring, she felt, like the lovers.

'Well, we'll see,' she said vaguely, feeling weary suddenly, and wanting The Girls to go home. It was callous but Anna had been disposed of and now their work was done. She wanted space round her, to pray through it all from the beginning. Marian suggested that they might all pray together but Grace didn't want that. Prayers had been said at the crematorium, she pointed out, and Anna had been consigned to God, clumsily no doubt, for the clergyman sounded very like the aged, fumbling individual who had dispatched Guy. But prayer had happened nevertheless, and it was valid.

'I would like the ashes here,' she told Marian as they said good-bye.

'Ashes: disposal of?' had been the last item on the funeral list. One of Grace's few literary skills was that she could read upside-down and she'd deciphered Marian's clear script with ease, across the kitchen table.

'Are you sure, lovie?' Ba was obviously uncomfortable and flicked a doubtful look at Marian. 'You don't need to put yourself through all that.'

'Quite sure.'

'What will you – '

'I don't know. Just ask the undertakers to send them here.'

With a slightly aggrieved air Marian brought her list out again and made a note to ring Harvey and Paine when she got home. Perhaps The Girls, having failed to persuade Grace to pray with them, had been planning some private devotions of their own, over the remains. Anna, Grace remembered, had said, 'I don't care, I don't *care,*' when asked what should be done with what was left of Guy. She did not know that Grace, some weeks later, had braced herself to go up to the old wind-blown cemetery at High Peth, had found the Beardmore grave and scattered the ashes there, like so much cat litter.

The day of the funeral was to be the last time she would ask Mrs Lumb to sleep in the spare room. She had a little dog, left behind with a neighbour, and she was obviously fretting about it now. Grace assured her she would be quite all right from tomorrow, that she was feeling calmer now and had much to do. She might even be going away in which case Mrs Lumb could have a little break, paid, she insisted on that.

She was planning to speak to Julia Wragg. She would try Stephen's wife Lynn again too, by phone this time, she never answered letters; and she would visit Mrs Dutt, his old landlady, to find out when she had last heard from him. All this she wrote down on a special list. Then, quite early, she took two of Dr Lucas's new pills and went to bed.

'May the Lord grant me a quiet night and a perfect end,' she said as she knelt down, committing into his care the day that had passed, the funeral and The Girls, Mrs Lumb, Buckle, all of them there. For Anna herself she found she could not pray. She was lost, and Grace didn't know where to find her.

6

At ten the next morning Buckle came back, on his own, this time, but
bringing a tape-recorder. He explained that Breda was working on
something else but sent Grace 'her good wishes, and love'. This he read
out word by word from a notebook, pinkly embarrassed. Though she
was still wary of him, remembering his former brusqueness, recalling
also that distinctly sexual look, Grace was touched by this meticulous
attention to the small humanising detail. He had surely not been
obliged to pass on that particular, peculiarly female message.

'Perhaps you'd be good enough to return my good wishes,' she
said cautiously, omitting the love. She didn't really want to start
anything with Breda Smith. There had been phone calls from her
after the earlier visit, offers of chat, cups of tea. She was clearly
anxious to renew the old friendship.

Now the funeral was over and the house empty once more Grace
felt curiously light-headed, but calmer. This morning she had prayed
for strength, strength for the day and continued strength, to carry out
a few investigations of her own, into Anna's death. Marian would no
doubt tell her that this relaxed heady feeling was simply delayed
shock. Grace knew it was the Lord.

Buckle handed her a copy of her original statement and took her
through it yet again. He was certainly kinder today, she thought,
more at peace with himself, his physical gestures easier. He said
finally, 'Now, is there anything else at all which might help us?'

'Yes, there is one thing. I should have told you before.' Her ears,
involuntarily this time, began their familiar nervous humming, and
there was a deep throbbing inside her chest. She desperately didn't
want them to harass Stephen, yet she knew she must tell him about
the phone call.

Buckle leaned forward. 'Yes?' he said.

'I phoned Anna at The Rock, on my way back here, that Friday
afternoon.'

'When, exactly?'

'About half-past four, I think it was just getting dark.'

'And?'

'Somebody answered.'

As Buckle adjusted the tape-recorder his hand shook. *So he was right.* So far Hallam's team had got nowhere with their enquiries and here he was, the side-kick, a local man merely conducting a routine interview, about to receive what could be the most important lead so far. Why had she not told him before? Breda had said she was 'sweet', but not too bright. Withholding information about this telephone call, in a murder enquiry, suggested to him that her intelligence was impaired. Unless she was protecting somebody.

He stared down at her large hands, neatly folded away in her lap, and a quiet shock went through him. Anna Beardmore had been strangled. She had no relatives and her entire estate had been left to this shy, nervous woman who now sat looking suspiciously at the tape-recorder with her marvellous dark eyes – a very large estate, it would seem, the value of which would steadily increase as much of it was in royalties and all Beardmore's books were bestsellers. The body had been mutilated and a hand removed, though no weapon had been found. But there had been violent sexual interference. So if the 'fantastic' theory he had idly propounded to Smith had some actual truth in it, and if Grace Bradley were indeed involved, she must be involved with somebody else, somebody male. Yet now she was calmly telling him about a phone call she had made to the scene of the murder the day the body was found, and that someone had answered – the man, presumably, whom she could have helped with the killing.

He could make no sense of it, but he knew that he could not ignore the possibility of her being implicated, not quite, not yet, crazy as the idea seemed, from all they knew of her. Everything was possible in a case of murder, and everything had happened. Money and sex were the classic motives for laying violent hands upon someone and this case could involve both. *Sex.* His fantasies of love-making with her swam up into his consciousness but he thrust them away.

'*So*, tell me what the person said, Miss Bradley,' and he bent over his file. His voice was calm but his hands were damp with sweat, his fingers sticking to the paper.

'Well, I spoke first. I asked if it was Anna, naturally, when the phone was first picked up.'

'And then?'

'There was quite a long pause and I could hear someone breathing. Then someone replied, a man.'

'And did you recognise the voice?'

'No, not then, though when I thought about it afterwards I wasn't *absolutely* sure . . .'

'What kind of voice was it, Miss Bradley? Did he speak with an accent, for example?'

'Scottish, just faintly.'

'But you definitely didn't recognise it?' He was thinking of Allen and watching her intently, seeing the deep colour rise slowly into her cheeks.

'I'm not quite saying that, Mr Buckle.'

'What are you saying, then?'

He was barking again, and she winced. 'I'm sorry,' he said hastily, 'I'm very sorry, only, this could be immensely important.'

She pressed her lips together, lacing and unlacing the long, strong fingers. Then she said in a whisper, 'It *could* have been Stephen Allen. He's Scots – well, you'll know that – and he's got a stammer, like the man on the phone. Only he spoke terribly quietly, you see, and there was a lot of noise outside the call box. It was one of those open ones and I – '

'Look,' he said urgently, 'for heaven's sake, *was it Allen?* Would you say you were . . . ninety per cent certain? It all adds up, you must see that. They're looking for him. I'm sure Hallam's people explained.'

'Oh yes, they did,' she said politely, 'but no, I'm *not* certain, not absolutely.'

'All right. So what did the man say?'

'Well, I asked if Anna was there and there was this very long pause. Then he said she couldn't come to the phone just at that moment, that he thought she was having a shower. Then he just rang off. I dialled the number immediately afterwards but it was engaged. I'm sure he'd left it off the hook. I gave up in the end.'

Buckle looked through his notes. Although the boy John Peacock had seen the body propped up at the table quite early on the Friday morning, when he should have been on a bus, going to school in Richmond, the police had not entered the cottage until early evening. It seemed he had fallen backwards from the window and gone crashing down, splitting his head open on some rocks and knocking himself out. A man called Bayles had found him, half lying in the stream, a twenty-five-year-old half-wit who was employed delivering milk. It was only because his dog had found the boy lying unconscious and barked over him that the man had actually seen the body at all. He'd been off the main track, unconscious and deeply concussed. His own mother was no use, she was asleep at the farmhouse up the valley, on some kind of sedation. Unable to bring him round Bayles had loaded him on to his milk waggon and driven him miles down Swaledale to his own parents. The last thing he should have done was to move him but then, this 'Daffy' clearly had several screws loose.

Hallam's people had interviewed the three of them and they'd all been terrified, the son locking himself in an upstairs room and having to be forced out and downstairs, to face questioning. It came out that there'd been a couple of 'incidents' years back, involving him. He'd exposed himself a few times, in a village street, then later a teenage girl who was already pregnant claimed he'd raped her one night in a field.

There was insufficient proof to bring charges so nothing official was ever done about it. But for months afterwards the parents kept him at home and out of sight. This job on the family milk round was only very recent and he usually did it with his father. But he'd been delivering on his own for the last few weeks; Bayles Senior was laid up with a bad foot.

Everyone interviewed in the dale had spoken well of Daffy Bayles and all had been very reluctant to talk about the girl, or the sexual side of his life, insisting there was no proof. 'But they close ranks, you know, these country people,' Keith Hallam reminded him. 'We can't discount him yet.' Buckle sensed from their phone conversations that he was already certain Bayles would prove to be their man, in spite of the hunt for Allen.

The young man looked likeable enough in his photograph, a bit of a comic with his shock of thick blond hair, craggy face, curly lips parted in a broken-toothed grin. Nevertheless, he remained a suspect, a huge powerful individual with shoulders like a prize bull.

'You didn't see either of these men, I take it?' Buckle passed over the photographs of Daffy and, again, of Stephen. Grace studied Daffy. 'I saw nobody at all,' she said, handing them back, having hardly looked at the second. 'And you showed me that one last time. *Why don't you believe me?*'

He saw her eyes fill with tears. 'With respect,' he said slowly, edging his way, 'you signed this statement last week as a complete record of what you remembered, and yet in the last five minutes you've just told me something which could be of immense importance. Why did you keep that back, Miss Bradley?'

But she was absolutely refusing to look at him. *Lord, guide me*, she was praying, *Lord, keep me from this, and keep Stephen in your perfect love. Lord, give me the right words.* But no words were offered.

'I don't know,' she whispered feebly. 'It was such a shock to me, about Anna, I was confused. All I can tell you is this, if it *was* Stephen I spoke to then he's got nothing at all to do with what happened to Anna. They were . . . they were lovers.' She pronounced the last word with extreme difficulty. He was touched. 'Lovers' and 'Love' were the words a woman like this would use for the act. She would never say 'have sex'.

They fell into a silence, Grace staring into the palms of her hands, worrying at an old cut with her fingernail, Buckle staring at the top of her head, wanting very much to look into her face, and read it.

She said, 'I suppose Stephen wasn't at the funeral?' He had not been on Marian's famous list and in any case Buckle would not have shown her that photo a second time if they'd traced him through that. It was why all those policemen had gone to the service, of course, they were looking for clues among those who had turned up. Marian had explained all that to her.

Buckle had arranged for a third policeman, Jim Wooding, to go along with him and Breda and, vaguely presenting himself as 'press', he had deliberately seated himself next to another newspaper man, a tall gaunt individual in an ill-fitting and rather dirty brown suit, someone who said he was on a paper in the north-east which had interviewed the dead woman only a few months ago. To Buckle's intense embarrassment the man had broken down and wept during the singing of the hymn. Fatherly old Jim had pressed his arm and offered him a large white handkerchief.

The man had drunk whisky during the reception afterwards, held in a private function room in a small hotel in the town, propped in a solitary corner, his eyes flicking here and there over the subdued gathering. Hallam's man had not approached him but Buckle thought it was worth having a word, that sudden outburst of child-like emotion during the singing of the hymn had interested him. Was it some raw new grief of his own or had it come from his contact with Anna Beardmore? It had been quite a lengthy interview with photographs, so the man must have spent an hour or so with her. But he had got stuck with Marian Stoker who was very anxious to tell him that he must be careful with Grace and careful about what the police said to her. She had stopped her daily newspaper and she had told them she was listening to no radio or television until the Anna story had been pushed out by something else. She did not want to know more than the essential facts. Just what she knew neither of them had dared to ask, but please could he bear her obvious fragility in mind. She had boomed it out, loud enough for the whole room to hear.

Buckle had stared at the large raw-boned woman towering over him with undisguised insolence and distaste, though she would not have recognised his feelings; she herself exhibited all the 'fragility' of an armoured tank. When he got back to the corner where he'd seen the reporter swilling down Scotch the man had gone. Irritated, he had made a mental note to get hold of the Anna Beardmore profile, and to arrange an interview with its author. But he had said nothing of this to Hallam. It was something he rather wanted to follow up on his own.

'Do you yourself have any theories as to what kind of person might have done this terrible thing to your friend, Miss Bradley?' he said, rather more gently now, for, in spite of her general composure, he could see that the upturned hands had started to tremble.

She stared at him, pulled her lips about with a slight shrug, and remained silent.

'You see, people kill for many reasons,' he went on, sliding into the old familiar jargon in an attempt to get some kind of response, and a lead into her relationship with Stephen Allen. 'Love . . .' he murmured, watching her carefully, 'greed . . . revenge . . .'

'Wickedness.'

'I beg your pardon?'

'But perhaps you don't believe in simple wickedness, Mr Buckle?'

'Well, should I?'

Should she? he asked himself. What could Grace Bradley possibly know about 'wickedness', she who had had no kind of life at all, hidden away for years in this cluttered and depressing house, manacled to a bitchy, demanding mother? She could never have grown up, she had had no chance.

'*The heart of man is deceitful above all things,*' she told him, '*and desperately wicked. I absolutely believe that.*'

'I see,' Buckle said, excessively polite now, through sheer embarrassment.

'I'm a Christian, Mr Buckle,' she went on, and now her voice was unwavering and strong. 'I believe in God and therefore I believe in the Devil too. Wickedness is the reverse of goodness, it's simple enough,' she added.

'So you think some kind of, er, evil person killed Miss Beardmore?'

'Well *of course*. Don't you? It must have been some kind of maniac. Who else would have . . . would have . . . attacked her body in such a hideous way?'

So in spite of The Girls' efforts she must know about the hand, possibly too about the rape. Had she been watching?

'He might do it again,' she went on, passionate now. 'He might do it quite soon, while we're all sitting here doing nothing.'

'Which is why we need your absolute cooperation, Miss Bradley, and why you should have told me about your telephone call before. This is difficult for me. Keith Hallam will ask questions, about my report.'

'Well, I'm sorry, but I've told you now, haven't I?' Her voice had a rising note of panic in it which Buckle recognised from the first interview. 'You think it was Stephen Allen, don't you?' she accused him. 'That he killed Anna? Go on, *say it*. I don't know what he was doing at The Rock that day, if it was he I spoke to, but truly, you're all mad to think it could be Stephen, he's lovely, and he was one of Anna's truest and dearest friends.' *And mine, And mine*, she keened silently. *But where was he?*

Buckle said nothing but watched the tape-recorder going round with private satisfaction. Perhaps, for all her show of innocence and outrage, this woman did 'protest too much'. Nobody had actually accused Allen yet but, as she'd just reminded him, he had been a close friend of the victim, once a lover. Therefore he could be someone who might help them to piece her last days together, if he could prove he had no connection with the killing. As to that, somebody sounding very like him had definitely been sighted in the Dales just before the murder had been discovered.

They sat on in the silence. Grace, who before had hidden her face away, now seemed unwilling to avert her eyes from his but had them trained on him, like some large and hungry animal. She was definitely strange, he thought, but her strangeness unnerved and attracted him equally. She was a woman of uncertain moods and passions and she possessed, for him, a certain mysterious strength. Perhaps she was not stupid at all, rather, if his wild surmisings proved correct, a fine actress and a quite brilliant liar.

He put his papers together, uttering vaguely about the need for a third visit. He could do no more now. There had been no official reason for this interview, he had already faxed her statement to Hallam's office and they'd sent a woman down immediately, to take her through the facts again, since when he'd heard no more from them. It was simply his good fortune that, for her own curious reasons, she had kept the incident of the phone call back until now.

He must tell Hallam. Perhaps, then, the case would pass out of his hands and they would take over here. That depended on how hard they were pursuing Allen, though, and on what Bayles was saying, if anything. For now, so far as she was concerned, he would leave all fluid, not intimate to her that he might not return himself, nor what his role was.

He would simply watch her, in his own time if necessary, and privately, and if she contacted Allen before they did then he would close in and show Hallam something. Innocent, wicked or mad, whichever Grace Bradley proved to be, he must see her again. If he was wrong, and someone entirely different was arrested for the murder of Anna Beardmore, then, in that heaven of hers, he must eventually pray to be forgiven.

After he had gone Grace made coffee and sat in the kitchen for a while, thinking about the empty day that now unrolled before her. The detective had certainly been kinder to her this time but she had still felt a tension in him, and she sensed it didn't arise from anything to do with the Anna enquiry, nor even her suppression of that phone call, but from something he felt towards *her*. Did he, to use Anna's vulgar phrase, 'fancy' her? Or was that imagination? It was not an experience that was familiar to her, for her knowledge of men was pathetically limited. In other circumstances she might have been flattered at such attention, but she had not warmed to him. Stephen was the only man who interested her.

Over her coffee she made a series of decisions. She would go into Peth today, but not to the shop. Marian had urged her to stick to her determination to show Frankie that she wasn't going to be pushed around any more, that she owned Bradley's and had every right to say how the shop should be run. But Grace had no heart to battle with the awkward manageress today, nor did she want to be seen in the shop. People who knew her would feel they must say something about Anna.

She would go across town to call on old Mrs Dutt, guilty that she had neglected her for so long and only going now because she was desperate for news of Stephen. She had been his landlady when he'd taught in Peth, a job Guy had found for him, as he had never ceased to tell people. It was at that time he had begun his curious aping of Stephen, not only in dress and physical mannerisms, but also his painting style. Grace knew nothing about art but even she could see that Guy's amateurish canvasses were lifeless. In the drawing room of her London house Anna had hung two mill town oils, one Guy's, the other Stephen's, side by side. The contrast was pointed and a useful conversation piece for visitors.

Grace felt Anna had intended it. It was part of that cruelty in her which she didn't like to think about. Guy too could be cruel; she had once heard him imitate Stephen's agonizing stammer, wondering at Stephen's mildness. He had actually smiled, she remembered, dismissing it as a joke. It was on this occasion that Anna, having rounded on Guy for his tasteless behaviour, went on to dismiss Stephen as 'a wimp'.

She was half-way to the front door when the telephone rang. It was Julia Wragg, a sprightly, young-sounding voice Grace thought, for somebody the other side of sixty whom Anna always referred to as 'old Julia'. She began by explaining her absence from the funeral, but Grace cut her off. 'It's all right,' she said, 'everybody understood about your having been in hospital. I didn't go either. I know it was awful of me, I just felt I couldn't. My friends coped marvellously, though. So how are you now, Mrs Wragg?'

'Listen, duckie, it's Julia. And may I call you Grace? When are we going to meet? There's so much I want to say to you. Do you ever come up to town?'

Grace rather recoiled at 'duckie'; it brought Anna back. In recent months she had started to use it herself, now and again, for her old friend, and the endearment had sounded so alien; this was obviously where it had come from. As she paused before replying she could hear little popping noises at the other end of the phone and remembered that Mrs Wragg was a chain smoker. 'I spend my time with old Julia coughing my guts out,' Anna had told her. Grace would too. Smoking made her feel sick.

'Not often,' she said cautiously, trying to remember how long it was since she'd visited Anna in London, 'but I'm quite free, and I'd like us to meet.'

'Well *do* come, come soon. I'm rather stuck here at the moment, convalescence and all that, though I've got work to do, of course. It never ends. Come soon,' she repeated.

'I will. I'll just need to book myself in somewhere.'

'Rubbish. There's nobody here but me, rattling around this great flat all day. You must stay here. Besides – ' and the voice paused, 'I imagine you might like to have a look at next door. Obviously the legalities'll take ages but I do have a key.'

So Julia Wragg knew about the provisions of Anna's will. Grace wondered what else she knew. She lived in a large flat off Haverstock Hill and Anna had bought the house next door, urged on, she had always suspected, by Julia. It was all the excited talk of its being a marvellous investment; Anna had been so cautious before, and very happy with her snug flat in Camden Town. It had sounded like someone else's advice, to Grace.

The new house was hers now, and yes, she certainly wanted to have a look at it. But whether she could quite face opening the door and seeing all Anna's possessions scattered over it as if, any minute, she might come walking in, she was not sure. It seemed rather insensitive of this Julia not to consider the timing more carefully, she thought, as the older woman rattled on about her exploratory 'op', in hospital, her two cats, her noise problems with the people living next door. But it was all, Grace concluded, a nervous cover-up for the unmentionable gap that was Anna. For what were cats and throbbing hi-fi systems and benign breast lumps compared with the enormous fact of their friend's death?

'Come tomorrow,' Julia said, suddenly interrupting her own spate. 'I'd love it. As I said, I'm rather stuck here, doctor's orders. Come this afternoon, why don't you?' and Grace heard her strike another match.

'Oh no,' she replied, her own voice carefully measured, 'I have things to do here. But I could come on Friday, for the weekend, if that's convenient?'

'Perfect. But you won't need to rush back, will you?' The managing, rather strident voice seemed to be saying, 'What for?' as if Julia knew, from Anna, all about the dull predictable pattern of boring old Grace's solitary life.

'Well, I'll see,' she said, making a note of the phone number, the address and directions about finding the house.

'Goodbye then, duckie. Marvellous to hear you. Lots of love.'

Grace stood in the hall trying to recall what Anna had told her about Julia Wragg. She was a widow, she remembered, and the small independent publishing firm of Wragg and Buckland had been founded by her husband George's grandfather. Since George's death ten years ago she had managed it alone. It was a minor but a prestigious company and it didn't put out any 'rubbish'. Grace could hear Anna telling her that very defiantly, for her own novels, with their enormous sales, were the most popular books Wragg and Buckland handled, though they were most definitely not in the pulp category. This too Anna had always been at pains to make clear.

She had told Grace that her Saddleford books had saved the company when it was having to consider merging with other larger houses to keep afloat, something quite alien to the independent old-fashioned spirit of grandfather's original venture. They had been able to resist only because of the Beardmore books.

For some years now Anna had been their most prized author, and she had drawn closer and closer to Julia Wragg. Grace knew that her own most deeply possessive instincts would rise to the fore when they met; she had long felt threatened by the growing intimacy, by what she imagined as the glittering literary talk, the gossip that went on which she could not share. But in her most jealous moments she told herself that she must have love, and remember all that this woman had done for Anna in the very early days when she was still a reporter, and when publishers were turning down her efforts on all sides; how Julia had regularly made long phone calls to her about the manuscripts, gone on encouraging, counselling hope, belief in herself and in her considerable talent.

But 'lots of love' she had said, in ringing off, to Grace, a total stranger. The fulsome declaration had made her uneasy and she wondered, as she unchained the front door, what their meeting would be like after such a foretaste. She must think carefully about what she ought to wear, perhaps buy something while she was out today. Julia Wragg had sounded very smart, very London. New clothes would give her some confidence. Also, she wanted to look her best for Anna.

As she was going through the front door the phone rang a second time. This time it was Breda Smith, her voice tentative and rather deferential. 'I just wondered how you were getting on, Grace,' she said. 'I'm sorry I couldn't come this morning. They'd put me on something else.' She had, in fact, been re-checking the information Grace had supplied about her movements in the Dales, the week Anna died. Buckle had put her on to it, following a request he said he had received from Hallam, though she rather suspected he was merely trying to keep her occupied.

Marian Stoker, now driving to Staffordshire, had been incommunicado but Barbara Savage at the library had given a very precise account of their daily programme which had tallied exactly with what Grace had said. She had spent all her time with them, except for the Tuesday on which she had visited The Rock. Barbara could not account for that day, she could only repeat that Grace had joined them for tea at about four o'clock and had reported on having had 'a lovely time', though she had said nothing at all about it. They had thought, perhaps, that she was simply tired, after the rather tricky driving. It was only afterwards that they had understood her silence. Anna's absence had been an embarrassment to her, a loss of face. She set such store by the friendship, Ba said.

Breda had dismissed Buckle's suggestion about Grace being involved as the most extravagant theorizing. She had used the word 'insane' to his face. But there were certainly gaps in the timing, hours that Tuesday when Grace had been on her own, driving from The Rock, shopping in Hawes, then driving to the old people's home to visit Miss Bruce. It was in those hours that Anna Beardmore could have been killed. If this request to re-examine Grace's statement did come from Hallam it could only mean that they were not quite satisfied. She rather thought it was Buckle's doing, though, that he was simply keeping her busy, and so out of

Grace's way. But he couldn't stop an informal phone call, between friends.

She had now read everything about the murder which had been sent through from North Yorkshire, and the coolness of her own emotions surprised her. She felt no personal anguish at the death of Anna Beardmore, only the shock the entire town seemed to be feeling at her outrageous end, and another unexpected shock at the loss of someone in her own generation. But in spite of the grisly facts, and the conscientious Breda had forced herself to read every word, her deepest sympathies were reserved for Grace. She felt angry that she should be implicated in such a hideous affair, and angry that selfish Anna had not been there to greet her that morning, even though her absence had been eventually explained by death. But Breda, irrationally she knew, and only because the old feelings of teenage inferiority had suddenly surfaced, resented that absence for Grace's sake, the reason in that moment being strangely immaterial.

Buckle was saying very little to her, now, about the case, but he was obviously interested in Grace and wanted to know anything Breda could tell him about the old days, when they were all at school together. Nothing of what she had told him had gone through to North Yorkshire, she'd noticed. She suspected that he was hoping to unearth something privately, here in Peth, and then present Hallam, his former chief, with some kind of coup. If he did find something it could surely have no bearing on Grace Bradley. She still refused to believe that his hints about her involvement in Anna's death were anything other than a poor joke.

'Have you any interesting plans for the rest of the week, Grace?' she said.

'*Interesting plans?*' Grace repeated, rather sharply, and immediately Breda knew that she must be careful. It was simply that Buckle had told her to check this out too, those had been his very words, and she had, without thinking how it might sound to Grace, simply repeated them from her notes.

There was a slight pause, then Grace replied cautiously, 'I'm going to London on Friday, I've been invited to stay with Julia Wragg, Anna's publisher. It'll be good to get away.'

'Yes, I'm sure it will,' Breda said warmly, writing the information down for Buckle, and loathing herself. She ought to ask how long Grace planned to stay in London but she felt it might sound too obvious. Let him ask for the information first. 'Well, bye-bye for now, Grace,' she said, 'and by the way, *do* look after yourself.' That bit was not Buckle, and she meant it.

Grace set off for Peth quite cheerfully, thinking only with charity of big Breda's kindness. Guiles and stratagems did not naturally feature in her estimate of humankind and it had not occurred to her for a minute that Breda might be acting under orders, or that anybody could think she herself was implicated in the murder of her best friend.

Mrs Dutt had obviously not seen Stephen for some considerable time and she didn't stay long. The old lady's profound deafness made communication almost impossible and Grace was made queasy by the smell of the filthy house where she sat all day in an untidy nest of cardboard cartons, with a narrow channel of floor between herself and the television set. After ten minutes' futile yelling, in an attempt to extract information, she crept rather guiltily away, pressing an envelope into Mrs Dutt's hand. The money would almost certainly be spent at the bookmaker's along the street. Stephen used to chide her about her passion for the horses but Guy had always egged her on. Anna had blamed Mrs Dutt for Guy's own betting, Stephen for his drinking. Nothing, after his death, could possibly be his fault.

In the town she spent some time looking at clothes. Black and grey seemed to be this year's dominating colours, relieved with the odd touch of red. Black didn't really flatter Grace, she was too swarthy. It had suited the pale-skinned Anna much better. She had nearly always worn black, after Guy.

She bought skirts, sweaters, a shirtwaister dress and a red Liberty scarf then, on impulse, a cashmere coat, also black. Everything came from Heelis and Heelis in Duke Street, an old family business where Mother had always shopped, a place that sold only the best. Afterwards she went next door to Duckhams and bought three pairs of shoes. When she got home she might pass some time going through her wardrobe, throwing things away. Gradually, she would buy new. Mother had always been very extravagant about clothes and it had driven Grace into frugality, almost meanness, when it came to her own. Anna had often ticked her off for looking drab, telling her she should make the best of her thick dark hair, her wonderful skin, her height. Well then, today she had obeyed, and spent several hundred pounds on clothes for her London visit, and it was not the tenth of the month either, when her director's cheque was paid in by Bradley's.

Anna would have approved, she thought sadly, lugging her packages up Beacon Brow towards the railway station where she bought a first-class ticket for London, for the Friday morning. Mother had always travelled first. She had not been thinking of her inheritance from Anna as she went round Peth writing large cheques. All that was still unreal, and Anna still alive. When she allowed herself to think about it at all she rather felt the money should go towards some kind of major Christian project, probably overseas. The Lord's work could be greatly helped by what Anna had left. In time she would confide in The Girls about it; and she would pray.

Buckle, driving up the hill as Grace walked out of the station, put up a hand and eyed her parcels with interest, but decided not to stop. He recognised the smart blue and gold carriers of Heelis and Heelis. Perhaps, later, Smith should pay them a visit.

For a while he waited around, then, from the ticket office, he obtained a list of the day's purchases so far and concluded that Grace was 'the tall dark-haired lady' who'd bought a first-class period return from Peth to London Euston and paid with an Access card. This certainly squared with what Smith had told him; that big lumpy girl had really done rather well. Before leaving the station he bought a ticket for himself, then drove to his flat, working out his new weekend timetable. He was off duty and he'd been due to go down to his mother next day, but she could wait. Half the time he got the feeling she was indifferent to his visits; they seemed to interfere with her own social arrangements, with bowling and bridge, and the Red Cross.

So the cautious, frugal Grace had been out spending money all morning, and now she was off to London. He felt a certain excitement at the thought of following her down there, also slightly sick, because of what her journey might mean, for she could be keeping some arrangement with Allen and he very much didn't want that; not only because he longed for her to be innocent in the Beardmore case but because he wanted her for himself.

Grace broke her new rule and watched television that night, in her dressing gown. But she changed channels when it came to the nine o'clock news, and again, at ten o'clock. It was unlikely, now, that details about Anna were still making national headlines, that would surely only happen again when they arrested someone. But she was taking no chances. She already knew very much more than she wanted to.

At half-past ten, when she was thinking about her prayers and bed, the front door bell rang and she heard the letter-box rattle. A bulky brown envelope was lying on the mat. Stepping over it she opened the door the few inches permitted by the chain. 'Hello?' she called out, not that she intended to admit anybody; but the bell had most definitely been rung.

Her voice fell into the night silence. She heard only the occasional swish of a car passing along the wet road at the bottom of the drive, an owl hooting in the big trees round Firs, the usual night rustlings. She shut the door, checked all the locks and bolts, and took the envelope back to the sitting room, switched off the television and opened it.

It contained several newspaper clippings, all about Anna, each one carefully identified and dated, by a typewriter. Her heart thumped queerly as she stared at them all. She did not intend to read a word and yet she could not help it, for the anonymous sender had used a bright yellow highlighter pen to draw attention to all the very worst details, the fact that the body had been undiscovered for several days and that it had been eaten by rats, a whole article about the survival rate of rats in this mild winter; the fact that Anna had almost certainly been strangled somewhere other than The Rock and that her body, with its right hand severed, had been propped in a writing position at her large pine table, the fact that some kind of sexual outrage had been committed on her body, possibly after death, the fact that a fifteen-year-old schoolboy had discovered it . . . All this, in her shock, Grace read, and could not but remember.

But reading itself was only the work of seconds. Running down the hall, tripping in the folds of her long kimono, she screwed everything into a tight ball and threw it into the stove. Then she banked it up for the night. The faint crackle and the gently burning flames as it ate all the paper were some comfort to her.

Perhaps she should phone Buckle. But he would no doubt tell her she should have kept the envelope and its contents, to be properly analysed and tested for fingerprints. He would think again what he had already made so painfully obvious in their interviews, that she was causing them unnecessary difficulties by suppressing information, further, that she was a fool. But surely the package was the work of a local crank who knew of her life-long friendship with Anna. The Girls had warned her at the beginning that she might get peculiar phone calls, curious people knocking on her door. The envelope was of that order. It was nothing that would have provided a clue to the murderer.

As she stared at the kitchen phone, wondering even so whether she ought to tell somebody what had just happened, it began ringing. For a long time she made no move, willing it to stop. Then she picked up the handset and put it to her ear, saying nothing.

The caller, a man in a phone box, was laughing, a low sneering laugh that chilled her. But remembering that Stephen might be trying to contact her, and that he could have started drinking again, she forced herself to listen, desperately trying to identify the timbre of the voice. As she listened, the strange laughter began to change, turning gradually into the most awful anguished weeping, a weeping that made her want to cry also. 'Oh, don't,' she heard herself pleading, 'Please, *don't*. Who are you? Let me help . . .'

There was a sudden pause, then the terrible laughter, almost devilish now, started again. Grace replaced the receiver and sank to her knees.

7

For the train journey she had equipped herself with a magazine, the day's paper and Anna's latest novel, the one that had followed her prize-winning *Miss Dixon*. But as they neared London all three lay unopened on her lap. *Christian Witness* had been the sole item of post that day and she had slipped it into her travelling bag at the last minute. But she had no heart to read about the glamorous couple on the front cover, drooling over their impeccable child, and how they had 'prayed for a pregnancy'; still less to read 'Why Wait?', the magazine's answer to the teenage 'sexuality crisis'. She viewed the cover with some distaste before putting the *Telegraph* on top of it. Since its change of editor it had become a solid family magazine with no place at all for what Marian Stoker rather belligerently labelled 'singles'. She should have stopped the subscription years ago; when she got back from London she would cancel it. Now she had accepted Julia's invitation, and was on her way, she was feeling altogether more purposeful.

She had brought Anna's latest novel because she felt she would be at a disadvantage with Julia Wragg if she hadn't at least looked at it. But this too she had not touched. Only the newspaper had interested her, with its lead report of a second murder in Yorkshire.

For a moment, on Peth station, she had thought there might be a link and she had read through the whole appalling story for clues, how a schoolgirl had gone out delivering newspapers two days ago, in a village outside Leeds, and disappeared, leaving no trace behind except an abandoned bicycle; but how, yesterday, her body had been found in an abandoned gravel pit, under the water.

The case seemed to have posed no problems for the police. A man, unnamed in the report, was already 'helping' them with their enquiries, but it was firmly stated at the end that any connection between this case and the Anna Beardmore murder had been ruled out.

Grace wondered how they could be so sure, and whether Buckle was involved in some way. She had written him a letter about the collection of news cuttings, and about the telephone call, but had only posted it on her way to the station, so that he wouldn't receive it until she was safely out of reach. She wanted the police to leave her alone for a while and in any case she was certain that both things were the work of some crank, nothing he was likely to follow up. The Girls had agreed with her, though Marian felt she ought to have kept the envelope.

'Mother's agony over little Janey,' the headline screamed, and a blurred photograph showed an anguished face. She stared out of the window and prayed for her, a forty-year-old housewife who had lost her only child to a sex killer. The girl had been just thirteen.

'If I am so quickly done for/What on earth was I begun for?' The curious, tricksy epitaph, carved on a baby's grave in the cemetery at High Peth, was something Anna had often quoted, when she was in one of her bitter phases about The Tragedy and had decided to get at Grace and The Girls, about Christianity. What indeed had Janey been 'begun for', Grace reflected bleakly as the blurred country-side flashed past the window, or Anna, or Guy, all dead before their time, and the dark thoughts lapped up again. But she pushed them away. For this meeting with Anna's special friend she knew that she must be strong. Like Ba's teenagers, she must bear the torch of faith.

Before the train finally drew in she spent a long time in the lavatory cubicle brushing her hair, redoing her face and nervously going through every detail of her appearance. The bright red scarf at her neck definitely relieved the sombre black coat and she was glad she had splurged at the last minute, and bought it. Anna, like Guy before her, had often talked of when she might die, but always flippantly. 'No longer mourn for me when I am dead,' she would quote, but smiling, as if that day were such a remote possibility that only the lightest thoughts were acceptable. Grace, the survivor, was wearing black on her first excursion into life again, since the murder. She wished she had tried harder, now, to find a more cheerful outfit. Death was a joyful thing after all, simply a passing from one room to the next. Except that the possibilities of that next room were infinite. And Anna was there now.

Julia Wragg was dressed in bright red and looked reassuringly over-weight, from the quick glance Grace was permitted before being enveloped in a long and close embrace. 'My dear Grace,' she heard, breathed into her neck, 'I've so longed to see you,' and she was held captive, rocking to and fro on a chilly North London doorstep, pressed tight against a soft bosom while the older woman let out little child-like sobs into her hair. The faint baby-powder smell and the comfortably upholstered figure reminded her of Marian Stoker and she was relieved, when stepping back, to see that Julia Wragg had large, warm brown eyes, not the small and calculating grey ones of Ba's domineering best friend. After the embrace she picked up her suitcase and travelling bag and followed Julia inside the house.

'It's all mine,' Julia called back, stiffly mounting a staircase, 'but we've always lived in the top flat. George never liked people living on top of him, and he wanted the views. Sorry about all the stairs. They'll do for me, one of these days. Bathroom on your left and there's another one just above, next to your bedroom. I'll dump these, then I'll put the kettle on. Or would you prefer a drink?' Now the initial greeting was over she sounded sharper and more business-like, perhaps even slightly guarded. Could she already be regretting those tears on the front doorstep? As she opened and shut kitchen cupboards, with Grace peering in at the doorway, she was definitely avoiding eye-contact. It was so like Anna, who had always refused to look people in the eye, and she wondered how conversations between these two had ever been conducted. 'Tea would be fine, thank you,' she said, rather timidly, trying to recall all that Anna had told her about Julia Wragg.

She'd been billed, she remembered, as a woman of enormous contradictions. 'A real softie inside but a keen businesswoman; and no one better when it gets down to the serious stuff of editing. I trust her.' Grace, remembering the first rapture of meeting, was not sure that she did. 'Lots of love,' Julia had said a few days ago on the phone, to Grace, a complete stranger. It was not her way, not at all.

She seemed very anxious to explain that they had the whole evening before them, and tomorrow the whole weekend; almost, it seemed, from her expansive talk, the whole of the rest of their lives. 'I have so much I want to discuss with you,' she kept repeating. Yet it was all vague, with no mention at all of the person who had brought them together, until Grace herself, with a kind of desperation, spoke Anna's name. 'I meant to read this on the train,' she said apologetically, pointing to the new novel she had brought with her. 'Anna was always going on at me for not reading anything, and I really did mean to read this one.' But, rather to her surprise, she had slept for much of the journey down. Grief had at last brought its own peculiar weariness and those hours alone were the first she had been given, encapsulated in time, cut off from friends, phones, interviews, to let her spirit rest. The sleep was denial, she knew, a signal that what had happened was as yet too hard for her. She hoped that this vigorous, bright, expectant woman drinking tea in the opposite chair would understand and not want to talk for too long about Anna, would not speak of the terrible things.

'You don't read,' she was saying, the large eyes staring hard, 'and yet you can write so well.'

'Can I?' Grace was genuinely puzzled. All she could think of were the letters she had occasionally sent to the house next door. She did not much like using the telephone for 'chats', she had always preferred to write to Anna, with her bits of news. Her notes then must have been passed on to this woman. *Why?* She felt uncomfortable.

'Oh yes, we both thought so,' Julia said unguardedly. Then she seemed to sense Grace's wariness and at once became selective. 'Well, for example, Anna let me see the wonderful letter you sent about Guy. *You will survive, if only because you must.* That was marvellous. Anna always said you could write like an angel, I remember. Between you and me, I think she was a little bit jealous,' and she smiled.

Grace stared at her, not understanding how her simple note could possibly be considered 'marvellous', and feeling deeply betrayed, because she remembered that letter, which she had sent in response to hysterical sheets from Anna, semi-incoherent ravings about Guy's death, and how she had laboured over it, writing and re-writing, until at last the words fell into some kind of order and she could do no more. In that letter she had daringly counselled confidence, to the agnostic Anna, that Guy, wherever he had gone, had at last found peace.

'*I believe Guy knows he is loved, now,*' murmured Julia, as if reading her mind.

'My letters were private,' Grace said rather stonily, 'I never imagined that Anna *showed* them to people.'

'Oh she didn't, duckie, she didn't, it was just the odd phrase, you know . . .' and they exchanged furtive looks, mutually acknowledging the lie and letting it go, to remain comfortable.

Since Anna's death Julia had been next door and gone through the papers she had left in her desk. There wasn't as much as she'd hoped, most of the stuff was presumably at the cottage, where she'd planned to write her next book. But there was one interesting file, a few letters and some diaries. These she had taken away, because of a plan she was slowly forming. But now she'd met Grace she realised she must be careful, choose her time carefully, wait, if need be. 'Tell me about Guy,' she said suddenly, deciding on a complete change of track. 'You must have known him pretty well. Did it surprise you, when he killed himself?'

Grace was silent for a moment. There were too many questions here. First, Julia must have heard from Anna about her feelings of antagonism towards Guy Beardmore, so there was no point in telling anything other than the truth, to ease the moment. His awful death had not suddenly translated him into a saint. 'Well, I never liked Guy,' she said flatly. 'Never. I just couldn't.'

'Why? Because of how he neglected your parents, I mean, after they had been so kind to him? Anna told me about all that.'

'No, I didn't blame him for that, neither did my parents. They were both so young and The Tragedy was so terrible for them, worse for Guy than it was for Anna because, you see, he came home to it. No, it was what he . . . sort of . . . turned into, when we'd all grown up and it was all behind him. Except that I don't really think it ever was "behind him". But it seemed to me that he made the tragedy of his parents an excuse for his whole life. And you can't do that, can you, however awful the past has been? It's a waste,' and she stared at the floor. 'He'd gone on suffering from it, though,' she said. Now she had told Julia the truth about Guy she found she was wanting to say more about the Beardmores. They were both dead and talking to this woman was a kind of release. She went on, 'Anna realised what he must have been through, when he died. It just added to her guilt. "I should have died instead," that's what she wrote to me.' Now she had, as if some terrible Christless justice had been forced to complete its inexorable pattern in the family.

'"The Hanged Man and the Woman Hacked About",' Julia said, turning over the pages of a loose-leaf file in her lap. It was what had happened to the parents that interested her most, and Anna had never talked to her about it.

'I'm sorry?' Grace said.

'Oh, Anna left some notes next door. I was looking through them the other day and the heading caught my eye. As her publisher her bits and pieces are obviously of some interest to me, I mean, as an indication of what else she might have done, had she only . . .' There were tears in her voice, but also distinct embarrassment. Grace was clearly beginning to look disapproving.

'As I think you know,' she said, suddenly quite formal, 'in her will Anna left everything to me. I would like all her papers, in fact I can take them back with me.' She would, and she would speak to Edward Pollitt about the legal position the minute she got home. She was not at all sure that Julia should have gone into the house, let alone taken away papers.

'Of course, *of course*, duckie,' Julia soothed, hastening to smooth over the awkwardness. Something had warned her that there might be difficulties of this kind. She had therefore taken care, last week, after the police had been through the house next door, to photocopy the bundle of notes on the Hanged Man, and to remove the letters and diaries. Each notebook covered roughly three months, though the early ones, and the one which must have included the deaths, were missing. Had she been able to read it for herself there would have been no need to question Grace, except that she'd been present when it had all happened, and, according to Anna, had a phenomenally good memory.

'Anna only ever spoke of her parents' death as "The Tragedy",' Julia said. 'Capital T. But I think these notes were to deal with all that, at last,' and she tapped the red file.

'The Hanged Man and the Woman Hacked About,' Grace repeated thoughtfully, glancing at it. 'It's not much of a title. Actually, I never liked "Saddleford" either.'

'Why not?'

'Oh, it always sounded phoney, to me. Perhaps that's why I never got very far with the books. I think that it must have reminded me of Saddleworth Moor, you know, where all those poor children were murdered. That's quite near Peth.'

Julia looked grave. Though she knew Anna would never have intended such a thing she had always made this connection herself, and she believed the reading public did. There was always violence going on in the Saddleford stories, though only ever off-stage. But Anna had seemed unable to leave the subject completely alone. In a queer way the Saddleford label was a strand, albeit a kinky one, of the immense success of the books. Publishing was never predictable. She had learned that long ago, from George. 'You say you've not read Anna's latest?' she said. 'Do I take it you've not read any of them . . . not your cup of tea, perhaps?'

'I did at first, but I, you know, got a bit bogged down. I read the short stories, years ago, *ugh*. . .' Death had certainly not been relegated to the sidelines in those. In her lurid early efforts Anna had indulged her taste for the bizarre and the macabre rather sickeningly.

'I know. They've never been published, of course. They could be, now, tastes change and she's a big name. But it was only when I got her to drop all that Gothic stuff that she produced something I could handle. She rather blamed me, I think.'

'What for?'

'For how the books *went*, you know, nothing too ghastly, nothing the average library-user couldn't cope with. Mankind can't bear too much reality, et cet, and it's true, if you study the bestseller lists. People like to be comfortable with a book. She complained in the end that I'd made her take the teeth out of her plots. But the point is, duckie, it *worked*, and she knew it. People adored them, couldn't wait for the next.'

'But she wanted to write another story like the one that won the award.'

'*Miss Dixon?* Ah well, yes, but it was a one-off book, that was; it often happens, you know, a writer does something they just can't seem to repeat, not that particular *trick*. She tried, but the story lacked guts, somehow. She needed the wider canvas, she'd adapted to it, I suppose.'

'She said to me, though, that she'd never intended to write the Saddleford series at all. She obviously felt she'd compromised with them. That's why she wanted to write a book about Guy, I think.'

'Hmm. The Hanged Man . . . I don't think it can ever have been intended as a title. As you say, it's too long. You knew all about it, of course.'

'About what?' But Grace understood the reference perfectly well, and Julia knew she understood, and was now expected to say more. There was a silence, then Julia forged on. 'About what Anna always called "The Tragedy".'

'Yes, I knew. But not from Anna and Guy. They never talked about it at all. Neither did my parents, they were very protective towards me. Anyhow, I was only fifteen when it happened, the same age as the Beardmores. All I knew at the time was that both the parents were found dead in the house and that my mother and father took them in, that night. Actually, my mother was in bed with shingles. Daddie did everything, and Mrs Lumb.'

'Who was she?'

'Our cleaning lady. She still comes to me; she went to Anna's funeral,' Grace added, with reverence.

'So you only heard the details much later? That was odd, surely? I mean, they were living in your house.'

'I'm sure they thought Daddie had told me; he just said act normally,' and Grace gave a dry little laugh. 'They talked to each other, of course, all the time. Anna used to go into Guy's room and they'd talk into the night. Sometimes they never went to sleep. They were very close, even though they were always arguing. It was something to do with being twins.'

'Anna shared with you?'

'Yes. The night it happened we both slept in my bed. Then Daddie moved another one in. She could have had a separate bedroom but she was too frightened to sleep on her own. In fact she shared with me whenever she stayed, until she went to university.' And in those first weeks, night after night, Grace had woken up and heard Guy weeping in the room next door.

Anna did not cry. In her diary, the day after the deaths, she had written, 'There is no just God that governs the earth righteously, but a God of lies, that bears witness against the innocent,' and she had shown it to Grace. While Guy hopelessly wept, she had needed to externalise. In the middle of the horror she had only missed one entry in her journal and that was because the notebook was at Firs and Mr Bradley could not get in to fetch it for her. She had asked.

'Anna coped better than Guy did, in the end. *That that I am shall make me live.* She wrote that to me after Guy killed himself. She was always quoting things at me, I'm sure she felt I needed educating, or something,' she added, slightly bitter. 'I don't know where it comes from.'

'Oh, it's Shakespeare,' Julia said at once, then, drawing back, 'er, *Troilus and Cressida*, I think. Actually, I'm not sure.' She was quite sure but she must tread carefully, remembering what Anna had told her of Grace's hang-ups about her truncated education, at the hands of her hypochondriac mother, and her own apparent lack of intellectual curiosity. She needed the woman on her side.

'So you didn't know about the parents for some time then?' she went on.

'No. I only really got the full story after Daddie died. Then I found all the newspaper cuttings amongst his papers. He obviously hadn't wanted me to know how much he had been involved.'

'So what did happen?'

'It was just before Christmas. They say that's when the really awful things often blow up, don't they? People with problems can't bear all the jollity, all the razzmatazz. It gets to them if they're depressed already. Guy died at Christmas too, you know, only a few days before.'

'But the Beardmores were suffocatingly religious, weren't they? Anna told me all about that awful chapel the father was so attached to. I'm sure she said they didn't actually *celebrate* Christmas.'

'Dr Beardmore was certainly very devout,' Grace said. 'The chapel was his life, apart from his teaching job at the prep school. He'd actually helped to build it. I don't really know where Anna's mother stood, I mean as far as religion was concerned. She'd been ill for such a long time. She had motor neurone disease, you know, she could hardly move and you couldn't conduct a conversation with her, her voice had gone. She was in a wheelchair when she was found.'

'So he killed her while she was sitting in a wheelchair?'

'Yes. His school had broken up for Christmas and he was at home with her. Nobody else was in the house that day. He just went into the drawing room, apparently, and hacked her to death.'

'What with?'

'Guy's army knife. He had this weapon collection on his bedroom wall. Most of the things were replicas but the knife wasn't. It had belonged to an uncle, or something. It had been confiscated a few weeks before, by his father. Anna and I had been in this play at our school, and she'd borrowed it for one of the scenes. Some boys fooled around with it and there was a big fuss. Anyway, it was only afterwards that they began to wonder how much had actually been planned, when they found out that Dr Beardmore had taken the knife away, and hidden it. But I'm sure nothing *was* planned, I've thought about it on and off for years. They said he might have been arranging to go away with Winnie, you see. But in fact, having killed his wife, he hanged himself in one of the outhouses down the garden, within minutes, they thought.'

'And who was Winnie?'

'Oh, she was lovely, a single lady from his chapel, little Winnie Carpenter. She'd been a Sunday School teacher, and everything.'

'But . . . they'd been having an affair?'

'Yes. For years, apparently.'

These Christians, thought Julia, remembering what Anna had said about the sex-starved, virginal Grace, about Ba Savage, more or less a married spinster, and about big Marian Stoker, *virgo intacta*, opening her legs to nobody but 'the Lord'; how dull all these religious people were, she had complained, how socially awkward, how drab; how, invariably, the Church took unto itself the halt, the lame and the blind.

'And what happened to her?' she asked.

'She died, just a few months after.'

'Not *another* suicide, for God's sake? I can't bear it.'

'No. But The Tragedy was responsible, I'm sure of that. The chapel people found out about her and Dr Beardmore, you see, and she was asked to leave. She went into hospital to have a minor operation, fibroids, I think, nothing much, and she never came out of the anaesthetic.

'My mother always said that deaths often came in threes,' she added thoughtfully, 'I do remember that.' But she did not repeat what else Mrs Bradley had said, that Winnie Carpenter's death was 'a judgement on her'. It would not help whatever image Julia Wragg had formed of Christians.

'Guy got home early that afternoon, from school. His term hadn't quite finished and he was supposed to be playing rugby. But the match was cancelled. Whether Dr Beardmore had relied on his being out of the house I don't know.'

'Surely he had? No one, no one on this earth would have deliberately exposed a fifteen-year-old boy to that.'

'No. Oh, I'm sure there was nothing deliberate or premeditated about it. Otherwise he'd have killed his wife more mercifully. He could easily have smothered her, for example, she was quite helpless by that stage. But there were rumours afterwards, about some anonymous letters about him and Winnie. I suppose he might have received one that very day and I think the complete hopelessness of the situation must have triggered everything off. He was in a trap till Mrs Beardmore died, and it was taking years. Yet he'd looked after her so marvellously, everybody said so.

'Guy found her first. One of his jobs was to do the fires when he came in from school. His father was very strict with him, not at all loving. Anna was the big favourite. He opened the drawing room door with a shovel of coal in his hand and found her there, dead in the wheelchair. That coal stayed in the doorway until the police finally locked the house up, hours later. Anna told me how everybody stepped round it. She couldn't get it out of her mind.'

'And the father?'

'I don't know how long it was before Guy found him. There's a mystery about the whole afternoon. The outhouse was where he kept his pet rabbits. He went down there to see to them, and found his father hanging from one of the beams.'

'So he hadn't summoned anybody, when he first found his mother?'

'Not immediately. Anna told me he talked to her.'

'*He talked to her?*'

'That's what she said. It was the only thing she did tell me, apart from his leaving the shovel of coal in the doorway. Guy was always strange, though, entirely unpredictable. Nobody understood him.'

'So his death wasn't a surprise to you?'

'Oh yes. I would have thought he loved himself too much. I really couldn't believe it at first, neither could Anna. Well, you know about that; she had to be persuaded not to come down here and see the body. There seemed to be no trigger at all for what Guy did, whereas, with Dr Beardmore . . . if the chapel really *had* found out about him and Winnie Carpenter, and he knew he had months, years even, of watching his wife deteriorate. Well, you can see how someone in that situation might suddenly snap.'

'But the violence of it, Grace. Was he a violent man?'

'I never saw it, though Anna told me he could flare up into great rages, just now and again. Guy was violent, though, and he got worse, as he got older.'

She suddenly remembered but, out of a curious loyalty to the dead Beardmores, couldn't bring herself to describe, how Guy had once hurtled a dish of hot food down the drive of White Lodge, at an old woman's head. A Mrs Reddish, an elderly lady from the Beardmore chapel, had brought a casserole to the house the day after the deaths, knowing that Anna and Guy had been taken in by the Bradleys, that the mother was in bed with one of her illnesses, and that the father was having to cope. Grace could well understand the silent, simple gesture that had so enraged Guy; the terror of the elderly woman in the face of the monstrous events at Firs, yet under it, her pity, her quiet determination to do something for those poor children, her wanting to give them a cup of cold water in the name of Christ. Old, crippled with rheumatism, she had not got away in time, for Guy had seen her from the hall window of White Lodge. And he had rushed out, picked up the homely brown dish and flung it after her. 'Take your fucking food, you fucking hypocrite,' he had screamed. 'You fucking well didn't come round here when they were alive. Don't fucking come here when they're fucking dead. Here, take your fucking stew, feed it to your fucking God in your fucking chapel.'

Grace had run upstairs and found Daddie. He was a small slight man and he'd had difficulty restraining Guy. Though he was Anna's twin he was much bigger and heavier. At fifteen he had been slim-waisted, though with enormous beefy shoulders and unusually large feet and hands. He'd had Anna's colouring, thick coarse hair that was sandy, almost pinkish in colour, a pale skin delicately freckled and the same small pointed features though set in a fleshier face, rather a chubby-cheeked baby face at fifteen; but in his adult years, through drink, he had gone to fat.

As she sat in Julia Wragg's untidy drawing room she suddenly saw him in old age. He would have had thick white hair like his father, but not the contained trimness of Dr Beardmore, a man, she had always felt – or was it only retrospection – with a secret, a knowledge which had suddenly broken upon him in an orgasm of violence and rage, of guilt and frustration and anguish.

'Was Guy ever violent towards you, duckie?' Julia wanted to know more, now, about this brother. Anna, though never exactly 'violent', had often had sudden inexplicable fits of intense irritability, usually about the handling of her books, quibbling over details of design, questioning contracts, rushing round to the production department at Wragg and Buckland, on several occasions reducing a junior copy editor to tears over some piffling, unimportant detail. And Julia had had to go round explaining and soothing, calming down ruffled feathers, yet all the time reassuring Anna that she had every right to say her piece. Privately she had disapproved of such self-indulgence, not really understanding these sudden flaring outbursts; except that she sensed they came from some massive unresolved tension deep in

Anna's subconscious which suddenly reared up and unleashed itself, raw and undiluted on some entirely irrelevant issue, anger out of all proportion to the fault. Perhaps Guy, whom Anna had been at great pains to keep away from her, was the clue.

'You know about the night of the Pritchard Award, of course?' she prompted, when Grace did not reply. That had certainly resembled violence.

'Oh yes, I watched it on television.'

'Didn't we all?' Julia said, with a little groan and, getting up, producing glasses and bottles from a cabinet. 'Come on, let's move downstairs and have a drink while I make a start on the meal.'

As she waited for Julia to join her, and sipped at a large dry sherry in a small conservatory, its door open on to the unusually mild evening so they could 'enjoy the last half hour of the garden' (evidently one of Julia's hobbies), Grace remembered her hurt over the Pritchard Award. Anna had been at great pains to explain how she would have loved her to have been the one guest whom writers on the short-list were allowed to invite but that, 'maddeningly', a word Grace also remembered, she'd felt obliged to give the invitation to someone else, a fellow writer, male, of course, of whom Grace had not heard. She never did understand why Anna had felt 'obliged', but her suspicion was that her own presence would have been an embarrassment. She was reserved for Peth. Guy had got himself into the award dinner with his characteristic sleight of hand, his uncanny plausibility. Anna would never have risked taking him as her guest. It was a glittering affair at which the drink flowed freely.

She had received the award, a prestigious one and quite valuable in terms of cash, for *Miss Dixon*, a short, painful book which was set in Peth but which could have happened anywhere. Grace had read it afterwards, because of the prize and because it was short. It had shocked her, though not because of the long explicit sex scenes. Contrary to what Anna had always glibly assumed, Grace was not a virgin.

The week Lynn had finally broken with Stephen for good and gone up to the island with their children, he had turned up distraught at Firs, wanting to see Anna. But she had just driven off to Newcastle to talk at some book event, and only Grace was there, at White Lodge.

After hours of rambling talk about his family troubles, Grace listening, Stephen pouring it all out, he had spent the night in her bed. The sex was gentle, pleasurable even, not at all the uncomfortable, difficult experience Grace had imagined and feared for so long, and he said that she was a great comfort to him. Nothing was said about the future and indeed Grace didn't want that. But she saw their unexpected coming together as a sign unto her, of what would one day surely come to pass: a permanent union in the sight of God.

She had always feared sex because it was the great unknown and because her parents had never spoken of it. Of course, one knew the facts, as one knew the facts of death, but, as she had discovered to her cost, nothing could prepare someone for how they would actually *feel* when the beloved passed away. She still remembered the horror of it, from Daddie. As for human coupling, that equal mystery for the uninitiated, she had once read that the sexual act was so ludicrous it must surely be ultimate proof that God had a sense of humour. 'All that pushing and shoving,' she remembered from a silly television film, 'and nothing much to show at the end of it, a bit like supermarket shopping.' With Stephen it was neither ludicrous nor futile, nor, when the moment came, did she feel at all frightened; she believed God had been in that.

She was preparing to go to bed, having said goodnight to him at the door of the spare room, and just slipping her nightdress over her head when he appeared in her doorway. He did not speak, simply came to her, put the nightdress aside and guided her to the bed. In the long wardrobe mirror she saw her own body and his, pitifully thin, with the defenceless small white buttocks of a child. He was so very thin she was amazed at the strength of his arms round her, and of his kiss. She had liked that best, and afterwards, when he buried his face between her breasts, pulling at them gently to give her pleasure. He wept at the climax; she too wanted to weep, for the joy of it, but she felt that he was in too much pain and that he needed her to be strong. So she simply held him in her arms. In her fingers the dark curls round the base of his skull were soft as down.

As she waited for Julia to come down from the kitchen she thought about it again, and she felt her cheeks warming. But why should she feel ashamed? Mother and Daddie would have been shocked, no doubt, but she knew the Lord in a way she felt they had not. *For the love of God*, she had crooned peacefully to herself, going about her solitary chores next day, *is broader than the measures of men's mind*. Her taking Stephen inside her had been entirely right, simply an image of the love she had long felt. She had no guilt about it at all.

Like the rest of the house Julia's garden room was lined with bookshelves, and she could see several paperback copies of *Miss Dixon* with the red and gold Pritchard Award ribbon slashed across the spine. Idly, she picked one out and thumbed through it. To her, the shocking thing about *Miss Dixon* wasn't the sex, it was the way Anna had lifted a story wholesale from a local newspaper and woven her novel around it. Though names and personalities had been thinly camouflaged anybody who knew the original story would recognise at once the pathetic case of Eleanor Beaconsfield, an ageing piano teacher who must have taught half the younger adults in Peth, including Guy Beardmore. That was where Anna had made a mistake.

Miss Beaconsfield had answered an advertisement in a magazine for 'a companion with a view to marriage', started a long, and, for her, happy relationship with a highly compatible middle-aged man at the end of which, to her amazement, a wedding was never arranged. The man, having used her for regular sex, simply debunked.

Unwisely, for the rather spicy court proceedings were bound to be picked up by the local press, Miss Beaconsfield, a steely and somewhat unyielding personality to her pupils, sued the man for breach of promise. She got nowhere, even though he had practised the same deception several times before in other towns, with similar respectable middle-aged women for whom, it seemed, he had a pronounced sexual proclivity.

Miss Beaconsfield gave up piano teaching for good soon after the court proceedings, suffered a total nervous breakdown and ended up in Raddon Court, the local psychiatric hospital. It had a library which Ba sometimes visited with books for the patients. She had not known The Girls then but Grace heard later that Ba had actually withdrawn *Miss Dixon* lest it should fall into Miss Beaconsfield's hands. She need not have worried, the woman was chronically depressed, not merely beyond reading but entirely indifferent to her own bodily functions. Grace thought she was still in the place.

Guy had been one of her most promising pupils and they were fond of each other. He had said nothing about *Miss Dixon*. Anna, aware of his jealousy and resentment of her growing success, had learned never to talk about her books to him. But he had clearly read of her Pritchard Award nomination. Uncluttered with the interminable family intrigues and quarrels which Grace had found so tedious in the other Saddleford tales, the sad little story of Miss Dixon stood out in the rawness of its pain, a slight but unforgettable drama of hope and trust that moved with devastating understatement to its unbearable conclusion. Anna had softened the ending very slightly, in the same summary fashion she dealt with anything unpleasant or difficult in the longer stories. Separation and divorce, life-threatening illness, God – all were relegated to the sidelines, Grace had noticed,

in the ones she had persevered with, the author always resisting the
opportunity of addressing the issues of life head-on. She hadn't known
till today how instrumental Julia Wragg had been in the shaping of the
Saddleford books. Anna had always praised her lavishly, but more for
her psychological support. She had kept very quiet about the literary
advice.

Apart from its slightly ambivalent ending, *Miss Dixon* was different
from the longer Saddleford tales. In its directness, its powerful linear
development, its concentration on a simple and pathetically hopeful
virgin, it stood out from the rest. 'A small masterpiece, quite perfectly
executed,' the chairman of the Pritchard Committee had announced
at the award ceremony.

Grace had watched it at home, on television, trying hard not to be
hurt as she watched Anna receive extravagant embraces from people
who were surely strangers to her. She had been going to switch off
after seeing her receive the cheque. It was boring, watching the
cameras range idly over long damasked dinner tables, over men
in dress suits holding inane interviews with aggressive, nervous or
simpering guests, most of whom seemed to some degree affected
by alcohol. Then someone lurched up who was really drunk. Guy,
in a stained shirt and a crumpled suit, bowtie undone and loosely
trailing, suddenly thrust his big face at the camera, appeared to
grab the microphone and belched into the lens. He had long ginger
stubble on his chin – he had moved in with Stephen since Anna had
stopped paying his rent and was starting to copy him again, she'd
reported to Grace, reverting to the adolescent years when he had
followed him round Peth Art School with doggy devotion, dressing
like him, becoming similarly shaggy and unkempt, even copying his
stammer, and of course, aping his painting style. Now he grimaced,
beast-like, at the viewers, farted loudly, took a swig from a passing
drinks tray and bellowed, 'Lock the door of the bog, I'm telling you,
when you strain at stool. Otherwise Anna Beardmore will be in after
you, with her notebook. She'll want to analyse your effluence, all the
waste products of your rotten little body, just as she anatomized Miss
Beaconsfield. And what harm had that poor old sod ever done to
anyone? Tell me that, will you? *She was my friend.*

'They fuck you up, this literary lot,' he screamed. 'Nobody's safe,
you know. So you lot, *out bloody there*, fucking well listen to someone
who knows what he's talking about. Of course, they won't take my
work, you know, these clever-dick publishers, they – ' But suddenly
the camera swung away, to another part of the hall, where somebody,
obviously unrehearsed, abruptly broke in on a group of dinner guests
and began to interview last year's winner. 'Tell me,' the hot-faced

young man said, 'what precise difference did winning this prestigious award make to you, Jon Hooker?' and the novelist, only momentarily startled, had already taken on that glassy-eyed expansive look that creeps over the face as someone prepares to enjoy the pleasure of talking solely about themselves.

Guy could have occupied the screen for only thirty seconds, at most, but the incident had caused trouble and the youthful producer who felt the drunken outburst made wonderful television had been sacked. Guy had boasted about it afterwards; he'd enjoyed the publicity.

Julia bustled in, with a bowl of nuts. 'Supper'll be a few more minutes, I'm afraid, I forgot to put the oven on. I do have a microwave, actually, but I've not sussed it out yet. Adam gave it to me, bless him. He's a pet. Come on, have a fill up.'

'Adam?'

'Oh he's a student, at UC. He stays here in the university term. I like having someone else in the house and he's really very good to me. We're great pals.'

So there was Adam. It seemed that everybody had a man, even the ageing Julia. Grace stared into her newly filled glass feeling again her profound loneliness, fearing for the rest of her life.

Julia was looking at her. Before settling herself in a creaking Lloyd Loom chair she leaned over and squeezed her arm. 'Come on, duckie, cheer up. We've got to keep going now, all of us.' But Grace felt the desperation in her voice, how it shook, was unconvinced. 'I know. I was just thinking about Guy, when he got himself on television. Poor Anna.'

'I didn't know anything about it until later that night. She didn't either, I suppose they didn't tell her. No, we only knew when we switched the video recorder on – Adam had taped it for me. We opened a bottle and all sat round. God, it was embarrassing. If only someone at the Beeb had *told* me. It was the end, so far as Guy went.'

'No,' Grace said. 'Anna's celebration party was the real end. I went to that.'

She had been surprised to have received an invitation but it quickly dawned on her just why she was needed. Anna had organised her evening round the food. 'You're so *marvellous*, darling,' she told her, coming into the kitchen and inspecting the little plates of canapés over which she'd laboured for hours, 'and I'm just *hopeless*. Thank you in advance . . .' and she hugged and kissed her. Grace went on arranging her plates. Over her new silk dress from Heelis's she was wearing rather a hideous floral overall of Mother's which she'd thrown into her case at the last minute, in case there was some extra washing up to do at the end of the party, forgotten by the caterers. But there were no caterers, just Grace, and she was not to remove the overall all evening.

Anna was wearing a pale blue floating creation, slightly glittery and on the flimsy side. 'You're so *clever*, Gracie,' she gurgled. She only used that name when she was nervous, and she was nervous now. Guy, who hadn't been invited because of the TV fiasco, had rung up that morning all smiles and told her he was coming anyway, and couldn't they be friends, for Christ's sake. She'd already started drinking and seemed slightly high. 'Clever old Gracie,' she repeated, extracting a prawn from one of the plates. Privately Grace reckoned that anybody who could read could read a recipe, and therefore cook. It was simply that Anna didn't *choose* to read, at least, not cookery books. They were obviously too boring.

Julia didn't come to the party. She'd developed a terrible migraine in the afternoon and been forced to take to her bed. Anna slipped next door a couple of times, to check that she was all right, taking a selection of Grace's goodies with her.

She sipped her sherry. Now she'd met Julia she very much wished she'd been there, that night. Beneath all the gush she seemed genuinely kind, and kindness would have helped, with the pain. For Anna, having made one early, half-hearted attempt to introduce her to a few guests, simply abandoned her for the evening, apparently forgetting that she was actually there, and when Grace, temporarily free from her kitchen chores, contemplated joining the awesome, yammering fray in the stifling drawing room, she shrank away from the close-packed bodies, the high-pitched braying and the cross-conversations, above all, from the large numbers of extraordinarily glamorous young men and women who, as she hovered by the kitchen door, still in Mother's hideous overall, flicked bland, uncomprehending glances at her, and glazed empty smiles, before turning back to their talk, and their drinking.

Nobody bothered with her at all, except Guy, who'd wangled his way in with flowers, chocolates and champagne, smooth-talking the two young men from Wragg and Buckland, boyfriends of Julia's typists, whom Anna had gigglingly referred to as 'bouncers'. He was the only person there who actually sought her out, coming into the kitchen at intervals and trying to prise her away from the sink. But, angry with Anna now, she insisted on staying there, hating the whole thing and determined to make her point. 'Oh, all right, *be* a bloody martyr,' he said at last, staggering off with a new bottle of whisky which he'd spotted on top of a cupboard and was clearly planning to keep to himself. It was early but he was already very drunk and not yet out of the aggressive stage which she knew would be eventually superseded by maudlin self-pity, and weeping. She told him that she wasn't being a martyr, but that somebody had to do the boring things.

'Yes, and that's what you are, Grace Bradley, bloody *boring!*' he yelled, so loudly that people in the drawing room turned round to listen. It was one of the last things he'd ever said to her.

'I blame Guy getting in on my migraine,' Julia said. 'If only Anna had been there. I don't know how he got past Chris and Ian.'

'No. He'd have got in anyway, honestly. Don't blame them. He had this *way* with people, it was really odd.'

Stephen had come to the party too, but without Lynn. Their marriage was 'cooling', that was the phrase he used to Grace when, unaware of any difficulties, she at last emerged from the kitchen and pushed her way towards him, the one person she was glad to see, kissing him and asking him how the family was getting on, sending special love to the children.

The reply forced from him by her bright, uncomprehending question had come grudgingly, as if squeezed out of an empty tube. He immediately picked up a drink and walked away from her, losing himself in the crush. Bewildered, and unable, quite, to believe in this uncharacteristic chilliness – they had not yet made love but she had always nursed a great tenderness for him and he had always treated her gently – she went back to the kitchen and started to wash glasses. Anna claimed to have organised people to do this, but someone had phoned half-way through the evening and said Miss Beardmore's booking was for the week after.

'I really thought Anna might have killed Guy, that night,' Julia said, tossing back her sherry and refilling the glass, before lighting a cigarette. 'I heard the windows break, you know, from my bedroom, and it's a hell of a way to fall, down all those steps.'

'I think she *did* want to kill him, in the end. She told me she did, actually.'

And now she could see Anna again quite clearly, in the middle of the drawing room in next door's house, her small hands quite flat, pushing Guy towards the front door. He was roaring drunk and she kept repeating through clenched teeth, 'Just *go*, will you, *go*. I've had enough. It's over.'

At first he only protested mildly, vaguely smiling, trying to push away the little hands, putting his arms around her. But Anna had become violent, her voice rising to a scream, the first frustrated tears coming. 'You're not going to spoil *this*, Guy,' she hissed. 'I'm not having a repeat performance of the other night, by God I'm not. I'm phoning the police.'

In the predictable fashion of highly embarrassed guests the people standing round the room were already, by instinct, forming small circles, turning their backs on the warring brother and sister, talking on, solicitously pouring fresh drinks for one another. But as Anna dialled a number an uncanny quiet came upon them all, broken only by the sound of tinkling glass. Caught between the drawing room and the kitchen, a tea-cloth in her hand, red checked and filthy like most of Anna's kitchen equipment, Grace stood watching in horror, praying that Guy would not see her.

'There's a hundred quid down the drain . . . fifty, that one, I should think . . . and this one? Oh, a couple of hundred for that, it's obviously a museum piece.' As Anna whispered into the telephone Guy was systematically chucking her precious collection of antique paperweights through the front window, into the street. When the oval mahogany display table was empty he gave a sudden roar at which the small polite circles, mesmerised now, broke ranks, and gaped. Unzipping his flies he urinated on the large oriental rug which Anna had bought to celebrate her award, an exquisite thing, a Tabriz, greys, inky blues and pale mauves, birds and animals at rest upon the Tree of Life. 'There you are, big sister' – she had been born ten minutes before Guy – 'now I've christened it for you. Say thank you nicely.'

Then, looking round for approval, he saw Grace in the kitchen doorway, holding the red cloth, her eyes on the steaming jet that glittered in the light of the table lamps, and he made for her, smiling queerly. '*Gracie*, old *Gracie*,' he said. 'Never seen a bit of cock before? Come *on*, here's your big chance,' and he started fumbling between his legs.

Somebody made a grab for him and Grace, turning away, heard him suddenly burst into childish tears. She heard Anna weeping too, the brother and the sister were weeping together, and it was years ago, and the night of The Tragedy. She wanted to go to them, put her arms round them both, and love them.

Then there was a general scuffle and her view across the drawing room was obscured by heaving backs. Wine glasses crashed to the floor, a table fell over, then some elderly woman with blue hair let out a high, piggy squeal. Seconds later, with Anna now sobbing hysterically but still somehow pushing away at the back, Guy was elbowed out by the two men from Wragg and Buckland and the front door double-locked. In the silence that followed they heard him rolling down the five stone steps that led to the street, taking milk bottles with him.

'Poor sod,' somebody whispered, as everybody gathered dumbly round Anna. Through the fug of wine and cigarettes the warm, familiar smell of urine wafted slowly across the room.

Grace swilled the last of the sherry round in her glass. 'It was the last time they saw one another,' she said, closing her mind down on the memory of it all. 'After that she refused to pay his bills, his rent, everything. She sent back all his letters, she even changed her phone number. Well, you must know all that.'

'And he killed himself, only two months later. Yet you say nothing triggered it off?'

'I don't think it was anything to do with Anna. He just moved in with Stephen, he started to milk him for money instead. It was typical of him. I don't think anyone else would have put up with it but Stephen, he's so easy-going – when he's well – and people have always taken advantage of him. I suppose that's why he was forever running out of cash, I mean, for the family. It drove Lynn mad, it was one of the reasons she walked out on him, well, so Anna told me. They say money often figures in marriage breakdowns, don't they?'

'Yes. Money and sex. Sex nearly *always* rears its ugly head at some point. Sorry, duckie, that's a bit rude,' and Julia laughed.

Emboldened, Grace said, 'Anna once hinted to me that she thought Guy might be homosexual . . . or bi-sexual. Is that the name for it?'

'Really?'

'Yes. Years ago there was some funny business in one of the prep schools he taught at. He had to leave, I think.'

'Are you telling me he was in love with Stephen?'

'Oh, I don't know, Julia. *Stephen* . . . well, I just can't imagine it. I mean, if you met him . . . Everyone was made welcome at their place in Meager Park, but he didn't have any particularly close friends. I think he just put up with Guy because he's like that. Of course, it was Lynn who had to cope with the practical side, and he never told her when all these people were turning up.'

'But let's get back to Guy, duckie. What did he actually *feel* for Stephen?'

'I honestly don't know. He certainly thought he was a marvellous painter, and he copied him. Mind you, it never did him any good. But it wasn't just the painting, he seemed, you know, a bit obsessed by him generally. He even tried to look like him at one point, the beard and everything, the long hair, the clothes – in the early days, that was.'

'But that's not unusual, is it? He was younger, it was a pupil-teacher thing, surely?'

'Not really. Stephen never actually taught Guy. Guy was chucked out of Peth Art College the year Stephen got the job there, and anyhow, he wasn't that much younger. He was a jealous person, Julia, jealous of anything other people had, or could do. And Stephen had Lynn and the children, then one of his paintings got into the Tate, and they made the TV programme about him.'

'Yes, Anna told me about that. He had a sort of *annus mirabilis*, didn't he? It was pretty short-lived though, wasn't it, this bit of fame and fortune?'

'But it happened,' Grace said loyally, 'and what I'm trying to say is that, with anybody else, that would have been *it*, so far as Guy was concerned. He wouldn't have been able to bear it, he'd have just gone off. That's why he was so vile to Anna, he was just eaten up by envy – he didn't even like *my* being friends with her, *me*, Julia. She told me that. Anyhow, he stuck to Stephen, I think he really did feel something for him. Mind you, he could be very calculating too. Anna gave him the push, after that awful thing at the party, but he didn't exactly waste time moping, not when he realised she was in earnest, and that he'd gone too far. I really don't believe he meant to end his life at all. He was drunk that night, the post mortem said so.'

'Hmm . . . he made a very thorough job of it, duckie.'

'He was *drunk*, Julia. I think he just meant to frighten everyone, Stephen included, well, *particularly* Stephen. I've told you, he loved himself too much.'

'Whereas my Anna loved people,' Julia said heavily.

Somewhere, Grace heard laughter and, in a neighbouring garden, somebody else, also enjoying the warm evening, struck a match, and the smell of cigarette smoke drifted through the creepered trellis. She heard money chinking faintly in a pocket and the crunch of feet on gravel.

She had the distinct feeling that somebody was listening to their conversation, and the noises seemed to be coming from Anna's side of the garden. She decided not to mention anything to Julia whose loud, rather penetrating voice suggested a degree of deafness and who seemed, from their earlier conversation over tea, highly nervous of intruders. But she still lowered her own voice, as she answered. 'Yes, but sometimes, you know, I rather think she loved the *idea* of people, not the reality, if you know what I mean.'

What she wanted to say was that Anna, at root, had been as selfish as Guy. True, he had made the tragedy of their parents an excuse for his entire life whereas Anna had shaken her fist at it, determined to survive at all costs, carefully saving up the small legacy she had been left, for example, so that one day she could buy time to write, whereas Guy had squandered his; getting a First at Durham while Guy was expelled from Cambridge, and then from Peth Art College for his anti-social behaviour and his refusal to work. And yet Anna had organised her life round herself just as determinedly as Guy. She had not sponged on people for food and money but she had sponged on their time, and on their emotions, if either could be used to advance her cause. Grace was a prime example and she suspected that the ageing Julia Wragg, who struck her as a very lonely woman, was, for all the 'good business head' quite probably another. She had clearly been rather dazzled by Anna.

Grace was feeling weary now. She'd talked long enough about the Beardmores and she was relieved when Julia went upstairs to dish up the meal. Agonising though her memories were of that last meeting with Guy, it was, strangely, him whom she pitied now, far more than she pitied Anna, raped and hacked about as she had been. Because he had truly loved some people. Eleanor Beaconsfield was one, 'Miss B', at whose fire he had been allowed to make toast on a fork, and Daddie, who had taken him down to the shop for weeks after The Tragedy, to keep him occupied.

In the basement under the showroom he'd got Guy cleaning silver and packing up orders with string and pieces of sealing wax. Daddie said nobody could do up a parcel as neatly as Guy and now, when she polished the White Lodge cutlery, the smell of the ammonia always reminded her of the fifteen-year-old boy with his crushed, bewildered face, and she heard again the suppressed weeping that came through her bedroom wall.

8

'So, do you think Guy had difficulties with sex in general?' Julia said. She had clearly not finished with him though they had made small talk while eating, at a rather rickety table she'd set up in the garden room, its doors still open on to the almost balmy evening. As she pondered her reply Grace looked out at the pretty walled garden, its last lingering flowers lit up, here and there, with lamps screened by fragrant shrubs and creepers, her ears still straining, though, for sounds from next door. The idea that someone was out there, eavesdropping, had unnerved her and in Julia's absence she had stood on her chair and peered over the wall, into Anna's forlorn and tangled empty plot.

'I don't know,' she said at last, 'I told you what Anna hinted about him, to me, but she never really went into it.' The direct question was rather a shock and yet, curiously, she warmed to it, as she'd warmed to the little joke. This woman at least could not regard her as a shrivelled sexless spinster, it felt more like a question between equals.

'Stephen was the only close male friend I knew about. Guy had plenty of girlfriends, in fact he got engaged five minutes after he went up to Cambridge. He seemed almost, oh, almost frantic to have "a relationship", you know,' and she crooked her forefingers at Julia, to indicate quotation marks. 'He hurled himself at women, really. Nothing ever lasted, it was just an endless string of broken romances. I don't know why nothing came of any of them, he was quite presentable,' and she remembered with pain how, in the early days, Guy would come home to show off his latest girlfriend to Anna, always with a kind of hopeful, desperate joy. He was even civilised to Grace, when he was seeing a woman, though like Anna he behaved towards her as if she herself had no sexuality of any kind. 'Good old Gracie' he called her in a hearty, back-slapping way, usually after a few drinks. But she'd known anyway that he would never have wanted her as a girlfriend, even though Anna had occasionally tried to push them together. She was the wrong kind of woman, too large.

'He always went for the same type of girl,' she said, 'the boyish, petite variety, never anybody remotely on his own scale.' Then she laughed. 'He always looked a bit funny with them, I thought, especially when he got so fat.' She had, inevitably, imagined the complexities of two people of such disparate shape and size making love; though, since her night with Stephen all the guilty, speculative thoughts about human copulation had quite ceased troubling her. 'Did you ever meet Lynn, Stephen's wife?'

Julia pulled a face. 'Mmm, yes I did, once. Can't say I cared for her very much; dull as ditchwater, I thought, apart from that gorgeous red hair, yet very domineering.'

'Yes. Well, she was the type Guy always seemed to go for, physically I mean. She started off as his girlfriend, actually, not Stephen's.'

'And yet they still stayed friends after the marriage?'

'Yes. Guy did rather trail round after Stephen. As I said, there wasn't that much of an age difference but it was definitely hero worship, with him.'

'I gather they met at Cambridge,' Julia said, plugging in a coffee percolator at her feet, and reaching for cigarettes. In the neighbouring garden they heard a match being struck, then a suppressed sneeze. Julia looked up, grimaced at Grace and leaned towards her. 'Do you know,' she whispered, 'I think there's someone back in Anna's house.'

'What do you mean, *back*?'

'Oh, we've had squatters in the street. Bloody cheek. Along comes a bit of an Indian summer and they not only move into the houses, they actually use the gardens too. I'll have to ring the police again. They won't like it, it's happening all over the place. Sometimes they don't even bother to come round. They take the view that you should secure your property more efficiently.'

'Let's go round now,' Grace whispered back, getting up. The challenge of it rather attracted her. It was outrageous for someone to be in Anna's house.

'*No*,' hissed Julia, obviously alarmed. 'That would be most unwise. Let's leave it to the police. The pair that got in when Anna was in Australia were real thugs. They pulled a knife on the man who came to get them out.

'*Honestly*,' she went on, puffing ferociously, 'I told Adam to go in and switch the lights on in the evenings, while I was in hospital. He obviously didn't, and someone's noticed. Round here you only need to leave a house in darkness two nights on the trot and they're in. It really is a bloody nuisance. I must phone the police, first thing tomorrow.'

Grace made no reply to this but she was quietly determining to go into the house tomorrow and confront whoever was there for herself. The idea of their using Anna's things, touching them, even, disturbed her deeply.

'Where were we . . .' Julia was stage-whispering now, her face embarrassingly close to Grace's.

'I think you were saying that Guy met Stephen at Cambridge. He didn't, actually, it was in Raddon Court.' Saying it, just like that, felt suddenly rather cruel.

Julia's eyebrows shot up into questioning half-moons as she blew smoke down her nostrils.

'That's the big psychiatric hospital outside Peth,' Grace explained. 'Guy was in because of his drinking. Anna was very tight-lipped about it at the time but I think they were drying him out, in a new unit they'd set up. He really was weird, he actually boasted about it afterwards, telling everyone that he was one of their first clients.'

'And why was Stephen there?'

'The usual reason, with him; one of his depressions. He didn't always need to be admitted, they used drugs as much as they could. The place itself depressed him, it's hideous, it should have been pulled down years ago. Anyway, he was really bad that time, so he had to go in, and so far as the friendship with Guy went, well, I can see how they might have become close, in a place like that.'

'Soul mates?'

'Sort of, yes. They had painting in common, and they always talked a lot about books, especially poetry, whenever I was with them.' Guy had ignored her whenever Stephen was present, he'd hogged him, often dragging him off to a pub for what he called 'a spot of serious drinking'. Anna always declined to join them. Grace didn't remember ever having been invited.

'Anna definitely told me they'd met at Cambridge.' Julia spoke defiantly, as if she thought the story of Raddon Court was a lie. She would do, Grace was thinking. Cambridge sounded rather better than a converted lunatic asylum.

'Well, that kind of friendship's a bit like a romance struck up on board ship,' Julia muttered, arranging coffee cups and spoons, clearly discomforted by the adored Anna's evident lie. 'It can't last. When you leave *terra firma*, you know . . .'

'It did, though, they were friends to the very end,' and suddenly, Grace wanted to go away by herself, and cry, for the end of fat Guy in that bloody London bathroom, for the young, unsuspecting Guy opening the drawing room door at Firs and dropping his shovel of coal, for Stephen at Christmas, opening that other door.

'*Yes*,' Julia said, leaning on the word rather heavily, and Grace saw that her eyes were beginning to close. They had eaten a heavy meal and Julia had drunk three glasses of sherry, and most of the wine. Also, she had not long been out of hospital. Mentally, Grace gathered herself together. It wasn't quite nine o'clock but perhaps she should suggest that she went to her room, then Julia could go to bed.

But suddenly, as if triumphantly catching hold of a long elusive thread, she rather shouted out, in slurred phrases, 'We never finished the story of what happened, duckie. Now where was Anna, exactly, when her parents . . . when Guy . . .' and she suddenly stopped. Grace was looking watchful again.

'She was at school,' she said dutifully. 'It was the Christmas play I told you about, Miss Bruce's *Dayspring from on High*. Anna was Isaac. It was the last performance and there was a party afterwards, so she came home late. The police were there and everything.'

And now she could destroy Anna, by telling the adoring Julia how eager she'd seemed to cash in, there was no other word for it, on the tragedy of her parents, using it to draw attention to herself; because she had been forbidden to go to that party, her father did not approve, not a party after a religious play. That wasn't the awful thing, though; a fifteen-year-old's wilful disobedience was mere high spirits, something Julia would have applauded. It was the day after, when Anna had insisted on going into school.

'She went back to school for the last day of term,' she said, almost whispering, because it had always seemed to her so terrible.

'But how *marvellous* of her, after what had just happened.'

'Yes.' But it was not, it was the beginning of Anna's life-long role of self-dramatisation. Anna Beardmore, tragedy queen. She had wanted everybody to know, to see her affliction. *O come and see if there be any sorrow like unto my sorrow*, Grace thought blasphemously.

Then, 'We've not talked about you, duckie,' Julia shot out suddenly. Grace's face told her that the Beardmore theme must be abandoned for now, though she sensed it was a vein by no means worked out and one which would be opened up again, when they next talked.

'Oh, *me* . . .' and she cupped her hands under her chin, still with Anna and Guy, and not knowing what to say.

'What are your plans, now you're . . . on your own?'

Grace shrugged. 'I'm not sure, there's been so much to sort out in the last few months, so much to think about.'

'Of course,' and Julia's eyelids were drooping again, as if too much oppressed by the stifling boredom of Grace's tedious routines at White Lodge. She would have been entertained by Anna, no doubt, about those.

'I might do some kind of church work,' Grace volunteered, loudly, to wake the other woman up. Both would be embarrassed if she actually fell asleep. Grace was thinking of Anna's money and wondering why Julia had not asked any questions about it.

Once more Julia opened her eyes. 'Ah yes, well I knew you liked a bit of church. I don't believe myself but I have great respect for religious people, as indeed Anna had.'

It was a lie. How they had giggled together in this very garden about The Girls, big butch Marian and simpering Ba, the dutiful female partner, and this curious brownie pack she ran, for adolescent girls.

'I may do more with our Wednesday Group,' Grace said, 'or with the Torch Bearers.'

'*The Torch Bearers* . . .' As she rolled the words round her mouth Julia suddenly fell sideways and gave a little snore. Grace studied her carefully. The woman was either terribly tired, or drunk. She began to tidy all the coffee things together on the tray. 'It's Ba Savage's youth group, at church,' she explained.

'Ah yes. They do good works, I gather,' said Julia, her eyes popping open again, quietly belching, then rubbing her chest as if in some kind of mild pain.

'They bear the light of Christ,' Grace said, 'to the old and the lonely, to anyone in need.'

'Ah yes, the light of Christ,' Julia repeated slowly, then she gave another little belch. 'I'm sorry, dear, but I think it's my bed time. Do stay down for a bit, there's TV, plenty to read . . .'

'No, I'll come up too. Should I bring the tray?' As she got up she heard a light cracking noise in Anna's garden, as if someone had trodden on a dry bit of wood. But Julia obviously hadn't heard anything and Grace decided not to mention it. This woman seemed to live in fear of burglars and break-ins, carrying a large bunch of keys round on her belt, janitor-fashion. She'd had a break-in herself, recently, along with several other houses in the street, and had all her locks changed. But she was rather past phoning the police tonight and Grace didn't want to send her to bed with unnecessary anxieties.

All the time they'd been sitting down here, though, she'd had a sense of a third presence listening in on their conversation, long before Julia had mentioned the squatters, or even before she'd heard that first match being struck. It was like the shades of all the dead they had spoken of, flitting in and out of their rambling conversation, a projection of her own sad imagination, she had thought. But she had not imagined the twig cracking.

'Oh God, Grace,' Julia announced tragically, heaving herself up at last from her wicker chair. '*Anna*. I don't think they'll ever find

109

out who did it.' It was the very first reference to the murder. Grace, after a prolonged, staring silence, made it clear that she had nothing to say, and wanted the subject dropped.

But Julia didn't seem to notice the look. 'The trouble with this lot,' and she jerked her thumb towards the bookshelves, 'is that their policemen are always so bloody clever and always get their man. But it isn't like that. *I know.* The people who came round questioning me were a load of dummies.' Grace laughed politely and followed her inside with the tray, having first slid an assortment of bolts home on the outer door, to save Julia bending. Her spirit was weary now and she wanted to creep upstairs, to say her prayers and be on her own.

Julia was laughing rather a lot for some reason. Out in the darkness somebody returned the laughter, but just too quietly and too late for either of them to hear.

9

In the small hours she had a nightmare. Someone in Anna's house came for her with a knife, a man whose face was neatly divided into two, one half Stephen, the other Guy.

It would be foolish to go next door on her own, she decided, waking with the dawn and lying chilly and rather uncomfortable in the large over-soft guest bed, while Julia snored loudly in the room next door. The woman was definitely on the verge of the neurotic about intruders, about bolts and bars and locking up. But she would surely not have been mistaken over the knife; and Grace herself had heard somebody in the garden.

It was very early but she was already wide awake and rather wanting to leave the house. While she had prayed last night the Lord had given her the strongest indication that she ought to visit Stephen's flat while she was down here. He had to be somewhere and he might actually have returned to his new home, which would be marvellous, or at the very least someone in the building might have seen him coming and going. In a drawer at Firs she had found Anna's master bunch of keys and brought it with her, managing to identify all of them except one. This, she had decided, could well belong to Stephen's flat. If it did then their relationship had gone on longer than she'd imagined, in spite of his 'pathetic' behaviour. Devious Anna.

She felt no guilt about taking the keys. Everything Anna had left behind was hers now, if not yet actually in name. Anyway, nobody had more right to go into Stephen's flat than she had, nobody seemed remotely concerned about him, nor had they been for nearly a year. If she were Lynn, she thought, she might have registered him as a missing person by now, but Lynn would only have done that if she had needed money and presumably Stephen was sending it through. When he was well, and painting, he had been a conscientious, almost punctilious partner, doing exactly what Lynn told him. She didn't see that this made him a 'wimp', as Anna had suggested. He was an artist. All he wanted was peace, to get on with his work. Lynn's life was easier, no doubt, with her husband off the scene. She had told Grace as much in their one brief telephone conversation.

She dressed quickly and made herself breakfast in the small kitchen. Julia, presumably anticipating that her various post-operation pills would make her sleep late, had left muesli, honey and bread in the middle of the ringed and sticky kitchen table. Before she left Grace loaded last night's supper plates and glasses into a dishwasher, filled dirty pans with cold water and swabbed down all the tiled tops. Like the rest of the flat the kitchen was rather chaotic, cluttered and a bit grubby. Julia needed, but would not employ, a regular cleaner. She'd had too much trouble with them in the past, she had explained, with people cutting corners, not turning up, stealing things. Now she preferred to manage herself. Adam had promised to clean for her till she was back on her feet; she apparently trusted him. But there were few signs of his having made an attack on this flat, Grace thought, emptying an overflowing ashtray into an extremely smelly waste-bin. As she watched the brown crumpled tubes drop into the mess of coffee grounds and banana peel she was back in the tiny kitchen at The Rock, with the stubs in the red plastic bucket, the uncanny smell of Firs, the rat in the corner, and she remembered the strange noise over her head 'like someone in a long skirt, dragging it across the floor'. When she got back to Peth Buckle would be round again, or the nice woman from North Yorkshire, Gloria Medlicott. She should have told them everything at the beginning.

Before leaving the house she took a cup of tea into Julia's room, but she was so deeply asleep she decided she ought not to wake her. Before taking the cup away again she examined the pill bottles on the bedside table, recognising the strong sleeping capsules from the agonising final weeks with Mother, and the equally strong painkillers, for arthritis. Now she thought about it, Julia did move rather stiffly and clumsily, though she had certainly not mentioned any pain. All these pills, plus the large amount of alcohol she had drunk with the meal last night, would keep her in this snoring state for some considerable time. In any case she was supposed to spend her mornings in bed, for the next month. It was surely all right for Grace to go out.

She left a note on the kitchen table explaining that she had gone across to Stephen's flat, spent a few minutes on the doorstep, studying her book of street maps, then set off for the Underground station. It looked a long and complicated journey, right across London, and a taxi would have been the easiest course. But if Stephen was at home she did not want to arrive too early. And when he was in the middle of a depression he didn't answer the phone. He might well be asleep. He spent whole days in bed when the real blackness was on him.

Half-way down the street she stopped, turned back, and went up the steps to Anna's front door. From the heavy bunch of keys she shook free the one that belonged to the house and inserted it in the lock. Then she stopped. It was foolish, deliberately putting herself at risk like this, yet, more and more, she was outraged. Some deep inexplicable anger about the violation of Anna's house, though by someone homeless, no doubt, had actually woken her in the middle of the night. She must know if someone was in there, then at the very least she could find the local police station and bring someone back with her, after she had been to visit Stephen. She suspected that Julia might still be coming round from her night's sleep when she got back, and would not have phoned anybody. Then she remembered the knife, slid the key out of the lock, bent down and peered through the letter-box, trying not to rattle the flap.

The narrow hall looked just as she remembered it from that one permitted visit, the weekend of the Pritchard Award party; the plain buff carpet, the pale walls lined with antique maps in gilt frames, another collection, which, like the paper weights, Anna had started with her early royalty cheques. Half-way down, opposite the staircase, was the mirrored Victorian hall-stand that had come from Firs. Anna's yellow mohair cardigan, the 'good-tempered' garment she always carried around with her, hung solitary on a brass hook, moving slightly in the air funnelling through the large letter-box, as if recently put there while Anna, perhaps, ran up the stairs or out to the little garden. Grace watched it settle. Anna couldn't be dead, merely 'sleeping' as it said reassuringly on the glossy black gravestone next to Daddie's, up at High Peth. The Bradley memorial had been cut from local stone and was now very mossy and stained, its own image of the unimaginable disintegration under her feet.

In Grace's mind Anna had not begun that necessary journey to decay. She knew that she was not allowing her friend to take her leave. For that reason alone she must eventually brave this silent house with its ghostly swinging cardigan. She must say aloud in the deserted spaces that Anna was truly gone, and was never going to come back.

As she moved away from the letter-box she saw a picture reflected in the hall-stand mirror, crouched down and looked at it. It was one of Stephen's small flower pieces, she thought, the genre Lynn had so despised, as their precarious marriage rocked and soured, dismissed as stuff executed solely for the galleries. Over the years Anna had bought several of Stephen's paintings, 'to keep the girls in knickers and socks', Lynn had said once, hating the patronage. Most of them were landscapes, thick, heavily-worked oils that Grace herself had not much liked. But she had always admired the flower paintings though Stephen himself had dismissed them shyly, saying he was no water-colourist. It made her quietly happy that these flowers, anemones she thought, were hanging safe in Anna's house. If he was in the flat she would tell him.

Some fifty minutes later, outside a leafy suburban Tube station, she consulted her pocket diary for Stephen's latest address. He had moved unwillingly into the new flat after Lynn's final departure for the island and now lived at Flat 5, 17 Dingle Wood, London SE19. It sounded more like somewhere in Peth, she thought, as she opened her A–Z and found the relevant page. Peth Dingle was the scrubby bit of wood on the edge of town where child sweethearts once held trysts, and where Daddie had taken her fishing for tiddlers with nets and a jamjar. It was still there, but with the raw bright bricks of a large housing development now showing through the bowed and knotted trees. Nothing was the same and she never walked there now. Perhaps she too would leave Peth. There were beginning to be too many memories.

This Dingle Wood was at the end of a long steep hill called Champion Rise. Grace plodded up it steadily and, as she gained height, her heart rose, in spite of all the uncertainties. The day was fine and warm, more like early May than the beginning of November. The heavy stuccoed villas had neat gardens with tidy flower beds and small ornamental trees. This was reassuring; Grace approved of neatness and order. In the sun the odd bird hopped and warbled, and an elderly man, washing his car in a driveway, looked up and smiled at her.

'Am I right for Dingle Wood?' she said timidly, stopping. She knew she was but she had a sudden need to break out of her silence. Her time with Julia had been somehow unreal, only happening because of Anna. All yesterday she felt she had kept company with the dead.

The man slapped his chamois leather on top of his car, put a friendly arm round her shoulder and traced her route in minute detail, making a major production of the very simple instructions. 'Thank you . . . *thank you*, very much,' Grace said, rather backing away. This was obviously a lonely little man who was desperate for a conversation with somebody. Grace knew the type. But she could now see the junction that must be Dingle Wood at the top of the hill, and she wanted to move on. 'Visiting relatives, are you?' he enquired nosily.

'No, just a friend. Stephen Allen, a painter at number seventeen. Do you know him?'

The man shook his head, a shade less friendly now, at the mention of something he could not assist with, something worlds apart from his own. Through the gleaming front window, with its fantastically looped and frilly curtains, Grace could see a hideous interior, and the print of a large Asiatic woman with a dark green face hanging in pride of place over the fire grate. Anna had poked fun at such 'art' in her Saddleford novels, and at such little men as these who burnished their Fiestas on Saturday mornings. A man like this would be unlikely to know Stephen or his paintings.

'Number seventeen?' He repeated, pulling at his small square chin. 'A bloke topped himself in one of those flats, last Christmas. Terrible business, that was.'

'*Really?*' said Grace. 'Well, thank you, very much. I know exactly where I am now.' As she walked, rather more slowly now, to the top of the rise, she wondered if she had enough courage to enter the building at all; and she prayed.

For a time, having located the block of flats, she stood on the far side of the road and simply stared at them, trembling slightly. She decided that a bomb must have dropped here possibly, during the last war, and the space remained unfilled until, in the fifties perhaps, they had built this unprepossessing 'Dingle Court'. On each side the familiar wedding-cake villas stretched away, encrusted, curlicued, tessellated. In their sheer dullness and squareness the flats resembled a large shoe box or the premises of some suburban branch library. It was hard to see how Stephen had ended up here. Money, she supposed. After the split Lynn had demanded her pound of flesh, Anna had reported.

Very slowly Grace crossed the quiet street and approached the entrance door. She did not like to think of what Guy, with his malicious eye for detail, might have said about these mean little flats. But he had been willing enough to move in with Stephen, when Anna's bounty had dried up; and he had died here.

Flat 5 was on the top floor. Grace decided that her one unidentified key must unlock the main entrance as well as Stephen's own front door. She let herself in and climbed the stairs. When nobody responded to her gentle tapping she inserted it in the lock. Then the door of Flat 7 opened and a large woman came out in a grubby dressing gown, almost at a run. She smelt of cigarette smoke and sour early-morning breath. 'Can I help at all?' she said, looking Grace up and down. 'I'm Mrs Batts. Well, I expect you know. I'm keeping an eye on things. The police asked me, like.' Her voice was very slightly menacing.

'Oh no, it's quite all right. I'm only visiting Stephen – Mr Allen. I have my own key, actually.'

'Nobody told *me*,' the woman said grudgingly, 'and the policeman that comes round said I was to tell him, like. They come themselves, regularly,' she added. This was definitely a challenge.

'It's all right, honestly,' Grace reassured her, sounding brighter than she felt. 'I'm a very old friend. I can just let myself in, and wait. Would you like my name? I can write it down for you.'

At this the fat woman seemed to lose interest, making Grace suspect that she was merely a busybody and that these 'orders' she had from the police were non-existent. 'No, 's all right,' she said. 'Not sure you'll be in luck, though,' as slippered feet shuffled back across the landing. 'I never see him coming and going. Creature of the night, that one. *Huh*, I don't know, I'm sure . . .' she muttered disapprovingly. 'First there was that friend of his, last Christmas, horrible business that was, and now this woman he was involved with goes and gets herself done in. What's all that about, for Christ's sake?'

'If anyone asks, my name's Grace Bradley,' she said rather desperately, pushing the door open. Inside she leaned against it until it clicked shut. When she got back she would have a business card printed, like Marian's. She was slowly making plans for the next few weeks and they would possibly expose her to suspicious interfering women like this one, with the foul breath. Something official would be a help, perhaps, in getting past such people.

At first, though she wandered from room to room, she actually saw nothing. She had been so hopeful that she might find Stephen here, the Lord had sent her here so clearly, but the place was empty. The flat faced east and sun was pouring in. On a wall the shadow of a large tree, still in full leaf, moved spikily, and under the window a straggling rosebush somehow flowered on. The brightness and bravery of the waning year filled her with a sudden awful hopelessness and she sat down in the main room on a striped canvas director's chair, slewed randomly in the middle of the carpet, looking about. Something felt wrong.

The flat was so bare. Stephen had had some pretty furniture, inherited from his parents. She'd noticed it on those two painful duty visits to his married home in Meager Park, not very far from this place. There had been a handsome brass bed, she remembered, and a fine Regency chest of drawers with shell handles, a collection of porcelain and several clocks. Old Mr Allen had dealt in antiques.

But Lynn had not cared for what she dismissively called 'old stuff' and the decor of the Meager Park house had been curiously split. There had been a featureless Formica kitchen, and both children's rooms and the main living area had been done out completely in modern pine with angular, rather ugly furniture, all tubes and polished hide. The porcelain and clocks, 'bric-à-brac' in Lynn's terminology, had been relegated to remote shelves and landings and all the old furniture crammed into one spare bedroom. Grace pondered. She would have expected Stephen to bring it with him after the split, but this flat was almost empty of furniture of any kind. Surely Lynn had not taken it to the island?

The flat had three bedrooms but only one bed and this was a folding affair of tubular metal, set up in the smallest, darkest room at the back, its window looking out on the blank wall of next door's villa, hardly twelve inches away. She stared at the unmade bed, then knelt down and put her face close to the sheets. They were stained and reeking and had surely not been washed for several weeks, the smell of them filled the whole room. Yet she stayed there, on her knees, breathing in the staleness, wanting to take in something of Stephen.

Along one wall there was a series of fitted cupboards. She opened each door in turn. One was full of remover's cartons and stuffed with files and papers, others contained books. In one she found a rail of Stephen's clothes. These too she brought close to her face, fingering them. They smelt of him, though only very faintly, a light sweat and the Imperial Leather soap he always used. She had noticed a jar of the familiar cream and red packets when she had taken a glimpse into the tiny bathroom. She had been unable to bring herself to go in there. Who had cleaned up? she wondered fearfully. Which poor soul had been paid to do that job, when Stephen had gone away?

As she ran her hand through the clothes she smelt cigarettes, then she spotted an empty packet on the floor, half under the bed. Stephen never used to smoke, though Lynn did. He'd always been telling her to give up. 'When you turn teetotal,' she had told him once, in Grace's presence. She could see his face now, blanking with embarrassment. Anna had been right about their marriage. He had wanted someone to dominate him, to run the practical side of his life while he simply painted. He'd never been much good at managing on his own. This flat had an air of transitoriness, impermanence. Nothing had been unpacked properly, or put away. He could not have accepted that he was on his own again, without his family structure, without his children.

Grace tidied up the bed, picked up the cigarette packet and threw it into a wicker waste basket. In it, rolled up, she noticed a glossy magazine. Idly curious, she bent down to pick it out, then withdrew her hand. It was obviously a collection of pornographic photographs, and the cover told everything, a young woman, beautifully coiffured, lying back on a richly upholstered chair, legs widely straddled, the pudenda decorated with tinsel which did not quite cover the pubic hair, deep auburn, Grace noticed, and perfectly matching the chair. Though smiling, the model had an inane, embarrassed look.

Grace folded the magazine into four and somehow managed to squeeze it into her handbag. The magazine was quite new, she noticed,

117

only last month's issue, which supposedly must mean that Stephen was around. But she did not believe that this, or the cigarettes, or the filthy bedding, were anything to do with him. He must be away, perhaps on one of those residential art courses where he sometimes lectured, and someone else was using his flat. Whatever the arrangement she was not going to have this magazine associated with him. If the police came round again they would notice it. She could spare him that, at least.

As she stood with her back to the wall cupboards the end door clicked and swung open eerily, exposing rows of white shelving, empty, apart from a small cache of objects on the middle shelf, a pair of tiny shoes in soft white leather, an antique baby's rattle of silver and bone that she remembered Stephen tying with ribbon to the bars of Debbie's cot, Debbie, their first born. Lynn had not wanted her to chew on such a thing though there were tiny teeth marks on the yellowing ring, Stephen's own, from his babyhood. There was also a polythene bag stuffed full of children's drawings. She took them out and looked through them sadly, a stick-like 'Mummy and Daddy', 'My Garden', all green and red blodges, 'The Queen', very stumpy with a massive handbag and a crown as big as her head. Each one was dated on the back in Stephen's handwriting, and carefully labelled 'Deborah' or 'Bridget'.

She put everything back, wandered into the long dark hall and looked at a pile of letters stacked by the telephone. The top few had been slit open and the contents read, presumably, and stuffed back. She picked up a couple of envelopes and examined them. One contained information sent in reply to Stephen's request for a credit card, another, literature he must have asked for about life insurance. She studied the dates and worked out that both items of information had been applied for, and sent, in the last fortnight. So he was definitely around, thank God, and planning for his future. And yet the loveless abandonment of these bare rooms somehow suggested otherwise.

She sat down again in the striped canvas chair and looked round at the heaps of packing cases and cardboard boxes, the toppling piles of books. In a corner was Stephen's easel, some painting equipment and a few unframed canvasses propped against the wall. She got up and looked through them. Nothing was dated but she thought they must be fairly recent, most looked only half-finished, a series of dark hill landscapes so heavily brown and black they could almost have been old sepia photographs. And the over-precise photographic quality was what was wrong with them, they were like poor copies of the Pennine series which, years ago now, had brought him his bit of fame and had led to 'Last Light' hanging in the Tate. A slightly

smaller version of it hung on the long wall of this room, positioned
to avoid the sunlight.

In a black folder she found a collection of small pencil drawings.
They were all signed and arranged in chronological order, the work
of recent months. The end drawing was only three weeks old. She
riffled through them rather guiltily, nervous lest he should suddenly
appear in the doorway and find her going through his things. He
was touchy about his work and on the two occasions she'd been
admitted to his attic studio in Meager Park everything had been
carefully covered up. These new drawings looked quite different from
anything he had done before, and she felt she understood them more.
They were compassionate, loving. He'd never drawn people before,
apart from the odd remote figure in his great brooding landscapes,
but many of these sketches were portraits, mostly of old men. A few
were complete figures, either huddled up in sleep or caught in harder
attitudes of anger or pleading, their knobbled beseeching hands thrust
out, their loose mouths hanging, and interleaved with the drawings
were short, simple poems about the people he had drawn. On the
cover was scribbled what was obviously the name of the sequence,
The Forgotten.

She shut the folder, tied the tapes up and replaced it, neatened the
stack of canvasses and stared down at the familiar scratched brass
and mahogany box he kept his oils in, suddenly thinking of that seat
Anna had erected in Swaledale. 'In memory of Guy Beardmore,' it
had said, 'who loved this dale.' It was not true, it was Stephen who
had loved it, and the bleaker, higher grasslands above, which had
inspired his best painting. Guy never went there at all until they
filmed Anna's first Saddleford novel, for television. Then he'd been
up fast enough, hanging round the film crew, drinking with them,
complaining belligerently about the quality of the scattered pubs,
and humiliating Anna by forcing something he'd written on to her
producer. All this had been kept from Grace until the final quarrel,
then Anna suddenly spilled it all out one night, at White Lodge. Anna
told lies, Grace had realised that years ago, and those about the dead
Guy were told to comfort and reassure herself, to fabricate some kind
of memory she could live with. He had not 'loved' the dale any more
than the television Saddleford had resembled Peth. It had all been
much too glamorous, too green and gold, too clean. On screen the
canals could not imaginably smell, nor dog dirt clog the gutters, and
the actors had looked too sleek and well-fed, too south of England to
be Peth people.

She was staring across at 'Last Light', wondering whether to leave a
note and go back to Julia's, when she heard voices in the outer hall and

a key being inserted in a lock. She leapt up, the flimsy chair folding as she caught the frame on her heel. But she left it and ran joyously across the echoing empty room towards the opening door, holding out her hands. She was right to have come; he was here.

'Why, hello, Grace. I suppose I ought to say Miss Bradley but we have met, and I am off duty. Strange who you meet up with, isn't it, on a weekend away?' It was William Buckle.

They unfolded the director's chair and restored it, and Grace sat down. Buckle took a seat on the carpet with his back against the wall, facing 'Last Light'. He was impeccably neat, as before, but clearly in his weekend clothes, cavalry twills, spotless and carefully pressed, checked open-necked shirt, fawn cord jacket, a cravat. From the chair Grace looked down on him, feeling lumbering and big, watching him produce cigarettes and a mother-of-pearl lighter and slide off cellophane wrappings.

'Do you object?' he said, with a tight little smile, flipping open the packet. She was surprised. A man of such fastidious appearance wasn't readily associated with the mess of cigarettes. But she merely shrugged and turned her face away, in her bitter disappointment, staring through the window. Only now had she really noticed the stunning panoramic views, right across London. This would be why Stephen had wanted the otherwise depressing little flat, this and cheapness. Though she had heard that nothing was cheap in London.

Buckle had either misinterpreted or ignored her signal because he went on smoking. He seemed very tense again, and his eyes kept flicking over her. The cigarette smelt peculiarly strong and she decided that he must almost certainly have visited the flat before, quite recently. As the ash gathered and fell he cupped it in his hand. Grace stared at him with distaste. 'When you opened the door I thought it was Stephen,' she said. As she pronounced his name in the silent flat her voice wavered. 'I telephoned several times, from home, but it was always unobtainable. Perhaps I should report it to faults again.'

'It's been cut off,' Buckle said, 'but of course they're not supposed to tell people that. Mr Allen has a few money troubles, I gather, a lot of unpaid bills,' and he stared at her. She was rapidly colouring up again, like the last time.

'Have you seen him?' *Let it be yes*, she pleaded. She could hear her own desperation.

'Not yet. But I think we're getting there. He's an elusive chap, your friend.'

'Has Lynn seen him – his wife?' They would obviously have contacted her. She thought of her now, 'Grim Lynn' as Anna had dubbed her, going through a police interview, contained and unweeping, and of the two obedient, bewildered little girls.

'No, though he keeps in touch, I gather.'

'*How?*'

But Buckle was clearly not prepared to say any more. 'Let's talk about you, Grace,' he said unexpectedly. 'Down here on business, are you?'

Now she knew that, in spite of the use of her Christian name, he must be mocking her. What 'business' could she possibly have here, in the wilds of South London? No, he had somehow found out that she had come to stay with Julia Wragg, and followed her here. With a sudden pang of enlightenment she recalled Breda Smith's casual phone call.

'I'm staying with Anna's publisher, Mrs Wragg,' she replied carefully. 'I just wanted to get away from Peth for a weekend, and she invited me down. I'd hoped Stephen might be here, and that we could meet up, so I slipped out after breakfast. Mrs Wragg sleeps in late at the moment, she's just been in hospital. But he's obviously not around, so I'll go, if you don't mind,' and she stood up. The walls of the room suddenly seemed to be coming in at her now, charged with Stephen's very absence. Underneath the choking feeling she could feel an inexplicable dread. If she didn't get out into the fresh air, away from the cigarette smoke and the stale heavy atmosphere of the stuffy rooms, she thought she might faint.

'Have you noticed the painting?' With one hand Buckle indicated 'Last Light', lighting a fresh cigarette with the other. Grace turned and looked at the huge grey-green canvas, the familiar sweep of the great empty fell, the solitary barn on the horizon and, beneath the black sky, the thick gash of dazzling yellow light.

' "And though the last lights off the black West went/Oh, morning, at the brown brink eastward, springs/Because the Holy Ghost over the bent/World broods, with warm breast and with ah! bright wings" ' she quoted. 'It's by someone called Gerard Manley Hopkins, Anna loved that poem, in fact I think she gave Stephen the title, for this. There's an even bigger version in the Tate Gallery,' she went on, proud for him, ' "Last Light" was his great breakthrough. He'd be doing wonderful things now, if it weren't for this damned depression.' She rarely blasphemed but his illness *was* damned, damned and evil. She believed it was the work of the Devil, like all sickness and brokenness. Only in God was there light.

But Buckle seemed uninterested in Stephen's career. 'I *meant*,' he said, getting up and stretching his legs, 'have you noticed what's happened to it? Look,' and he led her right up to the canvas, pointing to the

121

signature. Stephen always printed his name in black child-like capitals, but because this particular canvas was so very dark the signature had been executed in white paint, except that something had been flung at it, obscuring half the letters, and a jagged right-angled cut hacked round 'Allen', as if in an attempt to remove it. 'Someone's been playing silly beggars,' he observed, drawing on his cigarette.

Grace put a hand out. The mud, or whatever it was round the signature, had dried in thick lumps.

'*Don't*,' Buckle said sharply, and he pulled her arm away. 'Someone's got it in for your friend Mr Allen, unless he did it himself, of course. I hear he likes the odd drink,' he added slyly, looking for a reaction.

But Grace was still staring at the painting. Now she knew what the sweetish, stuffy smell in this room must be. It was not mud at all, it was human excrement. She sank back into the striped canvas chair, her cheeks red at first, then draining to white.

Buckle, remembering how she had passed out in the kitchen at White Lodge, got to his feet, suddenly anxious for her.

'I'm sorry. Are you all right? Can I get you some water?'

'No, I'm all right. It's just that . . .'

'I know. It's *sick*.'

In Peth, in her absence, he'd thought again about a possible link between her and Allen, though with less and less conviction as he recalled all that the solid Breda Smith had told him, and he'd said nothing whatever to Hallam, fearing he might seem foolish, obsessed, even. Grace alone had drawn him here, but not because he really believed she was implicated. It was clear now, anyway, that her alibi for those lost days in Yorkshire was sound. Several people had seen her in the dale. But then, this morning, he'd called on Julia Wragg, only to discover that Grace was actually on her way across London, to come to this flat. Immediately, uncannily, the tiny worm of suspicion about her had started to gnaw again, when he thought he'd killed it, and he'd found himself suddenly very anxious to get on his way. But then Mrs Wragg had delayed him by asking him if he would go into the murdered woman's house. Squatters, she thought, noises in the garden at night. He'd had a quick look, to keep her quiet, but had found nothing out of order, and nobody there. The only item of interest had been a postcard addressed to Anna Beardmore, mailed a couple of days ago in Blackheath, lying on the doormat. Taking it from his wallet he now gave it to Grace, explaining, and watched.

'The Artist's Room,' she read, 'Gwen John': a chair, a small rattan table, a window, some pale sunshine spilling over on to the order and neatness of a painter's studio. On it Stephen had scribbled, 'She was tidier than you – and a better artist than me. Love you. S.'

Slowly she lowered her hands on to her lap, still staring at the card. 'He's not well,' she muttered, 'I'm sure he's not well, Mr Buckle.'

'It's William, please. Now, why do you say that?'

For a second her eyes met his, in great pain, beseeching, and, before it had ever breathed independent life, the scenario he had worked out for her and Stephen Allen collapsed in his face. He felt immensely sorry for her, and ashamed that he had ever entertained the notion of such a woman as this being implicated in any murder at all. Now she was before him in the flesh again he saw that whatever the truth about the artist friend, Grace Bradley could have had absolutely no part in the Beardmore killing. She had clearly loved the woman, though he suspected misguidedly, and she clearly loved the man, and was ready to grasp at any straw which might reassure her he was close at hand. Her fingers were damp with sweat, he noticed, as he leaned forward to retrieve the postcard.

'Oh . . . can't I keep it?' she said.

'I'm afraid not, well, not at the moment.' But he rather feared, as he slid the card back into his wallet, that she might ask him exactly what *he* was doing here, with that sudden impressive hardening and purposefulness he had noticed in their last interview, when she had talked of her religion, and of 'wickedness'. Although he had cleared this visit to the flat with the local police, and so got past the fat woman across the landing, he'd not so far spoken to anyone up in Yorkshire about his unofficial trips down here, and he felt slightly ill at ease about the omission; though Hallam was still concentrating on Daffy Bayles, apparently, and plagued moreover by no less than three local timewasters who had come in to 'confess'.

He said 'Why do you say he's ill, Grace?'

'Well, it's the handwriting,' she told him fretfully, 'all *shaky*. My mother wrote like that after her first stroke. His is the same, when he's not well, I've always thought so. It was paralysis with her, she had to use her other hand for everything. But when Stephen was depressed, and taking all those drugs, he was terribly shaky, he couldn't hold a pen properly.'

'But it *is* his handwriting?' Buckle took the card out again.

She peered forward and scrutinised it. 'Oh, yes.'

'And the message?'

She shrugged. 'What about the message?' She sounded hurt.

'Well, is it, you know, his *style*?'

'I suppose so.' She sat back, her mouth set. Anna and Stephen had had their affair and she didn't want to discuss any aspect of it, and certainly not with this man. He had looked at her sexually, at White Lodge. She knew some men were like that, but she'd hated it. Nor

123

was she going to tell him that 'Love you' sounded horribly cheap, to her, and not at all the kind of thing Stephen would normally write. He couldn't have been himself, when he wrote this card.

Buckle was also thinking about the man's illness, and the depression that had apparently dogged him for most of his adult life. He'd like to get his hands on some hospital reports. But had Hallam got that far yet? He suspected not. All they knew so far was that Allen had been in psychiatric wards down here, and years ago, up north, where he'd first met Guy Beardmore. The boy had been only eighteen or nineteen, then, but he'd been in the same hospital, for what sounded like drying out. What he wanted to know was whether it was simple depression with Allen or whether there had been any mania, any schizoid behaviour. He'd got nothing from Hallam and the police down here said they had no information. They had shown him their report on the flat, though, and the picture was rather promising, particularly that stack of soft porn in one of the cupboards – thank God it had been out of sight when Grace turned up – and the celebrated painting decorated with shit. He was sorry she'd had to see that.

He ruminated. Now he had ruled her out he was left with an entirely motiveless murder, for the money all went to her. One piece of information that kept nagging him, though, had come from Julia Wragg, on his visit last weekend. Allen had quarrelled with Anna Beardmore, not long before the brother's death, 'violently' she had said, though he had decided she was a woman rather given to dramatics. When Allen's divorce papers had finally come through he had turned up on Beardmore's doorstep, not just wanting to move in but actually proposing marriage. Grace Bradley knew something about their relationship, her face had told him that, when she had read the postcard. She was jealous.

Perhaps he had been cruel to show it her in the first place, cruel to himself too, for there was clearly no chance for him, so long as Allen was around. But he felt desperate for some kind of response from her, she seemed so uncommunicative, so inert, just sitting there in the heavy silence. And yet her very passiveness was rousing him to rather violent thoughts, attractively sexual thoughts which he thrust away. Could she know that she interested him? What prevented his telling her, for God's sake? With shaking hands he took out another cigarette, and lit up.

'I'd like to leave a message,' she said suddenly. Producing a small notepad from her handbag she unscrewed a pen and began to write. 'You don't object, do you?'

There it was again, that formality, that strict regard for the proprieties. It was this unexpected side of her that Buckle recognised in himself, and warmed to, wanted to explore in her. It was a kind of emotional repression he absolutely understood. Perhaps, in the childish years, they had suffered the same.

'Not at all, though I'm not sure when he'll be back. Nobody's been here for some time, apparently.'

'Oh yes, the bed's been slept in.'

But she knew it was someone else who'd been using the flat. The stinking sheets belonged to them, and that magazine, and surely too, it was they who had defaced 'Last Light'. It would be one of Stephen's 'drifters', as Lynn used to call them. She had more sympathy now, if this was how they treated other people's houses.

'I came on the off-chance,' she wrote slowly. 'Sorry to have missed you. I'm back home next week. *Do* get in touch. We love you. Grace.'

Because she knew Buckle would read it she didn't actually bother to fold the paper but left it in the hall on the pile of correspondence, held down by a handsome *mille-fleurs* paperweight that was surely one of Anna's. It puzzled her. Guy had smashed them all, hadn't he, on the night of her Pritchard celebration?

She stared down at it, and at her note, while Buckle excused himself and went off to use the lavatory. No qualms there, about entering the room where Guy had killed himself. She supposed that was how he could be a policeman. Hideous death scenes were part and parcel of his daily bread.

'We love you,' she read, swallowing tears back, and the letters blurred and wavered. *But who had loved him?* Guy and Anna, Lynn, she supposed, for a season, his children, and his suffocating parents whom Anna had always blamed for his agonising stammer and for all the other, deeper problems of his life. Grace herself, *most*. She scratched out 'we' and substituted 'I', defiantly, not caring whether Buckle read the card or not. Then, certainly feeling queasy now, she let herself out of the flat and began to walk down the stairs.

'Finished in there, have you?' Mrs Batts, still in her nightwear, was leaning over the stairwell, two great breasts thrust obscenely upwards by the banister rail.

'Yes, thank you,' she faltered. 'I just need a bit of fresh air. Goodbye.'

Buckle found her standing against a garage door, outside the main entrance, her eyes closed, taking deep breaths. 'Are you all right?' he said, and he put a steadying hand under her elbow.

'Yes, yes I think so.' But she wasn't. Suddenly, up there in that hall, she had felt overwhelmed, stifled virtually to choking by her physical sense of loss, not only of Stephen and Anna but of Guy too, who had ended his life in this place, in some unimaginably hopeless moment, and the emptiness inside had thickened, become a rising blackness, physically thrusting her forth.

All the evidence was there to say that Stephen was close at hand, and yet she had felt he was dead, like the others. The panic had thrown her back to days of childish terror, days when, bathed and put to bed at six-thirty, she had crept down to the lower landing at White Lodge, spying through the stair rails for a sight, beyond the glazed breakfast-room door, of her parents by the fire, Mother embroidering a tablecloth, Daddie playing patience on his little table. Her terror always was that they would leave her again, as they had once when two cars had collided on the main road, at the bottom of the drive. They had run out to help, and she had come down because of a nasty dream and found the house empty. Huge, sick fear had swept over her then, a sense that they were both dead and that she would never be happy again in the whole of her life.

Buckle rang from Mrs Batts' flat for a cab while she sat on the steps in the sunshine. He was taking her back to Julia Wragg's, he insisted, before going on into central London to get his train north. She was a deathly white now, he didn't like the look of her at all.

She didn't protest nor try to dissuade him but, as the taxi set off down Champion Rise, she suddenly began to weep, huddled away from him in her corner of the seat. Awkwardly, unused, he patted her hand, then he put his arm round her, straining up on his small neat buttocks in an attempt to get himself level with her shoulders. She was so large and spreading, he felt so ridiculously small beside her.

Again, as she rubbed at her face with a tissue, he noticed her large workmanlike hands, remembering with embarrassment how he had first speculated, constructing an elaborate scenario about her and her lover Allen, and the hacked-about body in the cottage. He must pursue his few threads differently now. But it had helped to see the flat. There was violence here, and perversion, some kind of sexual obsession and a long history of mental instability, even if it were only straight depression, though an elderly prison psychiatrist had chided him once, saying that depression was never 'straight' but the most complex and unpredictable mental affliction in medicine.

It occurred to him now that Grace couldn't have known Allen very well, and that this obsessional, all-forgiving attitude she had towards him may be the by-product of idealistic ignorance and optimism, brought on by her religious faith. She had fallen in love with 'the first thing she ever met in trousers', or so Anna Beardmore had told Julia Wragg, he remembered from their conversation last week. He had not liked the publisher too well, with her slick, dismissive vocabulary, nor the sound of the novelist either; she seemed excessively malicious. But, personalities aside, he had gleaned from Wragg an all-important fact, that Anna Beardmore had turned down Allen's proposal of marriage only days after his wife had ditched him for good, at which he had obviously turned rather nasty.

He mustn't desert Grace, he must keep his eye on her, for her own protection. The pieces on Stephen Allen were still a long way from coming together but he could see a strengthening case for taking him in, if they ever tracked him down. When he got back to Peth he must find out just how far they had got with that. He didn't want Allen to get to Grace first, and certainly not if he was 'ill', whatever that euphemism meant. The other side of depression was violence. Allen might now be in a worse phase than she could ever imagine and turn against her, as he'd surely turned against Anna Beardmore.

After interminable traffic jams in the centre of the city they at last drew up outside Julia Wragg's house. Grace was obviously assuming he would come in with her, perhaps for more talk with Julia, but he had decided to go straight on to Euston. Composed again, now, though with sore eyes, she thanked him quite formally for bringing her back, and offered to pay the fare; but he waved the money away. Warmed by his unexpected kindness, she said, as he opened the cab door for her, 'Mr Buck – William, listen. There's something in Anna's house I need to get, and I don't quite feel up to going in there, just yet. I just wondered . . .' she was offering him some keys.

'Oh, well I'm not sure . . .' he began.

'*Listen*,' she repeated urgently. 'It's just an old cardigan, you'll see it, it's in the hall. Only . . . *please*. I want to take it back to Firs. She obviously forgot it.'

Bewildered, but very much not wanting her to weep again, he took the keys, went into the house, listened out for Mrs Wragg's 'squatters', then came down the steps with the yellow mohair jacket over his arm.

'Is this it?'

'Oh yes, yes,' and she almost snatched it from him. '*Thank you.*'

As the taxi turned round in the road she put her cheek against the soft wool. Buckle watched her through the back window, standing there on the pavement, cuddling the old cardigan as if it were a baby at the breast. He was moved.

10

'Oh, I'd forgotten. Your char phoned.' They were in the garden room again, eating a lunch of sandwiches and soup. Julia, all hugs and smiles on the doorstep, was still not out of her nightwear when Grace knocked, the fluffy yellow jacket stowed under her arm but not quite out of sight. If Julia had noticed it, she had not said so. Perhaps, thought Grace, she was being very sensitive. Then she decided not. The energetic, bustling Julia was – how had Anna described her once – very 'broad brush', not a woman to dwell upon the finer details of feeling. Had she done so she would surely have listened more carefully yesterday, and understood what Mrs Lumb meant to Grace. She would not, now, have dismissed her as a 'char'.

'She sounded rather panicky,' she said, pushing her plate away and fishing for her cigarettes. 'Asked you to phone her, some problem with the house, I gather. You could do it now, duckie, while the coffee's perking.'

'Thanks, I will, if you don't mind. I'm sure it's nothing but I'd better check.'

Mrs Lumb had become prone to sudden panics. If the cat went missing for a day she immediately decided it was dead on the main road, and spent hours looking for it. If the gas pilot in the oven blew out she was all for phoning the emergency number, fearing some kind of massive explosion. In constant dread of thieves and murderers breaking into her tiny house – ironically, like Julia, in this – she carried cash around with her in a home-made body belt tied round her waist, underneath her clothes. Grace had long ago given up trying to persuade her to open a bank account. She said writing out the cheques would 'worry' her.

Rather nervously she dialled Mrs Lumb's number. Perhaps there had been some obscene telephone call to White Lodge, about the murder, perhaps that man had rung again and laughed, or perhaps something rather more unspeakable than news cuttings had been pushed through the letter-box.

But all that was wrong was that Hibbert Engineering had left a card about the new boiler. They were starting work on the Monday, at eight a.m. 'I can come in, Grace,' Mrs Lumb said, her thin little voice wavery and defeated across the crackling line. 'But there'll be mess, they said, furniture to be moved, all that business, you know . . .' Grace could feel the mounting panic, the tears. Mrs Lumb had recently wept with frustration when she had dropped an old dish, smashing it on the kitchen tiles. Such small, inconsequential things distressed her now she was old. Nothing could interrupt the simple predictable flow of her narrow life without bringing on this tight-throated state of semi-hysteria. 'Shall I tell them not to come, Grace?' she whimpered.

'No, it's all right. I was coming back anyway, I can get a train home tomorrow. You don't need to come up specially, on Monday.'

'Oh, I will, I *will*. It's just that, well, on my own, with all the upset. You know . . .'

'I know, I know,' soothed Grace. 'And how's Binkie?'

'All right. Doing his pining, as usual.' When Grace was absent from the house the cat wouldn't eat. She was ready to go back anyway. She had realised in the taxi that she had only come to London in the hope of seeing Stephen. There was nothing to stay for now.

Julia was incredulous when she heard Grace was going back because of Mrs Lumb and a new boiler. 'For heaven's sake, duckie,' she protested, flapping small pudgy hands at the clouds of cigarette smoke, and coughing. 'Put them off. You're on holiday.'

'No,' Grace replied firmly. 'It's all right, I really must go back.' *But Lord*, she was pleading silently, *If I must live to be old, let it not be in solitariness, or in this hard widowhood. It's too awful. Let me remember you now, in the days of my youth, before the years come when I shall say I have no pleasure in them.*

'Well,' Julia said decisively, 'it doesn't leave us much time, if you really are going back tomorrow . . . *Grace*?' For Grace was staring dully into space, her mouth slightly open. Could she be saying her prayers, Julia wondered, slightly embarrassed. She did sometimes go off into little dreams like this, Anna had once told her all about them, with suitable comic imitations. She was definitely odd, and really a bit pathetic, with her boilers and her charlady.

'Yes?' answered Grace, turning to look at her, her eyes still glazed, and apparently absent.

'I'm saying that we've not got much time together.'

'No.' And she didn't actually mind. She would quite like to get away before Julia launched into any more heavy sessions about the Beardmores, though she had a strong suspicion that she was wanted here this weekend for some specific reason.

As if on cue Julia said casually, 'Oh, and Magnus is joining us for supper tonight. You'll have heard of him, I expect, from Anna?'

'*Magnus* . . . no, I hadn't.'

'Well it's Magnus Croucher. He's a dear. Getting on a bit now, but still absolutely on the ball. He's a journalist really, but he's done quite a lot of work for the firm, ghosting. He's extremely competent.'

'*Ghosting?*' Grace repeated warily, and wondering how his competence could be relevant.

Julia stared at her, then realised she must explain. (But how could anyone, she asked herself, be quite so bloody ignorant?)

'He writes books for people, you know, on their behalf, people who obviously *need* an autobiography but aren't quite up to it themselves, or perhaps haven't got the time. It's interesting work. He's got some very good titles behind him. He's just finished something on Mother Teresa, I think.' She dropped this in thinking Grace would thoroughly approve, though in fact Magnus's contribution to the book had merely been a short third-person interview, and she wasn't at all sure whether it was going to be published. 'Anyway,' she went on, getting no response but seeing a hard, rather suspicious look firming up Grace's lips, 'He certainly wants to talk to *you*.'

'What about?'

'Oh . . .' and she paused, for the moment uncertain. 'Let's wait till he comes, shall we?' Then the doorbell rang.

'That'll be Hilary. Did Anna mention her ever? I can't remember whether they actually met, Hilary Plant, she's a crime writer, you know, Golden Dagger Award, etc.' But Grace looked blank.

'The thing is, she's over from Ireland, flying visit, as usual, and I said I'd see her this afternoon, to go over a manuscript. I'm sorry it's now but I obviously couldn't say no, not to Hilary. Now, if you'd like to have the drawing room to yourself, I'll sit down here with her. She won't mind.' Then the doorbell was rung again, longer, and more insistently this time. Julia frowned. 'She's a tricky customer, our Hilary. We always argue. But she's one of our biggest clients, after Anna. Listen, I'll bring her down here and . . . er . . . perhaps you could clear the decks a bit?'

'No, don't,' Grace said. 'I can sit here and read, it's still quite pleasant. Or I might go for a walk. You go into the drawing room and I'll tidy up.'

'Well, if you're quite sure, duckie,' and Julia hurried off to open the front door. Grace was not to be introduced, she noticed. Anna had never sought to introduce her to the literary people either. She was home-grown and reserved for that other, earlier world where perhaps too much was known.

'*Darling,*' she heard as the door was opened, then a loud, rather masculine whoop, giggles from Julia, followed by a series of smacking kisses. She gathered the debris of their lunch together on a tray, waited till the drawing room door had clicked shut then carried everything upstairs, to wash up.

She spent the afternoon in the garden room, dozing and half-heartedly trying to read Anna's new novel. Julia did not reappear until nearly half-past four when she came downstairs with a cup of tea. 'I'd hoped we could all have a chat,' she said, in her stage whisper, though the doors were shut. 'But Hilary's being rather a pig about the new book, and she's got to go off somewhere else at six. You don't mind if I just carry on, do you, duckie?'

'Of course not. I'm quite happy here.'

'How are you getting on with that? Liking it any better?' and Julia nodded at the thick paperback in Grace's lap.

'Oh, you know,' she muttered non-committally. Then, 'I've had one thought, after our talk last night, about Anna and Guy's childhood.'

'And what's that?' Julia glanced at her watch. She was certainly very interested in Grace's view of Anna, but Hilary was upstairs, and in one of her bitchiest moods.

'Well, her father's religious views didn't allow them to have any kind of story books, you see. He felt it was false, somehow, false to real life, I suppose, and therefore wrong. He saw all fiction as lies. When there were school trips, to the theatre and things, Anna wasn't allowed to go, I remember. I wonder what her parents would have made of all *this?*' and she patted the book.

Julia's mouth puckered. 'That's *very* interesting . . . but listen, save it for Magnus. He'll be fascinated. See you soon.'

Grace smiled vaguely as she went off, then opened her book again, quite determined to say nothing whatever to Magnus Croucher who was obviously coming to pump her for information about Anna.

In her three hours alone in the garden room she read over half of the new novel. She hated it and, as she turned the pages, she began to have a sneaking sympathy with Dr Beardmore's puritanical mistrust of 'story', still more with Guy's bibulous attack on the night of the Pritchard Award. Two rather minor characters in this book were luridly portrayed on the jacket, though the main theme did not really involve them. It was another rambling mill-town romance, using characters resurrected from an earlier story. Grace stared down at the coloured picture. Here was a frumpish, middle-aged post office official bent over a counter and, in the doorway, her haunter and pursuer, a tragi-comic wanderer of the streets known locally as 'the shiny leather man', the women he terrorized always wearing patent leather shoes – though the story stopped short of actual assault and, she supposed, was somehow twisted round so all ended happily, to understand all being to forgive all in Anna's Saddleford.

The patent leather man was a genuine bogey, dug out of their common childhood. He had raped and savaged several women and, she thought, ended up in Broadmoor, though her parents had never spoken about it. The dreary post-office worker was most definitely poor Mollie McGraw. She had sold postal orders and stamps to Grace and paid over her mother's family allowance, screaming at her once in front of a long queue of customers because, on the way to do her errand, the child had carefully rolled the book up so that it had to be carefully and systematically flattened before the chit could be pulled out. Mrs McGraw, a childless war widow who lived alone, was brooding and threatening, sometimes violent, and entirely obsessed with minutiae. Anna had described her most cruelly, her yellow 'post-office' complexion, her claw hands, her little bulgy eyes like two blue marbles, and all the energy of her empty life consumed in issues the size of postage stamps.

Mollie McGraw had gone steadily and noisily mad, been retired from the counter and eventually put away like the rest of the local unfortunates, in Raddon Court. Mr Bradley, who had been at school with her husband, had occasionally visited her there. The grim hospital had obviously given Anna rich pickings as she sat working out her interminable plots.

'Anna Beardmore will be in after you, with her notebook,' Guy had yelled on the television screen, and it was true. She had been like a mothering animal, scavenging her lair for some useful post-birth detritus, some succulent piece of debris that could be fed into herself, to make her strong and rich. Grace suddenly remembered an unexpected cross-examination once, all about Mrs Lumb, and that she had clammed up, knowing instinctively what Anna was doing. Guy too must have been nervous, if he had bothered to read *Harriet Harker*, for example. For why should Anna stop with her friend? Her own family, which was his too, offered a plot worthy of Shakespeare. She had said that once. Grace remembered her bitter little laugh, she could hear it now, in the garden room. But bitter as she was, and scarred, like Guy, it had not stopped her using Peth and its inhabitants in her novels. And it seemed from this most recent story that she had become careless, not really seeking to camouflage her material any more. Anybody who had ever used their local post office at the end of Beaumont Crescent would immediately recognise poor Mollie McGraw. And she had sisters and brothers still alive. Mrs Lumb knew them.

132

In the end Grace put the novel aside, idly wondering how Anna's 'serious' book about Guy could ever have been much different. It would surely have falsified and glamorised, she thought, it would have evaded. All the raw and bleeding edges would have been doubtless cleansed and smoothed over, the nasty smells replaced by sparkling moorland air. Anna's moors were always too green, too glorious with gorse and heather, they bore no resemblance to the tatty dried-up grasslands above the real town, the hills that had never quite recovered from the Industrial Revolution.

Letting the book slide down into her lap she closed her eyes and dozed, making up for all the sleep she had missed last night. She felt strongly at odds with this place, and particularly with Julia, so friendly and yet, she felt, no friend. She was glad to be returning to her own house with its reassuring daily routines, and she would be genuinely glad to see Mrs Lumb, in spite of her panics about the new boiler. Also, on Monday afternoon, Miss Scotson, the visiting chiropodist, would be coming to do her feet.

She had imagined – though it was probably only the name – that Magnus Croucher would be skinny and small, a spiky sort of character bunched up in his chair, limbs neatly folded, grasshopper-like, compact and trim, perhaps, like Buckle. In fact his body was long and gangling, his face fleshy with great flabby jowls, the cheeks pock-marked and deeply pitted as if he had once suffered from some kind of skin disease. He looked very unhealthy, not merely because of his greyish-yellow pallor but because of the sweatiness of his skin. They ate in the kitchen, a cold meal and the room itself was coolish. But he sweated profusely throughout and, though he drank a lot of wine, left most of the food on his plate, Grace noticed, thrusting his huge face right up against hers, whenever she made a remark. He seemed nervous of Julia and to be taking refuge in Grace's less demanding presence and conversation. Not that she contributed very much. Nearly all the talk was of books and writers, and of various literary projects Julia's firm appeared to be engaged in. When at last he mentioned Anna's name Grace noticed how she skated nimbly away from it, immediately turning the talk to something else, her eyes flicking, lizard-like, on to his craggy face, to meet his, then slithering off again. Clearly Anna was not yet to be broached.

But left on their own, down in the garden room, while Julia cleared away and made coffee, Magnus plunged straight in, as if anxious to get something over with. He was clearly unsure of his ground and he kept swallowing, his Adam's apple huge and tight against the collar of his crumpled shirt. This, like the rest of him, was shiny and worn.

133

His jacket elbows were polished, his shoes cracked and creased. All of him was shabby and inside his clothes his large ungainly body had a cringing, defeated look, uncomfortably squashed as it was into Julia's old basket chair.

Grace had noticed that, when ordered to follow her downstairs, he had brought a battered briefcase with him. Now he undid it and drew out two bundles of notebooks tied up with string. 'You'll recognise these, I expect,' he said, almost sheepish. 'Julia thought they might interest me. You'll know what she has in mind, of course.'

'*No*,' Grace said heavily, and it was true. Julia had never mentioned any project connected with Anna. And yet she knew exactly what must be 'in mind', some kind of biography which this man would put together, a book based on Anna's letters and diaries, and on any other literary pickings that could be found. In normal circumstances such a book would surely be undertaken at the end of a long and fulfilled career. Anna had been young, but already famous, and her life had been hideously chopped off. Therein lay the crude fascination, she supposed. It was obscene. As yet there had not even been an inquest. She was dreading it because she knew she would be called as a witness.

'You've not *read* the diaries, have you?' She put even more outrage in her voice than she actually felt, for beyond her deep distaste was something bordering on disbelief, that anyone could want to cash in so suddenly, so soon. It was quite obviously Julia's project, and Magnus was her toy.

'Oh, no,' he reassured. 'I just glanced, realising that there was a great deal of ground covered, over very many years. It's impressive, I mean the sheer discipline. These begin when she was so very young, and it looks like a complete record, virtually. Wonderful.'

Grace glanced down at the familiar marbled notebooks, so small in his thick fingers, remembering how Anna had cleared a shelf for them in her own bedroom at White Lodge, when the brother and sister had moved in, after The Tragedy, and how she had pored over them, late at night when they were all supposed to be tucked up and asleep.

She said cautiously, 'What do you and Julia have in mind, exactly?'

'Well, some kind of biography, that's the obvious thing. People are interested in her, naturally. In her way she had become a phenomenon, and so quickly, and then, dying as she did . . .' But Grace was staring at him. 'Of course,' he went on, but stumbling, now that he had seen her face, and his pale greenish skin flushing slightly, 'I would do all the writing, but it would be marvellous to talk to *you* about all this, her childhood, the various influences on her . . .'

134

'The hanged man, and the woman hacked about,' she was thinking stonily, 'and the patent leather man and Miss Dixon, and poor pathetic Mollie McGraw, not to mention poor pathetic Guy.' Oh yes. It would make a good biography, very spicy, very fat. It would probably sell as well as any of her novels.

Getting to her feet she leaned towards him, took the diaries and hugged them to her breast. From the cardigan, which she had worn draped round her shoulders at dinner, came the faint smell of Anna. 'I'm sure you know,' she said icily but, in spite of her outrage, feeling a sudden unexpected pity for this shabby, rather frightened elderly man, 'that I am Anna's sole heir? All her papers are my property now,' though she realised even as she spoke that she was probably too late. She had the diaries, apart from the volume which Julia claimed was 'missing', but there were no letters with them, or literary files, and what Julia had not quietly stowed away she may well have photocopied for this man. Some day, somehow, the awful book would be written. But she would have no part in it.

'There's absolutely no question of my talking to you about Anna, Mr Croucher,' she said, her voice hard, and high with genuine anger. 'I hate the idea, I just *hate* it.'

He flushed deeply now, then said humbly, 'I see, I see.' Suddenly anxious, he added, 'You do realise, don't you, that it's only a question of our talking together? You need only tell me what you *want* to tell me. In time it could, er, make you a considerable amount of money.'

'I'm not interested in making money,' Grace said, carefully checking along the spines of the diaries to make sure no others had gone missing. If any had, then she would challenge him, if necessary through Pollitts.

Croucher did not reply but his blank expression told her that such carefree unworldliness was, to him, quite unimaginable. Miserably he picked a little thread off his thin flannel trousers and returned her cold stare in embarrassed silence.

Julia saved matters by bustling in with the coffee. Both leapt up at exactly the same moment, Magnus to take the tray, Grace to pull chairs round. 'Well, now,' she said cheerily, 'how've you two been getting on?'

'I'm afraid Grace isn't at all happy with the idea of the book,' Magnus said gruffly.

'OK, dearie, end of subject,' Julia answered smoothly, but with finality, almost before he could draw a second breath. 'It's too soon, of course, much too soon. We must wait until the time is right. Forgive us for even broaching the idea. Now then, it's white, isn't it, Grace?'

135

She said quietly, 'The time will never be right, Julia,' and stood up again. 'I'll just go and get my sweeteners. I left them upstairs.' They were actually in her bag, by her chair, but she wanted to remove the diaries. *Now*. In silence they both watched her go, Magnus's large lugubrious brown eyes resting on the tattered notebooks with, she felt, a kind of longing.

Up in her bedroom she put them at the bottom of her suitcase, then arranged the few clothes she had brought on top of them. She would go, first thing tomorrow, get the earliest train, even if it did mean leaving Julia asleep in bed.

Down in the garden room they were no doubt licking their wounds and planning their campaign, laughing about her too, probably, about her fondness for 'a bit of church', about her boiler and her concern over Mrs Lumb, about the chiropodist. As she took off Anna's cardigan and folded it on top of her clothes she shed sudden, hot tears.

Magnus had a large brandy with his coffee then left. Julia was very quiet afterwards, smoking more slowly than usual, Grace noticed, not lighting one from the half-stub of another as she did when she was in full spate. She made no reference to Magnus or to the planned biography, instead she asked about the visit to Stephen's flat.

'I gather that little detective chappie caught up with you,' she said. 'He came here first, woke me up, actually. As a matter of fact it was quite useful, having the law here. I got him to go next door. No intruders this time, thank God.

'Anyway, how did you get on? Funny bunny, that one, thinks he's the bees' knees. I thought so last time.'

'Which "last time"?' Grace asked sharply.

Julia seemed disconcerted. 'Oh, we'd met before,' she said eventually. 'He was up quite soon after the – after they found Anna. He came again, last weekend, just to chat. Quite informal.'

'What did he want? I thought the Yorkshire police were in charge.'

'Oh *yes* . . .' and Julia waved her hands about, 'but you know what it's like, they've all got their individual briefs but everything starts to overlap, as the plot thickens. A reporting to B, and B to C, and then C back to A. Read your thrillers, duckie.'

Grace winced, almost hating her. Here, in this house, Julia Wragg read too many fictions. Her mind seemed over-stuffed with subterfuges and stratagems. And yet, only a few years ago, she had been suddenly widowed. Like Ba, she was childless and in George she'd lost a cherished husband. It had been an idyllic marriage, according to Anna. She must surely have known the sharpness of death and yet there was a repulsive slickness about the way she talked of it now,

and with Anna's loss still so close, the wound still open and hanging.
She thought again of the austere Dr Beardmore and his extraordinary
dismissal of 'story', and a flicker of understanding glimmered. *Yes.*
There could be too much of it.

'He asked what I knew about Stephen Allen,' Julia told her.
'They're obviously very interested in getting hold of him. But you'll
know that, of course.'

'Yes, and it's quite ridiculous. They showed me his photograph and
everything. Simply because someone a bit like him was seen near the
cottage that week, I mean, that man could have been *anybody* . . .'

'Of course, of course,' clucked Julia.

'So why can't they just leave him *alone?*' Her voice was wavering
but she swallowed hard and prayed for control. She would not break
down in front of this woman. *She would not.*

'Grace, dearie, you must realise that he's got to be a suspect. I
mean, he disappears, for months on end, nobody has sight nor sound
of him, and there was that almighty row he had with Anna, and all the
money troubles, those spells in hospital. I mean, you can't just – '

'*Which row?*' and Grace did cry now, for sheer misery, when Julia,
taking her hand, told her of the quarrel, only days before Guy died, of
how, when Lynn had gone and the divorce papers came through, with
his Christmas cards, he had come to Anna and pleaded with her, tried
to wrest a promise from her that she would marry him, wanted the
relationship to start up again. 'You must surely have known about all
that, duckie?' and Julia, very soft now, squeezed her shaking fingers.

Grace nodded, 'I know,' but in fact she had not known. The thing
between Anna and Stephen was casual and temporary, like all Anna's
relationships, it had altered nothing. Stephen was hers, especially after
the love-making which had changed everything, for ever. And now
here was this woman, who had suddenly become monstrous to her,
telling her that he had really wanted to marry Anna, days after he
had been joined to *her*, in her room at White Lodge, when she had
felt so happy.

'I can't say I begin to understand,' Julia blundered on. She had
pulled her chair close to Grace's and had somehow managed to get
an arm round her. 'All I know is that the worst violence often happens
in the most intimate situations, between parents and children, siblings,
between married people most of all . . .'

'They *weren't* married,' shrieked Grace.

'No, dearie, but it was of that *order*, on his side, I mean, and with
all his many emotional problems I think – '

But Grace, unable to bear any more, cut her off. 'They'll find who
did it,' she said, calming down a little and fishing about in her bag for

a tissue, to blow her nose. 'The police are amazing, I think. I mean, they got the Yorkshire Ripper, didn't they? They'll get this man as well. Of *course* it couldn't have been Stephen. The idea's insane.'

But Julia's blank stare showed that she was totally unconvinced. 'I just hope they do find whoever it was,' she said quietly, 'before someone else suffers, that's all. I still can't bear to think of it, the poor love left there in the cottage so long, that hand . . . I suppose you know they found it in a school playground?' and a tear trickled down her face.

'Oh don't, Julia, *don't*,' and she got up jerkily, pushing away the horrific images, putting all the crockery on to the coffee tray, crashing cups and saucers together, spilling sugar.

'Will you sell it, the place up in Yorkshire?' With difficulty Julia got down on her knees and dabbed ineffectually at the sugar with a paper napkin, then tried to sweep it into her hand. After the sudden emotional outpouring, the tears, they were both embarrassed, taking refuge in simple mechanical operations.

'I don't know. I've not decided yet, about anything. But I do want to go back there, when I feel up to it.'

Julia stood up stiffly and let the sugar grains trickle down on to the tray. She said, with what felt to Grace like genuine concern, 'Don't go there on your own, duckie. Let me come with you. I'd drop everything at this end. Do let me come.'

But somehow the simple kindness did not touch Grace. She was still too stung by the biography project, by the prompt removal of Anna's papers from next door, and by the importation of Magnus Croucher. Julia had shed real tears with her at last, over Anna's death, yet she still suspected an emotional incontinence, like Mother after the last stroke, smiling and weeping together, ever in April mood. She would not have been out of the house five minutes, she predicted, when Julia would be on to Magnus, with some new idea about the book. It all repulsed her. And yet, 'Will you let me come with you?' Julia was repeating urgently.

She replied, 'As I say, I've not made any plans yet. I can't quite think straight. I'll see.' But she had thought, and her plans did not include Julia Wragg. She would return to the dale alone.

Julia did not come round until ten next morning. Then she showered and dressed, all set for a leisurely brunch with Grace. But nobody came when she knocked on the guest-room door, and she found it empty, the bed stripped and the sheets neatly folded. All that remained of her visitor was a coolly civil thank you note on the kitchen table.

11

Wearing one of Mother's old overalls – it was rather tight across the chest and she knew she had put weight on in the last few weeks – Grace pulled on rubber gloves and began to apply Brasso to the lectern eagle. She liked St Saviour's best when it was empty like this, the town traffic outside a remote hum, the faint clatter of shoppers on their way to the old market, inside, a faint, unobtrusive dusty light, the woody smell of Michaelmas daisies. Here, when she was fourteen years old, she had 'come forward' at an evangelistic rally, knelt down with others and prayed fervently for Christ to enter her life. At home that night she had summoned up all her courage and told her parents. It was hard because they were not churchgoers and the missioner had warned his new Christians that their people might not understand. They must expect to be made fools for Christ's sake, like the apostle Paul.

Mother had certainly been very silent, a look of pained embarrassment playing round her thin mouth. But Daddie had held her hand. And he must have written to Aunt Celia straightaway because, the very next week, she had sent a gilt and leather prayer book with her favourite text inscribed in the front: 'To the uttermost, He saves.' Aunt Celia was his older sister and the only religious relative they could lay claim to.

When the eagle was finished and gleaming she walked slowly up the nave, peeling off her gloves. Officially, she should do the cross too, and the candlesticks, but there had just been a wedding and all the altar brass was shining. She knew that she could have skipped the eagle but she had needed somewhere to go this morning, something to do, and the lectern was aways a cleaning challenge with its complication of feathers, its endless small crevices where the Brasso lodged, turning pale blue as it dried.

At White Lodge the boiler was installed and, with Mrs Lumb, she had spent two long days spring-cleaning the kitchen and the pantry. But in spite of the hard physical work she had not been able to sleep, not even with tablets.

As she stood by the communion rail, staring up at the ugly Victorian window behind the central cross, its hard bright colours depicting a ferocious-looking Christ in Majesty, she remembered the night of her conversion, the ecstatic weeks that had followed, the richness of her prayer times. How bleak it all felt now, how dead; prayer itself was a near impossibility. Whenever she knelt down to offer praise, to frame a petition or simply to listen to the Lord, her mind blanked out, as if an impenetrable curtain had dropped down between herself and the Almighty. She supposed it was simply depression, hard on the heels of the shock that had come with Anna's death.

She stared critically at the ornate cross, noticing a few slight smears, opened the gate in the communion rail and approached with her Brasso. When, years ago, she had first added herself to the cleaning rota, she had felt frightened, standing so close. It had not felt right, actually walking on the piece of rich Turkey carpet that lay spread beyond the place where she had knelt for so many weeks, so many years, to receive the bread and the wine; worse, actually to handle the candlesticks and the cross with her dusters and her tin of polish.

On that first cleaning day she had worked rapidly, wanting to finish and get away, a deep child-like dread gripping her that great bells might suddenly start ringing, a darkness sweep through the church, and a huge apocalyptic voice cry out, 'Take off thy shoes from off thy feet, For the place whereon thou standest is holy ground.'

Shyly, she had mentioned it to the vicar, thinking he might laugh. But he had listened sympathetically. Then he had made a surprising suggestion, that she might indeed remove her shoes, when she cleaned the altar furnishings, that this, perhaps, was what the Lord was saying to her, that the simple act of devotion might ease her spirit.

So now she stood as she always had, in stockinged feet, dabbing at the cross with a cloth and inspecting the floor behind the altar table for dust and rubbish. Often, on these visits, she had to pick up sweet wrappers thrown there by the choir boys, but there were none today, only dust and cobwebs as in any house.

And that was how it should be, it was only a building and the altar part of the building; these objects she had to polish were not holy relics, merely signs and representations of that great Love which had upheld her, along all the years. And yet she wished, as she replaced the empty cross and stepped back, that it was a proper crucifix instead. She needed to behold his hands and his feet. In her bleakness of spirit she was sharing, minutely, in his great suffering. She needed a visible sign that her pain was his.

Ba was coming to supper. She bought some food in Marks and Spencer, called in briefly at the shop (knowing it was Frankie's day off), and then, on her way to the car park, collected her new

140

business cards from the printers. She was pleased with them. She had had them engraved in flowing italic script with her name, Elizabeth Grace Bradley, and with two addresses, the shop below left and, below right, White Lodge. The actual name looked somehow unfinished. When she had ordered them the man had asked whether anything 'followed'. 'No,' she had told him, suddenly resenting the sketchiness of her education, Daddie's death, Mother's illnesses, all the domestic years. Anna could have added 'MA, Dunelm' to such a card, Marian SRN, Ba her library qualifications. Grace had one A level, a scrape, in RE.

At Firs, in the drawer where she had found all Anna's keys, she had found a box of similar business cards, obviously once ordered by Guy, just the address and 'Guy Beardmore, MA Cantab'. Whom, she had wondered sadly, had he fooled with those? If they ever met up again she might mention her pathetic discovery to Julia Wragg. She had seemed so unwilling to believe what she had heard about his early career, his drinking, his expulsion from his Cambridge college, all Anna's defensive lies. But would the woman actually *hear*? Julia, Grace had decided, heard only what she chose to. Her ears were stopped, like those with whom the Lord's prophets had pleaded in vain.

On the day after her return from London, Grace, guilty about her abrupt departure, had wired flowers and thanks. Julia must have picked the phone up to speak to her almost before the Interflora agent had returned to his van. She was all gratitude and concern, waving away Grace's apologies, 'entirely understanding', and making embarrassingly detailed enquiries about the installation of the new boiler. 'I hope you're leaving all the cleaning up to that little treasure of yours,' she had said. (It was no longer 'char' Grace had observed). 'I thought you were looking rather unwell . . .' as if they had known each other for years. Magnus, she had gone on to say, 'entirely understood' equally, about the book, and Grace was to give no further thought to it; which meant Julia had, and that Grace's refusal to consider it was something of a disappointment to her. Then she had mentioned an elderly client in Cheshire, someone who had been writing for them for years whom she really must visit soon. He was pretty old, and ailing, and she rather thought it might be the last time. Could she call in, she wondered?

Grace had explained that Peth was some miles away from the address she gave but that yes, she should telephone by all means. Perhaps they could go out for a meal together (she did not have the confidence to entertain her at White Lodge). And what about Anna's cottage? Julia had asked finally, rather demanding now. Grace did know, didn't she, that it was simply a matter of picking up the phone, when she decided to go up there? She would come along with pleasure . . . count it a *privilege*. Grace really shouldn't make that particular journey alone.

It was this phone conversation which had stopped her sleeping, for it had disrupted all her plans. She had drafted a letter to Julia Wragg but had not yet typed it out. (The typewriter, she felt, would give it more authority, for it was an important letter, about Anna's literary files.) In the rush she had forgotten that she was leaving everything behind except the diaries. What she most wanted were 'The Hanged Man' notes, not to read, at least not yet, for she felt that, like the diaries, they were still somehow red-hot. But she wanted them in her safekeeping lest some damage be done with them. In those notes, and in the missing 'deaths' diary (and had Julia removed it herself, perhaps, and lied?) was surely the essence of anything Anna would have said in a book about Guy and the days of The Tragedy. If anything at all was to be written now it must be written by Grace herself, the Lord was telling her that very clearly. Hadn't Julia Wragg praised her for her letters? Hadn't Anna said she wrote 'like an angel'? Well then. These were signs unto her that nobody else must attempt a Beardmore book. She wouldn't waste her time at Daddie's shop, arguing with Frankie, she would start thinking about this writing project instead. The book didn't have to be intellectual or high-powered, she would simply write down what she knew – and it was a great deal – in her own way.

So her diplomatic letter about the files had been drafted and then Julia had phoned, all sweetness and light. What was she to do now, about the rest of Anna's papers? She had wondered, on her return from London, whether she ought to get Edward Pollitt to send an official letter about her legal rights in the matter, but that would seem grossly unfriendly now, after the flowers and the forgiveness. Julia Wragg had rather cut the ground from under her feet.

Ba might have a view, she thought, putting her carrier bags on the doorstep and unlocking the front door of White Lodge. It was providential that Marian's old lady in Staffordshire had persuaded her to stay on for a while, otherwise Grace could not have invited Ba round on her own; she and Marian lived together, they were The Girls. But she did need advice about Julia, and her plans for a book, and Marian could be so opinionated, so bullying. The Lord had kept her in the Midlands. He was still watching over Grace, even though she could not feel him near.

Blessed are they who have not seen and yet have believed, she told herself sternly, going in. Then she looked down and stepped to one side. On the doormat were two postcards which had come by the second delivery. One was plain, the message typed, its signature illegible. The other, a colour reproduction of a painting, was quite definitely from Stephen.

She paced her movements, not allowing herself even to look at the cards until she had carried her shopping through to the kitchen, unpacked and boiled the kettle for a cup of tea. Then she sat down by the stove, poked the fire into life and received the purring, hopeful cat on to her knee. Tickling his ears she picked up the typed card first: '*The Loving Friends*: I quite understand your reservations at this stage. But if you have any further thoughts, do get in touch. I was very pleased to meet you last weekend. Yours,' and a bright blue scribble. Underneath was typed 'Magnus J. Croucher'.

Grace stared at it angrily. The door of the stove was open and she felt like tearing it into pieces and throwing them in. *The Loving Friends* . . . This, presumably, was some title he had dreamed up for the Anna book. Julia Wragg would not have been pleased with this card, after all her efforts to convince Grace that the idea had been shelved indefinitely. It was really rather unintelligent of him to send it.

Then she remembered him, nervous and ageing, hopeful in his shiny jacket, and she repented. She would write a stalling but polite postcard in reply, and keep his, at least until she had made a note of the address. The Girls had told her that sudden bereavement and shock could make a person act entirely out of character, and it was certainly true in her case. She had really been very uncivil to Julia, just leaving like that. There was no harm in writing back to Magnus, just so long as she did not mislead him into thinking she had changed her mind.

Only when the tea was poured and she had taken her first sip did she look at Stephen's card, and then, for a long time, only at the reproduction on the front. It was a tabby cat, a bit like her Binkie, curled round in sleep, its nose in its paws. Slowly, her heart flickering queerly, shortening her breath, she turned it over and read the back. 'Gwen John: Cat' it said at the bottom. He had written above, 'I missed you – "by a whisker" (joke). I'm pretty busy at present but do keep in touch. Heard on the grapevine that you've got Anna's cottage. Lucky you. Any chance of our meeting up there? Or anywhere? S.,' all in the same spindly hand that Mother had used, after her stroke.

She stared at the card for a long time, reassured at first. The feeble pun was like him, she warmed to the 'keep in touch', and she was glad that he was painting. The oddness was in the sentence about Anna. 'On the grapevine' rather repelled her, so did 'got', as if Anna's possessions were fairground prizes, tossed casually over the canvas to eager, waiting winners; and she cringed at 'lucky you'.

He was unwell, the handwriting alone convinced her of that. She had never talked to him about his bouts of depression because she had never spent long enough in his company, but she had discussed the subject with Ba, on their walk in Wensleydale. She had been ill after losing her husband and had had a few sessions with a psychotherapist. Grace remembered the 'wall of glass' she had talked about, which had, at that time, towered up, ever thickening, between her and ordinary life, the remote dream-like world she inhabited then, and the strange things she had done, like running away from old friends in the street, actually *running*, simply hanging up if phone calls became too difficult, and writing long rambling incoherent letters in the middle of the night, when she could not sleep. It was the letter phenomenon Grace remembered, as she sat looking at Stephen's card. It was, as a first communication from him since Anna's death, hugely insensitive. Therefore he was ill. She might actually show it to Ba, and get her opinion.

Slowly she stirred herself and began to assemble ingredients for the evening meal. How had Stephen found out about Anna's will? 'The grapevine' suggested that someone had talked, but she could not think who such a person might be. She had told absolutely no one and the only person apart from Edward Pollitt who seemed to know was Julia Wragg, and she had given Grace the impression that she hardly knew Stephen. Anyway, in what circumstances would she ever have talked to him about the provisions of a client's will?

Perhaps, she concluded reluctantly, he had been alone at some point in Anna's London house, found a copy and read it. But it was hard to imagine. Stephen had always been so muddled and casual which was why, she supposed, he had needed a woman like Lynn to organise his day-to-day affairs, to boss him. He was neither circumspect nor watchful, and definitely not a snooper. That had been more of a Beardmore characteristic. Both Anna and Guy had been in the habit of reading other people's letters, looking into their cheque books, listening at doors. Daddie had once caught Guy doing that, and shouted at him.

She pondered, rinsing pieces of broccoli under the kitchen tap, to make soup; then the doorbell rang. Clicking her teeth with frustration she went to dry her hands, glancing up at the kitchen clock. Ba was due in less than two hours and she wasn't nearly ready. Cooking, like all other physical tasks, Grace did slowly and laboriously. Whoever it was must be quickly dispatched. She wanted to make a really good job of this meal, for Ba.

Breda Smith was standing on the front step. 'I was just on my way home from work, Grace,' she said, flushing as their eyes met, for Grace had folded her arms and looked somehow as if she were barring the

144

door. Breda noticed, with a guilty satisfaction, that she was putting weight on. In the old days she, not Grace, was the fat one.

Grace said, 'I'm sorry, but I'm up to my eyes in cooking. I've got a friend coming for supper,' and she eyed Breda coldly, not opening the door any further. She was remembering the casual phone call, before her trip to London.

'It's all right, Grace, it was nothing really, only I was just wondering how you were. How was your weekend?'

'Did Buckle send you?' Grace's voice was icy.

'No. No he *didn't*. Listen, Grace, that's really why I wanted to speak to you. I realised afterwards what you must have thought. Well, it was very difficult for me.'

'Being asked to check up on me, you mean?'

'Yes. Anyway, I've asked to be taken off the job. So it's all right, and I'm sorry.'

Grace looked at her watch. 'Come in for a minute,' she said, 'but do you mind sitting in the kitchen? I've got various pans on the go.' She could spare half an hour and she wanted to know what had passed between Breda and Buckle. He had not made contact since she had returned from London, though by now he must have received her letter about the envelope of news cuttings and the weird phone call.

'It all smells very good,' Breda said politely, accepting a glass of sherry. Grace smiled to herself. Broccoli on the boil always reminded her of lavatories. Breda was obviously feeling guilty, wanting to make up.

'You said you'd asked to be taken off the case?' she said, pouring herself some apple juice. Not only was she rather indifferent to alcohol, she enjoyed keeping sober and clear-headed while drink made others fuzzy and loquacious. It had happened at Julia's.

'Yes. It was an uncomfortable situation, our knowing each other from school and everything, and, as I think I hinted to you, Bill – Superintendent Buckle that is – seemed a bit over the top to me, with his theories. I couldn't go along with them. Between you and me, I don't like the way he's keeping so much to himself, I mean, I'm not sure he *can*, it's not his case.' She shrugged. 'Of course, it's nothing to do with me really, I just do as I'm told, and he knows Keith Hallam. But he's young for the promotion he's just had, Grace, and he obviously wants to make an impression. He – '

'So what about these "over the top" theories?' Grace interrupted.

Breda paused. 'Well, they were ridiculous.'

'Do you mean theories about Stephen?'

'Stephen and you.'

'*Me?*'

'Well, at the beginning, after we'd been here, I got the impression that he thought you might be mixed up in it together.'

'Mixed up in *what*?'

'In Anna's death.' She whispered this, feeling that it was just too absurd to be spoken aloud. At the time she had been quite unable to come to terms with the sheer enormity of it, she had felt Buckle was merely theorizing, out of a kind of frustration, because it wasn't his case.

Grace, who had been standing at the stove stirring a pan, pulled a stool out from under the table and sat down. For a minute she scarcely had breath to make words. It had only happened to her once before, in the hospital when she had seen Daddie die. Her heart was pumping and the peculiar swimmy sensation was threatening to come on. She took a big gulp from her glass of juice then said, in a sort of dry croak, 'But Breda, that's *mad*.'

'I know, I know. But he's my boss, Grace, and he's very good at his job. People think well of him. What could I say?'

'Nothing. I'm not blaming you, and I know they've got to explore all avenues, just to eliminate people. I mean, they spent ages interviewing The Girls. Marian was furious about it.'

'I remember,' Breda said, 'I was there.'

'It's just that – well, *me*. But how did he know about Anna's will, Breda? I'm presuming that lay behind his little theory, the fact that I've inherited all her money. He discussed it with Julia Wragg, apparently.'

'I don't honestly know, but he got access to the information some-how. Presumably the Yorkshire constabulary passed it on. But the main point now, Grace, is that he seems to have put all his crackpot theories about you on one side. He's just anxious that you'll be, you know, OK.' She rather wanted to say 'safe'. It would only be a matter of time before they found Allen, and Buckle clearly regarded him as dangerous, with good reason, she suspected, though she would not say this to Grace. Buckle had told her, in his off-hand, inhibited way, that she was rather sweet on him, that he could do no wrong. 'They do want to talk to Stephen Allen,' she said, 'and they're still on the lookout for him, up north. It does make sense, Grace.'

Without comment Grace offered Breda more sherry, but she covered her glass. 'No thanks, I'm holding you up.' Though it was tempting to stay on, in the cluttered comfort of White Lodge, with its familiar smoothly-oiled routines, unchanged, it seemed to all appearances, since Mrs Bradley's death. The warm old-fashioned kitchen contrasted favourably with her box-like apartment in the new town flats where, tonight, another empty evening yawned in front of her. Sal had recently acquired a serious boyfriend and was planning to move in with him. This meant more loneliness for Breda. She would like to have started a friendship with Grace Bradley.

The night before, Buckle had taken her down to the pub, not wanting to discuss her scruples about Grace in his office, and she had drunk rather too much, going on about their schooldays at Peth High in a way that embarrassed her now, a way that had definitely been unfair to Grace. She had told him, she remembered, that some people had actually suggested that she might have been a little 'backward', though that word, she realised, was no longer acceptable now. But she had always had such difficulty with academic subjects and there were hints, sometimes, that her pass to the High might have been a clerical mistake. Such things were not unknown.

'And yet,' she had told him, 'she was always so lovely to people, so terribly kind. Absolutely *everyone* liked Grace.'

'Yes, so I gather, "pure gold",' he had quoted flatly, from a notebook on his lap. 'That's what the librarian friend said about her. She obviously thinks the sun shines out of her arse.'

Breda had felt very uncomfortable. Ba's phrase was beautiful, and he had cheapened it. But again she felt the curious tension in him, that she remembered from their long conversation after the first interview with Grace. His very belligerence, then, had been a give-away, and here it was again. She was occupying his thoughts rather fully, Breda suspected. 'So you're still not absolutely sure about her?' she'd asked.

'Oh, she didn't have anything to do with Beardmore's death, I just can't make my mind up about *her*. I suppose I don't *understand* people like that . . .' and he wanted to understand now, to anatomise, to possess.

'Women like what, Bill?'

'Well, she's so . . . *done to*, d'you know what I'm getting at? I mean, what sort of a life has she ever had, stuck in that house?'

'She was absolutely devoted to her parents.'

'I know, you said. But that's my point, they're *dead*, for heaven's sake, yet you get the feeling they're still around somewhere, keeping tabs on her.' He hesitated. 'I know what that's like, Breda, I've had some. You have to get away. She ought to sell up, buy a place with a girlfriend or something. I mean, what does she actually *do* all day, apart from seeing to the house, and she's got a cleaner to do that, remember, *and* she draws an income from the family business, though I gather she doesn't take much interest in it. Well, *OK*, if that's not her thing she could do something else, couldn't she? Especially now, with all the money that's coming to her. It's simply that I don't understand how she lives at all, with so little stimulation. I feel sorry for people like that, I really do.'

Breda looked at him. On the sticky pub table his fists were clenched into tight little balls and his smooth, normally sallow complexion had darkened, with two high spots of colour burning on his cheeks. His anger did not deceive her, it was Grace he wanted. Somehow, she had got to him, to this cold, impregnable man. She felt a deep stab of envy.

'I know her behaviour's a bit odd, Bill, but she's in shock, she's bound to be. Think of what's happened. You don't put a thing like that behind you in five minutes. She thought the world of Anna Beardmore. It's pathetic but really, she was Grace's life, especially after the mother died.'

'OK, we've already been through that. Just answer my question, I want to know. What the hell *does* she do, apart from running her bloody house. Christ, it's a depressing place. She's in a time-warp, poor woman.'

'Well, she's got the church . . . and this thing the Torch Bearers.'

'Oh, for God's sake, Breda,' and Buckle grimaced, irritably drumming his fingers on the table top. It wasn't merely that he felt personally confused and frustrated about his developing feelings for Grace, but the Beardmore enquiry was irritating him more and more. The most recent faxes from Hallam's office hadn't mentioned Allen and to his surprise two men had been taken off the case altogether. A group of government ministers were shortly to be going to Scarborough and a cache of Semtex explosive had been found on the North Yorkshire moors. General attention had shifted, on to possible IRA activities and Anna Beardmore was already last week's news. He could see the case, which had held so much initial promise, dragging on for months now, with nothing concrete achieved, for simple lack of manpower.

But he had to see Grace again. He did have one excuse, her letter about the news cuttings and the crank phone call, sent second class and wrongly addressed (deliberately, perhaps?) and so only reaching him that morning. This large Breda vaguely reminded him of Grace in her general plainness, her hefty bearing, but she was not nearly such a fine thing. Grace Bradley had a certain strength to her, a core.

It attracted him. In the London taxi, when she had wept for her friend, he had, in trying to comfort her, actually wanted to slide his hand up between her warm thighs, to draw apart the silk blouse and see her breasts.

*

Ba's views were unexpected, on the subject of Julia's proposed book, and she listened with great interest to Grace's idea of writing something of her own.

'I understand how you must have felt,' she said sympathetically, 'when they first mentioned their idea, and I agree that it's much too early . . . *years* too early . . .'

'Obscenely early,' Grace said harshly. 'It's obscene, Ba.'

'No.' Ba was cautious, but firm. 'I really wouldn't go as far as that. Try and think in the long term, Grace. The thing is, *someone* is going to write a book about Anna. If you don't, and if they can't get any genuine information, they'll simply make it up. I've just accessed a book about Cal Bethune, you know, that brilliant young pianist who died of leukaemia. Grace, it's hideous.'

'How is it hideous?' She had never actually heard of Cal Bethune.

'It's about the last few months of his life, and his relationship with the woman who nursed him. It's all extremely explicit, sexually I mean, and yet there it all is, in print, and people queueing up to borrow it. You wouldn't want a book like that to come out about Anna, would you? People can be entirely unscrupulous, if there's big money on offer. They just lie and lie. I think you could do a book yourself, love. I'd help, if you wanted me to, we could do it together.'

'Mmm . . . I'm not sure. I certainly got the feeling that Magnus Croucher wanted some easy money,' Grace said. 'What I suppose I ought to do is to get Edward Pollitt to send for all Anna's papers. I just had, you know, that *feeling*, about Julia . . .' She had confided to Ba, now, about the provisions of the will, and Ba had agreed, though rather nervously, not to tell Marian.

'What I would do,' she advised, 'is to tell her you want time to think about the whole thing, and send this man Croucher a copy of the letter. From the sound of it she won't make a move with him if she knows there's a chance of your agreeing to write something yourself. Then you can just, well, stall, until you're ready. As a matter of fact, pet, and I'm honestly not just saying this, I think you could write rather a good piece about Anna, you know, your own appreciation, Anna as *you* saw her.'

'But they don't want that, Ba, they want all the horrible stuff, they want things like Dr Beardmore and his affair with poor Winnie Carpenter, how he killed his wife and how Guy came home. You *know* that's what they're after, all the dirt.'

'Well if they do, you can't stop them, Grace, in the end.'

'I can. I can pray.' Though it was no longer true. She had once been able to pray but there was this awful white blankness now, spread over her mind and heart. Suddenly she said, '*Pray for me, Ba,*' and she squeezed her friend's arm.

Ba squeezed back. 'I do, love, every day.'

Before she went home Grace showed her Stephen's card. 'What do you think?' she said.

Ba examined it carefully. 'Have you shown this to Buckle?'

'No.'

'Grace, you really must.'

Then she knew that The Girls too thought that he could actually have murdered Anna. 'I think he must be ill,' she said plaintively. 'It doesn't sound like him at all . . . and look at the writing, Ba. That's the pills.

'Do you know,' she went on when Ba made no reply, 'not once, in all this, has anybody said anything about his coming home to the flat, and finding Guy in the bath? I mean, a terrible thing like that must have taken its toll on him, Ba.' And she recalled the note she had found on Anna's writing table at The Rock, about killing yourself being the most effective way of making sure you were never forgotten. She hated Guy for doing that to Stephen. 'On somebody like him,' she said aloud, 'someone so *sensitive* . . .'

Ba was silent, still staring down at the slumbering tabby cat, but privately she doubted. 'Sensitive' was one of Grace's words. What did it actually mean, though, in this context? What she ought to be thinking about was the impact of a suicide on someone chronically unstable like Stephen Allen. It might indeed have pushed him over the edge, but to a violent and entirely unpredictable act against someone whom, though only subconsciously, perhaps, he had reason to resent. He had apparently had a short but intense affair with Anna Beardmore. Grace had touched on that, when they had talked in Wensleydale, though she had clearly found the subject very painful.

At last she said, giving the card back, 'How little any of us really *knows* any one else, Grace. Do you know, I had been married to Phil for nearly a year before I discovered that I was his second wife. No wonder things went wrong.'

'How did you find out?'

'Oh, she wrote to him about something, and I accidentally opened the letter.'

'Why hadn't he told you?'

Ba hesitated. 'He said – he said he felt it wasn't relevant, yes, that was his word, *relevant*. They'd both been so very young and the marriage had only lasted about six months. He said it was a complication he felt we could both do without, that he'd concealed it for my sake.' She gave a little laugh. 'Odd . . .'

150

'Would you have preferred to know?'

'Oh yes. I never understood why he had kept it from me. It was always, you know, between us, afterwards.'

'And you think I'm deceived too, about Stephen? Is that what you're saying, that I don't really know him? You've been talking to Buckle, haven't you?'

'*No*,' Ba said hastily, taken aback at the unfamiliar shrewishness that had crept into Grace's voice. 'All I told him was about the day you went to see Anna, at her cottage. He did ask me if you'd been particularly friendly with Stephen and I said no, not to my knowledge. That's honestly *all* I said, Grace.' She could have told him, she supposed, that she and Marian rather felt that Grace had got some kind of adolescent crush on Allen. Certainly she had kept on introducing him into their conversations, on holiday, in the way one does at sixteen or seventeen, when one is besotted. Lovely as she was, there was something curiously young and unformed about Grace's personality, they had both decided, not that it was her fault. It was almost certainly the stifling regime imposed by old Mrs Bradley.

'If he did . . . kill Anna,' Grace said, getting the hateful words out with extreme difficulty, 'then why, Ba, *why*?'

'Dear Grace,' and she took her hand, 'I honestly don't know and I couldn't begin to imagine. But he has had profound psychiatric problems, now, you *know* that.'

'You mean depression? Half the world seems to have suffered from depression, it seems to me. You've had it yourself, you should know, and he's the gentlest, *kindest* man . . .'

'I'm sure he is, Grace. My prayer is that they will find whoever did it, and that the person will not be Stephen. That's what we're all praying for, isn't it?'

But Grace was not listening. 'Someone must have been jealous of her,' she said harshly. 'They cut off her writing hand and they stuffed her mouth with bits of paper. Did you know that? They raped her. Oh Ba, *I feel I can't bear it*.' And she wept.

Ba knelt down on the kitchen floor, at her feet, took both hands in her own and bowed her head. 'Heavenly Father,' she said quietly, 'Take all this pain. It is too much for us now. In your great wisdom and love resolve the torment Grace is in at this dark time. Put your loving arms around her, and around Stephen, wherever he may be. I commit them both to your infinite mercy. Amen.'

She did not go home until Grace was tucked up in bed and until she had seen her take a sleeping pill. The prayer time had brought them close, and she had very much wanted to stay the night. But Marian would be telephoning from Lichfield as she always did, last thing before turning in, and Ba had said she would be home from White Lodge by ten-thirty. She could see already that her loyalties might begin to be divided between the two friends. But Grace had seemed to need her so, tonight. She felt ennobled.

Much of the next day was spent drafting and redrafting letters, to Julia, to Magnus Croucher, to Edward Pollitt and to Stephen. The last was only a short note, on a picture postcard of the Swale cascading down over the great double waterfall near Keld. 'Lovely to have your card,' Grace wrote. 'I shall be in the north for a few days next week. Could we meet then?' and she had printed a phone number along the bottom.

The three letters she did not intend to post until Ba, who had offered to advise, had seen and approved them. But she was going up to the dale, immediately, but this time telling no one her precise plans. This was obviously what she must do next, instead of kicking her heels in Peth, waiting for Anna's papers to arrive from Julia: seek out those who'd had dealings with Anna in recent months, over the purchase of The Rock, new people she'd got to know, and talk to them. The brief Yorkshire period was important, in any account she might write; Anna had talked often of living at The Rock permanently, she wrote best there, she'd claimed. Whether Grace herself would have enough courage to go into the cottage she didn't know.

When she'd talked to people in the dale she would come back and start working systematically through the papers. It was the wrong way round, but what did that matter? Time was immaterial and she would organise her book in her own way. Nobody else had known Anna so long, nor so intimately in those early years when she was still learning to write. Grace had even typed out some stories for her, to try on magazines. She must have copies somewhere, things she could quote from. That would be a surprise for Julia Wragg. The more she thought about it the more certain she was that this was the way the Lord was guiding her, to write a loving account of Anna as Grace her friend had known her; and she would begin with The Rock, now. She very much wanted to get away from Peth and from the people in it, particularly the police, with their questions about Stephen.

She went out to mail Stephen's card but left the three letters untyped, in a file on top of Daddie's desk where she usually wrote her letters and paid the household bills. She would go back to Mrs Fawcett's in Wensleydale. She had said she kept on with guests until the weather broke and it was remarkably fine still, the late autumn days still mild and dry. She would phone this evening. Why wait?

On her way back to White Lodge she met Mrs Lumb. 'Hello,

Gladys,' she said, puzzled to see her there. She had done her three hours that morning and gone home as usual at twelve-thirty. She didn't usually venture out in the dark.

'Something came for you, Grace,' she said, turning scarlet, 'when you were at London. I forgot. I thought it might be important, like, so I've left it inside the porch. I'll see you on Friday.' She seemed very anxious to get away.

'No, no you won't, actually, I'm going off again for a few days. Don't worry about coming in, though, I'll ring you when I get back. I'll put Binkie in the cattery this time. I'm not quite sure how long I'll be away.'

'All right.' The old woman stood there on the pavement, unquestioning, mute, and Grace felt a sudden irrational urge of irritation at her complete subservience. She had had a child, and, therefore, sex. Had she turned her face away, perhaps, as Arthur laboured, disowning the lower portion of her body until his work was done, then, as he recovered, got up to cleanse herself from the distasteful act?

Calling goodbye, she walked home, hating the way such entirely inappropriate thoughts always seemed to force themselves upon her at times when she should be particularly kind and accepting, when the baser part of her nature was dictating whimsical anger and intolerance towards someone she owed a considerable debt. Then she reflected further, and her conscience eased. So long as she was enclosed in her physical body such thoughts would come. They were not of her, they were of the Evil One. What would someone like William Buckle say, she thought idly, if she talked to him about the Fall of Man? She rather wanted to.

In the porch she found the Tesco's carrier bag left there by Mrs Lumb. It contained a square cardboard box which she took out and put on the hall table, disappointed, as it was obviously not the green woollen suit she had ordered by mail from the *Sunday Telegraph*. She could have taken it away with her and worn it to meet Stephen. She felt he might come to the dale and she had given him Mrs Fawcett's number, just in case.

Inside the box was some polystyrene filling which floated about and stuck to her clothes as she took out a large white plastic drum, identical to the jumbo container of peanut butter she had bought recently from the health shop, but rather heavier. A neatly typed label on the side said 'Harvey and Paine, Manchester Road, Peth'. Across the top in permanent marker someone had scrawled untidily 'the cremated remains of Irene Anna Beardmore'.

153

12

Grace decided not to leave White Lodge until the afternoon. If she went too early in the day she could well get snarled up in motorway traffic and be forced to sit in interminable queues. Once, with Mother, the car engine had overheated and given up on her in the middle lane, and they had been towed ignominiously off the carriageway. Mrs Bradley, who was unwell at the time, had become rather hysterical about it all, and Grace had felt something of a spectacle. The car coughed and spluttered now as she circled the roundabout, entered the sliproad and eased herself out into the traffic. It was due to be replaced and she must start thinking about that, when she returned home. Suddenly, she thought of her new wealth. Papers about Anna's estate had started to come through from Pollitts, things for her to sign. Secretly, she had always rather liked sleek, fast cars and now she could buy anything she wanted. But she supposed she would simply replace the present Escort with a new one, though perhaps have a sunshine roof this time. That had been a little extra she had always fancied.

Now she was established on the motorway and, going a steady sixty, there was space to consider her present movements. She had no doubts at all about this last-minute decision to go up Anna's dale. Ba had mentioned her book project to Marian, who was still in Lichfield, and she too had offered help, saying that the very idea of outsiders doing anything was outrageous. Who better for such a book than Grace herself? And a break from Peth, after the funeral and its aftermath, was a sensible move. Grace tried not to ponder on Marian's excessive enthusiasm for the Anna project. Her trip up north would take her away from Ba, and Marian obviously wanted that.

Mrs Fawcett had remembered her, from when she had come with The Girls. She had said, rather grudgingly, Grace felt, that she could only give her bed and breakfast, not an evening meal. There were plenty of places around for that, she had added. There had been – or had Grace imagined it? – a certain hostility in her voice. She rather hoped nobody would try to telephone her at the farm. She had written 'in absolute emergencies only' on the note she had sent to Mrs Lumb. Then she remembered that she had also sent the number to Stephen.

154

As she drove north she thought about him again. The Girls obviously believed that the police might be right, that he might be implicated, and the knowledge appalled her. 'How little we know any one person,' Ba had said. Certainly, in places like Raddon Court, to which Stephen had once been admitted, years ago, there were very violent people, people who had to be secured in padded rooms for their own protection when their fit was upon them. She had actually heard that they still used some kind of strait jacket in such places, in spite of all the modern drugs. But these poor people had not *killed*. As for Stephen, she would not, could not, believe it. With Ba she had prayed that whoever had laid violent hands on Anna would be found before someone else suffered, found and healed, for with God nothing was impossible.

It seemed that she had the farm entirely to herself, though the sign swinging from the tree at the bottom of the long stony track said 'Vacancies', and she had certainly seen holidaymakers still around, bravely brewing up in front of their tents on riverside campsites, muffled against the wind in hats and scarves, or sitting inside neat caravans watching portable televisions. She would probably buy a set for The Rock. Anna had used the cottage for her writing, but for Grace it would be a holiday place which she would share with friends. Obviously The Girls would come, and they both had their regular programmes.

Now that she was here, and only a few miles from The Rock, she rather felt she would like to go and see it, not wait. She didn't think she could bring herself to go inside but at least she could stand and look at it. She should have asked Edward Pollitt about all the police procedures in a case like Anna's. Was she responsible for getting it cleaned up, for example? And would it be still as it was when they had first broken in and found the body? Surely not. At the thought of all that her flesh crept slightly. She must not dwell on it, or she would dream. So she busied herself unpacking her suitcase and laying her clothes neatly in drawers. The bed in her room was Victorian cast iron with brass knobs, like the bed Anna had bought for The Rock.

Heather, the girl who waited at table, had shown her up to the bedroom and offered to bring her a cup of tea while she settled in. She had said Mrs Fawcett was out but Grace had already seen her crossing the yard below the window, coming away from a washing line strung between two trees, with sheets bundled up in her arms. She wore a spotted overall and a headscarf under which, from above, the bumps of hair rollers were clearly visible, in rows. She was not 'out' at all. Could she be avoiding an unwelcome visitor? *Why?*

Thoughtfully Grace turned away and unpacked her Bible, her

ANN PILLING

writing things, and *His Living Word*, the little devotional bedside
book she read each day. She had got up late this morning and, with
so much to cope with before coming away – Binkie to the cattery,
then emptying the fridge, messages about milk and papers, some
last-minute ironing – she had neglected to read it. Now she sat on
the hard high bed and turned to the passage for the day: *As pants
the hart after the waterbrook, so longeth my soul after Thee, O God. My heart
is athirst for God, yea, even for the living God. When shall I come and behold
His face?*

She knelt down and buried her face in the tasselled bedcover,
breathing in its clean soapy smell. She had needed to come to this
place, if only for its deep quietness. At home, when she prayed, there
was always the traffic noise to distract her, the planes coming over
from Ringway, the air's thickness. Here nothing broke the stillness
apart from the odd fuss of hens pecking about in the yard, a bored
sheepdog yelping and occasionally rattling its chain. The simple room,
lovely now in its autumn light, held her, and behind her closed eyelids
she visualised the green sweep of the fells that enfolded the aged
farmhouse and its untidy settlement. On such hills Our Lord had
walked and prayed. He was her pattern.

'*Hope thou in Thy God*,' she repeated aloud, '*for I shall again praise
Him*,' and as she knelt by the bed she stretched her arms out, turning
up the palms of her hands in supplication. For the first time since
Anna's death she was at peace.

Heather, hearing what she thought was a muffled 'Come in' entered
with her tray of tea, then hesitated in the open doorway. The new
resident, a large, rather ungainly woman whose baggage she had
lugged up the steep stone stairs – two suitcases, a lot for such a short
visit, and a bulky plastic carrier bag from which she had seemed most
anxious not to be parted – was kneeling by the bed, her arms stuck out
across the counterpane, the palms of her hands turned upwards.

'Er, are you OK?' she grunted in embarrassment, rattling her tray.
'Here's the tea. Can I get you anything else?' Miss Bradley looked a
bit peculiar, all sprawled out like that.

The body by the bed merely shook its head, muttering grateful
thanks, so Heather retreated. It might be exercises, she thought,
like Auntie Brenda had had to do when she got arthritis, though this
woman looked a bit young for all that. She descended the stairs and
decided to report to Mrs Fawcett in the back kitchen. She would be
very interested. There was bad feeling about this particular visitor,
it seemed, not that Mrs F. had told *her*, she'd got it from her Gran,
down in Burtersett. She was here to lay claim to her property, Gran
reckoned, with that friend who'd been found dead at Foggett's not

156

yet cold in her grave, and the police still meithering Bayleses about
Daffy. That's what she'd heard, anyway.

Above her head, Grace, entirely peaceful now and deeply warmed
by a miraculous flooding of interior light, was going through her
devotions. 'Send out Thy light and Thy truth,' she hummed, making
up her own little tune. 'Let them lead me, let them lead me to Thy
holy hill.'

Heather, reporting to Mrs Fawcett, could hear a faint singing
filtering down through the floorboards. 'Screw loose?' she mouthed
to her interested employer, drilling an imaginary hole in her head
with a grubby forefinger.

Grace ate a large breakfast. She had not bothered to look for a place
to dine, last night. She had been tired and the weather discouragingly
windy and wet, so instead she had eaten fruit and biscuits in front of
the television. Mrs Fawcett had brought in a cup of Ovaltine on her
way to bed.

'More toast?' she asked now, smoothing down the front of her
overall. She was short and square with a massive bust which she
kept patting reassuringly, as if asking how it was getting on.

Grace could have managed another slice, but she said no. She
had a doctor's appointment in two weeks' time and she would
almost certainly be weighed. She did not understand Mrs Fawcett's
unfriendliness but she thought, perhaps, that the woman was determined to get her money's-worth from her late unseasonal visitor.
The rate she had quoted on the telephone was considerably higher
than they had paid last time. 'I wondered, Mrs Fawcett,' she asked
pleasantly, determined to ignore the coldness, 'if you could suggest
where I might eat tonight? I've jotted a few places down, from that
guide in the lounge, but is there anywhere you would recommend?'

'Where were you thinking of going? Some places have already
closed for the season.'

She passed over the list she had made. Mrs Fawcett frowned
over it, stroking her bust again, then the thick coarse hairs on her
chin. Instinctively, Grace's hand crept up to her own face and she
remembered how Buckle stared at her whenever they met. Was it the
faint shadow on her upper lip, so cruelly described in *Harriet Harker*?
'Well, you'd get a reasonable meal at Blackstone Hall. And Reed's
Country Hotel is all right, they've just done it up. Yes, I think I'd
go to Reed's. You'll need to book, though. Well, I'll clear away, if
you've finished.'

As she went through the door she stopped and threw a final remark
to Grace over her shoulder. 'Old Mr Reed used to own your place, as

a matter of fact,' she said, her voice harsh and accusing, 'but perhaps you already knew?'

'*My place?*'

'The cottage, up at Park Head, where your friend – '

'Oh yes, yes,' Grace interrupted hastily.

'His son waits on, some nights, though they don't really get on, him and his father. Funny family.'

There was a pay-phone in the front hall of the farmhouse and Grace used it to book a table at Reed's before she went back upstairs. It seemed that Mrs Fawcett knew that she had been Anna's particular friend. Perhaps The Girls had told her. But how, exactly, did she know that Grace had inherited The Rock, and why should she be so very hostile? Now she thought about it, it seemed bizarre that the woman had not offered some kind of condolence, however formal, when they had first met. After all, she had last come here the very week of Anna's death, and she would have known about that abortive Tuesday visit, from The Girls. They used to discuss their plans for the day over breakfast, consult her on routes, places to visit. She had been all friendliness then.

Anna had been murdered most brutally and thus Grace had lost the closest friend of her life, her best *loved* friend, after Daddie. It was true that Anna had never been very popular at school, which was when Grace had been closest to her. The other girls had never warmed to her, somehow, probably because they resented her brains. 'Selfish' was the word that had stuck, unfairly, surely. It wasn't selfish when a person struggled to survive after a body blow such as she and Guy had received. And Anna had not merely survived, she had triumphed.

The triumphs had brought glamour and money, important new friends like Julia Wragg and Sir Enoch Pritchard, administrator of the award, all those writing people. But Grace had always been the closest friend and now she had come back to this place so beloved of Anna much earlier than anyone could have expected, and with a courage that could have only come from the Lord, because she wanted to take Anna's home and Anna's adopted people to herself. And yet this woman seemed not to understand, seemed almost to hate her.

Buckle, she recalled, had told her of some of the local police's difficulties, when they had set about making their enquiries up here. The people were tight-lipped and unhelpful, it seemed, they had 'closed ranks' when questioned, that was the phrase he had used.

She thought about it as she brushed her teeth and put her walking shoes on, preparing to go out for the day. The dales were wide and stretched across endless miles but their actual population was thin.

Big news travelled quickly in such remote areas and with it, no doubt, ill-informed gossip. According to Breda, Buckle himself had actually considered the possibility of Grace herself being somehow involved in Anna's death, and if he could have conceived such a theory there was no telling what Mrs Fawcett might be thinking, especially of someone like Grace who, like Anna had before her, would come and stay at The Rock as a wealthy 'incomer'. That was the word here for people who greedily bought up second homes, then left them empty, for months on end.

Had the police considered that angle, she wondered, as they had turned over possibilities? Buckle, in attempting to explain all the possible motives to her, had certainly not mentioned it. In parts of Wales she knew that there was tremendous ill-feeling against incomers, she had discussed it with The Girls who had considered buying a cottage themselves, near Barmouth. People who had bought their way into the community had had their possessions vandalised, their actual houses burned. Could it be that some sick person had actually watched Anna as she played house at The Rock, some deprived, tormented soul who felt that her lot was rightly their own, and had been wrested from them? If only she could talk to somebody about the killer, and about what must have been in his mind, calmly, without weeping. If only somebody would *listen*. Buckle, now, seemed rather to be humouring her, she felt, and Ba, though she took Grace very seriously, clearly had her own private views. Marian simply treated her as the household pet. 'Good old Grace,' she would boom infuriatingly, at the end of any conversation, apropos of nothing at all.

She drove slowly over Buttertubs and past the layby where a few cars were parked, their owners staring down into the fearful echoing holes, small children tugging to be released, tired mothers snapping and pulling them to heel. At the bottom of the last hill she must signal left, then try to remember how to find Anna's hidden lane. But her courage suddenly deserted her and she turned right instead, in search of a tea-room in the next village along the dale, where she had spent several pleasant afternoons with The Girls. At the thought of The Rock her heart had suddenly started that curious sick thudding which had first sent her to Dr Lucas. Before making her pilgrimage she must feel calmer than this.

She soon found the tea-room, a converted brick chapel right on the road, ugly externally, with mean little windows and a ridiculously pedimented entrance, but inside freshly whitewashed and airy, with a selection of books on the area for sale, and pretty craft items decorating the walls. She had bought a corn dolly there last time, for Mrs Lumb,

159

Marian grinningly reprimanding her, such things being 'pagan', she claimed.

On a post, stuck in some rough grass by the door, a red and white notice said 'For Sale, A & D Black, Richmond'. But there were several cars parked along the verge and she could smell coffee, and hear china rattling. She went in, found a table and ordered a scone and hot chocolate. She might walk after she had been to look at The Rock, and this would do for lunch. 'I see you're selling up,' she said chattily to the teenager who brought her order, a red-faced bosomy long-legged girl with a two-inch pelmet of black skirt just showing below a baggy jumper, and she smiled at her, hoping she might be remembered, from her visits with The Girls. It was reassuring to be recognised.

The smile was returned, but blankly. 'Oh, yeah.' The girl's voice was whiny South London. 'We're moving to the Isle of Wight, Dad's bought a business. He's quite happy here but Mum wants to get back south; she says it's too cold up here, she doesn't like the winters.'

'Do *you* want to go?'

She shrugged. 'Dunno. Don't mind, really. There's more work down there, I suppose.'

'Do you – '

'Oh, 'scuse me . . .' and the girl's eyes flicked across the room to a table full of dirty cups and saucers where three sweaty young males in steaming anoraks and muddy boots had just sat down. 'Better get on . . .'

Grace smiled and sipped her chocolate, watching the girl totter away on high-heeled boots. Nobody ever seemed to have any time.

The wall opposite her, over the main door, still had the patchwork quilt they had all admired pinned up. The squares were irregularly arranged and of different sizes, obviously cut from random scraps of material. What was striking was the colour scheme which was entirely green but ranging from palest eau-de-nil through the turquoises and emeralds to a deep, blackish silky aquamarine. 'How marvellous,' Ba had said, 'it looks as if all the colour's drained to the bottom.' And Grace, proud of her bit of knowledge, had told them about a recent Lit. and Phil. lecture she had been to, about the way quilt-making could have a serious philosophy behind it, and how a person's whole life and beliefs could be sewn and presented in a patchwork such as this.

'Good old Grace,' and Marian, not listening, had examined the price-ticket. At a hundred and fifty pounds, she had declared loudly, no passing tourist was going to buy such a thing. Now Grace did, writing out her cheque for the astonished teenager among the cake crumbs. Dad got a ladder, climbed up and unhitched it from its moorings and it was rolled up and stuffed into a large black bin-liner.

Green had been one of Anna's favourite colours. Before Guy's death and all the black, she had invariably worn either yellow or green. She would have loved this beautiful quilt. Grace was taking it to The Rock. It was a love gift, for the house.

She left her car on the only straight bit of road she could find, near the seat Anna had erected, in memory of Guy, locked everything up and started walking, the quilt stuffed under her arm. On each side of the track the fells swept away, straw-coloured now as the year slowly died. High stone walls cut off the nearer view though there were occasional gaps from which short sheep-bitten turf rolled steadily back, down to the hidden river in the valley bottom which tumbled unseen through the glory of the late autumn trees, its rush faint from up here, more like the swishing of cars on a rainy night, along their main road at home.

She did not stop at Anna's red gate, looking resolutely away from the bit of house that showed through the trees, the massively slabbed roof, the twisted chimney stack, a casualty of lightning, Anna had told her, half a century ago. First she would visit Park Head and speak to Mrs Peacock, ask about John. She had one of her new business cards in her pocket.

The farm was long and low with a stone cow-house attached to one end, a taller stone barn on the other, breaking the line. It lay across the river and to get to it she had to walk over an ancient bridge that shot over the water with amazing sharpness, like a perfect half hoop. It was the width of a single car and she could see one parked outside the house, a rusty dented Vauxhall about fifteen years old, judging by the registration. Daddie had taught her how to work the years out. When she was a child they had done it on long car journeys, to pass the time.

Behind the house, dun-coloured treeless moors swept away on all sides, the brown shot through here and there with greenish streaks where water obviously trickled down from the tops. All the streams in the valley must drain into the river here, but first, she judged, they must find their way round the farmhouse, underneath it, perhaps. Its stone walls were covered with cracked rendering the colour of porridge, and from ground level swathes of green damp were creeping ever upwards in great mossy triangles.

She pushed a gate open and trod down long thick grass that had obviously once been a lawn, to reach the door. Nobody came to her knock so she peered through the letter-box: black and white plastic tiles lining a narrow lobby, a row of coat hooks with a couple of green waterproofs hanging up, a stale smell. The windows were tiny but low and, stepping to one side, she bent down, squinnying through. Now she could see a dark interior taken up with a bulky three-piece suite covered in green stretch Dralon, a massive television set, wall to wall carpet patterned in hectic swirls of brown and white. The heavy stone fireplace was identical to Anna's at The Rock but the original cast-iron interior had been ripped out and replaced by a coal-effect electric fire. It was all very neat, very clean.

Straightening up she knocked again. The brass clapper clattered noisily against the door, echoing round the narrow valley, and a dog barked in one of the outhouses. Disappointed, she moved away, staring round again. In the cleft of the brown hills a large bird was moving in slow easy rings, planing on the air, dipping and disappearing. She felt frustrated. Now she wished she had brought flowers so that at least she could have left something for Mrs Peacock, and a little note with them, perhaps, scribbled on the back of one of her cards.

As she stood looking up the valley a man came out of the barn, a dog at his heels. He was gangling and tall with a very large head and a ruddy weather-beaten complexion but, as he came close to her, she saw unexpectedly fine features, a straight, rather sharp nose, a wide mouth with a humorous curl to the lips, large brown eyes, the left much paler than the right. It at once reminded her of Daddie, whose eyes had been oddly matched too. He was wearing a shapeless cap which he raised slightly in greeting, uncovering dark curly hair, thick, quite luxuriant hair for a man of his age. He would be about forty, she thought.

He held out his hand and told her that he was Maurice Peacock. His greeting was firm, not like that of Buckle whose small limp fingers had somehow got embarrassingly tangled up in her own much larger ones. 'I'm very sorry,' she began, uncertain. 'I just came to have a word with Mrs Peacock,' and, fishing in the pocket of her anorak, she gave him her new business card. Suddenly, she felt foolish.

He glanced at it, then gave it back, embellished with an oily thumb print. 'Grace Bradley . . . you're Anna's friend, aren't you? I remember your name.' In the deep quiet of the little valley he flushed a slow, deep scarlet.

'I'm sorry,' Grace repeated, at a loss; and now she felt as if the terrible death was all her fault, in the way it had broken open this sealed and secret place, staining the loveliness, bringing the terror and the anger. Anna was dead and Guy was dead, so were their father and mother, and Stephen was sick and out of reach, playing some strange, silly game with her. Everyone who had ever loved Anna was either dead or gone away, except for Grace. She alone remained, the living link, and she felt that all the weight of death was resting on her now, like a great stone. 'I'm sorry,' she said again.

He said, 'My sister-in-law's in Darlington just now. Young John's with her. They'll not be coming back for a while.'

'I see. And how is John?'

'Well, you know . . . he's a grand lad.' She noticed that he did not actually answer her question but took refuge instead in contemplating his boots. Like his head, his feet were unduly large.

Buckle had said that the boy was still in deep shock and not talking much sense. She had thought of Guy when she heard. Now, as she stood in the deep grass by the blistered garden gate, feeling the sadness of the place, Guy and the Peacock child became one. She saw the shovel of coal in the drawing room doorway at Firs, the boy jerking away from the cottage window and falling down, Anna's bloody image branded everlastingly on his eyes, policemen breaking into The Rock with their cameras and their clipboards, ·Daddie, removing Mrs Beardmore's rings.

'I come each day to see to the animals,' the man explained, 'and to check round, you know. I check your place too, most mornings. The police asked me to, and it's as well to be sure. There've been some funny folk around, since. All's well down there, though.'

'That's very kind,' Grace said. *Your place* . . . So he too knew that The Rock was hers. 'It's odd,' she went on, trying to sound very casual, 'but everyone seems to know already that Anna left the cottage to me in her will.'

'Yes. Well, folk gossip, you know. It's the way of the world, isn't it?' Then he looked defensive suddenly. 'I've said nothing myself,' he assured her, 'nothing at all. Come to think of it, I can't think how I *do* know, now. I suppose one of the police must have let it out, or perhaps one of the newspaper men. They all did such a lot of talking.' He pushed back his cap and scratched his nose. 'Not that it makes it *right*, not a thing like that, someone's private business.'

'*No*.'

She sensed that he himself did not ever talk very much. His big peaceful countenance and his slow speech felt part of these wide fells, this unending bubble of water over untroubled stones, this sky. He was a bachelor, she remembered, and lived on his own further down the dale. 'Maurice Peacock, farmer, Low Farm, Swaledale.' It had been on Marian's computerised funeral list. He was the brother of Michael Peacock, the boy's father, the man who had died of a heart attack last year. The mother had become depressed, she remembered.

'A sweet man,' Anna had told her, definitely enthusiastic; she always preferred men to women. 'Very shy, salt of the earth type, do anything for you.' He had put shelves up at The Rock, fixed curtain rails, mended things. Typically, she had soon got him organised, and Grace could see how. There was a softness about him, an attractive uncertainty.

She said, 'Actually, I've got something here for the cottage. Could you let me in for a minute?' She had not brought the key, not intending to go inside this first time, merely to look, from a safe distance. But perhaps . . . with him . . . The deep peace she had felt yesterday as she knelt and prayed was with her still and this quiet, soft-spoken country man felt part of it.

He replied, 'Yes, surely, I'll just fetch the keys. I put a good padlock on for you. Hope that was all right?' But she had caught the flicker of surprise on his face. 'You're quite happy to go in there, are you?' he said awkwardly. 'I mean . . . you know.'

'Well, I think so,' she said, then, suddenly fearful, 'Is it . . . *all right?*'

'Oh yes, yes. The police won't be coming back, they've finished. It's all in order for you. Has been for a while.'

'Who sorted things out, Maurice? I may call you that, I hope. And I'm Grace, by the way.'

He smiled shyly. 'Yes, I remember, from Anna. She was a grand lass.' Suddenly the wide mouth quivered slightly.

Grace saw and prayed, *Don't let him say anything else about her, not anything*. In the silence they stared at one another across the gate. Anna was present.

After a few seconds he said, very matter of fact, 'I saw to things, like, when the police had finished. I really didn't know when you might come, to look the place over. It really is all right.'

She was grateful to him. Just what 'things' he had had to see to she dared not ask. All she remembered from the anonymous bundle of news cuttings was that the cottage had been thoroughly cleansed, stripped of all clues, presumably by whoever had killed Anna. 'Scoured' was the word used in the shortest, least sensational report.

He asked her to sit in his car while he locked up and found the key to The Rock. As she walked towards it the collie dashed past her, jumped into the back and sat erect, its nose shoved through a gap at the top of a window, yelping, eager to be off. She sat in front, nursing the rolled-up quilt between her knees. The ancient vehicle smelt strongly of dung and dog.

He apologised for it as they bumped down the track. 'It's a bit mucky in here,' he muttered, then he fell silent and concentrated on the driving.

'You've got the same cassette player as me,' she said at last. Now, as they slowed down and halted by Anna's red gate, she was beginning to feel very slightly sick.

'Oh, aye,' he said, glancing down at it. 'I got that put in specially. I've not much time for telly, don't have one, as a matter of fact, but I like listening to music. Do you watch telly much yourself, like?'

'Sometimes. I've got this tape too,' and she picked up a cassette of Bach's Double Violin Concerto. Anna had given it to her last birthday, together with a very literary collection of short stories. She had never given up attempting to educate her.

'Oh aye,' Maurice said, glancing at it. 'Your friend gave me that. It's got some bonny tunes.'

The field between the lane and the cottage was deep in mud so they walked across, leaving the car by the gate. Maurice carried the quilt. Before unlocking the door he went round looking in all the outhouses. 'Just making sure,' he said, coming back with a reassuring little grin.

'What about?'

'Oh, you get people sleeping rough round here sometimes, but it's all OK. When it's raining these old barns are a lot drier than a tent.' He was not going to tell her that he had called the police twice, to look at what someone had left behind. They had been annoyed, driving all the way down the dale to inspect bottles, cigarette packets and a load of shit. They'd hardly looked. After they had gone he'd felt foolish. Yet they were leading a murder enquiry. He had thought himself that nothing should be overlooked, even if it was only campers. It might not have been, that was the point.

While he went through his bunch of keys Grace stood behind him, clutching the black plastic roll to her breast like a shield. Anna's new wooden name-board was still in place but someone had daubed 'Foggett's' across it in white paint.

'Do the police know about that?' she said, pointing. She was shaking, now the time had come for the opening of the door.

'Oh yes.'

'What did they say?'

'Nothing much. They didn't seem bothered, really. As I told you, there've been some funny folk around lately. It'll be kids, that will. Nothing better to do.'

'What sort of people have been here, Maurice?'

'Oh, you know.'

She waited.

'Newspaper men mainly,' he went on, after a pause. 'They ask all the questions. One man really got up my nose – excuse my expression. Came round here one day, wanting a "story", asking to see inside the house. I couldn't get rid of him. In the finish I threatened to put the dog on him.'

'You don't remember his name?'

Maurice took his cap off and ran his fingers through his curls. 'Ee, you know, I don't. I think the paper was something like the *North-Eastern Gazette*. He said he'd done a long article about your friend, interviewed her about her writing and that.' Now they were so close to going inside, he too was getting nervous, for her, she felt. Touchingly, he was trying to depersonalise the situation.

She said, 'I think I read that. She sent me a copy. But you don't actually remember his name?' She would like to talk to this man about his hours with Anna, for her book, in spite of the nuisance he had apparently made of himself. The Girls had mentioned him, that he had wept at the funeral.

'Ee, I don't. Thin-faced feller, he was, a very bad colour. Not a well man, I thought. I didn't care for him, though, no, I didn't. Come to think of it, it was him told me the cottage was coming to you. Yes, it *was* him, up at the Ram. He did his drinking up there, stayed there some nights.' He sniffed disapprovingly. 'Tell you the truth, I really didn't care for any of those press people, trying to be clever. A bad thing like we've had here's better left to the proper authorities, I think. I'm sure they're doing their level best to get to the bottom of it,' though she thought that he did not sound quite convinced.

'Now then, here we are,' and he bent down with his key. Pushing the door open he stood aside for her to go first. She could see the tiny kitchen, shining and immaculate with its rows of blue and white china, its pine tops, its brand new Swan kettle and, framed in the far doorway, the big writing table covered with neat stacks of paper, beyond, through the window, the great waterfall crashing down, the glowing tree. She looked sharply away. *Dear Holy Spirit*, she prayed, *Source of all strength, all comfort, uphold me now.*

But she could not go inside. It was as if opening that door had unleashed something she had no strength to penetrate, some noisome, terrible presence, some thickness. At that moment she did not want merely to weep, but to scream, to release the voice of her own immense pain whose agony was being somehow choked to death deep inside her. 'I think I'll wait out here,' she said in a whisper, 'or perhaps we could just leave the quilt in the kitchen, for now.'

Maurice put a hand lightly on her arm; then he took the bundle.

166

'No, wait on,' he said, 'I'll take it up. I'll not be two minutes,' and he went inside.

In his absence she turned her back determinedly on the house and stared across an empty field, seeing, instead, the running white letters that had obliterated 'The Rock', restoring the place to what it had always been, to what it must remain. Anna had come and gone and there was bad feeling about her; perhaps, already, murmurings about Grace too. Should she sell the place, not put anything about it in her book?

She did not always understand the Lord's guiding. He had led her here and she had believed, until they had reached the actual threshold, that she had strength to go in. But when Maurice had pushed the door open it had been all devilishness, and heavy darkness.

He was soon back, with the black bin-liner folded up neatly. Carefully he locked up again, secured the new padlock, then guided her along the edge of the muddy field towards the gate. 'It's a bonny quilt, that,' he said. 'It looks grand on the old double bed. I slept in a bed like that when I was a child.'

The tears were running down her face. He saw, but said nothing, merely increased, very slightly, the pressure of his hand upon her arm as they approached the car. The sheepdog barked and scrabbled at the narrow slit at the top of the window, trying vainly to get its nose through. 'Dry up!' he shouted harshly, opening the passenger door to let her in.

She glanced across at him as he drove silently back along the lane to the spot where she had parked her car, by Guy's seat, seeing how the sunshine furred the little gold hairs along his arms. She wished that, in the field, he had stopped and put them round her, given her comfort.

The Ram Inn was quite a famous drinking place according to Maurice who sat in his car and chatted to her for nearly an hour before they parted at the seat, but as she drove up to it now she couldn't really understand the attraction. It was merely a rather decrepit-looking, overgrown cottage with a vast car-park at the side, abandoned on the edge of the road with bare brown moors stretching away on all sides and a muddy farm track leading up to the front door, which was flanked by a row of overflowing dustbins. The peace of the place was marred by the constant thrumming of a noisy electric generator. But it was the highest pub in the county, according to Maurice, in the entire north-east, some claimed, which gave it a certain distinction, and for that reason trippers stopped off there, just so that they could say they had been. The landlord did a good trade in T-shirts and embossed tankards, sold more of them than pints, he observed wryly. Reeds owned it now, he said, the same family which owned the country hotel below Buttertubs, where she had booked her meal. For a while the son Gary had been given the job of running it but the arrangement hadn't lasted very long. Apparently the father and the son had never really got on and old Mr Reed had more or less washed his hands of him now, though he still hung round the Ram. It had been a case of too much money too soon in life, an expensive education, two marriages in three years, heavy drinking bouts, a near-fatal car crash. 'You'll see him around,' Maurice told her. 'He's a good-looking chap, got one of them tans. That's all the foreign holidays. I don't know how he screws the money out of his father. The old man's very tight with it.'

Grace asked if it was Gary who had wanted to live at The Rock, that Mrs Fawcett had mentioned some family quarrel, about the sale of the property. He seemed embarrassed. 'Yes, but it was a daft idea from the start. The boy did want it, when he was running the Ram. It was nearby, you see, and there aren't many properties between Park Head and the pub, well, nothing you could really live in. Gary fancied it. He was keen to have his own place and he'd stayed there a lot as a child. His aunt used to live there, Mr Reed senior's older sister. When she died she left it to her brother though she'd always said their Gary was to have it. Nobody ever understood that. There was a real argy-bargy about that house. The old man never went near it himself, just left it to fall down. It got into a terrible state, over the years. Your friend spent thousands on it, new roof, the lot. Well, you'll know that.

'But Gary was always going back there. I used to see him. He'd bring friends with him and they'd swim, in the pool. They camped out in it some nights, with oil lamps. I saw them in there. Nobody bothered. But then the old man needed some extra cash, when he bought the hotel under Buttertubs, and he suddenly put it on the market. Gary begged him not to, said he and his friend would buy it between them, really begged him, folk say. But Reed said if he wanted it he could have it at the market price, said he'd got through enough of his money to buy twenty cottages, over the years. So it was put up for auction and your friend got it instead. They sold it off in the Function Room at the Ram.'

Grace made an embarrassingly noisy entrance because the front door of the pub appeared to be stuck, swollen with damp, she imagined. From the outside the whole place looked damp and there was bright green moss growing on the rough jutting boulders that formed the lower front walls. She wrestled with a massive doorknob, having to use both hands to twist it round, then finally leaned against the door with her whole weight, whereupon it gave suddenly, so that she more or less fell inside.

At the bar counter conversation ceased abruptly and three men perched on stools swivelled round and stared at her. Two more, sitting with pint mugs on opposite sides of an inglenook over a fire of logs, also looked up and ran their eyes over her. In a corner some youths in jeans and studded jackets were playing darts in a fug of cigarette smoke. After the briefest glance they went back, uninterested, to their game, one bending to feed coins into a machine, producing a burst of pop music. The only positive greeting Grace received was from an old dog, which got up from the fireside as she entered and ambled across the gritty slabbed floor, sniffing up her skirt. 'Whist,' the owner grunted from his chair, and the dog, cowering, slunk back to its place at his feet.

Nervous, she put on her brightest face, walked across to the bar and ordered a shandy. The man behind the counter grinned, rather slyly she thought, at his three other customers, as he set up a glass and mixed the drink. They remained silent and staring while she was alongside, only taking up their conversation again when she had retreated to a chilly corner at the opposite end of the room from the blazing fire. Then they resumed, a slow three-cornered drone that seemed to be all about tup prices and the legs of sheep.

It was cold away from the fire and rain was now lashing against the windows. Pewter-coloured cloud had settled very low on the fells and the road she had travelled on was fast disappearing into it. Up here it might easily be midwinter, and the sunlit valley she had left so recently imagination only. It was a depressing place and she rather wished she had not come. Did tourists really flock here in their hundreds, as Maurice had said? Yet there were the T-shirts and the crested tankards, displayed over the bar, and bright red car stickers that announced 'Hitchhikers do it at the Ram'. And Anna had often come up here for a drink, apparently. She'd called it her 'local', seemed to have liked it, for some reason.

Between Grace's corner and the door to the outside was an untidy noticeboard covered with curling bits of paper. Picking up her glass she walked over to it, turning her back on the drinkers at the bar. A sheet of bright blue notepaper gave details of a darts tournament in smudged Biro; next to it was a list of local church services for the month of November and underneath a leaflet about a choral concert which was to happen that night in Richmond. She hoped Ba would come and stay with her up here, perhaps at a time when Marian was away on one of her nursing assignments. She was interested in music and this concert was the sort of thing they could have enjoyed together. Now she was alone Grace needed someone to share things with.

Her eyes moved down over the noticeboard, and she suddenly saw Stephen, not a photograph but a pen and ink drawing, slightly cartoony in style but undeniably his face. She read 'Police Notice . . . wanted in connection with . . . death . . . Anna Beardmore . . . at the house formerly known as Foggett's . . .' But she turned away without actually reading it through, her eyes pricking. From the inglenook the old man with the dog was peering across at her.

'Would you like another?' The barman had come over to her corner with a cloth to wipe the table, and was offering to take her glass.

'No, thank you, but . . . there was something . . .' After all, it was why she had come up here and their silent hostility had merely hardened her resolve. She wasn't going to leave without trying to extract some information. From her pocket she took one of her new business cards and gave it to him. 'I was Anna Beardmore's friend,' she said. 'I came to look at the house, down at Park Head. She bequeathed it to me.' All unnecessary facts, she knew, for she had the strongest sense that this man, everybody in the room, for that matter, already knew everything about her. They would have heard she was around, from Mrs Fawcett, no doubt. They had probably watched her drive up, through one of these dirty little windows.

'I want to get in touch with one of the reporters who came up here,' she told him. 'I need some information, for a book I'm working on. He was one of the people who came after my friend's death.' She found she could say the phrase quite calmly and unemotionally now. God's peace had not left her, she was stronger, today.

The landlord, looking at her card, pursed his lips. The pop record on the machine had finished and the darts players were up at the bar, waiting for refills. There was a silence again in which she felt everyone was listening to them. 'Do you know his name?' the man asked.

'No, and that's the problem. But he came to the funeral, apparently.' She paused. 'I was unable to be present myself. I'd rather like to thank him. Also, he'd done a feature on her for his newspaper, the *North-Eastern Gazette*, I think it was. I need to talk to him about it.' Only now, as she spelt it out, did she realise the good sense of her decision to write something. She had known Anna since they were five years old, both as a friend at school and as the next-door neighbours' child. The families had been on holiday together. Over the winter she would look at some of Anna's very early diaries, her own school scrap-books, perhaps, and the Bradley family albums so carefully kept by Daddie. It could be a simple, loving, childhood memory, it need be neither distasteful nor dishonouring, and it could end before The Tragedy. Anything about Yorkshire could go in an appendix. She said, 'Do you keep a register of the people who stay here?'

But the landlord shook his head. 'Ne'er. It's just the one room, you see, nothing fancy, like. I remember the bloke you mean, though, thin feller, big drinker.' He smiled to himself. 'By God, that business in t' dale certainly brought folk out of the woodwork, and could they put it away . . .'

'Yes. I imagine it did,' she said primly. But her voice was hostile, she was issuing a warning, draping a protective cloak over Anna's memory, and the man clearly understood. Disconcerted, he looked away and began to rub vigorously at the sticky rings on the table top.

In the bar there was a sudden rattle of bottles, then a crate was dumped on the counter. 'Gary,' he called across, 'you remember that bloke who stayed here a few nights, after, y'know . . .' and he frowned, thumbing in the general direction of the front window.'That man from the *Gazette*, that reporter. You don't remember his name, do you?' and, giving the table a final polish, he returned to the bar. Grace heard muffled whispering, then an extremely small man came round the end of the counter, crossed the room and seated himself at her table.

'Gary Reed,' he said, extending his right hand. The left held a glass which he placed in front of him and immediately drank from.

He was neat and compact with pretty, almost elfin features, small dark eyes, turned-up nose and a girlish rosebud for a mouth. It felt chilly and dank in Grace's corner and the landlord was muffled up in cords and an Aran sweater. But this man wore thin summer trousers and an electric blue short-sleeved shirt with crossed tennis racquets embroidered in white on the breast pocket, clothes more suited for Mediterranean yachting, she thought, than for waiting on in a windswept hikers' pub, fifteen hundred feet up on the Pennines. His skin, of which she could see a considerable amount, for the shirt was half unbuttoned, was deeply and evenly tanned. He talked very fast, a curious fixed smile on the doll-like mouth, not answering her query about the newspaper man from the *North-Eastern Gazette* but asking questions of his own, about The Rock. He had heard a rumour that she was selling it and that this was why she had come up to the dale. He would very much like to make an offer. If they could agree a price privately it would obviously save in estate agents' fees. 'Of course,' he said, the rigid smile still in position, 'I realise that you'll need to think about it, and there's no hurry at this end. Anyhow, I'm having another. What are you drinking?' And he got up and went to help himself, from the bar.

'No, nothing thank you,' she called after him, but he was back almost immediately, with whisky for them both.

'Mr Reed,' she said, not touching her glass. 'I'm afraid you've been misinformed.'

'It's Gary, call me Gary.'

'The thing is, I'm not selling the cottage. Not yet, anyway. I've made no long-term plans.'

'Oh . . . *really?*' The facial glow faded slightly. 'I'd definitely heard you wanted to get rid of it.'

'I can't think how. I'm sorry.'

'I see,' and he paused, drumming his fingers on the table-top. Then he leaned forward, keen again. 'But you *might?*' He was very eager, his dark eyes bright and glossy, his small, even teeth very white against the deep tan.

She said slowly, 'Well yes, eventually. But I'm afraid I can't make you any promises. It's much too early to decide anything.'

Now he leaned right across the table, taking her left hand in both of his. His hands were very small, she noticed, and compact, like the rest of him, with short fingers but disproportionately wide, squarish palms, the nails very clean and closely clipped.

'I understand,' he said, with a sudden gush of emotion in his voice that rather repulsed her. 'But if you do decide to part with it, let me know. Promise?'

She nodded vaguely but said nothing. His instant friendliness, his set, ruthless smile rather reminded her of Julia Wragg, pouring out her instant oodles of love. As she silently contemplated her whisky she could think of nothing so much as of a large doll; and she remembered her childish disappointment when she had first discovered that her own dolls, on guilty inspection, had possessed no genitalia, merely an unexciting non-cloven pinkness between plastic thighs. This man too struck her as curiously sexless. He had been married twice, Maurice had told her, but there had been no children, both marriages lasting months rather than years; and the 'friend' with whom he had planned to share The Rock was definitely male, a Michael something or other. She pondered, looking at his clean neat fingers cupped round the whisky tumbler. Could he have killed Anna?

Then the sheer ridiculousness of it actually made her blush. She felt the blood creeping up her neck and, instinctively, her hands went up. And yet, though only momentarily, according to Breda Smith, Buckle had theorised along these lines about *her*. At the beginning of the enquiry absolutely no one could be ruled out, she had said.

172

Therefore, were her own thoughts, now, so outrageous? Not this man, perhaps, but *such* a man, someone whose ancestry had established them immovably among these unchanging hills, someone who had been forced to watch an intruder come in and steal the desire of his heart, pluck casually away that which, beyond everything, spoke peace to him. She saw again, as she stared at the face opposite, Anna's smart carved name-board defaced, the ugly white letters dripping down. Buckle should know that had been done. He should know, too, about the intense local feeling against Anna and her kind, about the auction in this very building, about Gary Reed's desperate efforts to buy his father out, how he had always loved The Rock, bathed in its waters, jumped down over its great stones. Not this man, perhaps, but *such* a man. She should tell him too about the strange lack of sexuality Reed presented. Such inadequacies, Marian had informed her, though only through heavy, pink-faced hints, lay at the heart of most sexual crimes, including murder. They would find, she had boomed confidently and entirely without pity, that poor Anna was the victim of . . . what had the phrase been . . . some 'lonely twisted little pervert.'

Grace asked, 'Did you know my friend?' And she watched him. It was obviously quite the wrong question, as she had rather hoped, for he tossed back his whisky and jerked to his feet so suddenly that he knocked his chair over, the weird flood of intimacy draining away as suddenly as it had come. 'No, I didn't. I saw her sometimes when she came up here for a drink, but we never really talked.' His voice was quite different now, neutral, guarded, and his little shiny brown eyes slid away from her as she searched his face. He was disquieted.

She said, determined to get a response, 'Her death was an immense shock to me, Mr Reed, as you can well imagine, and so far, the police are quite baffled. They have no leads at all.'

'And is that part of this little project of yours, then? Jack tells me you're planning to do a book on her.' His voice was a sneer, now, but under the tan he had coloured up, she noticed.

'No, of course not. It's going to be a kind of childhood memoir, for her publishers. We'd known each other all our lives.'

'*Because the mountain grass/Cannot but keep the form/Where the mountain hare has lain . . .*' he murmured.

'I beg your pardon?'

'Oh, don't you recognise it? It's a bit of Yeats.' He was wide-eyed now, mocking her. 'Much more in my line of country than your friend's books, though I've read them, of course. But then, there's no money in poetry, or I suppose she would have written that, instead of the novels,' and he gave a nasty little laugh. 'Never mind the quality, feel the width, eh? Well, see you around, perhaps. I'd be interested to know what you decide to do about the house.'

But as he went away she felt he was entirely *un*interested, that he had simply worked out some kind of secret personal anger on her, in the course of their bizarre conversation, which had moved in minutes from that initial cloying friendliness to an open hostility.

Might he be at his father's hotel this evening? That was where she would have expected him to be now, not hanging round here, heaving beer crates in and out of the cellar. He had once had management of the Ram, Maurice had told her, but he'd not been up to the job and an outside landlord had been brought in. So how did he pass his days, and where was his 'friend'? What had he been doing at the time Anna was murdered? Had anyone actually checked?

She left her seat again and walked to the door, stopping in front of the tatty notice-board, pretending to study it. A postcard in one corner advertised mountain bikes for hire in Hawes. *Bicycles* was the name of that horrific short story Anna had written one long vacation for a university magazine. Grace had typed it out for her on the big Olivetti, at Daddie's shop. She'd told Ba all about it, one night when she'd been to The Girls' for supper. There was an awful irony about the plot for it was the story of what Ba called a 'serial killer'. Marian had gone off rather huffily to prepare the meal. She always had a book on the go but it was inevitably some devotional work, and, though she had never said so, Grace suspected that she shared Dr Beardmore's extreme evangelical view, that mere 'story' was somehow suspect, and ungodly. She saw no purpose in drawing what Ba called 'life lessons' from mere works of fiction, 'mere' being one of her words.

In *Bicycles* a mild, inoffensive elderly man had committed a series of gruesome murders, one every five years, the fit always being brought on by the onset of warm weather, the start of the cricket season, and, in particular, the sight of young girls on bicycles. Grace didn't remember the dénouement very clearly, nor indeed whether the man was ever caught. What she did remember was that he had been quietly absorbed into the community during the years that elapsed between his spectacular outbreaks of violence, keeping the score for the local cricket team, growing prize vegetables for the annual produce show, and augmenting his old-age pension by repairing punctures for the neighbourhood children, mending their brakes, adjusting their gears. Inevitably, his young victims rode into his blameless life on bicycles.

Some murders were never solved, Ba had said so. In her library there were books about such cases in which the killer, like the man in Anna's story, simply melted back into his ordinary life, unmarked, unsuspected, believing, perhaps, when he read about his latest atrocity in the newspaper, that some other, wicked person was responsible. If such a man had murdered Anna he would kill again, in time, and after the same pattern, a similar motiveless, entirely spontaneous act growing out of his own ruthless inner logic, an act for which he would feel no guilt at all.

But Buckle, as well as talking to her about the psychopathic temperament, had talked too about motive, about greed and jealousy, about the destructive power of human love, concentrating on Stephen, one of her own loved ones. He could surely, with equal logic, she reflected, have turned his attentions to a man like Gary Reed.

Her eyes moved down from the postcard advertising mountain bikes till they rested on Stephen's face, in the police notice. But now she saw that it did not say 'police' but 'polite', and that the information below was not typed but very neatly printed, in black ink.

There was no way such a notice could be official. Someone, for their own perverted reasons, had done it themselves with immense care, come in here and pinned it up. Presumably the landlord hadn't looked at it carefully enough and thought it was the work of the local constabulary.

Bending down she removed the two drawing pins that held it to the frame and stuck them into the list of church services alongside. Then she removed the picture of Stephen, crumping it noisily in her hands while everyone in the room looked on.

Smiling round politely at them all she pushed the paper ball into the pocket of her anorak and walked out.

13

She decided not to go to Reeds that night. Her curious conversation with Gary Reed had unsettled her and, as she drove back to the farm, she decided she must write down what she could remember of it, to tell Buckle, for she felt that there was something wrong with it all, that none of it cohered. Then she started worrying about the evening ahead on her own account, and about eating alone in an intimidating hotel dining room. Reeds was expensive, she had gathered from Maurice, and rather showy, definitely the place of the moment. She was not sure she could face two or three solitary hours in such a place merely eating and drinking, spinning the time out to save face, a woman conspicuously alone. And her other fear now was that Gary Reed would seek her out.

Therefore she would not go. When she had washed and had her hour's rest upon the bed – a habit, now she lived alone, and something which helped to move the day along – she would phone the hotel and cancel her table. Then she would drive into Hawes and find something to eat there, a tea place, something quick. She would spend her evening reading Marian's book. Its title, *Solitariness*, was not promising, but Marian had enthused about it, the early life of some female church worker who was now prominent in ecclesiastical affairs in the north-west, a woman who had considered, but finally rejected, a monastic existence and who had had all sorts of 'adventures' along the way, according to Marian, including some kind of retreat on a remote Scottish island. Marian seemed to think her own celibacy was the final, approved state of affairs and, Grace suspected, wanted this for her also. And was Ba's marriage now regarded as a kind of temporary lapse, timely divorce intervening to save the situation, and to establish The Girls?

The farm was empty on her return. Heather went home in the afternoons and she had seen Mrs Fawcett's car parked outside a cottage on the main road, where a cousin lived. Before going up to her room she went to the pay-phone and cancelled her booking for the evening. Next to the unit was an ugly oak table with barley-sugar legs where bills for departing visitors were left on a plated silver tray. On

176

it she found a piece of paper headed 'Miss Bradley, phone message' in a looped, childish hand. She read, 'Mr Stephen Arnold telephoned. He has two tickets for the concert in Richmond. Please meet him in the theatre bar at seven o'clock. Yours and obliged, Heather Alderson.'

Slowly she mounted the ancient stone stairs and found her way along the dark passage to her room, staring all the time at the note. Stephen, always quietly spoken, had an infuriating habit of reducing the volume of his voice even more when using a telephone because he hated the instrument and only used it when absolutely necessary, to convey information, never to 'chat'. He must be Stephen 'Arnold'. Nobody else had this telephone number, apart from Mrs Lumb.

She looked at her watch. It was nearly four o'clock already and the drive along the deep country lanes to Richmond was inevitably slow, she remembered that from her visits there with The Girls. She would get ready now, then set off and find somewhere to eat in the town. Not that she expected to have much appetite. *Stephen* . . . The prospect of meeting him at last was already making her heart thud about, echoing inside her chest as if it were a hollow drum. Dr Lucas hadn't *said* so, but surely this was why she must take the yellow pills? Why did he treat her like a child still, never explaining? She would ask him about them, next time. She changed into her dressing gown and went along the passage to the guest bathroom. The brownish water that drizzled out of the tap was scorching hot but the pressure pathetically low, and the cast iron tub was huge. She left it running while she went back to put fresh clothes and shoes out, on the bed, and to fetch *Solitariness*. She had reached the point where Monica had been deposited on her island with a small tent and food for ten days in a cardboard box. Reading in the bath was soothing, and she wanted to drive calmly to her meeting with Stephen. She felt heady and light as she busied about, selecting matching separates and her new Liberty scarf from the wardrobe, Mother's pearls, her favourite, thick silver bangle and the new Bally shoes. Stephen was half a head taller than she was so there was no need to wear her usual flats tonight.

The bath was filling up so slowly that she abandoned the operation. There was no shower so she sat in a few gritty inches of water using an old enamel jug to sluice herself down. There was no time for *Solitariness*, she decided, abandoning the chilly bathroom rather thankfully and dressing in her room, in front of a rattling fan heater, though she would be interested, when she returned to the book, to know how Monica had coped with all the practical things on her island, the washing, the lavatory arrangements . . . She had always amused Anna, with her interest in these mundane affairs, on the rare occasions when they had discussed the actual mechanics of her stories. Anna had always told her that she could not make something she called 'the willing suspension of disbelief'. But now Ba had promised to help her with a reading programme; she was making her a book list. It was not that she wasn't *interested* but, in the past, Mother's illnesses had made that kind of thing difficult for her.

Before she left Fawcett's she tried phoning Heather at her grandmother's farm. They did bed and breakfast too, though only in the summer. The girl had left one of her brochures in the guest bedroom, in case Grace was interested, for another time.

She said, relieved when Heather herself answered the telephone – she had rather dreaded having to negotiate with the deaf grandmother – 'It's Grace Bradley, Heather. Thank you very much for the phone message. Er . . . I just wondered . . . are you sure about the *name*, dear? Was it Arnold? Or could it have been Allen, a Mr Allen?'

The girl hesitated. The man had whispered rather, and Mrs F's washer had been doing its fast spin at the time. 'Well I *thought* he said "Arnold",' she replied slowly, 'but there was noise going on in the kitchen. He didn't speak up too well, as a matter of fact, and he had a bit of a stutter . . . but I think he said "Arnold". Anyhow, he said to meet him at the theatre at seven o'clock, in the – '

'Yes, yes. I've got all that, Heather. That's fine. I know who it was, now. Goodbye, dear, and thank you ever so much.'

Gleeful, thrilled, she rang off, not wanting to prolong the conversation, eager to be on the road. When she left for home she would give Heather a generous tip. It *was* Stephen, with his telephone whisper, his stammer. Light-headed now, winged almost, she strapped herself into the driving seat of the Escort and moved bumpily down towards the main road, maddened by the slowness forced on her by the deeply-rutted track.

The journey to Richmond was even slower than she had expected because the dale was full of police cars, slewed up on to the narrow grass verges, and of uniformed officers with clipboards, talking to passing motorists. Eventually, just by the 'For Sale' notice outside the Coffee 'n' Crafts Cafe, where she had bought Anna's quilt, she herself was stopped. The young woman who spoke to her looked about sixteen years old, and put her questions with embarrassment. Did Grace own the car and what was her full name? Did she object to telling her where she had been and where she was going? Why was she staying in the dale at this particular time, and for how long?

She was obviously of no interest at all to them and almost immediately found herself being waved on rather irritably by a fat, bored-looking policeman who was stationed in the middle of the narrow road. But the sheer presence of all those official cars had given her a sick, uneasy feeling and she had felt immediate guilt as the uniformed teenager had gone, machine-like, down her standard list of questions. 'Just a routine check,' she had said when Grace, very tentatively, had asked what the questions were all about. But the answer did not somehow ring true. Could it be something to do with Anna? Had there been a fresh development? If there had, she would no doubt hear all from Mrs Fawcett, on her return.

Beyond the police block the roads were empty. The sky, clear again after the morning's rain, was already deepening towards evening and what traffic she saw was coming the other way, people leaving their work in the town and driving home leisurely to their snug villages, for the long, cosy evening indoors. She liked the unhurried feel of the place, the simple, low-lying cottages with their ancient slabbed fronts, the collie dogs lying across the doorways, the last-flowering geraniums on white-painted sills. Last time, with The Girls, she had felt she might one day call this 'home'. Now she was examining the thought again, though all was different and more complicated now, because Anna was dead. But Grace had The Rock, and all her fortune.

It was almost six o'clock by the time she had reached the centre of the town, parked in a side street and made her way across the vast cobbled market square, trying to remember how, from here, she would find her way to the theatre. She had been to it last time with The Girls, not to a show, merely to look round the place, tourist-fashion. Marian had read importantly from the guide book, informing them that it was one of the few remaining examples of a Georgian theatre still in use, heavily restored but in its way quite perfect. Grace had sat in a small green-painted box and looked down towards the tiny stage, then round at the rows of diminutive seats, feeling rather like an oversized doll. She had wanted to stay for a while, and daydream, quietly excited by the sheer ancientness of it all. Daddie had always praised her for her sense of history. But Marian had soon hurried them off to march round the castle, then to 'do' the town itself, systematically, street by street. She was an absolutely dedicated tourist. They had collapsed, finally, for a very late lunch in a health food restaurant back near the theatre, the restaurant Grace was looking for now, where she could pass some time before going to meet Stephen.

She found it, next to an estate agents where she stopped out of habit, to study the window. Since she had taken over Mother's affairs she had become rather interested in the value of her various properties. There was not only White Lodge, large and definitely imposing in its quarter-acre of well-kept garden in the best part of the town, but the shop, of which she owned the freehold, and the four terraced houses Daddie had inherited from his aunt, in a street near the station. Recently Edward Pollitt had advised her to sell them, to cash in on the recent spiral in house prices for which he was predicting a sudden sharp collapse, but so far she had refused to consider it. Great Aunt Grace, after whom she had been named, had lived in one of those houses all her life. She felt Daddie might not have liked her getting rid of it.

A glance among the properties, displayed in the window on revolving stands, showed her that Peth prices were low, compared with these. But then, it was a beautiful holiday area, full of retired people, who had savings rather than debts, while Peth, where wages were considerably lower than the national average, had once been described as 'the dustbin of Lancashire'. Guiltily she found herself working out what The Rock must now be worth, with its spectacular waterfall setting, its sheer antiquity, and all the expensive improvements Anna had lavished upon it. Then, right in the middle of the window, she saw a special display for what the agents described as a 'unique business opportunity', Coffee 'n' Crafts, a combined restaurant and craftshop, on a main tourist route but with an acre of land behind going down to a river on which there was a substantial three-bedroomed cottage 'in excellent order'. It was for sale at a price the modesty of which rather surprised her. It must mean that the property had been on the market too long and that the owner now must sell, and get to the Isle of Wight. Whatever the reason she knew that she must have the details, that this was why she had been brought along this particular street on this particular day. It was all coming together, the plan for her life. Eagerly she pressed down the door handle, only to find it locked and the interior empty and unlit.

In the doorway, though, she found a green dump-bin full of copies of the company's current property guide. She took one and leaned against a side window, leafing through it to find the coffee shop. Then she saw movement. A figure she had noticed when she had walked down from the market square, a man she'd half imagined might be watching her from a doorway across the street, had moved slowly off down the hill. It was the clothes that had misled her, the duffel coat and the black and purple varsity scarf. But the man was extremely thin, and rather shorter than Stephen, with a bush of thick dark hair, and wearing spectacles.

Even so, as he moved off, she peeped out of her own doorway and along the street. At the bottom of the hill she saw him stop again, then look up towards the estate agents where she was now pressed flat against the plate glass of the side window, nothing of herself showing. Slowly he crossed the road and disappeared, without another glance upward, under an archway where a bright gold sign advertised the Falcon. She relaxed, feeling rather silly. He had not been following her and she must not imagine that male passers-by trailed round after unattached women, simply because she needed a man. It was a kind of phobia, or so she understood from the sympathetic but sensible Ba, something endured by many 'singles', as Marian insisted on calling them, in her heartless, thrusting way.

But then she saw the duffel-coated figure again, as she sat in the window of the health-food cafe, spinning out a second cup of coffee before going to the theatre bar. She had felt much too nervous to eat anything, too tense about her imminent meeting with Stephen. He was standing on the other side of the road as before, pretending to inspect rolls of carpet in a furniture shop window, but with his body sideways on to the pavement, and twisting round at intervals to stare across at the cafe. When she saw him she turned her face away and focused on a mirror hung on the opposite wall, an art-deco pub glass painted with pink flamenco dancers and advertising a fizzy drink which they held unconvincingly level as they whirled about. Through the pattern of arms and legs and shooting bubbles she could see the camel of the duffel coat, the purple stripes and the face, only a blur from this distance, looking fixedly across the road.

She had not finished her coffee but she counted out the correct money and put it by her saucer. The waitress, with nothing much to do, spent most of her time in the kitchen chatting to an older woman who was washing up. Grace didn't want to be made late, waiting to pay. She got to her feet, shouted, 'Goodbye, and thank you,' towards the kitchen, and opened the cafe door. When he saw her move the camel-coated figure over by the carpet shop jerked into sudden life and moved quickly down the street, breaking into a slight run when she came out, setting a bell jingling. She followed him to the bottom, half-running herself now, and, reaching a junction, looked left and right. On one side was the arch of the Falcon Hotel, on the other, more shops with the theatre at the end, on a corner. There was no sign of the man.

She turned left and walked slowly past the shops, glancing into doorways as she counted them off. All were shut up and dark, the only movement was by the theatre itself. The doors were open and people were chatting outside on the pavement. They were smart, the men suited, the women perfumed and scarved. Anna, who had lectured here last year as part of an arts festival, had commented rather sarcastically on the dressiness, relieved that she hadn't turned up to speak in her usual casual writing clothes. 'The smaller and more obscure the venue,' she had said, 'the posher they all seem to turn out. I felt like the Queen.' Grace hadn't much liked it.

It was exactly seven o'clock. She found the small crowded bar up some steps, went in and looked round. The incident outside with the man, which she had definitely not imagined, had rather unnerved her and she felt, if she now saw Stephen, she might rush straight into his arms. He would not mind. She had watched him comforting his children after their little knocks and bruises, receiving from them the simple physical solace of touch that Lynn, who had always held apart, had seemed so unwilling to give. Besides, they were very old friends.

But he was not there. The only face she recognised was that of Gary Reed, who stood drinking at the bar counter. His Mediterranean yachting outfit had been exchanged for a dark grey suit, a lemon-coloured linen shirt and a silk cravat. He was talking to a much older man, who was similarly dressed, heavy and balding with a jowly, rather ugly face.

She was up at the bar, ordering her shandy, before she actually saw him. Then, too late to make an anonymous retreat, she blurted out a shrill 'Hello', rather expecting to be swept up into the flow of his conversation if not effused over, introduced to his friend. But he seemed acutely embarrassed and she knew then that he must have seen her come in. The friend was gruffly introduced as Michael du Cane, a solicitor who worked in the town. He told her that it promised to be a good concert, that the theatre had been lucky to secure this particular choir and that he hoped she would enjoy her evening. Then he turned back pointedly to his drinking and initiated a loud and technical conversation with his friend about Frank Bridge, the composer of a song cycle whose work they were to hear in the first half of the programme. Neither man addressed another word to her.

The bar area was not much bigger than the drawing room at White Lodge so, although she withdrew and found a seat as far from the couple as possible, she was still uncomfortably near the two men, and Michael du Cane had a thin but penetrating voice. They were obviously discussing her appearance in the dale. She heard 'Foggett's' quite distinctly, 'the Ram' and 'not selling'. Then, from Gary, she heard 'a big buddy of that crap novelist, Anna Beardmore'. Having examined every face in the room she went outside and waited in a small foyer lined with framed posters of past productions, *The Boyfriend*, *Carousel*, *Porgy and Bess*, *Bedroom Farce*. Anybody wanting access to the bar must pass through here. But Stephen did not come.

At seven twenty-five a bell rang and the orderly, well-groomed

crowd spilled out of the door and surged up the stairs towards the
minute theatre. Michael du Cane was one of the first to elbow his
way through, mumbling unintelligibly at her. Gary looked away. Not
knowing quite what to do next she went to the box office and asked
if there were any tickets in the name of Allen; they gave her a manila
envelope containing chits for two gallery seats. She removed one and
borrowed a pencil to scribble on the back of the envelope, 'Have gone
up. G.' Perhaps he had been delayed.

It was a concert of unaccompanied music given by a small choir
from York called the Minster Singers. She studied the programme
and was gratified to find that she had sung some of the pieces herself,
at school. It had never been strong enough for solo work but her light
soprano voice had been considered 'useful', and she understood that
she always sang in tune. She was not musical enough to know how
good these York singers were but they certainly looked professional
in their crisp black and white, and they came on to the stage without
music, which impressed her. She could hear every syllable too, and
she was fairly high up in the auditorium, sideways on to the small
stage. Gary Reed and his friend sat below her in the stalls, in the
middle of the third row.

The concert was entitled Seasons' Songs but they sang, inevitably,
of human love. One piece reminded her very much of Daddie:

Only a sweet and virtuous soul
Like seasoned timber, never gives;
But though the whole world turn to coal,
Then chiefly lives.

She missed him still, every day of her life she missed him, and,
looking at the empty seat beside her, she wondered how much she
really cared for Stephen Allen, whether Anna had been right in
dismissing him as weak and ineffectual and whether, if they ever
came together in marriage, she would actually be happy. Perhaps
she did not need someone like Stephen whom, like Lynn before her,
she would have to prop up, consider, endlessly organise, but a more
predictable, solid kind of man, someone more like her father, or like
Maurice Peacock. 'Seasoned timber' called up a picture of the kindly,
soft-spoken country man. There was a person with whom, unusually
for her, in the presence of a male, she had felt entirely at ease. She
would not be nervous of the sex-thing with someone like Maurice.
She had thought, when she had wept and he had taken her arm for a
minute, in the field, that she could love such a man.

Gary Reed and his Michael evidently loved each other too.

183

Glancing down into the audience she saw them peacefully holding hands as the choir sang its most melancholy piece so far: *No one is so accursed by fate, no one so utterly desolate/But some heart, though unknown, responds unto his own.'* It was lovely, but something she did not recall having sung in Senior Choir.

Intrigued by the hand-holding she found she was rather leaning over the balcony rail, peering down. Then she felt eyes on her, from the other side of the dim auditorium. Embarrassed, she withdrew, glancing across as she sat back on her seat. Someone opposite had moved slightly, obscuring himself behind one of the chubby wooden pillars which supported the upper balcony. *'O drooping souls, whose destinies are fraught with pain/Ye shall be loved again . . .'* the singers chorused reassuringly. But she had rather lost the thread of the song now and her eyes were creeping down again to the tier of seats opposite. The man behind the pillar was definitely the man who had spied on her in the street. He wore a black shirt and a wide sixties kipper tie, also black, and his duffel coat and striped scarf were folded neatly on his knee, but it was too dark to see his face properly.

As the music died away, still much of pain and unutterable longing, broken rather too early by hearty clapping, and the exit doors clattered open to mark the beginning of the interval, he moved very quickly. In the general surge of the crowd he was the first to disappear, she noticed, and, as the theatre filled up again for the second half – she had kept her seat till the bell rang, just in case Stephen should come – she observed that he did not return.

She drove home steadily along the dale, thankful that it was such a calm, fine night. She would be nervous in mist, and this was high country. Grace had received a loving but highly-disciplined upbringing, had always been made to write her thank-you letters on Boxing Day, to leave the bathroom as she found it, to clear her plate. But she had not endured to the end of the concert. The second half had been much heavier, and unintelligible to her, being sung entirely in German; and if Stephen had eventually shown up he would have found her seat empty. But her bones told her that he'd had no intention of coming, that he was still playing games with her and was probably still in London. Although the games must be part of his sick state of mind he was hurting her now. It was out of defiance that she had left before the end, with the beginnings of sympathy for the bizarre and hurtful behaviour that Lynn had had to put up with, all those years. Grace had always suspected her of exaggerating his strange moods. Perhaps she had not.

184

For most of the drive home she prayed. When the route was quiet and undemanding she found night driving lent itself rather well to prayer and meditation, though she would never have attempted any devotions on a motorway, or in the rush hour. But tonight the prayers rose upwards sweetly; talking to the Lord was easier than it had been for many weeks and she was filled with a new peace. She found she was bearing the necessary hurts better, that she was seeing with fresh eyes.

First, there was the plan for her life, which had suddenly clarified most marvellously. In Richmond, on her way back to the car, she had posted one of her new business cards through the estate agent's letter-box, having written on the back that she would like details of Coffee 'n' Crafts sent to White Lodge. Anna's money would not come into it, that must be set aside for the Lord's purposes. To buy the business she could always sell Great Aunt Grace's little houses, or she might sell The Rock which, for all its beauty, she could not really imagine living in alone. Quite apart from the memory of Anna it was too remote, whereas Coffee 'n' Crafts was in a bustling tourist village and the cottage which went with it was invitingly situated on the banks of a stream. Daddie had always told her that she would make a good business woman. Well, she would try. If she did go through with it, she was going to ask Ba to consider coming in on the venture. She was tired of librarianship and had often talked of opening a Christian bookshop somewhere, but she had no capital. They could sell books in the craft area, expand the already-existing local travel section, and reach out to tourists with the living gospel.

How Marian would feel about a move further north – for Grace would not want to split up The Girls – was something which would obviously need very careful handling. But she felt sufficiently confident to float her idea. She may well not get the place in which case the Lord would open another, better door. But she longed for it to be in this valley. More and more it spoke peace to her.

Her other, less comfortable thoughts were about Stephen, and her new realisation that he was not, perhaps, the man with whom she was meant to share the rest of her life. She truly pitied him, in the wreck of his marriage and the loss of his children and she had confessed tonight before the Lord that she really hated Guy for dying in the way he had, for the bathroom door which Stephen must have opened, for the hideousness from which he had fled away. Suicide: *simply the most extreme and brutal way of making sure that you will not easily be forgotten.* Yes.

But also, tonight, she felt that she was being forced to look honestly at Stephen for the first time. He was simply not interested in her, and never had been. He had only come to her that night at White Lodge because he had been unable to be with Anna, he had admitted as much. Anna had been the woman he really wanted, as all men had seemed to; even shy Maurice's face had fired up, in the little valley, when the magic name was pronounced. She wanted to think it was mere awkwardness, but no, there too Anna had made her mark. Next to her, men were not, never had been, interested in Grace.

But she did not understand what had happened tonight. The facts were that Stephen had made a phone call and an arrangement to meet her, and that the two tickets had been waiting at the theatre, with his name on the envelope. Then he had not come. *Why?* Either there was a practical explanation – he had simply broken down en route and had been unable to contact her – or he was behaving irrationally, as he had towards people many times in the past, because of illness.

Initially, perhaps, he had genuinely wanted to see her, had had every intention of doing so and made the concert arrangements when he had received her card and phone number. Then he had not gone through with it, because of embarrassment, she conjectured, after their love-making and because of his subsequent long silence. There had been silence after Guy's death, even though she was certain he had been there, that fleeing figure on the crematorium path, and he had offered no comfort when Anna died, sought no mutual support in her presence. Conscience, perhaps, had finally prompted him, on receipt of her card, to do the right thing by her; but at the last minute he had withdrawn again, unable to go through with it. *Withdrawal.* There had been days of complete withdrawal with Lynn, days when he was very depressed and had locked himself in his studio, she recalled from Anna, would not take his pills, drank, screamed abuse at the children when they came tap-tapping at his door in their pathetic, whimpering efforts at peace-making.

Distasteful as the thought of a visit was, Lynn remained the only person left to speak to about Stephen's state of mind. By the time she reached Fawcett's she had decided to travel on, up into Scotland, not go back to Peth. She was nearly half-way already, and it made sense. All she needed to do was to phone the cattery and Mrs Lumb, and tell them that she would be away for a few more days. There was just a chance that Lynn might have heard from Stephen, that he had visited, even. She had already studied the maps and the journey didn't look too complicated. Also, thinking that one day she might visit the island, she had the names of two hotels en route, in her address book, places where The Girls had stayed last month. The tiny island of Monica's *Solitariness*, she had discovered, was on Stephen's bit of coast too, and not very far away. If the good weather lasted she could take a boat ride out to it. Lynn, she was sure, would not want to spend very much time in her company. Perhaps she could take the children with her.

In the hall at the farm she found a feeble light left on for her and another telephone message. This time it was from Buckle, who had called while she was at the concert, asking her to ring back, if it wasn't too late. Calmly, she picked up the phone, feeling neither anger nor annoyance, for this was surely confirmation. His contacting her was part of the new whole.

As she drove to meet him next day, after a long morning of reading and writing up her notes in the farm sitting room – hours during which Mrs Fawcett had been conspicuously absent, Heather had served breakfast and dealt with her bill – she realised that Stephen could not have broken down the night before because he would have phoned the farm with a message by now. And the second ticket had not been collected from the box office; she had telephoned the theatre and checked.

In her bag she now had several pages of careful notes for Buckle whom she was to meet for a late lunch in a small hotel just off the M6. In what she had written she had made no attempt to defend Stephen. All she knew was that he had not killed Anna. But she hoped a man like William Buckle, who must surely from his work have some professional knowledge of lies and duplicity, of subterfuges and stratagems, of disturbed personalities of all types, might throw some light on the way Stephen had behaved towards her, might, by explaining, make it all easier to bear. She knew that from now on she must tell this man everything, whatever conclusions he might draw from Stephen's aborted attempts to contact her. He had something to tell her also, he'd said on the telephone, when she'd mentioned the notes she had made; 'Good news,' he'd told her enigmatically.

When he heard that she was driving on, up into Scotland, he apologised for taking her out of her way. The hotel was buried down a country lane, a few miles from the motorway. One of the service areas would have been more convenient for her, he knew, but he had wanted them to be as private as possible.

They had made small talk over the meal. Now, in the corner of a deserted lounge bar, he was barely talking above a whisper. He had spent last night and this morning with the North Yorkshire CID, he explained, as they found seats and he ordered coffee for them. Apparently there was 'big news'.

'*Good* news?' she asked, unfolding the notes she had copied out for him, and smoothing them on the table. 'That's what you said.'

'I thought so last night. Now I'm not so sure. The point is, Eddie Bayles is back in for questioning. This time I think they might bring charges.'

She stared at him. Now she understood Mrs Fawcett's absence all this morning. Whether or not Eddie Bayles had killed Anna, Grace, in her ill-timed visit, had been identified with 'the other side'. As she had finally driven away from the farm she had seen the woman staring down at her, from an upstairs window.

'*Anna?*' she said. Though the lounge was empty, apart from a man washing glasses behind the bar, she mouthed it nevertheless.

Buckle nodded. 'They contacted us early yesterday, and I drove up. There was a phone call, apparently, to one of their sub-stations, a one-man job, that's all. The message was that they'd find something if they dug in one of old Bayles's fields. It was all quite precise, a few feet out from the back wall of one of those old cow-houses, no problem. A piece of turf had been lifted, a hole dug, the stuff buried. It was there, all right. Eddie was in the house at the time, locked in a bedroom. They were on the road with him less than an hour later. Pretty neat work, I'd say.'

She whispered 'What stuff? Or can't you tell me?'

'Oh yes, it's out. Somebody blabbed, as usual, and they had to give the press something. It was on last night's local radio, I gather, and the papers have got it today. You didn't hear last night's news, then?'

'No. I was driving back from Richmond. A police-woman stopped me in the afternoon, though. Would that be it?'

He nodded. 'Yes. They were pretty damned efficient.' Otherwise, though, he was peeved because Hallam had rather elbowed him out of the way, seemed to wonder why he'd bothered to come up at all. From the beginning he'd been treated as marginal, only in on the case because Hallam had known him before, and the brusque reception at headquarters had made him feel his relative youth and inexperience all the more keenly.

'What was "the stuff"?' Grace repeated. Her eyes were fearful and large, her full soft cheeks deeply flushed. Buckle looked at her, then away, quickly, a sudden sickness in his heart. She whispered, 'Were they Anna's things?'

He nodded. 'It's very possible, but there's been no statement yet, and definitely no charges. They have to make various tests of course and – ' Then he stopped himself. He saw no point in telling her about the general excitement over the bloody garments, that some men secreted blood in their semen and that tests could successfully isolate such secretors, and so narrow the field, that samples would be

188

taken and tests done on them, from Eddie Bayles. Nor was there any need to tell her what had been wrapped in the bundle of clothing.

But she said urgently, as if on cue, 'Was there anything else?'

'Yes.' She could read the newspaper reports so he might as well be truthful now. 'There were two weapons, well, if you can call an axe a weapon; a little chopper. Father Bayles says it's not theirs, though.'

'And the other?'

'Oh, a kind of Scout knife, the sort that goes into a canvas holster.' He gave a humourless little grin and turned, with relief, to take the coffee tray from a hovering waitress. 'I was never in the Boy Scouts myself but you know the kind of thing.'

Grace did know, she had seen whole cards of such knives on display in a camping shop in Hawes, graduated according to size, hanging up on the door. Such a knife had been used by Dr Beardmore to kill his wife, the knife from Guy's 'weapons collection' that had caused such trouble at school, for *The Dayspring from on High* and for poor Miss Bruce. Weeks after the deaths it had been officially returned to Firs in a large brown envelope, together with various other things the police had removed from the house. Guy, begged by Anna, had gone out one night, climbed to the top of the cantilever bridge behind the house that took the East Lancs road across the Ship Canal, and flung it away in the darkness. Anna had written some verses about it, calling them *Knife*. They were copied out in the deaths diary. With her compulsion to externalise she had, within days, shown what she had written to Grace, years later reusing it in *Miss Dixon*. 'As for me,' the poem had ended, '*I have no tears left.*'

'But you said you weren't *sure*,' she reminded him. Now he had delivered the facts he had become silent and was making rather a great business of stirring sugar into his coffee.

'Well, nobody can draw any conclusions yet. It's too early. As I said, various tests are being done and they're taking Bayles through his statement again. It's not the father's axe, they say so, but it *was* found on their land. Believe me, it could mean anything.'

'Was the phone call anonymous?'

'Yes.' But he did not tell her that the voice was Scots and that the caller had had a pronounced stammer. She would hear soon enough, from the usual sources and, during this hour with her, he had felt she was rather easier in his presence, almost trusting him. If somebody, Allen he was certain, was framing Bayles, and this was the crudest attempt imaginable, then he would eventually make a mistake, and surface. He was already living dangerously, with his sneaky nocturnal visits to the London flat, his arty postcard to the dead woman, that curious conversation with Grace herself, at the cottage. It was as if, periodically, he *wanted* to be apprehended, like the loonies up here, who had already 'confessed' to the murder.

Then she took the wind out of him. 'Stephen's been in touch with me,' she said. 'Twice. I wrote the details down for you – not that there's anything much to say. He sent me a card last week, saying he was sorry he'd missed me in London, and I sent one back, when I knew he was coming up here for a bit. He knows this area, he's done a lot of painting in the Pennines. Anyway, he phoned yesterday, when I was out, asking me to go to a concert with him, in Richmond. I waited, but he never turned up. It's all in my notes. Here, you can keep them. I did them for you.

'As you know,' she went on, very formal now, with the crispness of speech he remembered from their first meeting, a curious precision which warned him that she was actually near her own private breaking point, 'I don't believe that Stephen has anything at all to do with Anna's murder, and I never will. I can't say I understand his present behaviour, but then, I'm not very clever about that sort of thing. Perhaps you understand better. All I know,' she repeated, 'is that he cannot have had *anything* to do with it. Do you understand?' And her voice shook.

'All right, all right . . . Grace.' He took the neatly written sheets from her, touching her hand lightly in reassurance as he leaned across. She was very near to tears and he was afraid. She must not cry, not here, nor anywhere. He couldn't cope with people's tears. Now, and for many years, he had been unable to weep. It was his parents' fault and it had been Fran's reason for leaving him, or so she had claimed, what she had described as his 'inhuman coldness'. But he wasn't cold, and there were people he loved. He thought he might love Grace and therefore he was frightened and so being deliberately cool with her. There were years of unshed tears in him, and of unspoken love. They were what made him so uptight with people. He couldn't help it, though. Fran, when she left him, had advised a psychiatrist.

Glancing dutifully through her papers without much interest he saw the name Gary Reed and mouthed it at her, raising his eyebrows. Hallam's people had questioned him and his friend du Cane at some length. At the time of the murder they had been on holiday in Umbria. Du Cane painted. How carefully their alibis had been examined he wasn't sure.

She said, 'It's just that he was so very odd with me, you see. He wants to buy The Rock, he asked me about it when I went to the Ram for a drink. When I said I wasn't interested in selling he seemed to turn on me . . . so suddenly . . . oh, such *hate*. Whoever did kill Anna, I wondered . . . thought . . . could it be someone like that, you know, very jealous?'

He did not reply but concentrated on reading her notes. He saw 'Welsh holiday cottages', 'local hostility'. Then 'right (*writing*) hand removed. GR very literary. Despised Anna. Cheated of The Rock in aunt's will.' He felt enormously sorry for her, and, suddenly, fiercely protective. All this was so obvious, so pathetic.

Then she said angrily, 'He called Anna a "crap writer", in the theatre bar. He said it loud enough for me to hear, it was quite deliberate. I should have reminded him about the Pritchard Award.' Her voice had a shrewishness about it now. 'Literature's obviously one of his things. He quoted poetry at me.' Like Anna, she had decided since, wanting to make her feel uncomfortable. 'He has a homosexual relationship with the friend,' she added, her cheeks colouring. 'In the concert I think they were holding hands.'

'Do you object?' He was interested, in view of her religious position, and he wondered, too, if she had thought of how she herself must strike others, with no male friends, apart from the tenuous link with Allen, and now conspicuously affiliated to The Girls; Marian Stoker was certainly lesbian, whether she recognised it or not, and the twitchy little librarian's male partner.

She shook her head emphatically. '*No.*' Though in fact, friendships of that nature secretly rather repulsed her. She could not quite believe they were of God and those who had them, she thought, always seemed so defensive, and never completely happy. 'I only mention it in my notes,' she said, 'because seeing them together set me thinking about such people's sexuality. I mean, the sexuality of whoever killed Anna.' He noticed that she articulated the word very precisely, as if sex was of immense private importance to her.

He said, 'You've obviously done a fair amount of thinking, Grace,' leaning slightly on her Christian name, though she did not react. She *had* thought, for her. Again he suddenly felt the need to touch her. Her large breasts were very full in the soft grey dress she was wearing. As she moved they swung slightly.

They sat on in silence. Grace played about with her coffee spoon but did not drink very much. Buckle concentrated on her notes. 'What about this man in Richmond?' he said eventually.

'At first I thought it was Stephen,' she told him. 'He was wearing a duffel coat, you see, and Stephen nearly always wore one. He seemed to be following me round. He was spying on me, when I was sitting in a cafe, he definitely was. Then he turned up again, at the theatre.'

'But it wasn't Allen?'

'*No.* This man was a lot thinner, as if he'd had an illness, I thought, and he didn't have a beard. Don't you think you should look into it, though? I mean, he'd got a striped scarf on too, like in that description you gave me. He was a bit creepy.'

'I will,' and he took out a notebook and wrote something down. 'About Allen, Grace. He was one of Anna's lovers, wasn't he?'

'One of the many.'

Yet again she had surprised him, in the way she had answered so immediately, entirely unembarrassed, looking steadily into his face with her marvellous dark eyes.

'And did you approve of her sex life?'

She shrugged. 'Well, obviously her way wouldn't be mine, but then she had nothing outside herself, you see, she believed in nothing. Where do you begin, when it's like that? I can't imagine really.'

'Obviously men liked her.'

'Oh, yes, they all liked her,' and she looked at him. 'You'd have liked her.'

He wanted to say, 'No, it's you I like, Grace,' but the words wouldn't come.

'Now listen, I'd be surprised if they hadn't already checked out this character in Richmond, it's not a big place and they'll know if someone's in the habit of making a nuisance of themselves. But I will speak to them.'

'Are you really saying that I imagined it? A man *did* follow me, in the street, then he turned up again in the theatre. He sat opposite, he was staring right through me.'

'But are you quite sure it wasn't Allen? Look. I know it must seem a ridiculous question but you haven't seen him for nearly a year, remember, and as you keep telling me, he's been ill, he could have lost a lot of weight.'

'It was *not* Stephen.'

'All right.'

From her bag she now took the card that had come to White Lodge and gave it to him. Then she unfolded a grubby sheet of paper and held it out. 'I found this, pinned up on a notice board at the Ram. It's obviously not official and I thought it ought not to be there. So I took it down. Someone's idea of a sick joke, I imagine. I was going to throw it away, then I decided you ought to have it. It says "polite", you see, not "police". I didn't notice at first but then I – '

'Yes, yes, I can see that,' he interrupted and he examined the crumpled sheet with care. 'Hmm . . . it's pen and ink. Nothing to do with us, of course. Well, I'll have to check up on this too, obviously . . .' and he looked at it again. 'It's really a very good drawing. Done from a photograph, I'd say. Whoever drew this has had some training . . .' and he looked at her. Allen was certainly living very dangerously now. He wanted to be taken in, though as yet, for his own curious reasons, he was resisting. Surely she must have made the connection?

He said gently, when he got no response, 'You were a very silly girl, you know, not to have kept those news cuttings. They probably *were* the work of a crank, as you said in your note to me, but really, you ought not to have thrown them away.' *Silly.* In the old days the word had meant 'innocent', hadn't it? 'Shepherds, leave your silly sheep.' Innocent, and helpless.

'I'm sorry,' she said humbly. 'I'll keep anything else that comes. I know it's important.'

'Good.'

'Backward' was the adjective Breda Smith had used of Grace, though deeply embarrassed at such disloyalty to a very old friend. But she was wrong. Grace was acute in her own way, and there was something steady and unwavering about her. She had thought of some significant details and she had forgotten nothing. What he felt now, as he contemplated her, was her genuine goodness; he wanted to be able to ask her forgiveness, for his ever thinking she might have played a part in Anna Beardmore's death.

One phrase had jumped out at him as he'd read through her notes. 'Stephen seems to be playing games with me.' Yes, and he believed they might be dangerous, desperate games. He did not want her to make any more arrangements to see the man, and he would make sure that the local police in Scotland knew of her proposed visit to the ex-wife.

'Grace,' he said, 'you *must* contact me if Allen gets in touch with you again.' But her face blanked as he spoke and he felt she had suddenly withdrawn from him. 'Now, promise me,' he said urgently, leaning across the coffee tray and laying his hand on hers.

But it was instantly withdrawn. Then, from her bag, she brought a small New Testament and held it up. 'I promise.' Startled, he glanced round to see if the barman had heard.

'I promise,' she repeated, adding silently, *For I am not ashamed of the gospel of Christ. For it is the power of God unto salvation, to everyone that believeth.* She knew now that this man William must be added to her prayers. There was much emotion in him and, she felt, a definite unhappiness. Part of her wanted the emotion to be for her but she sensed that it was all to do with his past, this curious hard energy, this thrusting quality of his that was forever pushing away feelings and issues which were too much for him to contemplate. She

193

understood that process, she had employed it over Guy's death, now over Anna's, too.

'Er, well, thank you. And you really have told me everything?'

'Absolutely everything.'

'Good girl.'

When she had driven away he went back to the empty lounge bar and ordered more coffee. She had been, he was sure now, entirely open and honest with him. Genuinely believing that Allen was not implicated, she had sworn on the holy scriptures themselves that from now on she would keep nothing from him, if the man should make contact again. And he was confident that she would keep her promise. Her faith in his innocence was total and these 'notes' she had made, which he would return to her after a decent interval, were themselves evidence of that faith, her own pathetic, amateurish attempts to explore every avenue of possibility, to catch hold of some stray thread that might lead to the killer.

He would keep her writings strictly to himself. He did not intend to expose her to any ridicule. Simple as they were, however, they evidenced more concentrated thought on the motive and psychology of Beardmore's murderer than had been apparent yesterday, when he'd talked to Hallam's people. The case had obviously cooled considerably since that Semtex cache had been discovered out on the moors north of Scarborough; the ministerial visit they had linked to it was still to take place, and security was getting most of the attention. Hallam had favoured Bayles from the beginning. Buckle had sensed that he was waiting for the conclusive test results with some complacency.

But now, whatever the outcome, he must go back to them, via the Ram, perhaps, with this curious pen and ink drawing Grace had given him. He was looking forward to watching their faces as he placed it beside the faked 'business card' Jim Wooding had been given at the Beardmore funeral, by the 'reporter' from the *North-Eastern Gazette*, who had then disappeared so abruptly, before he could make contact. Hugo Jolley, the name printed on the card, did not appear to exist or, if he did, had never worked for that particular newspaper. The interview with the dead woman had been done by a man called Skerrett who now worked for the *Sheffield Star*. Buckle had travelled up there, and interviewed him personally.

The card itself was hand-made, but so meticulously it would survive all but the most careful scrutiny. Tests would decide finally but he was quite certain that whoever had drawn the 'polite' notice had also fabricated the card. He believed it was Allen, but there had seemed no point in entering upon all this with Grace Bradley. She had told him 'absolutely everything'.

Pity, an increasing interest in her, against anything he could have predicted, and a sense that it was his basic duty to protect her, whatever he felt, had made him keep his suspicions to himself.

Grace stopped at the first service area going north, found a lidded litter container and thrust into it the plastic tub that had contained Anna's ashes, having first washed most of the name away in the women's lavatories. She had not lied to Buckle, in saying that she had told him 'everything' for what she had done early that day was nothing to do with anybody except her and Anna, and in any case, she knew now that any show of emotion embarrassed him. He would not have *wanted* to know this.

She had decided to take the ashes to The Rock but then she had seen Maurice's old car at the red gate and she feared meeting him there, the container in her hand. So she had gone back to Guy's seat and followed the river up the valley, away from the cottage, past a camping site with a solitary orange tent erected in one corner in the lee of a stone wall, past a roofless, deserted farmhouse, and on again, until she had come to a shallow waterfall where the beck widened out forming a deep pool and where, up above, stepping stones crossed over to the other side.

The flat brown stones were slimy with moss and she had taken off her shoes, leaving them on the bank. Then she had crossed to the middle, looking down into the steady dark rush of peaty water, the flecks of spray beyond it dimpling the calmer pool, a fish plopping up.

She had scattered the ashes all round her, like white seed. Some had flown upwards, caught on the wind, but most had dropped down by her feet and been carried away by the water, down into the pool, then beyond into the hurrying beck that in time became a greater river and at last, miles on, joined the sea. In such a way Anna's own soul was at one now with the deeps of Almighty God.

Tears came as she stood scattering, but not of grief. In that moment she simply wanted to praise Him and she broke into quiet singing as she stood, ankle deep, in the bubbling stream:

I love you, Lord, and I lift my voice
To worship you, O my soul, rejoice.
Take joy, My King, in what you hear,
May it be a sweet, sweet sound in your ear.

She did not know, quite, how long she stood there, but suddenly, she was startled by someone plucking insistently at her skirt and a cheeping high voice said, 'What are you *doing?*' Then she heard a deeper voice, male, cautioning in embarrassment, 'Come away, Simon . . .'

'I want to go on the stepping stones like that lady, *I* want to, my own self . . .' and the childish plea became an angry roar as the small boy was dragged by his father towards the distant orange tent.

'But, what's that lady *doing?*' Grace heard, staring after them as they disappeared through a gateway. 'Why's that lady . . . why's that lady . . . *crying?*'

14

She had never understood why Stephen had bought the bungalow. It was ugly, meanly-proportioned and it had no view, which was tragic in view of the sweeping grandeur of mountains all round it, and its proximity to the sea on which it turned its back. All she could remember was that he had been happy on this island as a child. His paternal grandfather, a crofter, had been born on it and Stephen had been brought up for holidays, until the old people had died. Afterwards, it seemed that his parents had never gone back, that his father had spent the money from the croft on a seaside cabin in some south coast resort, to please his mother, who had never got on with her parents-in-law, and who had found the long journey north tedious and uncomfortable. But Stephen had always been very bitter about it, claiming that he'd been 'untimely ripped' from the island, vowing that he would one day return there.

When 'Last Light' was hung in the Tate and Channel 4 had done a short programme about him in their *New Faces* series, his paintings had started to sell and he'd gone up to Scotland to investigate the property scene. At the time the only place for sale was the Craig, this bleak-looking elongated box with metal-framed windows set in a patch of scrubby grass, overlooking a steep hillside that was perpetually in shade, where sharp white rocks erupted from the thin turf. But it had outbuildings, which he needed, and an acre or two of land on which he had vaguely talked of rearing beasts, like his grandfather. And it was cheap, the money from 'Last Light' and the television programme would pay for it, with some over for immediate repairs.

He had bought it on the spot and gone back in triumph to Lynn, at home with the children in Meager Park. At the time their outstanding bills ran into thousands and the London house needed a new roof. But he had been depressed for several months, and was unable to paint.

Anna had always dated the final phase of his marriage break-down from this secret purchase of the Craig. He had not gone straight to Meager Park to tell Lynn but had sought out his pub cronies, to celebrate. When, in the small hours, he had woken her up to tell her, drunkenly waving the documents under her nose, she had not believed him. In the morning, perusing them more carefully and realising that it was true, she had wept.

It was ironic that Lynn now appeared to have installed herself at the Craig with Debbie and Bridget, leaving Stephen to live in London. It was he who loved the island, she who had always complained about it, refusing to consider his ultimate plan, which was to sell up in London and settle there, he to paint, she to make pots. They had met through Guy, when Stephen was lecturing at Peth Art College; she had been a student in the ceramics department.

As Grace walked up the track towards the bungalow, from the boat, her heart pounded rather at her own daring. She was worrying more now, about her heart. Apparently she had what Dr Lucas had very vaguely described as 'a slight irregularity' which occasionally made her breathless and sometimes caused palpitations, though that was nothing, Ba got those too. Since Mother's death she had been taking a pill each day, and she had to have regular check-ups. She knew she'd put on weight and she really must lose it before she next saw Dr Lucas, otherwise, he would nag her.

But this particular thudding inside her chest had nothing to do with her 'flutter', nor with the steepness of the track as it wound round the rocky hillside, leaving the marvellous vista of mountains and sea behind as it entered a dark, sullen little valley of its own where there had been just enough flat space to build the monstrous bungalow. She was fluttering with nerves at her own audacity, in simply turning up on Lynn's doorstep with her overnight bag. But she had felt there was no other way. Had she telephoned, the conversation would have been cut short, without ceremony. It had happened before.

Outside the house was a newish Land-Rover. It wasn't Stephen's, he'd never learned to drive, had never had the necessary courage to try, something Lynn had always rather despised him for, just as she had mocked him for his phobia about using the telephone. When they came to the island everything had to be lugged up this track from the boat, though Stephen had found an enormous high pram and pushed it along cheerily, sometimes sitting the children on top where they squealed with nervous delight. She could see the pram now, in a rusting heap by one of the outbuildings. On the grass by the front porch were two little bicycles, child-sized trikes with cheerful red wheels and blue saddles.

Before knocking she glanced through a side window, into a passage that ran the whole length of the house. Directly opposite was a half open door and beyond it what appeared to be the family living room. The curtains were closed and an enormous television screen flickered in the gloom. Debbie and Bridget sat in front of it, side by side, totally absorbed in the manic gyrations of a row of pink cartoon elephants.

Grace stepped back. The afternoon was slowly slipping away now, but the sun still warmed her face. As yet the marvellous weather had not broken and she had driven north in a calm, golden light, watching it illuminate first the fellsides of the dale, then the bleak Pennine uplands, then the greater Scottish hills, seeing the clouds move silently over the wide land, patching the heather slopes with huge patterns, like a hand laid on the earth from on high. And she had gloried, as lochs and seas and mountains endlessly unfolded, in the sheer extravagance of what God had made.

She looked down at the abandoned trikes. The Craig, for all its immediate ugliness, was surely in paradise. The darkened room with its great screen and the two curly heads transfixed before it saddened her.

On the other side of the front door she looked through a window into a modern kitchen. Here was much evidence of Lynn who had always seemed propelled by a compulsion to control her immediate environment, in the soul-less white Formica tops, the spotless cork floor, the stainless-steel cooking utensils hung up and burnished in orderly rows. The only concession to the 'artistic' was a shelf of the thick rather ugly-looking brown-black cooking pots she made to sell.

This bungalow suited the Lynn approach well enough, but Stephen must have surely fought with her over it. He would fight too, if only he would come, about the installation of the gigantic television set. One of his few triumphs, in the general war between them, was that he had never allowed television at Meager Park. He believed it was a destructive thing, especially for his children. Lynn had defied him, though, by sending them off to a neighbour's to watch, several hours a day, so she could have 'some peace'.

It appeared that the children were in the house alone, for all was silent as she walked along to the other end. The bungalow was smaller than it looked. It had a kitchen, the room with the television, a child's bedroom with pine bunks, and next door to this a small immaculate bathroom. At the end was a last, larger room, its door shut.

She went round the side of the house and came to a curtained window. As she turned the corner a startled sheep skittered away, bleating. It had a pale, bony, lugubrious face, quite different from the pert enquiring Swaledales she had got so used to, scattered over Anna's valley.

The curtains were pale straw. Everything Lynn chose was bleached and colourless, Grace remembered, tuning in with the clothes she wore. They had been pulled across hastily and did not meet at the bottom, quite why Grace could not understand for a steep bank rose up only feet from the glass. A narrow triangle between the two drapes permitted her to look in.

The room was quite dark but she could see that a double bed more or less filled it. On top of a white woven counterpane she saw two people, naked. The man kneeling over the woman was Stephen. She saw him only fleetingly, in profile, but recognised the soft ring of tender dark curls at the base of his skull, the otherwise balding head, the small beard and the long sharp nose, grotesquely parodied below in his erection. She watched as, with a kind of roar, he turned and flung himself upon the woman who opened her legs momentarily then clamped her knees snugly round his hips. The soles of the feet, Lynn's feet, were very dirty against the white bedcover. Then she saw how his small, painfully thin buttocks began pumping, silently pumping, and she heard a stifled female cry.

Sharply, she turned away and stumbled up the steep bank, colliding with the amazed monk-like sheep, then with the green tin eminence of an oil container. The slope got steeper as it rose up and she found herself on her hands and knees, clawing at the turf in an effort to get away, sliding down again and dislodging stones that fell rattling against the tank. When at last the bank levelled out she started running, until the bungalow had disappeared from sight.

Only then did she stop, flopping down exhausted on to a flat white rock, to stare out over the rusty roofs of the out-buildings, across the wooden landing stage with its decrepit black hut alongside, to the dark sweep of water and the mainland, with its layered backdrop of purplish blue mountains.

Her heart was thudding painfully now, and she rather wanted to be sick. Certainly there was some relief in the fact that Stephen was here but more, there was her own humiliation because she had not immediately turned away from the window. Stronger than either feeling was her own envy and desire, her unutterable longing, both for the sex she had seen and for her to bear a child, out of such an act. When Stephen had come into her at White Lodge, in love she had foolishly believed, then, she had hoped, in spite of all it would mean – the general astonishment, the impossible position she would face amongst her friends – that she might have conceived. But within days the hated blood had come flooding down, the blood of her barrenness.

She was crying. Getting up from the rock she made her way slowly down the slope towards the house. Her overnight bag was by the front door, where she had left it. She would take it and slip away, down to the landing stage. If she was quick she could get the last boat. It was hard, just leaving the children, she had brought them gifts, she wanted to love them. But now, with the complications of Stephen's presence, and of what she had seen . . . she felt they would somehow know she had watched.

Then the door opened and Lynn came out, zipping up her jeans. Grace slipped and sent a shower of small stones rattling against the side of the water tank. Lynn looked up, put a hand to her forehead to shade off the glare of the sun which, in a final burst of brilliance, was sliding down behind the mountains. Grace waved. 'It's me . . . *hi!*' she shouted, in a desperate attempt to sound casual, and she carried on picking her way down the slope. By the door Lynn was toeing the overnight bag suspiciously, with a bare foot.

'I was up here,' Grace said, 'having a long weekend, so I just thought, you know . . .' She hoped Lynn wouldn't ask too many questions, expose the fact that she had come specially, from Anna's valley. Could she know about the will? Her talk, always, was of shortage of money. What Grace had seen of the bungalow showed that the purse-strings were still being drawn very tight. 'Cheap and cheerless' had been Anna's spiteful description of Lynn's approach to home-making. But then, her own money had bred confidence, also a kind of hardness.

'Where did you stay?' Lynn had now seated Grace at the kitchen table and was spooning instant coffee into mugs.

'Moffatt. The Girls . . . friends of mine . . . recommended a B and B there. It's a gorgeous little town. I bought this sweater. I thought it was rather fun.'

She looked down at her chest, pulling at the coarse Shetland fibres. It was bright red, decorated with little black sheep. Anna had often told her to wear more cheerful colours and red set off her thick dark hair. 'I brought sweaters for the children too,' she said, unzipping the overnight bag. 'Hope that's OK.'

'Where's your car?' said Lynn. She herself had not sat down but was standing rather rigidly at the opposite end of the shiny kitchen table with her arms folded. Her voice was very slightly menacing. Presents for the children obviously suggested a plan to stay overnight.

Grace looked at her fearfully, letting the packages drop back inside the bag. Lynn was much thinner than she remembered and her face had aged rather terribly. It had always been quite deeply lined, now it looked ravaged, the heavy downward creases that framed the mouth were more profoundly engraved, the neck scrawnier. She did love him but Grace knew that Stephen, though not through his own deliberate fault, had made Lynn suffer. The lips were puffy, she noticed, and there were sore red marks round them, from the kissing. She looked hard at the scrubbed table top. 'I left it in that car-park, by the landing stage,' she said, 'where I caught the boat. They said it would be all right overnight. But if you're doing things I can go back. I'd just like to get a glimpse of the children . . .'

'Oh, you can stay here, if you don't mind a camp bed,' Lynn said ungraciously. Then she pulled her mouth about. 'But don't mention Anna, for God's sake, and definitely not Guy. They don't know anything. What with Stephen doing a bunk, and then the police coming round, I just couldn't face it. They were very fond of old Guy, you know. They ask about him more than their father.'

Grace was silent, remembering the last time she had seen him with the little girls, at Meager Park. One of them had had a birthday – it was soon after Mother and she had been at Anna's Camden Town flat for the weekend. They had gone over with presents. Anna was Debbie's godmother, though she had tried hard to resist the honour, saying it was a farcical idea, in view of her agnosticism. But Lynn, a biddable middle-of-the road Anglican, to whom making her weekly communion had seemed as inevitable as opening her bowels, had somehow got her way. Anna never forgot her duties, always sent lavish gifts and had left both children money in her will. Edward Pollitt had let this slip, though Grace supposed she ought not to know. Would Lynn mention the bequest, she wondered? Might she be jealous?

On the day of the birthday party Guy had hung on, drinking. Stephen had been on a dry spell at the time so there had been no alcohol in the house. Everyone had drunk mineral water, about which Anna had complained, though she had submitted. Guy had brought his own bottle.

When the children were ready for bed Grace remembered their being brought down to say goodnight, and how Guy had ignored Lynn, going out with them into the garden, and walking on his hands up and down the patio, then doing backward springs, whooping Red Indian fashion while they squealed with delight. He had not, he explained, been able to buy Debbie a *new* present, not like Auntie Anna, the horrid men at work wouldn't pay his wages. But in the hall, in a very old box, was something very secret, very special, something he'd had when he was a little boy and had lived with Auntie Anna at Firs, the great big house next door to Auntie Grace, which Auntie Anna had been able to get back from the people who had used it as a home for all the grannies and grandpas, now she was so terribly rich and famous.

'Guy,' Anna had whispered, pulling at him as he danced inside and up the hall with the two entranced little girls. 'Guy, don't . . .'

202

and Lynn had stood at the top of the stairs, holding Mickey Mouse toothbrushes. '*Bedtime*,' she had rapped, 'Come on, Steve, bring them up.' But Guy had already enlisted Stephen's help for his project and they were both down on their knees, fitting rails together. He was making a complicated route all along the hall complete with signals, stations, and wayside houses. Debbie and Bridget, their eyes huge with expectation, kept opening boxes and finding little painted people, trees, sheep and cows, which they arranged reverently along the shiny track, which now snaked in and out of doors, up banks, through cuttings, completing a huge loop that entirely filled the hall.

By now, everyone except Lynn was waiting eagerly for the clockwork train to set off. She had stormed into the kitchen with the toothbrushes and slammed the door on them all. But Guy, winding up the engine ceremoniously with a large brass key, found it wouldn't go. 'Come on, come *on*,' he said irritably, 'for Christ's *sake* . . .' and he banged it against the wall. Stephen, who had watched him drinking, and was obviously anxious for the children, unscrewed the base plate and tried to get the machinery going. 'It's all rusted up, I'm afraid,' he said. 'Never mind, pets,' when sudden tears welled up in Debbie's eyes. Bridget was sitting by a signal box at the far end of the hall, patiently waiting for a train to come along the track.

But Guy suddenly exploded. '*Shit*,' he screamed, '*fuck the bloody thing*,' and pushing past the children, squashing the rails as he did so, walked into the sitting room and flung himself into a chair. 'It's always the shitting *same*,' he roared. 'Try and give the little buggers a treat and – oh bloody *hell* . . .'

Grace had helped pack the rails, the cows and the people back into their boxes. Stephen had made comforting noises and cuddled the weeping, frightened children. Guy too had wept, she remembered, by the fire with his whisky bottle. 'Don't come *near* me,' he had warned Anna, when she had tried to approach him.

And yet, Lynn said, the little girls remembered him with love; not Anna, remote and queening it with her lavish gifts, but Guy who had walked on his hands and had exciting secrets. 'How strange the change, from major to minor,' Stephen had hummed sadly to himself, fiddling with the rusted-up engine, when Guy, like the two children, had eventually fallen asleep.

Grace had loved him for the way he had toiled for hours over the little Hornby train, straightened the crushed rails and, by the time she'd left with Anna, to go back to the Camden Town flat, got it running importantly round the legs of the kitchen table, all ready for morning.

Now she was opening her mouth to make some reassuring comment

203

on the return of Stephen when she realised that she did not officially know he was there, so closed it again. Then the kitchen door opened and he walked in. Except that it was not Stephen.

She saw at once how she had been mistaken. This man was of the same slight build, bearded and roughly the same height. He had the same dark baby hair that grew in a circlet round the base of his skull. She remembered its curly softness, how her fingers had played happily with it as Stephen lay asleep beside her, in the bed at White Lodge. But when she had looked through the bungalow curtains it had been rather dark. She saw now that this man's nose was very slightly hooked, and much narrower than Stephen's, how the slightly ridiculous goatee beard was trimmed to a neat little point, how the balding head itself was pointed. The whole face reminded her of a large hornet.

'This is Colin,' Lynn said, unhooking another mug for coffee. 'Colin, this is Grace, you know, Grace Bradley. She came to have a look at the children.' The curious phraseology was Peth language, a reminder that Lynn too had originated in the dreary little town of Grace's birth, had gone to the local art college, met Guy, then Stephen, had moved south, had carefully modified her accent. 'Looking at the children' sounded discouragingly temporary. There seemed no question of staying over, in spite of the grudging mention of a folding bed.

Colin came over and shook her hand. He said, rather quaintly she thought, in view of the fact that he was fresh from another man's bed, 'You're very welcome. But I remember you, don't I? Didn't we once meet in London?'

'I don't think so.'

'Yes, you were at the party, when Anna won the Pritchard Award.'

'I'm afraid I don't remember you.'

'But you can't have forgotten the night?'

'I'm sure nobody could forget it,' she said rather frostily, feeling the reference, between perfect strangers, was a gross intrusion.

'I was out of work at the time,' he went on, quite easily, sliding away from her obvious disapproval. 'I couldn't get a job down there, even though I'd been told they were crying out for teachers in London. Anyhow, I've got one now. I teach at the little school here, over on the mainland.'

'The girls go,' Lynn said, 'but later we think we'll have to send them away. It's all right here at primary level but they'll be bored when they get older. Anna left them some money. We thought we might use that, for the fees. Didn't we, Colin?'

She gave him a mug of coffee, sat down beside him and slid her hand through his arm. Her air, like his, was proprietorial. She wore a ring on her wedding finger, a thin silver rope. 'Colin made this for me,' she said, when she saw Grace looking. 'We're getting married when the divorce comes through. He's living here.'

I know, Grace wanted to say, I watched.

Lynn said, 'I don't suppose you've seen Stevie Boy, by any chance?'

Grace shook her head. 'Not since Guy's funeral, and I didn't speak to him then. He avoided everybody, just went off.'

'That's Steve all over,' Lynn muttered, with sour confidence.

Grace disliked his being called 'Steve' but it was typical. Bridget and Deborah were usually 'Biddie and Debs'. She was suddenly grateful for her own plain monosyllable, and for its meaning: unmerited favour, the love of the Lord that she had done nothing to deserve, like the sun that had poured down on her throughout this long journey.

'I didn't think he'd have gone to that. We heard nothing for ages, afterwards.'

'But he *found* Guy, Lynn. He found him in the bath.'

'I know.' Lynn's mouth was a shrunk line, pressed fiercely against any threat of emotion; but Grace saw how she had tightened her hand on Colin's arm, and how he took it in his own, and stroked it. There was clearly no hope, now, for Lynn's marriage with Stephen. She had come to rest in this Colin; they loved each other. Grace marvelled at how easily other women found men to replace those who had died or fallen by the wayside. She never met spare men. In all her life only Stephen, she felt, had shown real interest, and now she knew that he had not wanted her either.

She said, feeling her way, 'I just wondered if he'd had to go back into hospital, you know, the shock of it and everything . . .'

Lynn shrugged and shook her head. 'I wouldn't know, Grace,' she said stonily. 'He certainly didn't show up at Guy's inquest. I don't know where he was.'

'*You* went?'

'Yes, to see him, to be honest. Huh, that was a laugh. I thought at least we could get on with the legal stuff. He won't answer letters, you see, he's impossible. I could never get him at that flat, and then they cut the phone off. We're no further on now than we were when Guy died.'

Grace whispered, 'Was it awful, Lynn, I mean the inquest?' She needed to know. In the New Year she must attend the one on Anna.

Lynn's face worked. 'Straightforward, no surprises. It was obviously suicide so it was all over pretty quickly. When the coroner gave his verdict the doctor in attendance was reading a newspaper, I was sitting just behind him. He was checking the racing results, I think. I suppose he'd made a bet. That was poor Guy, *finished*.'

Suddenly she stood up, and twisted away from them. Grace had never seen Lynn weep before, but she was clearly weeping now, and, as she came back to the table, making no effort to rub away the tears that coursed silently down her pale, tight cheeks. At last she said slowly, carefully wiping her face on a tissue, 'The thing I could have done without was the headmaster they suddenly wheeled in. They asked him about that thing at Bellingham, with the boy. Do you remember him, Col? Colin came with me,' she added defensively. 'He was a real smarmy type, and you could tell he was lying through his teeth. They tried to make out that Guy's problems were all something to do with that business at the prep school. But I mean, it was years before.'

Grace nodded. 'I remember.' But just what she remembered was cloudy, there had been so many 'businesses'. Guy had used the French he had acquired at Cambridge to teach in a series of little prep schools, obscure country establishments with dubious academic credentials, where pay was low and the absence of a degree an irrelevance. At least two of these he had left suddenly, in mid-term, always running to Anna with some bad luck story. Grace had never asked questions because Anna had never volunteered any information. But she had always assumed the 'problem' must be associated with drink. Now, it seemed, from the hints being thrown out by Lynn, that his misdemeanours had been sexual.

Lynn, of course, would have known about Guy and sex. It had been a prolonged relationship, and she could not believe they had been chaste. She thought of the long succession of girlfriends Guy had brought home for Anna's inspection. He had always favoured rather boyish women, the voluptuous female had never been to his taste. But the idea of there being some homosexual element in his relationships with these boy-women had never occurred to her. 'Were you surprised, Lynn, when Guy killed himself?' she said, trying hard to sound gentler than she felt. She did not want her to weep again.

'Only that it happened then, not that he actually did it. He'd talked to me about it years ago, when we were, you know, going round together.' She flicked a look at Colin and he smiled reassuringly. He was saying, 'It's OK, I know all about that, and about Stephen, but we've got each other now.' They were impenetrable in their smugness. 'He'd never got over his parents, you know,' she went on, 'not like bloody Anna. She just cashed in on it all, well, she was *going* to. That was one of his fears, I think, a book about what happened. Oh, I just don't *know*, Grace. I mean, you could never tell what a bloke like Guy would do next. They told him he had a personality disorder, that time he was in Peth Hospital for drying out. Great psychology, don't you think, telling a man a thing like that when he was doing his level best to give up the booze? It's more than Steve ever did.

'Guy never forgot it, it became a kind of label, I think, something he tried to live up to, in a way. The bloody psychiatrists told Steve the same thing. I mean, hell's teeth, what does any of it *mean*? That you can't control yourself? Well you can, I *have*. I've had to, being left with the kids. I've stopped smoking for a start. Hope you're impressed. Couldn't afford them any more. *Depression.* God, I'm up to here with it . . .' and she put her hands round her throat. 'Anyone can shut themselves up in a room for days on end, not eat, and refuse to come out. That's what Stevie Boy used to do. It was bloody marvellous, I can tell you. Come to think of it, he and Guy were a good match for each other. Mutt and Jeff, that's what dear Anna used to call them.'

'So, er, Stephen's *not* been in hospital?' Grace said cautiously. It was curious but Lynn was definitely more concerned about Guy. Grace had the distinct impression that the missing husband was now simply something of a nuisance. Love had clearly died long ago.

'Not as far as I know. I think the police would have told us.' It was 'us' not 'me', Grace noticed. Colin was absolutely established. In time he would take over as the father of Stephen's children.

'They've been up several times,' he said now. 'They actually seem to think that Stephen – '

But she cut him off. 'I know what they think.'

'Can you *imagine*, though?' Lynn said, with a dry little laugh, flinging out her hands in mock astonishment. 'My ex-husband, some kind of sex killer? I mean, well. *Steve* . . . he's not got it in him.' She spoke as if the sadistic murder of Anna Beardmore was some admirable feat of strength. 'That's what I told that man Buckle. Odd bod, he was. It's not his case, actually. You told him straight, didn't you Col? Queer as a coot, we thought.'

'I quite like him,' Grace said. The remark rather took her by surprise but, after her initial wariness and his own hard-edged officiousness, their general misunderstandings, she felt more sure of him, had believed, when they had talked in the hotel, that he was genuinely concerned for her, had sensed some slight sexual interest which was flattering, even though she found she was unable to respond to him.

Lynn stared at her curiously. 'Oh well, takes all sorts . . .' she said vaguely. Grace recalled something she had quite forgotten about this woman, how she drew upon a small store of stock phrases, in order to communicate. It was on a par with her furnishing the different places she'd lived in from mail-order catalogues. If her supply of cliches and glossy brochures suddenly ceased to be she would become both homeless and dumb. People's marriages had always been a mystery to Grace. Stephen's choice of Lynn quite staggered her.

'You know they've arrested Bayles, do you?' Colin said, 'Here, it's in this,' and he pushed a newspaper across the table.

'I did.' Though she was not going to say how she knew, or what. Instead she asked, 'Do you think that's the end of it? That they've got the right person?'

'Could be,' he said slowly. 'In a way one would *like* to think that the solution was rather more interesting. This man sounds a bit pathetic, and a boringly obvious choice, I'd say.'

'What do you mean, *interesting*?' She was beginning not to like the feel of this conversation. Colin and Lynn, when not fornicating in the end room while the children watched TV, had obviously spent some time considering the identity of Anna's killer, as they might consider a chess problem, or ponder a crossword clue. Removed from London by hundreds of miles, snug and orderly in the Craig, with Stephen not impinging, except for his irritating unhelpfulness over the divorce, they had obviously mulled over the possibilities, between bouts of sex, perhaps. Lynn, she remembered, was addicted to crime stories. 'I think it's some nutter,' she now declared, adding confidently, 'Oh, they'll get him, bound to . . . but perhaps not soon enough,' and her small, shrouded eyes glittered queerly. 'It'll be the same all over again, I think. First he rapes her, then he chops a hand off. *Ugh!*'

'You don't think,' ventured Grace, sickened by the evident relish in Lynn's pronouncement, 'that the hand was connected with her writing? I mean, she was terribly well-known, and there must have been all kinds of people – '

'*Ne'er*,' Lynn cut in scornfully. 'He's into mutilation. He stabbed her, or something, didn't he? He's a nutter, Grace. The hand is just a trade-mark. Anyhow, a psychopath wouldn't necessarily be much of a *reader*. Your average criminal's got a very low IQ, remember. Read your detective novels. He'll just be another perve. Pity old Anna got in his way. Mind you, she was asking for it, holing herself up in the middle of nowhere.'

Grace looked at her with loathing, remembering Marian's similar pitiless dismissal. What she hated was not so much Lynn's dogmatism but the apparent gusto with which she had embarked on her crude analysis. And she had embroidered the facts. There had surely been no mention of any stabbing in the press reports.

There had always been a considerable antagonism between Lynn and Anna and she had attributed it to Lynn's jealousy of Anna's worldly success, which had increased in exact proportion to her own miseries with Stephen, particularly their chronic shortage of money. Now she knew, from Julia Wragg, that Stephen had been in love with Anna, had wanted marriage with her when his own had failed. Julia also, she recollected, had bidden her look at novels if she wanted to understand what had happened at The Rock. Here it was again, the same curious advice from Lynn.

What, though, did this woman actually understand about the psychology of a sex murderer from all these thrillers she read? Only one aspect of the hideous affair was predictable: that in time the man would kill again, and after the same pattern. She recoiled inwardly, thinking of the *Bicycles* story, and of solitary women in expensively-renovated cottages, busily writing books. 'How little we know of any one person,' Ba had told her. Killers, she believed, could be the gentlest of men. Stephen was gentle.

'*Anna*,' Lynn began again, 'always struck me as rather – '

'Shh . . .' Colin said, putting a warning finger to his lips. 'The little ones are on their way, I think.' As the door opened Grace noticed that he removed the newspaper that contained the leading article about Bayles's arrest, naming Stephen as a remaining suspect. 'They both read well,' he said proudly, 'wouldn't want them to see this.' Grace was marginally reassured. In other circumstances, and without Lynn, she felt she could have liked him. She just wished she hadn't seen him on the bed. She kept on seeing it now, and what they had done, and it made her want sex. It wasn't fair.

At first the two little girls treated her as some miraculous object. When she saw her, Bridget, the younger one, immediately scrambled on to Colin's lap and started sucking her thumb.

'*Baby*,' snapped Lynn, 'take it out. It's only Auntie Grace, you must remember Auntie Grace,' and she poked at her.

'Leave her, Lynn, she's OK,' Colin muttered. At least he had more spark than his predecessor. Stephen would have meekly removed the offending thumb.

'Isn't Auntie Anna coming?'

'Not this time, she's very busy,' Grace said.

Deborah stared at her in silence across the table. She had always been the more solemn of the two children. Bridget was very chatty, very confident, but it had never been easy to win Deborah over. There was a remote look about her now, a kind of stricken quality in the way she stood listening, quite separate in the doorway, as the questions poured out from her sister.

'Is Uncle Guy coming?'

'Not this time, I'm afraid.'

'Have you seen Daddy?'

Grace shook her head and opened her overnight bag to find the presents. Stephen's continued absence was a considerable problem but they should have told the children that Anna and Guy had died, just died, unexpectedly and sadly, as grown up people do. There would have been no need to talk of any horrors, and she believed they would have absorbed the knowledge into their own more limited world. The deaths of these two exciting but remote people, who broke into their little routines only rarely and arbitrarily, would not bring that weight of pain which came with all the years of knowing. Not telling them, forcing her to talk always, for as long as she was here, as if all was pre-Guy, pre-last Christmas, gave a feeling of agonizing unreality to it all. It took her back to Peth market-place where she had cheerily reassured Carole Newton that Daddie was 'fine, just fine', when all the time he lay dead in the hospital. She did not want to talk to the children of the living brother and sister. Guy she had not really grieved over, except for the pain he had been to Anna. Anna, for all her faults, she loved and needed still. She could not bear to resurrect her, and yet these people were forcing her into it.

'I didn't know . . . I wasn't sure . . .' she muttered, rooting about in her bag. Then she put the two bottles of wine she had bought in Moffatt on to the table, very much wishing she had chosen something else. All the talk of Stephen and Guy, from Lynn, had brought the old days too vividly back. She knew it was a tactless choice. But Colin said, 'Great,' and seized the bottles. 'I'll put them in the fridge, we can have them with supper.'

'It's only spaghetti,' Lynn said coldly.

'Can *I* have some wine?' asked Bridget, sliding off Colin's lap and reaching up to open the fridge door. Deborah was eyeing the bottle sadly, a little quiver playing round her mouth. Grace wondered what scenes she had witnessed between Stephen and Lynn, what she must have heard, remembered and stored up. She hated herself for making such a silly choice. Anna had sometimes told her she was silly.

'I brought you girls something,' she said. 'Hope they're not too small, you're so *big* now, aren't you?' The sweaters were produced and immediately put on, Bridget parading round the kitchen. 'My one's got trains on,' she said. 'Uncle Guy's got a little train. Daddy tried to mend it. *Will* Uncle Guy come, Mummy?' Deborah, whose sweater was several sizes too large, carefully turned the sleeves back and pulled it up in bunches round her waist, so that it looked as if it fitted.

'It's too big, you look silly, Debs,' chortled Bridget gleefully, still admiring her trains.

'No it's not, Thank you, Auntie Grace,' the older child said dutifully.

Bridget ran over to her. 'Thank you for mine too,' and she reached up for a kiss. At last Grace took them both in her arms, holding Bridget on her lap, hugging Deborah. 'Can we show you our bedroom, Auntie Grace?' she said shyly. 'We've got bunks now.'

'That's a good idea, girls,' Colin said. 'Auntie Grace'll be sleeping in your room. I'll have to get the Z-bed out. Why don't you go and make a space?'

'Yes, come on, I'll take the luggage,' Bridget said importantly, dragging the red zipper bag along the cork tiles. 'Come *on*, Debs . . .'

When they were in the passage Lynn shut the door on them, but Grace could hear her talking to Colin. '. . . just turning up . . .' she caught. 'Who the *hell* does she think she is?'

The bedroom, like the rest of the bungalow, was uncannily neat and tidy. Pine bunks and hanging cupboards occupied one long wall, the other was fitted with a series of white interlocking melamine cubes for the storage of toys and books. Bright curtains with a small print of dancing teddy bears hung at the window, and a fish mobile twirled round. It all had the look of some recommended scheme carefully copied from a home furnishings magazine, and it was in quite remarkable order, for the room of two small children.

'Mummy likes us to keep our room neat and tidy,' Deborah said quietly, picking a stray book up from the carpet and restoring it to a shelf.

'Yes, she gets very cross if we don't put away our things,' parroted Bridget.

Grace saw that the top shelves were filled with paperbacks of Anna's novels. She pulled a couple out. They had obviously never been read and she had difficulty opening them flat. Deborah watched her. 'Auntie Anna's clever, isn't she?' she said.

'Oh yes, very clever.'

'Auntie Anna didn't send me a present on my birthday,' Bridget whimpered, in a sudden burst of petulance, 'and Daddy promised she would. It's not *fair*.'

'Oh shut up, Biddie.' Deborah was wandering rather aimlessly round the bedroom, straightening things up, rubbing at marks on the white shelving, casting the occasional shy look in Grace's direction.

211

Bridget was busy collecting armfuls of picture-books and dumping them on her duvet. 'Auntie Grace can't read all those,' Deborah chided, 'don't be so silly.'

'You will, won't you, Auntie Grace?'

'Well, not all of them, pet. Listen, let me ask Mummy if she needs some help with the supper first. We can't leave her to do all the work, can we?'

'Oh, she'll be all right, come *on* . . .' and Bridget smoothed her first book out at the first page. Grace sat down beside her and looked at the coloured spread obediently. She had forgotten the heartless selfishness of the very small child.

Then Colin came in with the folding bed. Deborah leapt up nervously. 'We've not made the space yet, come on, Biddie, help. She never helps,' she whispered to Grace.

They moved toy boxes away from the window so that he could unfold the bed. 'Hope you won't be in too much of a draught, Grace,' he said. 'We're going to fit double-glazing eventually. It might be a bit chilly tonight, though. D'you mind the sleeping bag? We're a bit short of bedding. *Stephen never sent half the stuff up,*' he whispered. '*You can only go on wrangling for so long, can't you?*'

'That's fine, fine,' said Grace. 'Does Lynn need a hand in the kitchen, only I think Bridget's rather keen to have a story.'

'No, it's OK. I'll help. You stay with the girls. They'll be in bed straight after the meal so there's not that much time.' Lynn had made it clear to him, perhaps, that Grace would definitely be leaving tomorrow.

'I *love* Uncle Colin,' Bridget said passionately, when he had closed the door. 'Sometimes we pretend that he's our Daddy, don't we, Debs?'

'We don't, we *don't*, Auntie Grace,' and suddenly Grace found Deborah was clambering on to her knee, hiding her face against her.

'Sweetheart,' she said, 'it's all right. Daddy'll be here soon. He writes to me, and phones. It's just that he's very busy with his work, that's all,' but against her neck she could feel the child shuddering with tears. They were warm, soaking through the rough wool of the bright new sweater.

She clung there, all through the stories of Postman Pat. In the end Bridget grew bored, and went off to see what was happening in the kitchen. The minute the door was closed Deborah slid off Grace's lap. From the top of a wardrobe she took a hinged box covered with coloured paper. On a label stuck to the top she had written, 'Very Private and Secret. Keep Out. Deborah Fiona Allen'. With reverence she carried the box to Grace and laid it on her knee. 'I didn't want *her* to see,' she said vindictively. 'She's too young.'

The box contained letters and postcards from Stephen, all written in the same spidery hand she recognised from her own cards. The child had arranged them in date order and they covered the months of his absence. He had never written very much, simply cheery messages of love and reassurance. Many of them were embellished with drawings done in fine black line, rather cartoony. She remembered the 'polite' notice in the Ram and a sudden chill went through her. 'These are lovely, Debbie,' she said, but rather desperately for she knew where her duty lay, it was to show them to Buckle, she'd promised. But how could she betray this child?

Deborah said, 'He sent us dresses for our birthdays, but they didn't fit. Mainly he sends us money, but Mummy puts it in our post office. I'm saving up for my own personal stereo. Have you got one, Auntie Grace?'

'No pet, no I haven't.'

'Daddy said he would come at Christmas. Biddie and me went down to the ferry our own selves, but he didn't come.' Again the wide mouth puckered and trembled.

Grace thought of that last Christmas, of how Stephen had found Guy's body in the flat, of the silence that had followed, of his non-appearance at the coroner's court. She said helplessly, 'He'll come soon, Debbie,' and she watched as the very secret private box was restored to its place on top of the wardrobe where nobody, not even Lynn, would meddle with it. She wanted to put her arms round this child, to let her weep and weep. From now on she ought to pray, not for any personal future with Stephen, but for him to be restored to these children, for Colin to be somehow removed and for all to be made right. Such prayers must be a torment to her, bitter and hard, like the agony of the Lord himself. But she knew that those whom he loved best he chastened, and asked to suffer with him. Now Anna was dead perhaps she ought to be godmother to these two children, pray for them every day, use Anna's money to help them in their lives. They were the Lord's. Only this morning he had given her a marvellous word in the Moffatt guest house. *Fear not, for I have redeemed thee. I have called you by name. You are mine, precious in my sight, and honoured, and I love you.*

'Debbie,' she said, stroking the child's hair, 'I'm sure your daddy *will* come back.' But the eyes that looked up at her held an awful certainty that he would never return.

'Food time!' shrilled Bridget, bustling in.

*

213

To her surprise, Lynn gave thanks for the dish of spaghetti. 'Hands together, eyes closed,' she ordered the two girls, the old formula jerking Grace back to childish days. 'For what we are about to receive may the Lord make us truly thankful, Amen.'

She pondered. Lynn was the daughter of a clergyman, high Anglican, long since dead, who had once presided over St Simon and St Jude on the other side of Peth. The place was still spiky, according to Marian; 'Pongs and gongs,' she had said witheringly, 'the whole silly caboodle.' Lynn had been anti-church in the days when she had gone about with Guy, and her parents had allowed her to be, believing that she would one day 'come back'. Now it would appear that she had. There had been the elaborate christenings of both children, reported to Grace in malicious detail by Anna ('white socks, darling, hair ribbons, even a two-tiered *cake* . . . oh, God . . .'), then the Sunday School classes on the mainland described so enthusiastically by Bridget in between bouts of Postman Pat; now Grace before Meat, as Daddie had always described it. Colin, she noticed, had bowed his head reverently as the words were pronounced. Perhaps he belonged to the Lord. Therefore, should her prayers now be that he should become the father of this family? Should she accept that Stephen would never again have a place here?

But if she accepted that it must force her to reconsider her own position, review her long-cherished hope that she might one day marry him herself. And something was wrong with that, something that belonged to the deeply-rooted conviction which she was trying, unsuccessfully, to ignore, her dread that Stephen was never going to return to these children, nor come to her, nor to anyone. It was part of that terrifying darkness that sometimes lapped round, quenching the necessary light. She could not share her fearfulness with The Girls, they would make her discount it, pray over her, perhaps, talk of her 'hunches', insist it was not 'of the Lord'. In her more hopeful moments she felt Stephen might be in waiting somewhere, waiting for Anna's murderer to be tracked down and exposed or even, voluntarily, to come forward. Buckle had said this might happen. Only then, perhaps, would he come to her and to these children, be seen in the light again. He had always been a frightened person and the consistent accusations against him must have paralysed him with fright, brought back his own darkness.

During the meal, which Lynn conducted like an irate Victorian governess, constantly rapping and snapping at the two children for gobbling, for speaking with their mouths full, for interrupting, all references to Stephen were carefully deflected. The questions – when was he coming to see them, had he visited Auntie Grace and did he know that Uncle Colin had come to look after them – all came from Bridget who kept up a stream of prattle parallel to shovelling in huge forkfuls of pasta. At her side Lynn kept wiping her face with a paper napkin and making disapproving clucking noises. Deborah, picking half-heartedly at her own plateful, asked no questions, Grace noticed, and at one point, when Bridget banged her fork on the table saying, 'I want to see my *Daddy*,' poked at her, and whispered that she should shut up.

Lynn packed them off to bed the minute Bridget's plate was empty, and Deborah's abandoned. Colin got up and shepherded them out of the kitchen. 'He'll see to them,' she told Grace. 'He's absolutely marvellous,' pouring out more wine. She had drunk a fair amount during the meal. Now she didn't smoke Grace supposed she needed a substitute of some kind, but alcohol was ironic, in view of Stephen and Guy.

She said tentatively, 'Lynn, I thought I might go to Eilean na Naoimh tomorrow. I've been reading about it. I could take the girls if you like.' On a blackboard, on the mainland quay, she had noticed that someone ran boat trips to Monica's island. She had thought she could buy some nice food for a picnic, give the girls a treat. 'Do let me take them, Lynn,' she urged. 'It'd be a break for you, and I'm sure they'd enjoy the boat ride. I'd really love to do it.'

But Lynn was frowning. 'Oh, I don't think there's much doing on Eilean na Naoimh,' she said. 'It's just ruins, and anyhow, the kids travel on boats all the time. They've no choice, living in this place.'

Grace had forgotten how thoroughly Lynn had crushed Stephen.

'Anyhow,' she went on suspiciously, 'what's the great fascination? Birdwatchers go there a lot, I know that, but I wouldn't have thought it was exactly your scene, Grace.'

'Well, it's a sort of pilgrimage, really,' she said with difficulty, as Lynn's eyes narrowed. 'I'm reading this marvellous book about it, by Monica Sale. She made a retreat there.'

'Oh *yes*, she was a real holy Joe, she was. Our minister knew her. Into women priests or something, wasn't she? He didn't much care for her, I remember that. Bossy type, apparently.'

'She's a deacon,' Grace said carefully. 'Women can't be priests, not yet. Listen, do let me take the girls. We could have such fun, and it's ages since I've seen them.' But she sensed that, however hard she tried to persuade, other plans would be made. There was definite resistance to the innocent scheme she had devised. Perhaps Lynn didn't trust her not to talk of Stephen, or of Anna and Guy, perhaps she feared prying questions about Colin, or even some curious religious indoctrination from Grace herself or from another 'holy Joe' who might be making his retreat on the island.

When Colin came back Lynn announced, loud and rather belligerent, red with all the wine, 'Grace wanted to take Bid and Debs on a boat ride to Eilean na Naoimh tomorrow but they're spending the day at Josie's, aren't they? I had her lot last Saturday and it'll give me a chance to catch up on some orders. What time were you planning to go back, Grace? There aren't so many boats at weekends.'

Grace shrugged. 'I'm staying across at the hotel tomorrow evening,' she said. A night at the bleak-looking concrete hostelry by the harbour had not been part of her plan and she hadn't booked, but Lynn was leaving her no choice. 'Then I can make an early start for home on Sunday. I'm staying in Moffatt again, on the way down.'

'You could buy another sweater,' Lynn said, with a queer little giggle. She was definitely rather drunk. 'I wish *I* could buy some new clothes, but that's not on, not with what Steve sends. I don't know what he thinks he's playing at. He's bloody mad to think we can survive on it.'

'Now come on, love,' Colin chided, obviously embarrassed. 'He always sends something. It'll get sorted out. Anyhow, we're managing, aren't we?'

'Yes, but that's not the point, Col,' Lynn flashed, thumping the table. 'Who the hell does he think he is, sending dribs and drabs in envelopes, when he feels like it? Fifty quid one month, twenty the next, *in little brown envelopes*, Grace, can you credit it? He sends the kids pound coins wrapped in bits of paper. I ask you . . .'

'Children love things like that though, don't they?' Grace said rather daringly, determined to defend Stephen. 'I expect it's a bit like treasure to them, lots of gold coins.'

'Oh for heaven's *sake*,' Lynn snapped, upending an empty bottle over her glass and watching the remaining drops slide into it. 'Does he send you pound coins too? And those silly little cards?'

'Not *silly* cards,' Grace said calmly, but feeling her way now. Lynn had definitely drunk far too much and she recognised this precarious stage only too well. Soon the peevishness would deepen into anger, then turn to weeping. She had witnessed the process in Guy many times, in the White Lodge days and once, at Meager Park, in Stephen. 'He's sent me the odd note,' she said, 'and there was the – ' But she stopped, not wanting to betray Stephen, or herself. Lynn ought not to know of the abortive meeting in Richmond. What good could it do?

But she was too late. 'Then there was *what*? Go on, you were going to say something.'

'Oh, nothing. It doesn't matter.' But she felt herself blushing.

'Then there was *what?*' Lynn's voice was unpleasantly shrill, and she had thrust her face up close.

'Leave it, love,' Colin said wearily, beginning to stack plates. But Lynn was waiting.

'I was in Yorkshire last week,' Grace said, shrinking back. 'I'd told Stephen I'd be up there, in a letter.'

'Had you gone to lay claim to Anna's cottage, then? We heard you'd got it, via one of Steve's stupid cards. Lucky Jew.'

Grace winced and Colin said rather tetchily, 'Oh, for heaven's sake, Lynn, grow up.' Having carefully swabbed the table clean he was now donning an apron, and running water into the sink. But still Lynn didn't budge.

'He said he was going to be up there too, and that we could meet, at a concert. It was in the old theatre at Richmond, a choir from York. Well, I went, but he never turned up.'

'Typical.'

'But Lynn, I think he's ill.' She wanted to say 'have pity'. Colin turned from the sink and looked at her sympathetically. He said, 'I'm quite sure he is, Grace, he's obviously hallucinating. He *meant* to meet you, no doubt, probably thinks he did, now. It's all part of the same behaviour pattern.'

'Oh *balls*,' Lynn shouted, getting up and rooting about in a cupboard. 'Colin's an amateur psychologist,' she said, with heavy sarcasm, 'he's rather interested in Stevie Boy, thinks he's got him all sewn up. But he can't bloody explain why he won't bloody show up, and do his duty by his two kids.' She came back to the table with a bottle of whisky. 'Anybody want some? Speak now, there's not much,' and she sloshed several inches into a tumbler.

'No thanks,' Grace said.

'And Colin'll say no, and that I've had enough. I know, I know . . .' and she rammed the bottle back into the cupboard.

Quite suddenly, as Grace had feared all along, she began to weep. Colin abandoned his washing up, pulled out a stool and put his arm round her. On the other side, Grace held her hand. 'I think,' Lynn mourned, pushing the whisky away untouched, 'I sometimes think I'd have been happier with old Guy. We had some great times, Grace, we really did. I've still got all his poems, you know.' Then a cackle of empty mirth cracked round the kitchen.

'Please, Lynn, leave it. Let's all go to bed,' Colin said.

'Bed was what Guy was no good at, Grace,' Lynn bawled. 'It would have been OK otherwise, but *in bed* . . .'

'I liked his poems,' Colin cut in rather desperately, 'a bit Larkinish, but I did like them. He lost his way, I think, footling about in those wretched little schools. He should have persevered. He'd have got into print eventually.'

'I didn't know Guy had written any poetry,' Grace said, grateful for the diversion. But Stephen had, she'd seen that verse sequence interleaved with the drawings about the old men in the London flat. They had shared much, she reflected sadly, these missing men; painting and versifying, drink, a certain sexual inadequacy, and this woman Lynn with the flaming hair, so unutterably wretched now under the thorny exterior. And suddenly she started up all over again. 'In *bed*, Grace . . .' she said, raucous and very deliberate.

'That's where I'm going,' Colin announced, standing up.

'I think I will too, if you don't mind,' Grace said. 'I had a terribly early start this morning,' and she went to the door.

'Use the bathroom first, then, I'll get you a towel,' Colin called after her.

'No, it's OK, I've brought one. Er, I'll go then.'

But before she had quite shut the door on them, slowly and carefully, so as not to wake the children, Lynn had started yelling again. 'What she needs is a bloody good *fuck*,' she heard, as she tiptoed away.

The next evening, in a small back room at the Bay Hotel, she sat in front of a small television set, trying to concentrate on a news bulletin. Someone important had been shot in the Lebanon but Grace didn't actually know where the Lebanon was. More than once The Girls had hinted that, as a Christian, she should be more informed about world affairs. But she couldn't concentrate on what the man was saying, nor on the marvellousness of Monica's island from which she had just returned. All she could think about was Lynn's cruelty.

When she had woken up that morning, very late, after an initial struggle to drift off in the suffocating sleeping bag, a struggle which had finally given way to profound sleep, she had found the house empty and a note to say Lynn had taken the girls across to Josie's, wherever that was, on an early boat. There had been no sign of Colin. She would have no doubt insisted on taking him along, whether or not he had tried to resist. 'Don't quite know when we'll be getting back,' the note on the kitchen table had ended carelessly. 'Ciao, if we miss you.'

She had been the only passenger on the small motor launch that went across to Eilean na Naoimh. The man that took her over had agreed to drop her back on the island, instead of going straight to the mainland, though rather grudgingly, and for a fee. That way, though, she could at least get a last glimpse of the children, before going to the hotel. But when she had reached the bungalow, in the

late afternoon, she had found everything locked up and the red zipper
bag, which she had packed that morning, dumped in the front porch,
by the abandoned tricycles. A second scribbled note was attached to
the strap 'We're all staying at Josie's. Party on. Hope you enjoyed
your boat trip. Lynn.'

She had slung the bag over her shoulder and set off down the track.
Rounding the last corner to meet the sea she had spotted the ferry
still moored to the ramshackle landing stage, but the boatman was
handing his last passengers aboard. She had shouted out, run the last
few yards at a pelt and arrived panting painfully. There had been
curious glances as she stepped aboard and found a seat, put her bag
at her feet and closed her eyes. Her heart was knocking hard, deep
in her chest, and she had the new sickly feeling she had experienced a
couple of times before. It was surely the silly burst of running, nothing
to do with her 'flutter' which Dr Lucas had assured her many people
had, without even knowing it. Even so, she should have waited for the
next boat, not made a sweating red-faced spectacle of herself. But she
had wanted to leave the island, the unkind note and the shut house;
those tricycles.

Now she switched off the television and stared at the blank screen,
thinking of Eilean na Naoimh and of the endless rocky steps up which
she had laboured, the steps to the sanctuary with its broken cross,
its huddle of curious hive-shaped cells in which and under which,
in minute subterranean chambers, holy men in ancient times had
contemplated the mysteries of their Lord. He had wanted her to go
to Eilean na Naoimh, and in spite of the pain of Lynn's behaviour, he
perhaps had meant her to go alone from the beginning and not with
the two little girls who would no doubt have run up the winding stone
stairway, chattering and twittering, and racing each other to the top.
Nobody else had come in the boat to the tiny sea-lashed island with
its murderous cliffs, its minute solitary patch of bright green grass
where a crofter, the boatman had told her, had once tethered his
lone cow to a post, for fear it should tumble into the sea and be
drowned.

She had ascended slowly, thinking of the Lord on his way to
Calvary, wishing she had brought some deliberate burden to carry, as
Monica had carried her tent, her box of provisions, her clothing. She
too had wanted to enter into the Lord's own heaviness as, stumbling,
he had carried his cross.

At the top, outside the walls of the ruined chapel, now nothing
more than a huddle of stones marked by what must once have been
a Celtic cross, the cruciform ringed with a rough inner halo but all
weathered into stumpy shapelessness and latticed by lichens and

strands of moss, she found, after much searching, the fresh water spring described in Monica's book. At first it seemed a mere patch of wetness in the grass, but when she bent down she discovered stones among the bright green blades and water bubbling gently over them, cupped into a tiny pool which someone had hollowed out and lined with pebbles, to catch the precious drops.

She knelt, scooped up some water, and splashed it on her face. Then she made the sign of the cross, a bold, broad sign with great sweeping gestures, standing upright now for there was no one to see, gazing out across the heaving blue-black water to the neighbouring island, a glaring white guano-covered outcrop with shooting rocks like great needles, inhabited entirely by gannets. The holy men had caught and eaten them, according to Monica, rowing across to the screaming colony in their coracles of tar and skin. She herself had brought rations for her retreat but, as the solitary days rolled by, she had come to want very little food, and had drunk only water from the spring. Like the holy men before her she had come to be busied only with God, taken up, as time passed over, marked only by the divisions of day and night, with her still, deep contemplation of the Lord himself, and of what he had created in this water, this land, in its stones and its birds, its silences, its very *thisness*; taken up, too, in her prayers for the world beyond this still, small point of absolute calm, the world that heaved endlessly like the waters, *the world*.

Grace too, like Monica, had felt the centuries of prayer on Eilean na Naoimh, felt the sheer weight of intercession offered there, for the dead and the unborn, for the broken. She felt it again, in this ugly room, saw the monks at their devotions, huddled in the tiny dank underground cells beneath her feet, where they had mortified the flesh, bending double as they crawled into the darkness to remind themselves how their Lord too had bent meekly under the last agonising yoke, prayed with blood and sweat that the final cup be taken from him. There had been blood on these stones also, for marauding pirates had landed on the island with long-prowed boats and slaughtered the holy men in their sanctuary, roasting their flesh for meat. In the holiest places Satan broke in, raging around his prey like a roaring lion, endlessly seeking whom he might devour. As he had ranged round Anna's valley, breaking it open. That too was a place of sanctity, another Eilean na Naoimh where, under all the horror, she had felt Christ's peace.

As she stood in the sanctuary she had put her hands on the ruined cross, needing to steady herself as the remembrance of the death once more swept through her. At her feet the miraculous clear water bubbled into the grass, gulls screamed round and, far below, against invisible rocks, the sea hurled itself at the island in a dull monotonous roar. Then a sunburst suddenly split the thick grey of sky and water, brightening the great litter of stones all round with points of light, and she felt another, different light flaming somewhere inside her, light that first dappled, then began to thin the lapping interior darkness that had crept ever closer, threatened ever more nearly, since Anna's death, light that seemed now to grow from the roots of Love itself, nourished by all the people who had dedicated themselves to Love on this rock. Those ancient prayers had been for her and for now. It was why she had come.

As she clasped the shattered cross the Lord gave her a word quite clearly. *Because he cleaves to me in love, I will deliver him. I will protect him, because he knows my name. When he calls to me, I will answer him; I will be with him in trouble.* She had read it that morning in the children's room, at the deserted house. As she thought of it again the goodness of God broke over her, like the waves of the sea.

She knew now beyond all doubt that she must leave Peth and live in Anna's valley. If when she returned home, the craft shop had been sold to somebody else, then so be it. There would be another work for her to do and another place for her to live in. It might be The Rock itself. With or without The Girls she would go there soon. She was as certain of this word, and of this sign, as she was that Stephen had not murdered Anna.

Carefully, but with a lighter step now, and a with a little spurt of joy bubbling endlessly inside her like the high, secret spring, she made her way down the rocky steps to wait for the motor launch. It was raining hard and the wind flung water against her cheeks like little handfuls of stones, and the boatman seemed suspicious of her. But she had her word, and it warmed her.

Now, in her room, she tried hard to focus on Eilean na Naoimh, on the moment when she had stood by the cross, the sun splitting the clouds. There was no point now in dwelling on Lynn and her deliberate spite, or on why the kindly Colin had weakened and let her be abandoned so churlishly, or of how the little girls must feel, for she had, unwisely she realised now, mentioned her idea of a picnic on Monica's island, and it had excited them.

By the tray of tea-making equipment lay a shiny Gideon Bible. She picked it up and turned to the Psalms, feeling she should read her special, personal word from the Lord over again. But then the telephone rang. It was reception, telling her there was an outside call. Would she please hold the line.

Let it be Lynn, she said, Colin or Lynn with some explanation, perhaps a possibility of seeing the children again, of loving them. Or let it be Buckle, with the news that Bayles had been charged, or Gary Reed, anybody but Stephen.

It was Marian Stoker, loud and rather formal. In her absence there had been a break-in at White Lodge. She mustn't upset herself but they felt she ought to know, and not come home unprepared. 'We can't tell just what's gone, of course,' she brayed with a certain enthusiasm (Marian, Grace always felt, rather relished bearing bad tidings. She had noticed the zest with which she had spoken of her various 'cases'). 'But they only seem to have been interested in your drawing room. The rest of the house looks OK, according to the police. I'm afraid your silver's gone, though.'

'From the drawing room? You mean the display table?'

'Yes. They've emptied it, I'm afraid.'

That seemed cruel. Everything was insured but the glass-topped table had contained Daddie's collection of watches, which could not be replaced. He had started in the trade as a fourteen-year-old assistant at Blackshaw's, the only other 'quality' jeweller in Peth. The old watches, all lovingly restored by him over the years, had been specially assigned in his will to Grace, who as a child had sometimes been allowed to polish the gold and silver cases. After The Tragedy he had allowed Guy to give them a good clean, patiently taking one of them apart to show him the movement, anything to keep the boy occupied.

She tried to concentrate on what Marian was saying, telling herself that the stolen watches were only 'things'. But she kept thinking of Daddie, and of Guy, leggy and pale in his school blazer, of all the pain in that face, only given voice at night when he lay in the room next to her own, and she heard him weeping.

'They've gone through your desk pretty thoroughly too, I gather, papers all over the place et cet. Buckle says they were definitely after money, it's classic,' she added authoritatively.

'Did he say anything else?'

'Not really. He'll obviously be round to see you when you're back. When's it to be, by the way?'

'Monday. I'm spending tomorrow night in Moffatt. But I'll be home lunch-time, the day after. You don't know when Buckle's coming, do you?'

'Didn't say, I'm afraid.'

'Would you let him know I'll be back Monday lunch-time?'

'Will do.'

Grace was obliged to ring off without speaking to Ba, who had not been offered. It was typical of Marian to take charge of an official, grave communication like this. Also, for all her practical kindness, Marian, Grace sensed, wanted Ba for herself. She was not to become one of The Girls.

She pottered around the bedroom, switching on the electric kettle for a cup of tea. She would ring Buckle herself before she left the hotel. He had given her his home number, said she might speak to him at any time. It would be easier returning to White Lodge if she knew exactly what had happened, and he would know more than Marian. Also, she found she was rather wanting to hear his voice again, just to *hear* it.

In the night she dreamed of many men, and of sex with them. All were silent and smiling, curving over her in a white bed. She was aware that her feet were muddy and bruised, from scrambling over rocks, yet still the men smiled. When the climax came she cried, full of a joy and a certainty that she had not known she lacked. The faces were those of Stephen, of Buckle and of Maurice Peacock, Guy's face also, more often than the others, very young and not twisted by The Tragedy. As he curved towards her the silver watches hung on his coat pressed against her breasts, hurting them.

15

Calmly she drove south, finding that she was not unduly worried about the intruders at White Lodge, apart from the loss of Daddie's watches, which was a grief to her. Before the visit to Eilean na Naoimh such news would have been devastating but now she carried a new peace round with her, a new joy, welling up inside like that secret water in the high grass of the little island. *For I know the plans I have prepared for you, plans for good and not for evil, to give you a purpose and a hope.* The prophets had eyes before and behind. Like the great beasts of Revelation they were all eyes; all ears too, to discern what the Lord had to say to them as they endured endless days without meat or drink in their terrible mountain fastnesses.

But in these days it was not always very clear what the Lord was saying to his people, and she had always envied some of the women in Wednesday Group who so often described how the Lord had spoken to them, advising this, advising that. Now, though, she believed that she too had discerned, after months and years of waiting upon God for some incontrovertible sign of His will for her. As she approached her violated house it held no terrors, nor did its likely condition nag her as she entered the familiar outer suburbs of the town, nor the mystery of Stephen or Anna's death crowd in on her as before. It was as if the Lord had assigned them to the past, along with White Lodge and all that was in it. By spring she would be living in the valley, would have started her new life.

Marian must have been on the look-out for her because the front door opened even before she had switched off her car engine. 'We've not got much time, I'm afraid,' she said, coming down the steps, 'but Ba's done soup and sandwiches. We're both due back at two. Good journey?' in that order, and grabbing the blue suitcase and the red zipper bag. This time there was no embrace for which Grace was thankful. Marian was clearly in business mood, the protuberant eyes bright under the shaggy brows, the large teeth gleaming. 'Only obviously,' she said, 'we didn't want you to come back to an empty house, in the circs.'

Muttering thanks Grace followed her inside. The rest of the reception committee consisted of Ba, Binkie, who immediately came rubbing against her ankles, an extremely youthful policeman called David Jespersen, and Mrs Lumb. When she saw her walk in, the old woman suddenly burst into tears. 'Oh, for heaven's *sake*,' Marian hissed through gritted teeth. 'Why does she have to make such a production of it? I've told her, it's happening all the time, especially in an area like this, these big old houses, well screened from the road. You ought to get a dog, Grace.'

Grace smiled vaguely, saying nothing, but inside something warmed her. She was moving on soon so there was no need to think about dogs. That was why, before inspecting the house, she must look at her post. But first she put her arms round Mrs Lumb. 'It's all right, Gladys,' she whispered, 'honestly. I – what? Oh, *silly*. How could it possibly be your fault?'

Ba, rather nervously, she thought, had crept up and sneaked in a furtive peck on the cheek before disappearing down the hall after Marian, with talk of warming soup. Grace felt her plan for suggesting that The Girls might come in with her on the valley enterprise was rather less hopeful now. Marian would definitely oppose it. When the three of them were together she was watchful, clearly wanting Ba for herself. And Ba was always nervous with Grace, loving, but somehow never to the full.

She tried to comfort Mrs Lumb, who was still jerking out dry little tears, rigid in her arms, almost as if the bodily touch, even though it came from someone familar and trusted, were some kind of obscenity. But Grace hung on, believing that the old woman needed arms round her, having no one to touch her now, no one to stroke her, or to awaken love. 'There's absolutely nothing to worry about, Gladys,' she kept repeating, 'just a little bit of silver they said. I mean, it could have been so much worse. You hear some terrible stories. What . . . I can't hear you, darling?' The old woman was mumbling something about the bathroom window, the wash-house, the key in the usual place.

At her elbow the pink-cheeked young officer was awkwardly hovering. Some instinct made Grace draw Mrs Lumb aside, and sit her down. She dropped her voice and Mrs Lumb obligingly whispered back. It seemed that the wash-house key was missing and that it was all her fault because she'd not checked round as she usually did, after coming in on the Saturday, to see things were all right. That's how they'd got in, the police reckoned . . .

'I told her, Miss Bradley,' the young officer said rather helplessly, taking refuge in his notebook. 'They'll get in if they really want to, whether there's a key handy or not.'

225

'Listen, I'm not at all sure that key was still there, Gladys,' Grace told her, trying to sound equally reassuring. 'I've not used it for months. I just can't remember . . . now *don't* worry. Come and have a sandwich with us.'

'Oh, no. I just came to see you, like, see you'd got back safe and that. I'll be off now,' and she knotted a headscarf under her chin and buttoned up her mackintosh. The suggestion of her breaking bread in this house with a policeman and The Girls seemed to hold some kind of terror for her, from the way Grace's kindly suggestion had made her suddenly cower back. 'I'll be in Friday, then,' and she let herself out through the side lobby. Grace could not persuade her to use the front door like everyone else. She had this need to abase herself.

'Goodbye, Gladys,' she called after her. 'Mind how you go.' She knew that there would have to be further worried talk about the missing key but not until they were on their own. 'The usual place', an empty paint can up on a shelf in the old wash-house where Daddie had cornered the rat, had contained a spare front door key for as long as she could remember. Apart from herself, only Mrs Lumb knew it was there. Then she recalled that Stephen had used it to let himself into the house, on the night he had come inside her. She had been at the women's Wednesday Meeting and had told him where he might find it, just in case she was delayed. She had not been, but he had reached the house early.

'Grub up,' Marian said heartily, popping a round red face out from the kitchen end of the long hall. 'Will you join us, David? As I said, our timetable's rather tight but we didn't want Grace coming home hungry, to a cold house.' *David.* The little intimacy amused her as she glanced through the letters neatly set out on the telephone table. Marian would have no doubt dealt with him as she dealt with one of her 'cases', taking over at once as they went systematically through the rooms of White Lodge to find out what was missing, suggesting computerised lists, perhaps. She really couldn't ever live with Marian, nor with the way she repeated everything two or three times, like an infant school teacher, or someone training dogs. Puppy-like, the gangling young officer was already shambling down the hall. 'Well yes, thanks very much. I'll need to check things through with Miss Bradley but a spot of lunch would be very nice, if you can spare it.'

'Good-oh. This way then. Coming, Grace?'

She went after them slowly, reading a letter from the Richmond estate agent. The craft shop, he wrote, was indeed still on the market. He had noted her interest and would suggest an early appointment to view. Full details were enclosed.

'Anything exciting, Grace?' Ba said, ladling out soup. As she entered the kitchen she had slipped the long buff envelope into her bag.

'Not really. This smells good,' and she pulled out a stool, aware, however, that horse-eyed Marian was eyeing her with suspicion, having picked up that this answer was not wholly true.

Grace had rather hoped that she would be allowed to go over White Lodge without The Girls, that was, sans Marian. But she rushed them all through the food, cleared away, then chivvied them in the direction of the drawing room.

'If you're short of time, Miss Stoker,' the young policeman said tentatively, 'perhaps we should leave the desk until last. Only I shall need Miss Bradley to go through it all quite carefully,' and he stopped at the bottom of the staircase.

'Good idea.' Grace was relieved. The drafts of her letters to Pollitts, to Julia Wragg and to Magnus Croucher were inside the desk. She had planned to consult Ba about them, would still do so, but she didn't want advice from Marian. Boldly she led the way up the stairs, with Marian on her heels, checking her watch and muttering that the drawing room was 'key'.

To her disappointment, Grace suspected, nothing was amiss in the bedrooms. She pulled out drawers, ran her eyes along familiar shelves, inspected mantelpieces. All was in the customary immaculate order achieved by Mrs Lumb's cleaning labours and her own fastidiousness. As she slid drawers back on carefully folded garments and closed cupboards, on endless racks of polythened dresses and coats, on boxed shoes, boxed gloves, boxed scarves, she felt a certain pride. Then she thought of the old song, 'For No One', and knew that at last she had discerned wisely. Everything here must go. It was all barenness and sterility. It led nowhere.

Downstairs took rather longer to check out but here too it was obvious to her that nothing had been touched. Her valuables, all Mother's jewellery, the silver and various bundles of policies and certificates were permanently stored in an old green safe in the rear pantry, the safe Daddie had always called the Iron God. Nobody had attempted to broach it. There was no logic in leaving the watch collection out of the safe when she went away on holiday yet she invariably did, and nobody had ever touched them before. But on the faded blue velvet of the display table was now an intricate pattern of darker circles, where the cases had rested.

'Anything else missing, Grace?' said Marian, as she stared down at it sadly, feeling her foolishness. She looked carefully round the room.

'No. No, I don't *think* so . . .' then 'Oh *no*. Aunt Celia's clock. It was always on that little window ledge. Funny . . . I'm amazed anyone even noticed it. It's such a dark corner.'

'And couldn't be seen from the garden. Humph. Neither can your display table.' This was Marian, hockey legs apart on the hearth rug, arms folded, thrusting. 'It suggests an inside job to me.'

Her sense of high drama rather made Grace want to giggle, in spite of the loss of Aunt Celia's pretty French carriage clock, a silver wedding gift to her parents. 'Marian,' she said very firmly, 'the only person who knows this house from top to bottom apart from me is Mrs Lumb, and you're surely not suggesting – '

'Oh no, no. David's already questioned her, of course.'

Gently, very gently, hoped Grace. The young man looked mild enough but he was quite obviously dismayed by the barging Marian.

Ba was looking at her watch. 'Sorry, darling,' she said, coming up to Grace, 'but I'm due back at work in ten minutes. Marian's dropping me off. It's on her way.'

At the front door Grace asked if they could come round to supper the following night. She wanted to tell them about her move though not, she felt now, to suggest they might come in on the craft shop venture. It wouldn't work, not the three of them together. But now she was definitely leaving Peth she wanted to share her plan with somebody, talk it all through. Sharing it would make it real, and they could talk about the book on Anna, too. 'I'd love to,' Ba began warmly, but Marian interrupted. 'No, we can't. Don't you remember? It's the banner meeting, at Ailsa's.'

Ba looked blank. Ailsa Birch was a fellow librarian who occasionally came to St Saviour's, someone who didn't yet know the Lord but whom The Girls were working on. 'I don't remember saying we'd go to that . . .' Ba said vaguely, definitely uncomfortable and avoiding Marian's hard eyes.

'Oh yes, dear, yes, and we must. She'll have baked, and everything.'

'Well, perhaps the day after, then?' suggested Grace. 'My week's quite free.' It was not true about the banner meeting, surely. Ailsa was very much on the fringe of things. She wouldn't have been asked to host a sewing group.

'Look dearie, we'll ring. Must dash now,' and Marian bore Ba away to the car.

She had lied about their promise to go to Ailsa's, and she knew Grace had caught her out in the lie. The large hazel eyes with their slightly bloodied whites had slid rapidly away from the accusing stare of Grace's dark brown ones, the glossy eyes with the amazing milky-blue pupils, so admired by William Buckle.

Grace had not been able to reach Buckle by phone from Scotland, but it was clear that he had been fully informed about her movements, of the visit to Anna's valley, and to Lynn on the island. He had come to White Lodge himself just as soon as they had told him of the break-in. Jespersen was obviously impressed that someone so senior should have taken such an interest. He did not mention Anna or Stephen, she noticed, or hint at any connection. Presumably, he had his orders.

All the papers in her desk had been pulled out of their various drawers and pigeon holes and lay in a crumpled heap on the worn red leather top. 'Sorry it's a mess,' Jespersen said, 'but we couldn't touch anything, not before you came.'

She touched it now, smoothing out the letters she had drafted before going to the valley, her polite note to Magnus Croucher about the projected book, various questions to Edward Pollitt about how she stood exactly, in relation to Anna's will, her request to Julia Wragg that all the literary papers be sent to Peth. The sheets had been screwed up into hard little balls. 'Funny,' she murmured, carefully flattening them out, and reading over what she had written.

He said, 'You didn't keep any money in this desk, did you?'

'No, but . . . oh *no* . . .' and she opened a little drawer, then a second and a third. 'How *stupid* of me . . .'

'What's the problem, Miss Bradley?'

'Well, just before I left I got a cash-card from the building society. They've installed one of those machines in town. I'm sure I put it in this drawer.'

'And it's not there now?'

'No.'

'But presumably you've got the PIN number? It's no use to anyone without that.'

She shook her head, embarrassed. 'It's ridiculous, I know, exactly what they tell you *not* to do, but I'm afraid when it arrived I put it with the card. Look, here's the envelope. I left in a bit of a rush.'

'Go and phone them, Miss Bradley. They'll cancel the card for you.'

Obediently she went off, her heart flickering. When she came back she felt sweaty and hot and there was that rough grating inside her throat that always signalled tears. 'They've cancelled it,' she said dumbly, 'but it had been used. Three withdrawals of two hundred

229

pounds each, over three days. I, well . . .' She shrugged. 'I asked for it, didn't I?' She searched his face, then the silent, thickly-draped room, saw the niche where Aunt Celia's clock used to beat, saw the faded velvet of Daddie's empty clock table and felt afraid. Ba had been robbed once and for many weeks afterwards she too had lived in fear. She said it was how she imagined a rape.

Jespersen was writing in a notebook. 'We'll have to get full details of the withdrawals,' he told her, 'when, where, et cetera. They're quite used to it, and they're usually very good. You could get that silver back, and the clock, if they can trace him. Someone might have seen him using the machine, you see. That'd be good, wouldn't it?' he added kindly.

'Marvellous.'

She handed him the building society envelope with a brave little smile, pressed quite extravagant thanks upon him for all he had done and showed him to the front door. But inside she was wanting to scream. She'd not thought she minded very much about the burglary, but now she had seen the state of the desk and discovered the various thefts there was a worm of panic gnawing. She kept thinking about the vanished wash-house key and of the night Stephen had let himself into the house, had sat in his old duffel coat at the kitchen table, waiting for her, a glass of wine in his hand. She thought too of the money that had been stolen with the plastic card. Had some of it been translated into gold doubloons and sent to the island in little bags, to give joy?

Buckle came in the evening, while she was sitting over the remains of Ba's soup, on his way home from work, he claimed, but she knew that he rented one of the new town flats in the same block as Breda Smith. There was no way White Lodge could be on his route.

When she opened the door to him he seemed, though only momentarily, at a slight loss, less master of the situation than before, limper, and his face somehow apologetic, she thought, and grey with fatigue. She had come from the kitchen with a spoon in her hand. Now she stood on the front step feeling rather foolish, carefully holding it away from her cardigan, to avoid drips.

He said, 'I'm sorry, you're obviously in the middle of your meal,' but he didn't move away; rather, she felt, he leaned towards her slightly. 'Only, I have one or two things here . . .' and he fingered a paper file under his arm. 'Jespersen's followed up the cash-card. The three withdrawals were made locally. So far, that's all we've got. It was very bad luck, that was.'

She was grateful to him for she knew that he must think her extremely stupid, and yet she sensed he was different with her, less on his guard, and he definitely wanted to come in. The minute she issued an invitation he was over the threshold. 'You could have some soup,' she said. 'It'll save you cooking when you get home. Ba made it, there's plenty.' Without demur he left his raincoat on Guy's chair and followed her along the hall to the kitchen.

While he drank the soup he fed her with questions about her visit to the island, and because she had sworn on the scriptures she told him everything, everything except for the moment she had peered into the bedroom and watched the love-making, and her time of ecstasy on Eilean na Naoimh. The picture she presented of life at the Craig exactly matched what they already knew – the installation of the school teacher, Colin Semple, the wife's abortive attempts to contact Allen and the fact that she too now seemed to have the beginnings of a drink problem. This had come from the minister of the mainland kirk. A queer twist, the drink, in view of her sufferings with Allen. Grace told him of Deborah's secret box, of how Stephen regularly sent the girls little letters, and money. She did not add that the 'polite' notice at the Ram closely resembled the cartoony drawings on the collection of postcards. He could pursue that himself. She would not be instrumental in bringing yet more policemen to the island, rocking the precarious peace of those two children.

He said, 'How did the little girls seem?' He rather liked small children, had found, whenever he visited friends with families, that they liked him, crept on to his knee, brought him books and toys, snuggled up. *Bloody life*, that had loaded Allen's innocent ones with all these horrors.

She shook her head. 'I couldn't tell. Lynn's a good mother, very good, and the boyfriend, Colin, seems to think the world of them. My feeling was that this is *it*, you know. As soon as the divorce is finalised they'll marry and he'll take over. Well, he already has. It was all very, oh, organised, terribly *organised*. Lynn obviously didn't like me turning up out of the blue. I suppose I should have phoned to tell them. Only, I just wanted to see the girls. I feel so sorry for them.'

Her voice shook and she stared at the table, chasing breadcrumbs round in a circle with a damp forefinger, seeing again the locked door, her bag dumped in the porch, those trikes. He saw her face work, the lips puckering, then pressed tight. Always, with this Grace, there were tears around, dammed up behind those remarkable eyes, if not actually shed, and now he sensed again the enormous vulnerability, the passion in her that had no apparent object, throttled as it had been through the long years of sacrifice in this stifling ugly

231

house. He wanted to release her, reach out and stroke her, penetrate.

Inwardly he shivered slightly, opened his file and sorted through paper while she made coffee. The skin of her face had flushed an even darkish pink. Apart from the faint shadow of hair above her upper lip, described in the *Harriet* novel he remembered, and suitably exaggerated by the cruel Anna, it was a flawless skin, that of a child. She seemed uncomfortable, moving jerkily round the kitchen; perhaps he had been staring too much. Reaching inside his jacket he produced his reading glasses and put them on. 'I followed up that man you mentioned,' he told her, 'but the Richmond police didn't know of a character like that, I'm afraid.'

'Did you tell them about the duffel coat? And the scarf?'

'Of course.' He read through his notes. Bayles was out of it, the forensic tests having established that the bloody nightgown buried in his father's field could have no connection with him, nor with his seed. Hallam was now disgruntled and tetchy, once again cheated of a kill, and he had shown minimal interest in the 'artist's impression' of Allen which Grace had taken from the Ram, dismissing it instantly as the work of a crank. Buckle was glad he'd made a photocopy, before handing it over. They seemed to be getting nowhere with the Beardmore killing, and there was nothing new at all on Allen's whereabouts. Now they were re-examining Reed and du Cane's statements because Hallam claimed to be 'dissatisfied' with the tapes sent over by the Italian police. 'Not that man, but *such* a man,' Grace had written in her notes. She could be right. The obvious explanation was often the one the police came back to, shame-faced.

As he stirred his coffee he mulled over the list of names in the latest report. None of these other people was a murderer, it was Allen, Allen they must look to, even though Grace had said she would stake her salvation on his innocence. Allen was an artist, his work hung in the Tate. He said casually, 'By the way, I showed that little drawing to Hallam.'

'And?'

'Well, it's gone off to the experts.'

She raised her eyebrows.

'Handwriting,' he explained. 'I think the author of that notice you gave me is possibly this mysterious reporter who's been around.'

'But you saw him, you saw him at Anna's funeral.'

'Yes.'

'And it wasn't Stephen. You've got photographs, you'd have recognised him.'

Buckle was silent. They had not of course had any reason to photograph 'Hugo Jolley', the vanished pressman who claimed to have written the article on the dead woman, a piece which he had since traced to one Geoffrey Skerrett on the *Sheffield Star*, and certainly there was no immediate resemblance to what Jim Wooding remembered of the man and to their recent photos of Allen, who was so heavily and shaggily bearded that all but the eyes and the rather pronounced straight nose was more or less swallowed up in hair. But, as he had pointed out to her once before, it was nearly a year since she had seen him. He could have lost stones in weight, changed the colour of his hair, shaved it all off. According to the wife he had worn a beard for the last ten years and people who removed beards were often unrecognisable, at first. The new emaciated Allen, 'not a well man' according to the farmer Maurice Peacock, who had talked to the elusive 'reporter', might well be unrecognisable to Grace.

She said boldly, secretly claiming her new freedom in the Lord, her new trust, 'I think you should know that the missing key, the one I kept in the wash-house, was a secret. Nobody knew it was there apart from Mrs Lumb and me . . . and Stephen. He knew about it because he called to see me once, unexpectedly, just about this time, it was, last year. I was at a church meeting but I told him he could let himself into the house if he arrived before I came back. I've worked it out, you see, and I think he might have been here and taken my things, so he can send money to his children. I know he didn't kill Anna and that's why I feel I can tell you about the key. He's sick, you see, William, and I want you to find him. Actually, I think he *wants* to be found.'

Buckle, realising what this speech must have cost her, and warming to her use of his Christian name, slid his hand across the table and took her fingers in his own. This time she did not withdraw from his touch, she simply sat there, heaping up the scattered crumbs again, trying to shape them into a rough cross. He said, 'I understand, and we *will* find him. Now, if you would like someone to stay in the house with you for a while, at night, I could easily arrange that. Breda Smith would come.' He had wanted this because, after the discovery of the break-in, they had investigated Firs and found the massive brass furniture of the front door smashed off with a great stone. Someone had slept in the house, there had been blankets and candle-ends, the remains of a fire in the drawing room grate. Firs, he had discovered from Pollitts the solicitors, had not belonged to Anna Beardmore outright. There had been a complicated convenant in the parents' will about it and after their deaths it had become the property of a charity who had left it empty for some years, then converted it into an old people's home. Only three years ago the dead woman had managed to get a lease on it, saying she wanted to live in it again. This had been a cause of great bitterness between the sister and the brother. Guy Beardmore had interpreted the reclaiming of the death house as a ghoulish, horrific act, also evidence of further greed, for she already owned two properties. In any case, Edward Pollitt had told him, with obvious disapproval, that in spite of big talk of returning to the family home, she had never lived in the place for longer than a week at any one time; yet to do this she had driven out the old folk.

Buckle was not going to frighten Grace tonight by telling her what they had found next door, but he felt uneasy about her staying on at White Lodge alone. Breda, however, was obviously not an acceptable companion. She was shaking her head vehemently, clearly wanting no relationship to start up in that quarter. 'No, it's all right, I can ask Mrs Lumb. When I've been ill she's slept here the odd night. You needn't arrange anything special for me, really, I've lived here alone for nearly a year now.'

Besides, she was going from the house and she was going soon. When she could arrange it she would make a day trip to Anna's valley and look at the craft shop and its cottage; and she would speak to Pollitts about the financial arrangements as soon as Edward could see her. Meanwhile, she would endure here. She would fill her days and her evenings, she would see people, spend more time with the Lord, and all manner of things would be well. She had absolutely no need of Breda Smith.

'All right.' He very much wanted to take her into his arms now but he could not. As yet it was too early, he felt he had not read her quite fully and he feared rejection. So he pointedly checked his watch, tidied his papers into the file and stood up. 'I must go,' he said, 'you'll want to get on,' though he sensed that the evening held no more for her than it did for him.

She said, looking through the kitchen window into the blackness, 'I hate these short days. I particularly hate November, don't you? "No light, No sun, No fun, November," someone said.'

He smiled. 'That's good.'

'Daddie – my father used to quote it. He loved poetry. Not that it's much of a poem.'

'Nice, though.'

'Yes. What do you do at Christmas? That's another thing I rather hate, I'm afraid.'

'Oh, do you? Why? I'd have thought, with your views – '

'No. People don't really understand. Christmas is just an invention, to get people through to the New Year, a sort of psychological prop. It's nothing to do with the Lord. I mean, he's always there.' He felt she spoke of 'the Lord' as if she really loved him, passionately, in a way that shut him out.

'Well, I suppose that's right. I'm always glad when it's behind me, I must admit.'

'So, what do you do?' she repeated.

'Oh, I spend it with my mother, on the south coast. We don't really get on but, well, you have to, don't you? Nothing changes, does it? That's what I find,' and he gave a shy smile. 'What about you?'

'Oh, I think I'm about to make rather a big change in my life,' she said, nervous, but suddenly anxious to tell someone, *anyone*, about what she'd decided to do, and she explained all about the craft shop scheme and her plans to sell Christian books. 'I'm not absolutely sure yet,' she said cautiously. 'I've got to see the house and look at the finances of the thing, and there are friends who may be persuaded to come in with me. I've got to talk to them, at some point. But I definitely feel, once we're into the New Year, that I may well make the change. I suppose that's why I'm rather keen to jump over Christmas, this time.'

'But you wouldn't live at the cottage, would you, at The Rock?' He had not himself visited the scene of the murder but he knew it was very isolated, not at all right for this woman, surely. Besides, he didn't want her to go away and start this tin-pot one-woman crusade to convert the passing tourists. It sounded mildly lunatic, to him. He didn't want her to go away at all; she mustn't leave him.

'Oh no. There's a house attached to the business, by a stream, and it's in quite a large village. I think I'll end up selling Anna's cottage. It's a lonely spot.'

'That sounds sensible.'

'So I'll have Christmas with my various old ladies, as usual,' she said with a wry smile. 'Then . . . then I'll *see*.'

'Well, I'll be very interested to hear how it all turns out,' he said politely, following her towards the front door. At Guy's chair he stopped to pick up his mackintosh and she helped him on with it. She was slightly taller than he was, he noticed, not that it would matter.

On the step he pressed her hand. 'Grace, take care of yourself, and let me know if you change your mind about Breda staying here for a night or two. Otherwise . . . well, I'll be in touch.'

Standing on his toes he lightly brushed her cheek with his lips, then walked away quickly to his car, not looking back. She stood in the open doorway and stared after him, waving as the car disappeared round the loop of the drive. Then she brought her hand to her face and stroked it. But it had been the kiss of a brother to a sister. That was all.

For the rest of the long dark evening she thought about it as she pottered rather aimlessly round the house, settling to nothing, not knowing whether she would have liked more from him in that moment, nor what she wanted now.

16

In Wednesday Meeting, the following week, Nellie Wade had a vision. She was an ugly hump-backed little woman who lived in a condemned terrace near Peth railway station, a perfect example of 'the halt, the lame and the blind', all the human debris that the church inevitably got lumbered with, as Anna had noted in more than one of her novels. Grace had tried to slide her eyes over the spite but now she saw poor Nellie the memory of it flared up unresolved, like a sore not thoroughly healed.

Nellie was simple. Quite what she derived from Wednesday Meeting Grace had never understood, for the group often studied books, writings on prayer or the life of Our Lord, some missionary biography like Monica's, and she was almost certain that Nellie could not read or write. She had once attended some adult literacy classes which Ba had organised at the library but she had given up, saying tearfully that it was all 'too hard'. Sometimes the whole meeting would be devoted to prayer, for people present who had special burdens and for others whose needs had been laid on their hearts. Some of the women prayed very beautifully, weaving into their petitions the most marvellous sentences of scripture, beyond anything Grace herself could manage. Nellie prayed too, but her prayer was only ever a heartfelt 'God help me'. When she spoke, though, she lifted up her hands on high and a kind of radiance flooded over her worn, ugly face. She was, Grace felt, very holy.

Marian disapproved of Nellie and had apparently suggested to Mr Cutler, the new curate who now presided over Wednesday Meeting, that she might somehow be 'removed', clearly thinking he was young and green enough to be bulldozed her way. But Mr Cutler was too busy doing rather exciting things to worry about Nellie. In the absence of the vicar, who was at home recovering from a serious operation, he was taking the opportunity to nudge St Saviour's more towards his own charismatic view. Guitars and jazzy modern songs had been introduced into the services, sketches by the Youth Group sometimes illustrated points in his sermons, and the ladies of Wednesday Meeting were now making banners to decorate the walls of the church. Privately, Grace thought them rather hideous, weird semi-abstract designs suggesting candles or chalices, made up of scraps, pieces of leftover curtaining and discarded cushion covers, all cobbled together and worked into a picture in harsh, bright colours, bearing texts in uncertain capitals, the words sometimes leaning sideways and falling off the bottom. *Wise men still seek Him* and *The Lord is my light.* She had much preferred the plain white walls of the early Georgian church unadorned. But people generally seemed rather wild about the banners.

Nellie, Marian had explained to the new curate, was something of a broken reed. She never studied the set books nor made any kind of contribution. True, she helped with the banners, but her crude ugly stitching had regularly to be unpicked by Ba at home. Ba was an excellent needlewoman but quite frankly she couldn't afford the time. Besides, as they all knew, there was this unpleasant *problem* about Nellie. Others were starting to comment and it wasn't good for those on the fringes like Ailsa Birch, whom they were hoping to bring in.

The 'problem' was that Nellie's little house had no bathroom so that she could not wash as thoroughly as other people and therefore gave off a strong, stale smell. Recently, unknown to Marian, Grace had been instrumental in trying to get a bathroom put into the house in Nelson Street. It was not going to be pulled down for at least two years and she felt it was worthwhile. The landlord, a friend of Edward Pollitt, had grudgingly agreed to the improvement, warming to the idea when he was told that someone in the church had anonymously offered to pay the cost. Grace had been determined to stop Marian driving Nellie away from Wednesday Meeting, she loved it so. But when strange men had arrived unannounced to measure up, draw plans and give estimates for the operation, Nellie grew very frightened and hid. She went to see Mr Cutler and begged him to ask the people to go away. She didn't understand about the bathroom, didn't want it at her age. Others in the street had had them installed and they'd got bursts, all sorts. One woman had to call the Environment. Nellie wept.

The Girls were not altogether happy about Mr Cutler's new line in worship and they did not always come to Wednesday Meeting. Grace was thankful that Marian wasn't present when Nellie had had her vision, though she rather regretted Ba's absence for she still nursed a tiny hope that one day the two of them might share the cottage by the stream without Marian, and the vision was clearly about the new plan for her life.

Nellie had not spoken it out loud, she had whispered it to Mr Cutler during the prayer time and he had written it down carefully. When the prayers were concluded he had read out exactly what she had told him. 'Nellie has been given a Word,' he informed them gravely, 'and it is this: *'I see a woman walking by streams of living water. In her hands she carries a golden book. It is the word of the Lord. "Ho, everyone that thirsteth," she cries to all those who pass by. "Come and drink of my waters," and she is clothed in fresh new garments.'*

Before he had quite finished Nellie interrupted him. A low monotonous moaning noise was coming from her half-open lips, her eyes were closed and, as she moaned, she stood up, waddled to the middle of the room and raised her pudgy little hands with their hacked black fingernails to heaven.

The moaning went on and on while everyone sat patiently waiting, staring fixedly ahead and trying not to catch anyone else's eye, but at last her voice ceased and she stood there, swaying slightly on the faded fireside rug, her eyes still clenched shut. She had spoken in tongues and the group sat on in silence, waiting for an interpretation.

Then Rachel Bowman, the senior classics mistress at Peth School, a scared rabbit of a woman with thinning mousy hair and cruelly buck teeth, who had come to Wednesday Meeting for as long as Grace could remember but had never contributed a single word, suddenly rose from her chair, joined Nellie on the rug, and put an arm round her. The other she stretched towards the ceiling. *'Behold,'* she said, *'the tabernacle of God is with men, and he will dwell with them, and they shall be his people, and God himself shall be with them, and be their God. And God shall wipe away all tears from their eyes; and there shall be no more death, neither sorrow nor crying, neither shall there be any more pain; for the former things are passed away. And he that sat upon the throne said, "Behold, I make all things new. I will give unto him that is athirst of the fountain of the water of life freely, and I will be his God, and he shall be my son."'*

That night Grace wrote down the vision in her journal. Mr Cutler had given her the precious scrap of paper and she would keep it for always, for Nellie, who could neither read nor write, had spoken from the Revelation of St John the Divine. Rachel, who had interpreted, presumably knew New Testament Greek but, though she understood little of 'Tongues', Grace doubted that it was in the Greek that Nellie had spoken. At such blessed times the language the Lord gave to his people was not always that of men, but of angels.

Through the tedious dragging weeks between the night of the vision and Christmas Day, Grace kept Nellie's word in her heart, praying over it each day, and hoping for another Sign, because when she visited Edward Pollitt, and discussed her plans with him, he was distinctly discouraging. Yes, he said, he had indeed advised her to sell Aunt Grace's property but just now was a bad time to choose, the deadest time of all for buying and selling any house. He advised her to wait until spring. Also, she should get the accountant from Bradleys to investigate the commercial soundness of this rural craft enterprise. It looked attractive enough – she had brought the illustrated brochure to show him – but all would have to be carefully investigated. Timidly she had suggested that some of Anna's money might be used to buy the new property. That way Aunt Grace's terrace need not be sold off until prices were more buoyant. But he explained that Anna's estate was extremely complicated and that she could not expect any money to be realised from that quarter for a very long time.

Hearing this she didn't dare tell him that she had already been to The Rock, had a key and had made vague plans to go back there, for he suddenly asked her not to continue with her routine visits a to Firs, saying that the firm would make sure that the empty property was not interfered with.

'But why not?' she asked. 'Anna asked me to keep an eye on it for her when she first got the lease. I always have, you know that, Edward. I mean, I'm only next door . . .'

But he was curiously insistent, vaguely muttering about 'talk' and the 'appropriateness' of the situation. Better to keep away from the house, he said, until she was officially in possession of the lease, then of course she must decide what she wanted to do with it.

She knew that someone had recently broken into Firs. Buckle had told her of the general mess, the smashed locks, now replaced. So it was hard to decide whether the elderly solicitor was simply being over-scrupulous about the legal niceties of her inheriting Anna's estate or whether he was obeying some instructions from the police. But she did as she was told, and stopped going round there.

Through the fogs and damps of the dying year the dark pile of the death house loomed over the more compact White Lodge. Anna's sudden decision to get it back, to furnish it again with some of the family pieces that had been stored for years in a damp ex-cinema belonging to Pickfords, had surprised Grace. Anna had obviously fancied the idea of reclaiming her family home but had not seemed to enjoy the reality. Her visits to Peth had been very infrequent and she nearly always stayed with Grace at White Lodge, finding it impossible to heat Firs.

It had not been popular as an old people's home. They wanted noise and traffic, apparently, shoppers walking past their windows, a bit of life. The gardens of Firs were flanked on all sides by the ancient conifers which gave the house its name. For the week she had stayed there one old lady had screamed every night, saying that the trees had left their places and walked across the lawns towards her ground floor room with outstretched strangling hands. Grace had understood. Had they lived, she would not have wanted her own parents incarcerated in the gloom of the Firs Eventide Home.

Both The Girls had parents in Homes, which had always been rather a puzzle to her. Ba's father was bedridden but, so far as Grace knew, in his right mind. Marian's mother had survived a severe stroke but needed constant attention. Grace didn't think that either of them had ever looked after these parents in the way she had looked after Mother, though Marian was a nurse. But of course they both had their careers, and the money they earned paid for nursing elsewhere, while they made their home together. To her, though, it was still odd.

She had hoped she might be invited to them for Christmas. After church, on the day, she would visit her old ladies, Mrs Dutt, Nellie and Mrs Lumb, but the rest of the time would be free. Last year she had spent it in the hospital with Mother; now she could go anywhere.

But before the end of November Marian, who had already written and stamped their Christmas cards (they sent jointly), told her, in Ba's absence, of their Christmas plan. The day itself would be spent in the Homes, Ba with her father at Southport, Marian in Lytham St Anne's. On Boxing Day they would meet up and drive north-east, towards Scarborough. Just inland from the resort, in a moorland village, there was a splendid Christian conference centre which took guests over Christmas and New Year. They were spending a week there, to enjoy fellowship and teaching, it was marvellous and the people were marvellous. It was to be their third year there.

Grace tried hard not to be hurt, telling herself that, because she had twice been invited away with The Girls, she must not assume that she had any special claim on them. They had obviously taken her on holiday twice this year because they had felt so sorry for her, after Mother, and, in Marian's phrase, wanted to 'jolly her along'. They had rushed to her side when Anna died and again when the house was burgled. But in more recent weeks she had sensed that Marian, if not Ba, was rather regretting the new intimacy, the generous widening of the charmed circle. This Christmas plan, which totally excluded Grace, was a seal on that friendship with which, obviously, she must have nothing to do, though she did wonder how readily Ba had agreed to it. She rather despised her for caving in.

She knew that she would have felt more robust if other things were happening to her, and if her plan had moved on. But, like the year, all her projects seemed to have died. William – rather unexpectedly, he'd told her, and with what sounded like genuine regret – had been sent to Liverpool for six weeks to lecture on a police training course, a replacement for some senior person who was sick. He would not be back in Peth until New Year. Once or twice a week he telephoned her, to ask how she was and to report that there was no fresh news on the Anna enquiry, but if he returned to the town centre flat on his days off she knew nothing about it, for he never visited. Sometimes she thought of his hand round her fingers, of the gentle kiss, and wondered if she had imagined too much.

So far, she had done very little about the book. On receipt of her letter about Anna's papers and the legal position, Julia Wragg immediately parcelled up several box files which she said contained all the notes in the house and posted them to White Lodge. Then she telephoned. She was postponing her visit to the ailing client in Cheshire until New Year, she had decided, but when she came north could she visit, and might she also bring old Magnus? By then Grace would have had a chance to go through everything, and perhaps they could talk. She was interested in the idea of a memoir of childhood about which Grace had written another letter, *wonderful*; but Magnus too had been having thoughts. He thanked her by the way for her kind letter and was keen to meet up again.

Grace smiled as Julia rang off. She had sent Magnus Croucher the briefest, most non-committal of notes. In no way was it 'kind', nor a letter, and she had already told Julia Wragg it was much too early to publish a book on Anna. But all had been changed and wilfully misinterpreted, and she sensed that, between them, they had worked out new tactics to get their own book off the ground.

She was grateful to have the files at last, though no doubt Julia had photocopied the entire contents. She didn't plan to read them yet, she knew she couldn't. What she did was to look quickly through the four boxes for the missing journal, the notebook in which Anna had written of the death of her parents; but she couldn't find it.

The day the files arrived she wrapped them in a large polythene bag and put it in the spare room wardrobe where she had already hidden the diaries, finding she couldn't actually bear to look at the papers yet, or even be in their physical presence. It was as if they were somehow giving off heat; in the night she feared they might glow in the darkness. She had never had any kind of ghostly experience yet she felt that the material in those black boxes had a threatening, independent life. Once they were safely in the spare room she shut the door on them and avoided going into it.

Nothing happened about her stolen goods, or the cash card. If someone answering to Stephen's description had been seen using the machine in Peth then Buckle was keeping the knowledge from her. Nobody attempted to sell the watches, or Aunt Celia's carriage clock, and she eventually filled in insurance claims. She would not replace anything but she would need ready money for her venture into the New Life, and it could be set aside for that.

Twice she had arranged a day trip to view Coffee 'n' Crafts but each time it had snowed, blocking all the roads into the valley. On the television news she saw film of helicopters dropping food to remote farms. This gave Edward Pollitt, who was really no more than a fussy old woman, she had decided, a fresh opportunity to state his case. It was all very well living in such a place in good weather, he argued, but come the end of October everything would be shut down for several months and the tourist flow would cease. What would she do then in such a place?

Privately, she was confident that there would be plenty to do, and village life had always attracted her. She had never felt she was a town person and anyway, the village she had in mind was reasonably large with a church, a chapel and a school. It also had an old literary institute where there was a small lending library and where evening classes were run in the winter months. Then there was Richmond with its music and its plays, only half an hour's drive away. She listed all these attractions for Edward Pollitt but without undue attempts to persuade. Her reason for living in Anna's valley was other, a prompting from the Lord who would reveal his purpose to her in due season.

After all, in her vision, Nellie had seen her clothed in fresh new garments. She would so like to have asked whether the woman who walked by the stream with the golden book had walked alone, or whether another walked by her side, but that would not have been appropriate in Wednesday Meeting where there were so many 'singles', not least toothy Rachel Bowman who had interpreted the Word.

So many awkward, isolated women, she thought gloomily, and so many of them in the church, as she began to make her simple Christmas preparations. For Nellie, Mrs Dutt and Mrs Lumb she had bought mohair scarf and glove sets, from the sweater shop in Moffatt. Now, as she packed them up, she thought with dread of her Christmas morning visits, the filth of Nellie's house, the cheerful slovenliness of Mrs Dutt's, sitting among her cardboard boxes, and of the joylessness of Mrs Lumb's ugly scoured interior as she waited with a hurt, proud expression for a telephone call from the adored son Mike who had not visited for several Christmasses. She saw that in time, if she remained solitary, she too could become smelly and confused, or worse, grow like Mrs Lumb, quite unable to yield to the touch of love. Money and intelligence would not necessarily save her. *To the uttermost he saves.* She must cling to Aunt Celia's favourite text, and she must go back to the valley, just as she had planned. It was surely significant that so far no other party seemed interested in buying the craft shop. The estate agent had promised to phone if there were an offer, while pressing her to come and view, just as soon as the snow cleared.

To Scotland she sent shocking pink sweat-shirts decorated with little white pigs. Deborah loved pigs particularly and had a little collection of them on her bookcase. On the day of her visit Grace had read aloud to them the closing chapters of a book called *Charlotte's Web* in which a clever spider had saved the life of a pig by writing words of witty approbation in her web. Both girls had wept at the end, when the spider died. But lo, up in the rafters of the barn, silvery threads came floating down in millions, each one a new spider, a child of the noble Charlotte who had yielded her life that others might live. She had said, closing the book, 'That's what Jesus did, isn't it?' But unconsoled, Deborah had continued to weep for Charlotte, curiously mature in the knowledge that death, whatever joys came after, was at the time unanswerable and hideous.

With the sweaters she enclosed a Marks and Spencer's gift voucher, labelled 'for the house'. She dared not risk anything personal. The nearest branch was probably a day's drive away from the island but she couldn't help that. She could hear Lynn saying '*ridiculous*' as she opened the envelope, and no doubt thinking too that the pig garments were impractical because the colours would run in the wash. Anna had once said of Lynn that she hadn't a scrap of poetry in her and that this was the basic problem, so far as Stephen was concerned. Yet Guy had obviously written some poetry to her, and Stephen had painted her, several times. She marvelled again at the weird chemistry of sexual liaisons, wondering why the Lord had always chosen to keep her free of them.

On Christmas Day she got up early and walked across the silent town in the rain, to St Saviour's. Mr Gardiner, the vicar, was now recovered sufficiently to take the occasional service and today he was presiding over an eight o'clock Prayer Book Communion. Later in the morning it would be family church. Mr Cutler was organising this and there would be guitars and general razzmatazz, dozens of toddlers scrambling over the pews clutching their Christmas teddies. She had heard whisper that the curate himself was planning to pop up out of a large hamper, decked out as Father Christmas.

Today she couldn't quite bear that so she sat in the chilly side chapel with a scattering of old ladies, going through the motions of the service but with her mind completely detached, the comfortable words sliding over her unheeded. She felt lonely. The Girls were at their Homes. Anna, who had talked of their spending this Christmas together, in London, was dead, so was Mother, so was Daddie. Buckle had presumably gone to his mother and she'd had no word of Stephen for weeks. She would like to telephone Lynn to find out whether he had been in touch, but she feared a rebuff.

After her three morning visits and the distribution of the scarf sets, she returned to White Lodge and cooked scrambled eggs on toast. On her most recent visit Dr Lucas had behaved rather mysteriously. He had changed her tablets and asked her to return in three months, not six, making rather a fuss about her increase in weight. Yet he still wouldn't answer any direct questions, simply told her, rather brusquely, she thought, to 'go carefully'. So now, in defiance, she ate only half her scrambled egg, irritably pushing away the glass of wine she had dispensed for herself, from a box, in recognition of the fact that, even for her, it was Christmas Day. In spite of Nellie's vision, and of her own Word on Eilean na Naoimh, she had never felt more desolate than now. And at this moment she rather hated Dr Lucas, who was overweight himself and a heavy smoker, also the chairman of a local wine club. What right had he to warn her about her habits of life? And if there was a problem, she ought to know. Testily she scraped the congealing eggs off the plate into the waste bin. Then the telephone rang.

The operator told her that a Mr Allen was ringing from a York call box and would she pay. 'Oh yes, *yes* . . .' she whispered, and her heart lurched, squeezing away her breath. 'You're through,' said the voice, then added endearingly, 'and a Happy Christmas.'

The operator had sounded very near, her heavy Yorkshire vowels could have been coming from the next room. But Stephen's voice was faint, and she kept having to ask him to speak up. The brief phone call was agonising, because of his stammer, and as she waited for him to get his words out all her anger and hurt at his 'tricks', particularly the Richmond fiasco, drained steadily away. She just wanted to see him. 'Where are you, Stephen?' she said at last. 'What on earth have you been doing with yourself?'

'I've b–b–been helping on a p–p–p–painting course,' he said, 'a residential thing at the university while the c–c–c–campus is empty. Not very thrilling, nobody can draw a s–s–straight line, actually, but it's money. Anyhow, this week's free. Were you thinking of c–c–coming up at all? We could m–m–meet?'

She paused, suddenly wary, realising that she hadn't quite forgiven him. 'I'm not sure, Stephen. The weather's not very marvellous, is it?'

'Well there's no sn–sn–snow here. You know how it is, they've got to have *something* to t–t–talk about on the telly, especially over Christmas. It's OK up here, honestly. The M6 is open anyhow so it can't be all that bad. Listen, why don't we meet at the c–c–cottage? We could spend New Year together, it'd be like old t–times. Go on, Grace . . .'

'I'm not *sure*, Stephen,' she faltered. She didn't understand. She had never once spent New Year with him, he was rambling, though he didn't sound drunk. He must be thinking of his Scottish New Years, bagpipes in the heather, firstfooting and sitting up all night, bacon and eggs at six o'clock in the morning. Guy had shared one wild Hogmanay with him, at the Craig.

'I'll be there N–N–New Year,' he repeated, and this time she thought she detected a slight slurring of his speech. 'You be there too, and we'll celebrate. See you.' Then the line went dead.

'Stephen . . . *Stephen* . . .' Desperately she juggled the black buttons of the phone cradle up and down.

'Your caller has rung off,' a voice said, male this time, and distinctly unseasonal. 'Please will you replace your receiver?'

She havered, hoping something else might happen to make the decision for her. Eventually she rang Buckle at his flat but the line was connected to an answerphone, asking her to leave a name and number. In the background she could hear a cat mewing resentfully. He liked cats, apparently, and he had made a great fuss of Binkie. She hadn't known he owned one himself. He was emerging as rather a different person from what she had originally imagined, and she was certain, now, that she interested him. *Why didn't he come?*

The Girls had left her their phone number at the holiday centre but she decided not to consult them. It was only to be used in an absolute emergency and all she really wanted from anyone was confirmation of the fact that she should go to the valley, for she knew that she had already decided, the minute she heard Stephen's voice, in spite of her careful hedging.

He may well not turn up again but that didn't matter. A & D Black in Richmond had said they would show her over the craft place any time, apart from Christmas and Boxing Day, so when she got there she would phone and arrange something. She would certainly be seeing the valley at the coldest and deadest time of the year, something Edward Pollitt had strongly advised, if she were really serious in this plan to make her home there.

On December 30th she set off in crisp, very cold weather. More snow had fallen on the northern hills but all the main routes were open. In cardboard boxes she had packed a selection of food from the freezer, also a few frivolities, chocolates and nuts, a box of crystallised fruits, and some bottles of wine to toast the New Year, just in case, by some miracle, Stephen kept his word. Then she drove without incident up an empty motorway, doing the journey in record time without the usual impediment of lumbering juggernauts.

But by the time she had left the M6 and turned towards Brough the thin steely light, which had lit her way since Peth, had muddied considerably and darkened into a thick yellowish cloud that sat heavily on the fell-tops. The first flakes of snow were falling as she left the trunk road and started weaving her slow way across the wild treeless moors that eventually dropped down into Anna's little valley. Her car radio was broken but, had she been able to tune in to the local weather report, she would have heard that she had the alarming distinction of being one of the last cars permitted to travel east on the A66 that day. Within an hour of her leaving it, just as she was bumping up the track towards the cottage, painfully slowly because of the thickening snow, she would have heard they had closed the road.

The Rock was still securely padlocked but she had anticipated this and had brought Daddie's toolbox with her so that she was able to unscrew the iron hasp quite easily and lever it off the wooden panels, bringing the padlock away with it. Laying the new ironwork down on the snow she inserted her key, pushed the door open and walked straight in. She must be very resolute now and not think of that terrible moment before, when Maurice had gone inside with the quilt, and the thick darkness had rushed out at her.

Inside all was neat and just as she remembered from the last time, and there was a smell of lavender air-freshener mixed with furniture polish and pine disinfectant. Maurice had a lady who came to clean his own house in the village. Grace suspected she had been here too. The place had been 'bottomed' with the thoroughness of a Mrs Lumb.

The inter-connecting door was ajar. She nudged at it with her foot and went through. Again the same neatness, a fire laid in the grate, all the cushions plumped up on the deep window seat with its amazing view of the rushing water, and a large potted fern which somebody had recently watered. On the table blocks of paper and new notebooks, card-indexes in boxes, everything she remembered from that Tuesday morning, except for the notebook labelled 'Novel 7' and the note about suicide being the most effective way of ensuring that you are never forgotten.

She didn't know, exactly, how the police would have gone about their grisly business in this cottage, but she did know that Guy Beardmore's knife, for example, had been dutifully returned to White Lodge, some months after The Tragedy. Whatever they took away they restored eventually, she presumed, to the rightful owners, when they had had their way with it. The Rock was spotless, orderly, and, with its well-worn comfortable furniture, its old prints and its bright rugs and curtains, cheerfully welcoming. These things did not hold the weight of memory for her which they must have held for Anna – not that she could have minded the old associations very much, or she would not have brought them up here. There had been a pronounced lack of sentimentality in her.

But for all its homeliness she decided not to ascend to the upper storey of the cottage. She didn't know where Anna's body had been found but she remembered vividly that peculiar dragging noise over her head, the day she had come to visit. Before leaving Peth she had thought carefully about her sleeping arrangements. She had brought a sleeping bag and pillows and she would spend the night on the settee, by the fire. Off the kitchen was a minute washroom with a basin and lavatory, so there was no actual need to ascend those treacherous-looking stone steps.

She found matches, lit the fire, and carefully made a nest of small coals round the first flames to bring it on, just as Daddie had taught her when he had first allowed her to help with fires. Then she switched on various electric heaters. She would leave them on all night, she thought, for the cottage was icy cold, and as soon as she had unpacked she must put more layers on. How had Anna survived in this place during the winter months? She had, though, and she had claimed to have done some of her best work here. That must go into the book.

Grace thought of the four black box files in the back of the car. Tomorrow she would look at them, though not at the diaries or letters. Those she felt she ought to destroy before anybody saw them, she could burn them on the fire. That way they would be safe for ever from the clutches of people like Julia Wragg and Magnus Croucher. She believed that such acts of destruction in the past now caused literary scholars considerable anguish, but that was when they were dealing with the works of a great writer. She was no judge, of course, yet she knew that Anna Beardmore was not and never would have been 'great'. What she wrote lacked the bowels of compassion.

It was not yet five o'clock but already the dark had come down. She went round the house switching all the lights on to cheer the place up. An outside spotlight suddenly illuminated the waterfall, dream-like now as it whitened the darkness, big snowflakes dancing about over it like feathers from the breast of some great bird.

When she had brought in her various bags and boxes and deposited the food in cupboards, on shelves and inside the ancient chugging refrigerator (that too she recognised from Firs, and she smiled at Anna's economy), she went into the main room, seated herself at the writing table and pulled the phone towards her. First she would speak to Maurice Peacock, in the hope that he might call on her and dig her car out of the snow, if need be, for as yet what had become quite a blizzard showed no signs of easing off. She would phone the estate agent to fix up a meeting for the following day, then she would try and contact Stephen at York University, ostensibly to ask if he was coming to The Rock but in fact to find out if he had actually been there, and if there had ever been a painting course. At last she knew she was turning against him, and in a strange way she was glad.

She turned up the local directory and wrote down the Richmond numbers on one of Anna's blank pads. Then she picked up the phone to dial directory enquiries, to get the number of York University. But the line was dead.

She stood up and peered under the table. The white flex had been neatly zig-zagged together and bound up with a wire tag. It had been cut off about three inches from the wall socket and the remains still projected. Both ends of bare wire were rusty and crumbled into flakes when she touched them gingerly with her forefinger. It must be some time since this phone line had been severed. Presumably the police knew about it, but had had no reason to tell her. Officially, of course, she should not be here.

She went outside and looked at the snow, floating about in quite huge flakes now in the stream of light from the rustic lantern over the door, drifting upwards, it seemed, rather playfully. And she thought of Stephen's children loving it too, if it was snowing on the island, and suddenly, of a film she had once seen when a girl, pregnant too young, had danced in front of a bonfire, writing her name on the darkness with a giant sparkler, trying to be little again. Then she went inside. The heaters were already penetrating the cold and the fire was blazing nicely. She would not panic. She would have a quiet evening, snug by this fire, go to sleep early and in the morning make her calls from the phone box at the end of the lane. However bad the weather Maurice would have to come, to attend to the beasts at Park Head. She would get up early and listen for him.

The four black files lay on the table but still she could not bring herself to look at them. Instead, after a quick meal of tinned soup, fruit and bread, she settled down by the fire and finished *Solitariness*. After Monica's heady time on Eilean na Naoimh, however, the thrill of it all rather lessened and there were tedious passages of sickening piety to be ploughed through, about her work with down-and-outs in northern cities.

At ten she banked the fire up for the last time and went through to the kitchen with her washing things, into the lean-to that had been converted into a tiny cloakroom. It had no heater and the air was icy cold. Hurriedly she washed and brushed her teeth in freezing water because the immersion tank was in an upstairs cupboard and she would not go up there. As she dried her face she heard scrabbling, skittering noises in the roof space over her head. *Rats*. Birds or mice would have made a lighter sound. Occasionally a bird got trapped in the loft at home, above her bedroom. She knew what birds sounded like.

She fled back to the main room, poured an inch of neat whisky into a glass (she had found a half-empty bottle in a cupboard by the fireplace), and swallowed down four capsules of sodium amytal, double her usual dose. Then she settled down into the sleeping bag on the lumpy maroon settee that had once been in the breakfast room at Firs, clicking off the remaining lamp. The outside spotlight she left on and, as she drifted into unconsciousness, she took with her a vision of the whirling snow, the arch of gleaming white water slicing the blackness. *Lighten our darkness, we beseech Thee, Oh Lord*, she prayed, *And by Thy great mercy defend me, Grace, from all the perils and dangers of this night*, personalising the ancient collect to include, particularly, those busy rats over her head, the thought of which terrified her. For with Him, without whose knowledge no sparrow fell to earth, nothing was too silly, or too trivial. And He was watching over her, for she slept deeply.

In the morning, after a hurried breakfast – much later than she had meant, but the sodium amytal had drugged her too deeply – she set off to walk up the valley, to Park Head Farm. She had thought, as she came round in the sleeping bag, that she'd heard the noise of a car engine quite near, just across the field, but when she reached the track she saw that the deep snow was still virgin. Nothing had been driven along here since yesterday.

Even so, she turned right at the gate and plodded off towards the farm. In places the soft snow came over the tops of her wellingtons and her feet were soon soaked. A car could not possibly get up here in these conditions. If need be Maurice would come to see to the beasts on his tractor. She could wait for him at the house and ask him to tow her car down to the main road. He had told her that it was usually kept clear in winter and, if her car was left there, she should have no problem about driving down to the village to meet the estate agent, and ultimately getting out of the dale, and home.

But there were no beasts to be seen at Park Head. All the outbuildings were empty, one of them with its door hanging off, and the dismal, damp house looked as deserted as before. Carefully she looked about. If no vehicle of any kind could get through this tremendous snow then perhaps Maurice had walked from his farm, and transferred the animals to some other cow-house nearer the road. She understood that country people still walked long miles for the sake of their beasts. In the old days some of them had also mined lead, knitting as they trudged to their work under the ground with candles in their hats. Maurice himself could knit, he had shyly confided; his grandfather had taught him.

But here too there were no footprints in the snow, nor anything to suggest a person or a vehicle had recently been to the house and its fields. She decided that the sister-in-law's animals must have been taken to his farm along the dale and she started to walk back.

Half a mile beyond Anna's red gate the snow had drifted and suddenly became deeper, as high as her knees in places, impossible to walk through. She could see the top of the telephone box but she couldn't get to it, so she tried climbing on to one of the dry stone walls so that she might walk along the top, but in scrabbling up she dislodged what proved to be one of the large key stones and a whole section came rumbling down, the great lumps disappearing with dull thuddings into the endless snow.

Back she went to The Rock, stepping in her own footprints, fetched the coal shovel and returned to the lane where she spent the next hour digging out a little channel for herself, so that she could reach the phone box. When she eventually got there she was sweating hard and she had a creasing stitch deep in her side. In the booth she leaned against the door for a few minutes, partly to recover her breath but also because she now had a deep dread that this phone too would not function. Edward Pollitt had been right to advise her to come to this valley while the elements raged. She thought of the helicopters dropping their bundles to men and cattle, thought of her own small supply of food at The Rock, of the blisters on her hands where she had wielded the snow shovel and, lifting the cold handset, felt afraid.

But a miraculous steady purring came down the line. Joyously she inserted coins, took the list of phone numbers from her pocket, and tapped out Maurice's. She let it ring for a full minute by her watch but nobody answered, and she found herself thinking of that time on the motorway when she had phoned Anna at The Rock, and Stephen had spoken to her. No one spoke now, and at last she put the phone down. He could not, surely, have gone to his sister-in-law in Darlington, the snow would have prevented him. No doubt he would be round the farm somewhere, attending to his own beasts.

Next she rang A & D Black in Richmond and was peeved to hear a chirpy recorded message wishing her the compliments of the season but advising that the office was closed until January 2nd. 'Any time except Christmas and Boxing Day' the young man with whom she had corresponded had informed her. In annoyance she slammed the phone down, consulted directory enquiries, then dialled General Office at the University of York. Here at last she did get an answer. As she listened she knew she must have been expecting it, for she heard what the man had to say with no surprise whatever. There was not and never had been a residential art course at the university this vacation. Somehow she had been misinformed. He was very sorry.

A few yards beyond the phone box was the seat Anna had erected in Guy's memory. Now she trudged down to it, observing with some relief that the tyres of some large vehicle had recently marked the snow, pressing it into shiny little patterns that gleamed like the top of a Christmas cake. Below, on the road that wound along the valley to Richmond, she could see in the whiteness a crawling blue lozenge that must be the top of a car or van, heard the faint thrum of its engine as it disappeared. So her escape route was open, just as long as there was no more snow. But she must keep trying Maurice and get him to bring his tractor up, to pull her car out. It had more or less disappeared into the snow now and resembled a fairytale haystack, blanched by an enchanter's spell.

She cleared snow from the seat and from the ugly little plaque so that people could read Guy's name, and sat down for a minute, staring into the valley. All was softened now and the hills were like two breasts, liquid and drifting, as when a woman lies down to sleep. In the dark cleft where the river ran the trees were mere bobbles, shapeless under their great burden. Only the sky was alive and marvellous, a stunning bright blue, a summery sky, fleeced about with fat little balls of cloud, like floating snow trees.

But the cold was intense and although she didn't want to believe it she feared more snow might be on its way. In the phone box she tried Maurice's number again, this time letting it ring even longer, in case he was in an outbuilding and might be running at this very moment to pick it up. At last she abandoned the attempt and picked her slow way back to The Rock through the channel she had made, slipping occasionally because it had started to freeze. She would not stay here beyond tomorrow. If only she could get help with the car she would quite like to return to Peth now, but, by the time anyone came, she supposed the dark would be falling, and there was no way she would risk the wintry journey at night.

For the rest of the day therefore she would 'hole up' at The Rock, to use Anna's phrase. She would read a bit, keep herself warm, and let in the New Year which, for all her present disappointments, held such promise for her; and she would make all the preparations for Stephen, just as she had planned, even though her heart was telling her she would let it in alone.

At nine that evening all was ready, apart from the steak which she had planned to flame at the table in the special pan which she had brought from home. The dish had been meant for Stephen, so had the avocados, each now fanned out on its plate in a perfect circle with a delicately sculptured radish at the centre to relieve the green; so had the crème brûlée which she had made at White Lodge, and the two bottles of superior Cabernet Sauvignon which Frankie from the shop had presented to her, as a Christmas gift.

The wine was open, the first course in place on two plates at opposite ends of the big writing table which she had cleared and spread with a festive red cloth, setting red candles in the old brass holders she had taken down from the mantelpiece. She had even polished them.

Now she sat down and poked at her avocado without appetite, staring at the opposite wall with its waiting empty chair and at the poster Anna had pinned up, the photograph of the curious modern sculpture called Broken Path. She knew what it meant now for she had at last looked through the files sent by Julia Wragg, and matched them up with some notes still on the writing table. *Broken Path* was to have been the title of Anna's book about Guy, and the boxes contained interminable though fragmentary notes about his life, from the minute of his birth to the minute of his death, a life that had been enclosed in her life. It seemed very important to her that she had been born a few minutes earlier.

'It's not the dead I pity, it's the living,' she had written on one sheet of paper, with great savagery, it seemed, for the pencil had ripped through the paper. 'The dead cling to them, and won't let go.' But it was evident in the rambling notes, the scraps of memories, the reconstructions of childish days with their little joys and sadnesses, and of the months after The Tragedy, that she felt towards the dead Guy both pity and guilt. 'Poor sod,' someone had whispered on the night of the Pritchard party. Anna had obviously heard and remembered, and here the night was, quite agonisingly described but with herself, not Guy, the villain of the piece.

253

There was no synopsis for the projected book, and the diary which must have dealt with the days immediately after The Tragedy was not on the table with the other writings which the police had presumably restored to their place, when they had finished their work. Without reading every word of the semi-illegible scribbles it was hard to work out just how Anna had intended to shape her narrative, though it was certainly to have been a novel, Grace remembered. The words 'Broken Path' highlighted in yellow kept leaping out at her from the closely-written pages. 'This path,' she had mused in one place, 'a lovely thing for the eager young to walk on, a path shaped by loving hands, each minute piece set in its place with love, awake in the sunlight with warm life: this is the diamond path along which the boy treads unwarily, his heart open to joy. Then, a great uninvited sorrow and, though the years pass over, memory works ever upward, mole-like, until the lovely diamonds are flung apart, shattered irrevocably. Away from the path, a shoe. He has walked out of life.' Under this she had written in enormous capitals, 'Father, forgive *me*, for I knew not what I did.'

Grace had already drunk one glass of Frankie's wine, now she poured another and went to sit by the fire with it. In spite of all her efforts the basic cold of the thick-walled cottage was taking over and she found that she was shivering. She pulled her sleeping bag out of her suitcase, unrolled it and got inside; then, setting the alarm for 11.50, she made herself as comfortable as possible on the old settee and closed her eyes. She didn't expect to sleep but in fact she did, quite soon, dreaming of Anna and Guy at Firs. They were happy and young and there were no strangling trees to frighten them, instead endless lawns stretched down to a meadow through which their pretty mother, uncrippled and her face shining, walked to meet them with outstretched arms.

At its appointed time the electronic alarm bleeped courteously but she woke up at once, checked the hands, clicked it off, then switched on the radio. She must take her tray and be out of the door before the first stroke of midnight, and, only when the chimes had started, could she come back again. Of course, it was not as it should be. One ought to leave by a back entrance and enter by a front, that's what Daddie always did. But The Rock had only one door. Still, the going out and coming in were mere symbols, as were the three objects assembled on the tray, a lump of coal, a piece of bread and a coin. Warmth, food and prosperity, these she hoped to take into the New Year and all, she acknowledged, came from the Lord. 'Of Thine Own do we give Thee,' she said aloud, picking up the tray.

Over the radio came a voice: '*I said to the man who stood at the gate of the year, "Give me a light that I may tread safely into the unknown." And he replied, "Go out into the darkness and put your hand into the hand of God. That shall be to you better than light, and safer than a known way."* '

There was a short pause, then the same voice announced that in London the hands of Big Ben were just coming up to midnight. Out she went into the darkness, Anna's old yellow cardigan slung round her shoulders, and stood with her three gifts looking up at the thick stars, then down at the luminous bluey shine on the crisp snow. Behind her, in the cottage, the BBC voice said, with some emotion, she thought, 'May I wish you all, wherever you may be, a very happy New Year.' She thought of Daddie, and how he had always hugged her very specially at this time. 'My little Grace,' he used to say, even when she was grown-up and much bigger than he was.

The cold was quite savage and she turned, hurrying back inside, quite peaceful now, knowing that this valley was her place and that she would drink deeply here, of the waters of life, taking the loveliness into herself, drawing strength from it. In the kitchen she shut and bolted the outer door, left her tray on the draining board, then went back into the main room, to warm up again.

But now a man was sitting at the table, on the chair in front of 'Broken Path'. His grey emaciated face had a lop-sided, twisted mouth and his dry-looking black hair was growing back to its natural sandy ginger at the roots. He was wearing a dirty camel duffel coat and a purple and black university scarf. In her absence he had poured himself a glass of wine.

When she came through the door he grinned broadly. 'Hi, Grace, Happy New Year.' Then, '*Hey*, that's Anna's cardigan. Hell, you don't waste anything, do you, lady? Well . . .' waving a hand expansively over the pretty table, 'this is all very nice. Can we eat?'

She stared at him in horror, backing away, then crashed into the door and gobbled at the air for breath as a wave of huge pain came up suddenly, inexplicably, from deep inside her chest, splitting her in two, squeezing at her neck as if she were being garrotted. Then she clutched at her throat with both hands, trying to push the monstrous pain away, to give herself ease before her legs buckled beneath her.

Now she understood, saw it all, knew why, all these months, she had felt that suffocating darkness, knew why she had been so certain that Stephen could not have killed Anna and why she had known that he would never come back. He couldn't, because he was dead already.

The man who now sat at her table so smilingly, drinking her good wine, was the man who had followed her round Richmond, peeped

255

out at her round the columns of the little theatre. But it was not
Stephen sitting in Anna's old chair, nor was it Bayles or Gary Reed
or Maurice, all of whom had been questioned about the murder. It
was Guy.

In great agony, as the excruciating pain robbed her of speech,
she cried out, '*Jesus*, Jesus, remember me when you come into your
kingdom.' Then she fell down.

17

When she didn't move he went over to her and knelt down on the icy flagstones. Anna had kept these, though they had been taken up, then relaid in concrete to minimize damp. She had been spending money like water in the end, *like water*, when he had had so little.

Gently he pushed at the woman on the floor. 'Grace, for God's sake, *Grace* . . .' Then, appalled, he straightened up, nudging at her with his foot as one might gingerly investigate the corpse of a large animal. Suddenly her head rolled to one side and something came out of her mouth.

He sank to his knees again, feverish now, prised her lips apart with his fingers and felt round inside in case she wore a dental plate, dentures even, for she could choke on them in this position. But she had fine teeth, very even, very white; it was strange that he had never noticed them before, they had known each other most of their lives. But she had never attracted him physically. He had always found large women particularly threatening and in her case his lack of interest was compounded by her religious fanaticism. He was sad for her now, though. He'd been into White Lodge twice, first to steal the watches and the clock, along with her cash-card; later, when he was running short of ready money, to see if there was any in her desk. He'd made this second visit when she was at eight o'clock Communion and he'd had time to read all the business correspondence meticulously arrayed in various files, as well as notes about Anna's murder which she seemed to have prepared for the police. She had obviously been planning to move up here, buy that shop which was up for sale along the valley and convert the tourists. But it would not happen now; her God had let her down badly.

Holding the lips apart he clamped his mouth over them and blew air into her. Then he sucked it into himself, sucked harder, then blew out again. At the same time he slid his other hand inside the thick sweater she was wearing, bright red, decorated with jolly little sheep, positioned his palm over her breast bone and rammed down hard again and again. But now he was very close he could see the beginnings of white slits between her eyelashes. If he let her head fall

257

back the eyes would open fully and he couldn't bear that. Besides, in spite of Anna's fancy new waterproof screed, it was very cold on the floor, and Grace was cold. He took his mouth away, did his best to close up the awful flopping lips, and cradled her in his arms in an effort to warm her.

Once, at Firs, he had gone down the garden to feed his rabbits and found Snowball, the oldest and best-loved pet, lying dead and stiff. Not understanding he had taken her into his arms to warm her back to life, as he now took Grace; as he had taken his mother in the death house, in spite of all the blood on her.

Snowball had been his first death. Afterwards there had been other rabbits, wilder and more wilful creatures that were always escaping from their cages and eating the vegetables. They had been gambolling about gleefully in the straw of the old hen-house where he kept his pets when he had opened the door and found his father gently swinging there.

Carefully he eased Grace's head back on to the cold flagstones, stood up, and looked at her. Once, at Bellingham, a middle-aged woman who helped serve dinners to the boys had had a heart-attack in the dining hall. He had been on duty that day, watched, tried to hurry the children away, then rushed to her side with Dickie Tomlinson, the senior master. So he knew what had happened to Grace, remembering the same clutching at the neck, the hideous choking noises, then the limpness. Rose, the Bellingham woman, had made a good recovery. But Grace was dead. Why hadn't Anna *told* him there was something wrong with her? It figured, old Mother Bradley had suffered from a heart complaint too, it must have been the only one of her ailments that wasn't imaginary. But Anna might not have known about Grace. If she had known she wouldn't have much cared, all the notice she'd taken of the poor woman in recent years. She'd cared for nobody but herself.

The walls of the cottage were faintly knobbled; under the new plaster he could see the shapes of great round rocks. *Fake.* Why not have left them bare, or else have had a smooth, honest finish? Why did Anna always have to pretend? This woman at his feet, this *good* woman, was at least straight. Anna had not deserved her, he had come to tell her that, and to tell her that they might make something of this place, together. He could sell his paintings, she could run her little shop, and they could manage without Anna's money, and be happy. It wouldn't matter about the sex.

But she had died on him. It was the shock, what else could it be? Oh, he should have thought everything out better, but he'd decided it would be all right, coming to her like this, quietly, in the night.

He *had* thought about Grace, he *did* think about people, unlike bloody Anna, that was why, in the end, he'd not approached Grace at the concert. He'd felt it would be the wrong moment, too public for her, too sudden. So he'd slipped away before the end. Then, in the Falcon, a nice old pub that, he'd got drinking, couldn't remember . . .

Now she lay grey-faced on the slabs, her awful floppy mouth accusing him, her hair spread round her in dark glossy meshes. He felt faint and sick, and he leaned against the wall for support, the great boulders cool to his trembling hands. *Christ*, why couldn't he die too? He ran against the wall and crashed the flat of his head against it till the blood streamed down his face, hopelessly crying. Why had nothing ever gone right for him? Why hadn't even this gone right? For, truly, he had thought about Grace, in his long months alone, about how he had misjudged her, about how all of them had misjudged and undervalued her, realising that she alone was whole among them. And he had come to make amends, for them all.

He knew that he shouldn't have played those cruel tricks on her, made silly phone calls, sent the cards. He'd been ashamed afterwards, stopped drinking altogether, for a while, when he realised what he'd been doing and how he must have frightened her. A woman like Grace had deserved better. But, please, *didn't she understand*? He'd had nobody else to turn to, after Stephen died, and he would have turned to her, not kept going off again, just when he'd plucked up the courage to come clean, if he'd not been so terribly afraid. Policemen frightened him, he kept seeing them at Firs, stepping over the shovel of coal; and newspapers frightened him, and what he might see on the television. Tonight he'd been going to be very brave, though, to have told her everything from the beginning, and thrown himself on her mercy. Mercy was something she understood.

'Grace . . . *Grace*. Come on . . .' Gently, with one foot, he pushed at her, but her face lolled over again, rocked slightly with a little crunching noise, against some grit on the floor, and was still. He must tell someone. Turning away he went to Anna's writing table and picked up the telephone, a warm relief suddenly flowing over him. Now at last they would believe what he had been trying to tell them all along, and come, and the fight would be over. He had tried, nobody could say he hadn't tried. He'd sent letters explaining who he was and how, last Christmas, it was Stephen Allen who had died, not Guy Beardmore, the famous writer's brother, the bum she'd disowned who had never made anything of his life. One night in Newcastle he had even gone into a police station and told them his story, but he'd been rolling drunk and they'd simply slammed him into a cell for the night. In the morning they had given him a cup of tea and sent him on his way. The loathsome Julia Wragg had been right when she said the police were a load of dummies. He'd heard her say that himself, when he'd listened in the garden of Anna's London house, the weekend Grace had come to stay and they'd talked of writing a book. She'd been against it; he'd wanted to thank her for that too, tonight. Anyhow, the police deserved all the shit people threw at them. If they'd not been so dumb when Stephen died he would never have got away with the last year.

The phone was dead. Of course, he had cut through it himself. He went to the table, opened the second bottle of Cabernet Sauvignon and poured some out. Then he made the fire up and sat down. Music was what he needed now, to calm him, also, to strengthen him for dealing with Grace's body. It would stiffen and he must do something with it, not leave it lying there in the doorway. Not yet, though.

He looked along Anna's new bookshelves for something to listen to. There were records, compact discs, tapes, and a very expensive hi-fi system. He looked at it all critically and did a quick calculation; three or four thousand, this lot was worth. She had always treated herself nicely, the bitch.

He picked out a tape which he had given her himself, years ago, the Bellingham chapel choir singing Durufle. Stuart was on it. *Ubi caritas et amor, Deus ibi est.* Yes, and he, Guy Beardmore, had also loved, in his way, and had shown charity. That was the only God there was. The voices rose as one but he could hear only Stuart and suddenly the tears began pouring down his face. It was because of Stuart that he'd been forced to leave Bellingham, his last school, the place where, at last, he had been truly happy. All the children there had loved him and they had been gentler than any of the women in his life, unthreatening, so much less greedy in the exchange of love. He would have liked to have married and to have had children, sons, if he could choose, but he was no good with women. Only with Anna that one time had he succeeded properly. It was beautiful then, because of their grief, but always, afterwards, she had sent him away, saying that Grace in the next room might hear, that it was wrong. She had had many men inside her since, Stephen among them, and he'd found that hard to forgive, he had never really got used to it, not Stephen, his only friend, having to be shared with Anna. But he had been the first, and the one who had loved her best.

In the folder of work he had prepared for Julia Wragg he had put his poem to Stuart and with it his charcoal sketch of the sunlit clearing in the little wood. It didn't really fit with the rest, *The Forgotten*, his verse sequence about the homeless which he had put together over these last few months, drawing the men in the various hostels he had stayed in as he moved from town to town, drafting the poems at night, while the rest of them slept. They had been alcoholics, discharged psychiatric cases thrown back on the community, petty criminals who hopped in and out of prison. But they had accepted him. Old Guy was always good for a laugh, they said, and besides, he usually had money. They had even praised the drawings he'd made of them. Interesting, that, how perceptive the old lags had been, he knew it was his best work. The oil paintings he'd attempted, heavily derivative of 'Last Light' but with none of Stephen's amazing fluency, had been hopeless crap, *shit*. In anger one night, at the Dingle Wood flat, he supposed when he was very drunk, he thought he had flung his own excrement at one of the canvasses, though he couldn't quite remember now, he could have dreamed it. There was so much he couldn't remember any more.

Stuart. The real Stuart had been a local paper-boy, assaulted and murdered early one morning outside Bellingham village, by a young garage mechanic, and hastily buried some miles away, in a shallow grave. The police had been three days finding him. His own Stuart's parents were stinking rich and their boy had had no need of a casual job to earn extra pocket money. Even so, when he'd seen the local paper and heard the name he'd been sick with fear until it was confirmed that nobody from Bellingham School was missing.

> *Though you still slept, I laid*
> *My hand upon your face.*
> *They had found him and my heart*
> *Warmed with a shameful happiness that he*
> *And not my child*
> *Lay in that place,*
> *Covered over with leaves*
> *Beside a lonely road.*
> *Why was he not found before*
> *When the trees from which they fell*
> *Must have cried aloud?*

He read the poem through then put it with its drawing on top of *The Forgotten*, opened up Anna's small portable typewriter and wrote a short letter to Julia Wragg. The enclosed, it explained, had been amongst some of Anna's papers in a drawer at Firs. Did she think there might be a little book here, the verses interleaved with the black and white drawings? The name Beardmore was sure to help, wasn't it, and surely the material was worth publishing anyway, in its own right? If they wanted a 'Beardmore book' this could be it. Just a thought, of course, and absolutely no urgency for a reply.

He took Grace's building society cash-card from his pocket and practised writing her name on a piece of paper. He was good at forging other people's handwriting, he'd had a lot of practice on Stephen's. When he was depressed he couldn't control a pen and his writing was spindly and faint, the querulous copperplate of an octogenarian. After hours of practice he'd perfected it and started writing to everyone, Anna and Grace, Lynn, the police. He'd perfected the stammer too, it had been mentioned in the papers, in the reports about Anna. He was proud of that.

It had been rather good, being Stephen for a year, easier than being Guy, who couldn't paint, or keep friends, or make love to women. Only now did he understand how deeply he'd envied him, and wanted to be like him. Years ago there'd been a big scene. He'd struck Anna for taunting him about his love for Stephen, calling him queer. All right, so what if it was true? What had she ever understood about love, or about painting, for that matter, about any of the arts? She was just a pulp writer and she knew it. At least what he'd achieved in *The Forgotten* was honest.

When he was satisfied with the signature he signed his letter, typed 'Grace Bradley' underneath in capitals, then burned the samples. In the drawer of Anna's writing table he found paper, Sellotape and stamps. Carefully he made a neat parcel, thinking of Grace's father in the basement room at Bradley's shop, in the weeks after the deaths, patiently showing him how to wrap orders up to be posted off. He had loved using the sealing wax, and cutting the great rolls of brown paper to size with the 'special' scissors which were always kept in the parcel room. Bill Bradley had been kind to him then. Grace had called him 'Daddie', years after he'd died. Pathetic.

When the parcel was ready he stuck all the stamps on, three pound's-worth, more than enough for something so light. It was extravagant of him but nobody here would be needing stamps any more. Besides, the wine, and the Christmassy music on the Bellingham tape was making him frivolous. Stepping over Grace's body he went into the kitchen and propped his neat package up on the draining board, to the left of the outer door, so that he would be sure to remember it when he went out. Then he returned to the main room, poured out the last of the wine and flicked the hi-fi system over to 'radio'.

Schmaltzy Happy New Year music was suddenly interrupted by a news bulletin. There had been another bomb explosion in London, this time in Trafalgar Square, the third since Christmas Eve. Seven people were known to be dead, three of them children. The IRA had claimed responsibility. He liked children, he had loved Stephen's little girls, it was for them he had stolen, so that they could have things and believe that their father wasn't dead. He wasn't all bad.

Children were canny, of course, so he had never risked speaking to them on the telephone. But he was a bloody clever mimic, even his father, who had never praised him for anything in all his life, had grudgingly commented on that; Father, who had merely criticised and wanted more of him than he could possibly give, and had compared him with Anna. If his parents had only lived they would have seen him go to Cambridge. He *did* go, except that the silly buggers sent him away after a year for fluffing a stupid exam. Anna, on the other hand, was a classic Oxbridge reject, though she had never accepted the fact and had insisted on her mediocre A-levels being re-marked. Pollitts had had to pay, out of the money their parents had left. She had ended up at Durham, a place that aped the dreaming spires. She'd not liked hearing that but it was true; he'd had the better brain, more flair altogether, and he'd certainly fooled Grace with his phoney voice, speaking through a handkerchief with the handset held a few inches away from him.

Regularly, since Stephen's death, he had written to the children up in Scotland, sent them postcards with little drawings on and sometimes funny poems. When he'd had money he'd sent that too. He could see now why they said that prison was not a good idea. In the hostels he'd met plenty of people who had been 'inside'. They'd given him very useful advice, told him exactly how he could realise cash from the things he had stolen, which dealers in the area to avoid and which might be relied upon to pay up, no questions asked. When the two cash-cards belonging to Stephen had stopped paying out money he had systematically sold off his treasures, all the beautiful old stuff left him by his father, the clocks and the porcelain that Lynn hadn't wanted and had tried hard to persuade him to sell off, when money got tight. How had either of them ever fancied such a woman? She was a bitch too.

Daringly, he had also sold off the good furniture, though he'd not risked going to the Dingle Wood flat himself, when the dealer came to collect it. A man he'd got to know in a bed and breakfast hotel had negotiated the sale for him and had waited in the flat until they came to take the stuff away. For his services he'd received a fifteen per cent cut of the profits, which had been more than generous, for a total of one hour's waiting. But then, Guy Beardmore had always been generous and had not wanted anything in return for what he gave, unlike Anna whose acts of bounty were always finely calculated, and whose gifts were invariably given at a price. Look at the shitty way she'd treated poor Grace.

Stephen's little girls would have had a very good Christmas this year. For each of them, in shiny gold paper, he had wrapped one hundred pound coins, put the packages in small padded envelopes and sent them to the island. The remaining four hundred pounds of Grace's money he had posted off to Lynn. 'Our mummy would like some new things,' Deborah had written plaintively in a letter she had sent to Stephen at the flat. 'She wants some boots and a new dress, and the washing machine keeps stopping. Uncle Colin's trying to mend it.'

He had been planning to explain everything to Grace this evening, over a quiet drink, about letting himself into White Lodge, and about what he'd done with her money. He could easily have spent it on himself, bought a few bottles, had a bit of a party with people, but he hadn't. He wasn't as black as Anna had painted him and he'd wanted to tell Grace that, tonight. It would have been easier between them now, now that Anna couldn't come barging in, telling everybody what was what. Fucking know-all. And he'd not sold the carriage clock, or the watches. He'd brought everything back.

When he was being Stephen he hadn't forgotten anything, the post for example. He'd been careful to keep up a flow of mail coming to the flat in Dingle Wood, for anybody who might investigate. He'd sent regularly to insurance companies for information about their policies, filling in questionnaires about his credit worthiness, applying for cash-cards. Whenever he'd used the flat as a base he'd slept in the little bedroom, the one with the window that looked out on to next door's blank wall, and he'd been careful about showing lights at night. Nobody had bothered him, though, or come poking round. It was only after Anna's death that he knew he must keep away from the place for a while, and he'd found other places to sleep in, hostels again, and a series of cheap bed and breakfast hotels where whole families were sometimes crammed into one hideous room.

Occasionally he'd used Anna's London house, to which he had his own key. She had given him one in the euphoria of her new purchase and, after the quarrel, had forgotten to reclaim it. He had not often stayed there; with the watchful Julia on the other side of the party wall, it would have been too great a risk. But now and then he had gone in, to pick up something he could sell, wandering at leisure through the freshly painted rooms and, on Grace's weekend, smoking a quiet cigarette in the garden, listening to their talk, laughing aloud at some of it, especially when they'd talked about those dumb-dumb policemen. Perhaps they'd heard, and wondered who it was; and he'd only narrowly escaped confronting Grace too, when she came to The Rock on that Tuesday in late October. Had they met then, perhaps all would be different now.

That morning, when he let himself in to the cottage, he found a note to Grace, from Anna, saying she had just gone up to Park Head with

Maurice, to have a look at a prize ram he'd bought at Hawes auctions. Would she walk along to meet them and see it? It was bound to be interesting. It was typical of her to have buggered off on an impulse. She'd always preferred male company to female, a ram to a ewe.

Mischievously, remembering Grace's rooted disapproval of him and all his works – and he'd tried to be nice to her, to include her in things, really he had – he destroyed the note to confound her putting in its place, like some ghastly *billet doux*, a scrap of paper in Anna's handwriting, a quotation about suicide being the best way of making sure that people never forgot you. Let the woman sweat. Then he took advantage of his sister's absence to poke around the place. He wanted to see what she had been spending all her lolly on. Knowing she didn't drink any more, because of him, he'd brought a couple of bottles along. Now he opened one, poured himself a glass of wine, and wandered about, a cigarette in his mouth. That was another habit she disapproved of, prissy devil. Eventually he went upstairs and he was admiring the antique brass bed when Grace arrived. He decided to frighten her off, treading heavily on the floorboards then stroking his hands along them, hoping she would think it was rats. He had remembered her terror of them, from childhood, and the famous incident in which 'Daddie' had bravely cornered one in the wash-house, the place where, conveniently, a spare key to the house was still kept, after all those years. Poor Gracie, she'd never grown up, never had a chance. And he could have helped her.

When she had gone he typed a coolish note to Anna, from her, though he'd not signed it, but typed in the name rather prettily, with large spaces between and a couple of crosses, to show there was no real harm done by her friend's casualness. The letter said she had had her friends with her and they had all agreed that three of them traipsing up to see his new ram might be too much of a crowd. In any case, they were actually on their way home, there had been a change of plan because of someone's elderly mother being ill. He hoped it sounded plausible. There was no real need to elaborate further. Grace had become something of a burden to his sister in recent years, she'd more or less told him that, *cow*. Oh, it was OK when someone could be useful to the great Anna Beardmore, but Grace was outliving her usefulness, now that Peth had lost its charm and London beckoned. He'd hated the way she'd been made to skivvy, at that party.

Anna would not pursue her too hard, especially since Julia Wragg was due the next day. Whether she had actually bothered to phone the poor woman he didn't know, but he had not returned to The Rock until much later when all danger from her, and from those friends whom she killingly called 'The Girls' was over.

In the course of his wanderings he had also, finally, gone to Firs. For this he could find no key but he had smashed the front door lock off and got himself inside. He had made a fire in the drawing room grate and slept there all night, hoping his mother might come to him across the familar red carpet with its border of grey leaves, be young and untwisted again, untouched by what his father had done. But there had been no kindly ghosts, only the bloody ghost of a corpse squashed down horribly between the arms of the wheelchair, its head between its knees, and the ghost of the shovel of coals and kindling, dropped in the doorway, over which the ambulance men and the police had stepped so discreetly. Sometimes he got frightened at night and at Firs he had slept with his knife under his head, as he always had done, since the day they had returned it to Mr Bradley, after The Tragedy. It had not been thrown into the canal; he had used another knife for that, a replica. Anna had not seen in the dark; she wasn't as clever as he was.

From Firs he had gone to White Lodge, letting himself in with the wash-house key, removed the silver watches and the clock, then gone through the desk, reading the drafts of Grace's letters. He'd been angry, not with Gracie but with the odious Julia Wragg. It wasn't enough that Anna had planned to write of their love in her new novel, oh no; together with some creep called Magnus, Julia was evidently trying to persuade Grace to let her do something at Wragg and Buckland. The book would have Grace's name on it perhaps, but they'd have twisted everything round. They'd have crushed Gracie, people always did. Here she lay, on the flags, her face hideous now, greenish, the cheeks all sunk as if she was sucking in air, and what had come out of her mouth starting to crystallise, like a great scab.

The collection of watches and the brass carriage clock were here, in his duffel bag, all ready to give back to her. He'd been going to suggest she kept them here. This place needed a few homely touches. Anna had been crap at that kind of thing. He and Gracie would have tackled it together. Tomorrow he would dispose of the stuff down one of the deep mine-shafts he had seen on his walks along the fell sides; neither he, nor she, nor Anna needed them now.

The men in the hostels had told him quite good things about prison. Some of them did a bit of thieving at this time of year, to get themselves back inside for Christmas. If only they still hanged people. Prison would go on too long. They would release him after a few years and then the whole of the rest of his life would be waiting, to be lived through. Death was better.

The news flash about the Trafalgar Square bomb had been extended to include a statement from the Prime Minister about the 'inhuman

depravity' of the IRA. He switched off in disgust. He had reason to
be very grateful to them. It was they who had been responsible for
the cache of Semtex explosive which the police had discovered on the
North Yorkshire moors, a discovery which had reduced the manpower
deployed on the enquiry into Anna's death and so taken the heat out of
the hunt for Stephen. He had always known he would turn himself in
eventually, but he had found that he was unexpectedly relieved when
things suddenly went quiet. It was because he was working so well on
his collection of drawings, better than he'd ever done in his life, as if,
in dying, something of Stephen's greatness had come into him. And
the poems were taking shape too. He'd just needed a little more time
to complete his work before the end came, and the IRA had given
it to him. As *The Forgotten* took hold of him he knew he mustn't be
interrupted before it was finished, yet always, underneath, there was
this fear that, wherever he was, the police would one day knock on the
door and come for him. That was why he'd played one of his 'tricks'
on the CID and buried the knife and the axe in Bayles's field, just to
ginger them up and keep them all away from him. Anyhow, it had
been fun reading about Eddie's arrest in the paper.

It was Grace who had called them 'tricks', in those notes she'd
written, for the police. There were copies of everything in her desk
at White Lodge, everything except Anna's will but he'd found that
earlier, in a filing cabinet at the London flat. Stinking rich, Grace
was going to be . . . would have been. They could have shared it,
that's what he'd been going to suggest, though they could have lived
very simply here, investing what they didn't need for their old age.

The night Stephen had died there'd been a massive gas explosion in
South London, only a mile away from the flat in Dingle Wood. A tower
block had crumpled and sagged like something made of a kid's building blocks, fantastic. He'd been to have a look, when all the fuss had
died down. They'd blamed the good old IRA for that too, at first, but of
course it wasn't. Nobody in those tacky flats had been worth bumping
off, they were nobody special, they were like him, the nowhere people.
It was a leak and a large area had been evacuated, dozens of streets.
More or less every policeman in the area had been called to the
scene. A suicide in Dingle Wood was very small beer in comparison,
especially when the man reporting it was obviously drunk. Nobody
had come to the flat for a good two hours and when they did show
up they were very off-hand with him. He supposed it was because
he'd been drinking heavily and there was vomit all over the hall.

On an impulse, without ever having planned such a thing, he had
identified Stephen as himself, telling them that the body under the

water was Guy Beardmore, the friend he shared the flat with. Asked for some proof of who he was he had taken from his pocket Stephen's cash-card for the Trustee Savings Bank and a library card he'd borrowed which fortunately bore no photograph. He had been using the cash-card for his own spending. Like Grace, Stephen had foolishly kept the PIN number with it because he couldn't memorize the digits. This was part of his depression, the condition for which he was being monitored by his doctor and given tablets which Guy knew that he did not take. It was when they said that Stephen's own doctor would have to come and see the body before signing the death certificate that he thought the interesting game would be up, almost before it started. But in fact another doctor came, a partner in the practice, in lieu of the other one who was in Austria for Christmas, skiing. This man, who had never seen Stephen, would apparently do. He was not making an identification, Guy had done that; he was simply there to do the paperwork.

Of course, he knew exactly what the crap psychiatrists would say, and they had had enough of psychiatrists, him and Stephen both. They'd say he'd been acting out his obsession over Stephen for the last year, playing out his need to identify with him, all that shit. They'd forced it out of him once in a hospital, at a group therapy session, they'd made him cry. *Group therapy*. They were just saving on the wages, that's all they were doing. Anyhow, everyone had cried at those, it was awful. Not that it mattered, nothing mattered now.

Stephen's kids had mattered, though, and he knew now that the false identification, and all that had come from it, had come from a determination to spare them for as long as he could. Asked, out of politeness, he sensed, for neither policemen nor doctor seemed to have any time to spare for him, why he thought 'Guy' had killed himself, he simply said that he had been very depressed for a long time and had tried it twice before, once an overdose then, horribly, an attempt to put an electric fire in the bath which the real Guy had only just prevented. 'Third time lucky, then,' the doctor had said, unnecessarily, he thought.

When they had gone he had destroyed the two letters he had found earlier that night on the kitchen table and read before going into the bathroom for a pee, where he had found the body under the pink water, its gaping wrists turned upwards, the hands breaking the surface as if in supplication to some unanswering god. One letter was from Anna, short and harsh, refusing to discuss his 'ridiculous' proposal any further. He was still married to Lynn, she had reminded him, and even if he were free it would never work between *them*. It was a very bad idea for them to meet, now or at any time. She would be in London at Christmas, with Julia. New Year she was spending alone, at The Rock. She was planning a new novel. She was being honest with him, not trying to hide anything, but please would he not embarrass her by turning up or by behaving stupidly.

The second letter was from Lynn. If he was determined to come to them for Christmas then she had no way of stopping him, she wrote. But he couldn't stay in the bungalow, Colin Semple would be there. He might as well know that Colin had now moved in permanently and that the girls liked him. For the first time in years she was actually looking forward to Christmas, though a bit of money would come in handy. The hotel might have a room, or he could always stay in Jean Cameron's B and B on the quay. Whatever, he would have to fix things up himself, but she actually felt it would be less disruptive for the children if he stayed away.

He had told the police that there were no notes. Alone again he had torn both letters into tiny pieces and burned them in an ashtray. Then, from the pocket of Stephen's jacket, he had taken the railway ticket he had purchased for his Christmas trip to Scotland and burned that too. In the hall was a gay carrier bag full of cheerfully-wrapped presents. The sight of it, with all its hope and jollity, was somehow unbearable to him. He carried it downstairs and dumped it in one of the dustbins. Then he returned to the flat and went through Stephen's pockets and drawers, removing his credit cards and his cheque book, his passport and all the other documents which bore either a signature or a photograph.

He would have liked to have worn his clothes but he was much too fat. The camel duffel coat had always been too big for Stephen, though, so he took that, and his university scarf. The clothes wouldn't have been a problem now. Food no longer interested him and over the last year he had shed nearly four stones in weight. He looked sallow and gaunt these days and his face was a permanent putty colour. A farmer called Peacock at the Ram had very kindly enquired after his health, when he'd been up there doing his reporter bit and sneaking his 'polite' notice on to their pin-board. That had been another bit of fun. Peacock hadn't been so friendly when he'd turned up at The Rock, though, in fact he'd threatened him with the dog. *The Rock.* Bloody silly name, that. He'd painted the original name back. Anna had been a pretentious cow.

'Stephen seems to be playing games with me' Grace had written in the notes she had prepared for the police. She seemed to keep copies of everything she wrote which had been useful to him. One of his 'games' had been his brief appearance at the crematorium, at the end of his own funeral service, though at that moment, when she had called out to him on the path, he had almost gone to her, revealing the whole insane deception. A better one had been turning up at Anna's in the role of the mythical Hugo Jolley, though he knew now that he had very much wanted them to apprehend him that day, couldn't understand why nobody there had recognised him even though his naturally sandy hair was coloured a dark brown and he wore fake spectacles with tinted lenses, like someone in a film. Surely Wooding, the elderly policeman at his side, must have wondered about him when, during the hymn, he had burst into tears? 'Oh Love That Wilt Not Let Me Go' they had sung, the choice of the two Lesbians, he supposed, for Grace had been too distraught to arrange the affair herself and had not been present. But 'Oh Love' was the hymn they had sung at his parents' funeral to which, dumbly, he had been dragged by Anna who had been on a hideous, screaming sort of high. They must be brave for Mummy and Daddy, she had whispered. But those two women had sullied that hymn for him now; it was cruel of God.

He thought that he was now drunk enough to deal with Grace but he must go very carefully and not fall over. There must be no injury to her, no suggestion of physical assault. What exactly had been wrong with her? Had she really died of shock? Anna had never wasted time talking to him about Grace Bradley, she was merely a useful but rather boring friend. She was certainly rather overweight, which had turned him right off, but no worse than many people. Shock could kill people, though; 'heartbreak', the poets called it. If only that had happened to Anna instead. Listen, he'd never meant to harm a hair of Grace's head, showing up at The Rock. It was merely intended to be one of these little tricks of his, that had so bothered her. He wished he'd never started them now.

One of the things he had liked least about Anna was that she had become middle-aged before her time, set in her ways with her own times for doing things. She got very angry if her personal schedules were interrupted, even though they were selfish, anti-social schedules. For example, she had not liked it when, unable to sleep, he had sometimes telephoned her in the middle of the night, to chat. She was his sister, after all. But she was often writing then, she said, working to meet one of her deadlines. Silly, greedy bitch. She was a liar too. She'd spread lies about him getting drunk and behaving obscenely the day she'd been given that big prize on the telly, and afterwards, at her precious party, when she claimed he'd peed on some bloody rug and smashed all the windows. None of it was true and his friends knew it. Anna and her fucking writing.

She'd been writing when he came back to The Rock, even though it was two in the morning the day after poor Grace's abortive visit, an event not important enough to note down in her desk diary; he'd checked, afterwards. Julia Wragg's visit, starting the following afternoon, had been blocked in in yellow high-lighter, though in the event she had been too ill to make the journey. Pity. What he had left behind at the writing table had been meant for her, not for young John Peacock. He regretted the boy, still having psychiatric treatment in some hospital, because of the shock of what he had seen. That was never meant to be. Perhaps, before he left, he should write to the mother.

He had let himself into the cottage with the key he'd had made from Grace's. On one of his visits to Peth he had stolen it from her desk and had a copy done. The Rock was all lit up, even though it was two in the morning. He could hear water running upstairs and the quacking of a radio. She would be in the bath. When she had cleansed herself she would no doubt trip down in some floating evening garment, make tea or perhaps pour herself a drink, then resume work.

Spread out on the writing table were her notes for something called *Broken Path*. He looked at it and saw that it was the same material he had pored over in the London house. These were the scattered notes that were to be turned into a book about his life.

Tonight, evidently, she had been re-reading her very early journals, and making notes on them. Under a large glass paperweight was the deaths diary, the volume which covered the three-month period during which his father had killed his mother, then killed himself, and the Bradleys had taken them in. He had never seen it before. She had somehow kept its hiding place a secret, carrying it round with her at all times, as Grace carried a copy of the Holy Bible.

He didn't need, didn't want, to read it, for he could not bear to see what she had written of their love-making, that night in White Lodge, of that supreme act of consolation in the raw of their grief. In her hands, and with only the thinnest of disguises, it would surely become just another Saddleford episode, cheapened and misrepresented, for she had done the same to so many, to Mollie McGraw at the post office, to the patent leather man, to his own Miss B., now a vegetable in Raddon Court; and now, for money, he was sure, and perhaps also to work some curious guilty anger out of herself, she was preparing to do it again, but this time to her own, to his mother and father and, most of all, to him. It would probably be made into a film, it had everything, love, adultery, murder, incest . . .

'*No!*' He took the deaths diary and ripped it in two, then stuffed it on to the fire. Upstairs Anna called out nervously, 'Who's that?'

and he heard the floor creak over his head. Without knowing he must have cried his angry defiance aloud.

He said nothing but took from a hook on the inner door a long silk kimono, black, wreathed with gold dragons breathing fire, pure silk. Her books were in Japanese too, now, she'd been to Japan twice, to lecture. *Christ*, what would they understand of her tin-pot mill town yarns? They all read comics out there, didn't they?

He had been in his walking clothes all day and he stank. Now he removed them, enjoying the fire as it warmed his nakedness, folding them neatly on to a chair with his boots balanced on top. Look at this room. She was a slut compared with him, fouling every nest she'd ever had, as if neatness and order were somehow beneath her, too boring, insufficiently cerebral. Going to the bottom of the stone steps and clacking the curtain aside he coughed loudly. 'Who *is* it?' she called. He smiled. She was frightened now.

He made no reply but slipped on the lovely kimono, swirling the dragons round him. A draught was blowing in from somewhere and the silk sucked against him and clung, outlining his great cock. He had shown it to Grace at the party. Well, he'd wanted her to feel she was a woman, that was all. But he'd upset her, Anna had told him so in that terrible last letter. He'd never meant to.

He decided not to tie the kimono, let her see him as he was. In the grate there was a fresh little spurt of flame as the paper he'd stuffed on to the fire sagged down and burned its last. She could never, now, write of their tragedy, at least he'd saved them both from that. But she had planned to, here, in this house. He was very, very angry with her.

He began to climb the stone steps, to where she was, trying to control his rage and not move too fast; he was still smiling a little. She had always said that he had a particularly kind smile, that it was like their mother's. Though they were twins she was much more like her father. She looked like Dad now, as he reached the top step and saw her face in the light of a bedroom lamp.

She didn't respond to the smile but instead started to scream horribly, her head bobbing from side to side like the head of a carved wooden puppet animated by a coiled spring, and she repeated his own word, '*No*', but endlessly, retreating into a doorway then falling back on the high brass bed, sending the lamp crashing down, just screaming and screaming. She wore only a thin nightdress, the sleeves were puffed and it was printed with a faint scattering of tiny flowers. Her body was still damp and steamy from the bath and she had the sweet smell of a very young child.

She tried to cover herself up but he grabbed her hands and pushed them behind her head, drove her foolish, twitching legs apart and thrust himself inside her, but it was not as before. She had welcomed him then, stroked him as he wept, and he had buried his face between her little breasts, sucking at the small dark nipples until peace came to him. But now she clawed at him and tore at his hair, stiffening herself against him and drumming on his thighs with her small hard feet.

He withdrew quite suddenly, hating her now and seeing his father in her face, his father copulating with the chapel woman in some prim front bedroom in Peth while at home his mother endured. All this she was planning to write about. Why didn't the silly bitch stop screaming?

He took her right hand, ink-stained with the hard writer's callous on the inside of the middle finger, and bent it back at the wrist until it cracked. She cried out in agony but now he felt he could bear it no longer, he must end the sound. So he put his great square hands round her neck, pressing with his thumbs just below the lump in her throat till the passage of air was cut off, and held them there until she stopped moving beneath him and there was no more noise.

There must be no blood in the house. Keeping his eyes away from her face he pulled down the nightdress, humped her over his shoulder fireman fashion and made his way down the precipitous stairs. Once outside he began to pick his way round to the front of the cottage. The great waterfall was illuminated by a strong floodlight hidden somewhere in the grass. By its light, and with agonising slowness because the path down to the beck looked almost sheer, he made his way down the wall of retaining boulders until he reached the water. He had brought his knife with him and the small wood chopper he had found lying behind an antique coal bucket by the fire.

Her body was warm against his and, as he laid her on the bank, reassuring gurgling noises came from her belly as if, surely, there was still life there. But she was looking at him with dead bulging eyes and she had stuck her tongue out at him, just as she used to do when they were little at Firs, before she ran to her father for protection. Blood was trickling from her mouth.

He had expected a great jetting of blood but she didn't bleed very much at all when he removed the hand, first cutting the skin all round with his knife then hacking, untidily, with the little axe. It was lethally sharp, perhaps that man Maurice had sharpened it for her. People said that he was generally helpful and kind. Guy always remembered kindness.

He dragged her across to the deeper water and dangled the stump of her right arm in the fast-flowing stream, so that any more blood which came out would be washed away. Then he cupped water in his hand and washed the blood from round her mouth. He pulled off the nightdress and made a parcel of the axe and the knife, wrapping the flowered fabric round it. Then he carried her naked body back up the rocks.

She had always been very untidy and her day clothes were scattered round the main room. Perhaps, before bathing, she had lain naked in front of the fire, like someone out of a D. H. Lawrence novel. That would be very typical. He picked up a bright blue Shetland sweater – not her usual style, surely, she'd always fancied herself in rather more subtle colours – and pulled it over her head, thrusting the heavy arms down till they protruded from the cuffs, one hand, one bloody stump. Then he sat her at the writing table.

At first she fell to one side, then sagged forward; he pushed and pulled at her to get the effect he wanted but too vigorously so that her head fell right back and a deep choking sound came from her throat. At last he was satisfied that the writing posture was secure, the back straight, the head slightly stooped, the left hand fanned over an open book. The stump held down some blank sheets of paper. It was hard forcing her tongue back inside her head. It kept sliding out, however much he pushed at it, in a kind of silent mockery. But at last he knew the answer. He had torn up some of her notes into little pieces, also the scrap of paper describing how suicide ensured that people never forgot you, the one he had left for Grace.

All this paper he now moulded into a small hard ball then forced it between her lips, but still the tongue crept to the front and stuck out at one side. So on the other, for symmetry, he pulled down a couple of strands of paper, gleefully imagining Julia Wragg's entry to the cottage.

He didn't look at Anna again but switched the radio on, found some pop music, and turned it up very loud, to fill the sudden appalling silence. He smiled as he listened to the brainless din. It was the kind she detested, the kind she always said made her want to go out and murder somebody.

For an hour or so he pottered about, washing down the stone steps, though he could see no blood on them, picking up Anna's scattered clothes and restoring them to the old press in her room, brewing a pot of strong coffee to keep himself awake, for he must get to Richmond and on to a bus before the light came, and he must walk over the fells, not go on the road. In her room he carefully straightened the tumble of sheets on the high Victorian bed. He could smell hair and blood, and his own semen.

In sudden revulsion he left the bedroom, almost fell down the murderous stone steps and ran out of the cottage, sliding down the great rocks to reach the water where he threw off the silken kimono and plunged in. The cold was paralysing but he splashed about, not in the harsh light of the expensive lamp Anna had rigged up but in the milder, kinder light of a big moon. Then he pulled the gown on again and went to warm himself by the fire, before putting on his clothes, and to find a flash-light for his walk through the darkness.

He glanced at the blue hunched back of the figure at the table, intent upon her writing, banked the fire up and burned the kimono, then left the house, Radio One still blaring. In his duffel bag he had the bloody bundle of clothing containing the knife and the axe.

He walked fast because he was lean and fit now, he'd never felt better, and in less than half an hour he'd reached the village where Maurice the kindly farmer lived. Before striking up on to the fells he took the ink-stained hand from the pocket of Stephen's coat and flung it over the ornamental railings of the local primary school.

He was thinking of that now as he laid Grace gently on Anna's bed and covered her up with the green patchwork quilt. It was very beautiful and reminded him, in its infinite gradations, of a kind of tone poem about the sea and the sky, about the earth and the leaves and about the trees that nestled between the breasts of the gentle valley. He too would have liked lovely things but he had never earned enough money to buy them. Anna, on the other hand, had always treated herself very kindly.

No child had found the hand because it had been a half-term holiday and the school was closed. If there was a God He must surely have been in that kindliness. Guy knew he shouldn't have flung the hand into the yard, he loved children. But when he had done it he had been crying out against all the anguish of his life. 'Look at *me*, love *me*,' the hand had been saying. All the children, gathering round, would perhaps have been told his story, and known his pain.

Now he locked the bedroom door on Grace, put the key in his pocket and went downstairs. All he had brought with him was his duffel bag. It contained a few clothes, his washing things and the Bradley watches and clocks. It wasn't very heavy and he could easily take it with him, but nothing was needed any more. He had cared too much about possessions, been too jealous of Anna's, but it was all too late now. Grace's God, knowing what he had done, had punished him for the hand in the playground and had slyly drawn him back to The Rock when he thought he had left it behind for ever.

After leaving Anna he had spent two days and nights in a motor hotel off the M1, staying in his room all day and having meals brought up to him. Each morning and evening he had swum in the indoor pool but the smell of his sister's blood and of his own seed remained on him. He had passed the time working on his poems and drawings but there was a television set in the room and he had watched all the news bulletins and also had the newspaper delivered to him each morning. But nobody, it seemed, had discovered what had happened at The Rock.

On the Friday he had gone back, still wearing Stephen's duffel coat and scarf but with his face shaved. He had thought the removal of all that heavy hair would take away the sex but as he walked up the track he could smell it still. It was obvious that nobody had been to the cottage. He didn't go near Anna or look at her, simply removed what he had come for, a pair of Georgian silver bonbon dishes that stood on a side table; they would realise several hundred pounds and keep him going for a few months. He'd noticed them on the Tuesday, for they had belonged to his mother and in the will everything had been left to them jointly. Why had *she* taken them? As he was stuffing them down into his duffel bag the telephone had started ringing and he had eventually picked it up and had a conversation with Grace. His last act, before leaving the place, had been to cut the line. Bending down to do this he had caught sight of his sister's small feet, dangling under the table but curiously foreshortened now, and drawn up towards her stomach like the paws of his dead Snowball when he'd found her stiff in the hutch. The smell of her body was worse nearest to the floor and when he'd got outside he'd been sick in the grass.

He locked the cottage and began to walk, stopping only to put his parcel to Julia Wragg on top of the postbox which was fastened to a stump by 'his' seat. He had wrapped it in polythene to preserve it from the weather and now weighted it down with a large stone. The postman would collect it tomorrow and take it to Richmond. Even if there weren't enough stamps, Julia Wragg would get it. She could pay the difference.

Snow was falling again, whirling thickly round his head in the light of the small torch he carried, all he had been able to find at The Rock. He had left Stephen's coat and scarf behind at the cottage together with most of his own clothes and he was deliberately very thinly clad, no hat or gloves, bare arms, flimsy summer trousers. Almost at once, as he struck out, the intense cold bit into him.

He trudged steadily through the snow, able to follow the path only because the ancient painted stones set along the track centuries ago still poked up defiantly out of the heaped whiteness. Gradually the skin of his face turned numb. He drummed his fingers against his sodden trouser leg, noting that he couldn't really feel them; nor could he feel his toes or his knees and great shudders kept jarring him. He had never been so cold in all his life. It was good.

Below the seat marked with his name a minor track broke off the hill and went to the old mine workings at Marlin End. He had found, on the day he had come to The Rock and scared Grace off, the deepest shaft he had ever seen. Its dangerousness was acknowledged by the fact that huge lumps of antique iron work, presumably the remains of old machines, had been dragged across its great mouth to obscure it. But he had examined the shaft very carefully. A beast could easily slip down between the rusted red bars, also, a man.

Once off the hill his way was flatter and easier. In October he had walked this way on delicious springy turf. He went slower now because the cold was taking hold of him, his skull felt as if someone had stunned him with one great driving blow and his teeth were clashing together inside his mouth. After another mile or so of steady walking the path suddenly broke off, the way to the old mine workings being separated from him by the wide river. Last time he had removed his boots and waded across. Now he simply slid, in his thin sneakers, across a great sparkling curve of ice.

He no longer needed the path, he could see the humped white shapes of the ruins at Marlin End quite clearly now, under the moon. In their midst was the great shaft and he began to run towards it all, slipping about in the soft new snow, an unexpected joy warming him through.

Then a dog yelped somewhere. He stopped and looked across to the neighbouring fell where, even at this hour, lights gleamed yellow in a farmstead. Bounding along the broken path and skidding over the ice came a dark blodge that eventually materialised at his feet as a black and white collie, fluffy and young, sniffing at his crotch and wanting to play.

He stamped at it and gave a little roar, shook it off and made his way towards the ruins. But it followed him, though with difficulty now because they were in a broad trackless meadow where the wind had heaped the snow up into huge drifts.

At the shaft he knew he could not hesitate and he was now so very cold he wanted the end to come quickly. The hole was so tremendously deep he knew that down below water would still be flowing. He would simply fall and let it lap over him, let it be his friend, not fight it. He couldn't fight anything, any more. He squeezed through the tiny space between a massive tubular bar and the side of the shaft, swinging there in the darkness, the dog now puzzled and whining, licking at his ear. Then he let go.

But someone had thrown something down the ancient shaft, to get rid of it, something hard and unyielding which he could not see but which had broken his fall agonizingly, ramming his knees up under his chin and digging into his testicles, the pain bringing vomit into his mouth. Below, though, he could definitely hear water running. He stretched down a hand to try and touch it but it was too far away.

Contentedly, as the terrible pain slowly eased, he sat doubled up in the darkness then, ludicrously, the small dog thumped down into his lap, yelped, licked his face and suddenly urinated against his chest, the little stream warming him. For a while it scrabbled about, making pathetic leaps towards the mouth of the shaft. But he wanted peace now very much so he took it in his arms and stroked it. Gradually, making quiet grunting noises, it fell asleep.

He too wanted to pass into sleep, into the welcome blackness and the welcome cold, and, as the last inner darkness lapped up and sent its first gentle waves over him, he thought of Grace and of what she had cried out in her pain. *Jesus, remember me, when you come into your kingdom.* Was she there now, and was Anna with her? Could he come too?

As he fell asleep a change came over his face, for he was dreaming of his mother and his father, and of Anna, of all of them in a lovely place where nothing bad was happening, nor ever could again. It was the face of a little child, unblemished and smooth with its own intense and hopeful inner light, a face on which the marks of pain, and of love, had as yet left no trace.

Epilogue

Fifteen months later two teenagers who were staying at Keld Youth Hostel took ropes and went down the great shaft at Marlin End where they found the remains of a man and of a small dog. Although all evidence at The Rock suggested Stephen Allen, an examination of his dental records indicated that the body must be that of another man who, at the time of writing, has not been identified. Eventually Lynn registered Allen as a missing person, later telling her children that he had died in a road accident. To this day she believes that the police were in error and that the Marlin End body was that of her first husband.

In the same week that the remains were discovered Wragg and Buckland published *The Forgotten*, a collection of poems interleaved with drawings by 'G.B.' In her introduction Julia Wragg spoke of Heaney, of Larkin, of Hughes and of R. S. Thomas; she mentioned also the war-time Underground sketches of Henry Moore. 'Yet in both verses and drawings,' she argued, 'we hear a voice and see a hand that is entirely the author's own. When this book fell into my hands I knew I was handling something unique, something which, though minor in scope, signified a genuine literary event, and we can only regret that G.B. did not live to fulfil the promise in these pages.' Anna Beardmore's novels sell in large numbers. *The Forgotten* was remaindered after three months.

At Grace's funeral Buckle stood between Mrs Lumb and Ba Savage. The Girls had evidently had some kind of major quarrel and Marian Stoker did not attend. The elderly clergyman who presided, who had known the deceased for many years and her parents before her, spoke of her supreme though simple faith, of how she had always called her beloved father 'Daddie', 'Abba, Father,' in the same way as Our Lord himself had talked familiarly to his Father in Heaven. For his scripture reading he took a passage which, so her friends had told him, had come to have special meaning for her, in the last weeks of her life: *'And God shall wipe away all tears from their eyes; and there shall be no more death, neither sorrow nor crying, neither shall there be any more pain; for the former things are passed away.'*

Buckle wished he had not doubted his own love for her, deliberately putting time and distance between them in those last weeks before Christmas, accepting the lecturing job which had taken him away from Peth, but he had needed to be sure. When he returned to his flat and heard her voice on his answerphone, and of her plans to go to the valley alone, in a last attempt to meet Allen, he knew that he indeed wanted her. But he had not been able to reach The Rock because the high wild road over the tops from Kirkby Stephen was blocked with ten-foot drifts. Others, not he, had found her body in the cold locked room, under a green patchwork quilt.

Oh, Grace. As the hideous canned organ music died away and her coffin slid slowly out of sight, red plush curtains moving silently across to fill the space, he found that he was weeping. Later, when the congregation was asked to kneel, he tried also to pray.